THOSE FRIGHTENING THINGS
YOU SHOULD LET WIN

BY CLAY BERRY

PUBLISHER'S INFORMATION

EBookBakery Books

Author contact: clayberry4@gmail.com

ISBN 978-1-938517-81-5

© 2018 by Clay Berry

For all the Barbs and Tamaras amongst us
whose suffering seems insurmountable,
yet whose wisdom may teach us all what it means
to be a little more human.

———————————

"There are those frightening things you should run from.
There are those frightening things you should stand up to and defeat.
And then, there are those frightening things you should let win."

— Barbara Fletcher

A NOTE FROM THE AUTHOR

Dear Reader;

This story continues the narrative begun in *Through a Shattered Looking-glass*. At the end of that book, the Baxter family had just returned from New Hampshire, where they sought healing but faced a crisis that both shattered them and initiated their rebirth. Tamara, the daughter of Aimee and Terrance Baxter, had been struggling with various mental disorders which unsettled the aspirations of her parents who are both Wall Street financiers. On a weekend getaway in the White Mountains, the family nearly came to an end. Were it not for the intervention of a gracious old woman named Barb, they might have lost their daughter altogether.

It will be obvious to most, but needs to be said to all, that this is a complete work of fiction. This is also a story that deals with extraordinarily sensitive issues for many people, so a few other things must be said.

Where I can bend a story towards a hopeful outcome, for so many who suffer from mental illness the prospects of resolution and relief are too often fantasies simply not coming true. No one gets a day off, not the person who suffers or those who care about them. The grinding, daily work of moving forward would seem insurmountable but for the fact that so many people simply do it as they struggle to get out of bed and on with their day.

This story is for those who struggle in their minds to discover peace, purpose, and meaning. It is written for those who are seeking consolation, inspiration, and motivation as they push forward to discover something new in those experiences that may seem so utterly empty. Most importantly, it is written out of love and with the deepest respect for those whose lives have been so impacted by the kinds of experiences depicted here.

For Tamara Baxter, her search for restoration becomes a quest of faith, a pilgrimage toward one whose greater suffering can contain and heal her own. The story is written from a Christian faith-perspective, but it is offered to all as a source of encouragement. The book rests on a simple premise, that our most important sources of help come from beyond us: family, friends, community, and God. Then, from within, we discover a hope at work that inspires new life.

Lastly, while the characters raise questions about medication and questionable decisions are made in the story, I wish to emphasize that this is an important issue that needs to be faced in consultation with one's caregivers, family, and medical professionals. No position is taken by me concerning the value of medications; the story simply explores the decision made by the characters as they sort out their particular circumstances.

My prayer is that all who read this will be deepened in their sensitivity to the suffering of others and will bring to that suffering the hope that comes through facing it together with grace and sacrificial love.

Clay Berry

CONTENTS

PART ONE

1

Dreams from Which
No One Could Awake

TAMARA OFFERED TO POUR OUT (as if any these other so-called "guests" would demean themselves to do such a thing). She handed the first tea-cup across to Stamey, a paunchy, snobbish bear who truly dressed the part. He refused to recognize her kindness, and she had a good mind just to tip the cup in his lap.

Sanderford, the gaunt gorilla (he had lost a great deal of stuffing over the years and now, in his old age, was but a shadow of his former glory), turned his cup on its head refusing tea altogether. He snorted something foul, so Tamara turned her full attention to Thorafura, a long, sleek, purple snake. She was curled tightly in her chair with her graceful neck extending tall above the other table guests slowly swaying in place awaiting her tea. She was most gracious when Tamara set the cup in its saucer before her. Nodding her diamond-shaped head in appreciation, she gracefully bowed to her cup and took a dainty sip.

Tamara then offered around the thin sandwiches, cucumber mostly, but there were a few with spiced ham and well-aged cheese. Chocolate cheesecake waited at the center of the table for later.

"There is to be a new moon tonight," wheezed Heatherwhinny, the old lady-horse with the paisley saddle blanket. She had just slipped through the door without apologizing for being late, then she said in hushed tones: "The granthyrs will be out tonight."

"Pish," muttered Stamey. "Stay in your stall and they'll leave well enough alone. Even granthyrs wouldn't soil their claws in there."

Sanderford snorted his assent.

1

Heatherwhinny scowled at Stamey the bear. "Jaunt couldn't join us?" she asked in her nasally voice.

"He's in a tiff over some berries," griped Stamey.

"Eat too many again, did he?" asked the elder horse.

"No. I ate them for him," replied the arrogant bear.

Thorafura, however, remained quiet and looked malevolently at each one there. This isn't just any new moon, she was thinking. It would also be a Twirthy Moon, its darkened mass hiding the serpent's eye in the constellation Naeddra. It would mean a night darker than dark, perfect for slitherslaying and slurping egg-juices or even… mmmm. She was losing herself in her ruminations.

The room was growing grim as the sun continued to set. It was now well past tea time, and if the she-snake could hold each of them for a few more minutes longer, then this pesky Heatherwhinny will have whined her last complaint. As for that insufferable Stamey, the sinking of the sun will settle his snobbery for good. And what about Sanderford? she mused. Leave him be. Without these other snots for him to snort at he'll just die a miserable, slow, and lonely death all on his own.

"Tea, Heatherwhinny?" asked Tamara, growing uneasy at the change in temperature around her table.

"Herbal, please. Lemon grass would be best. And no honey, though a sugar cube would be perfect if you have any left."

"Sorry, old girl," sniped Stamey, "but it's Constant Comment tonight as you can tell from the banter around the table."

"Then I'll just have a sandwich, if you please," said the horse.

Thorafura's tongue whipped across her lips. "Delicious tea, Heatherwhinny. You should expand your culinary palate and join us for a cup while it's hot."

But Heatherwhinny ignored Thorafura and sat herself down to enjoy her cucumber sandwich.

"It's getting dark, Tamara, how about a little light, otherwise you won't be able to enjoy the finery I wore to grace your table," pleaded the snobby bear.

"Candle-light would be best," said Thorafura. "This setting screams for a little candle-light, and if I know Sanderford, he would prefer it to the glaring artificial light of the human bulb-stick."

Tamara found three candles and set them in the middle of the table. She lit them just as the last bit of sun had done its job to keep them in light.

Stamey took his napkin from his lap and, as daintily as he could, wiped the corner of his mouth just as Heatherwhinny shifted in her seat and knocked it from his hand onto the floor. The paunchy bear groaned and struggled to bend sufficiently to fetch it.

"Oh, allow me," offered Thorafura, whose slender, striking beauty was highlighted perfectly by the dancing light from the candles. Her eyes glistened as her sleek neck curved downward beneath the table and out of view. Slowly, her body untwirled itself and she emptied the seat in which she had been sitting. As the trailing end of her torso gave way to tail, she snapped it skyward and slashed it across the table hurling the candle sticks across the room toward the drapery. In that instant, she sunk her face into the protruding belly of the horse and pierced her with long razor fangs filled with poison. Then, with the speed and snap of a ringmaster's whip, she twined herself around the bear, tightened her powerful body around his and forced his last squeal out of him. As she squeezed, she raised up and towered over Tamara. Thorafura's eyes reflected the fire filling the curtains, and her ferocious jaws, dripping with horse-blood, soared at Tamara, intent on striking, but the snake halted inches before her face.

"Thank you for the tea. Now, best tend the fire," hissed the serpent. "I'll be back. Trust me."

Tamara thrashed her way back into some cognition and found she was being held down by Aimee. She was hot, and her t-shirt was damp. Her hair was matted with sweat, and she was in no mood to have her waking moments invaded by her mother. Aimee kept a heavy hand on Tamara's shoulder trying to steady her shaking body. As her daughter came more fully awake and grew calm, Aimee lightened her pressure.

The room was still dark.

"What time is it?" asked Tamara.

"Quarter to four. You okay?"

Tamara involuntarily looked over at her curtains then whispered, "I guess so," though her head felt like it was on fire. She squeezed her temples hoping to push out the pain building behind her eyes.

"You're sure?" asked her mom.

Tamara released a semi-positive groan, enough to reassure Aimee it was a bad dream but nothing more.

"You've still got a few hours before you have to get up. Think you can get some more sleep?" asked Aimee.

"Not likely," moaned her daughter, still seeing Thorafura's burning eyes and naked teeth ready to strike at her.

Aimee turned on the small lamb-shaped night-light, so she could see her daughter.

"Can I do anything?" implored her mom.

"You can cut this head from my body," replied Tamara.

"Hey!" Aimee shot back, then she tempered her tone. "Want to talk about it? What was it?"

"Mom, surely by now you're over asking idiot questions like that." Tamara rolled over and turned her back to her mother.

"No. Actually, I'm not, especially when I think it might help."

"I've had it with walking everyone through my dreams and hallucinations and psychotic vacations from reality, especially at four in the morning," protested Tamara. "Why are you here?"

"Because you called me," said Aimee.

Tamara rolled back over and looked quizzically toward her mom.

"You never do, is my point," Aimee explained. "Usually, when you're in crisis, you just lash out at whatever is going on inside you as if you could beat it back into submission. But a little while ago, you were shouting my name loud enough to wake us. Your whole tone was different."

"Sorry," said Tamara, who became introspective. The fear elicited by Thorafura evoked a powerful response, but it wasn't to fight, nor was it to flee. She could feel the cry for help tingling within her even if she had no memory of vocalizing it. Even so, where that help would come from was still up for grabs. As much as she wished her mom might make some kind of a difference, Tamara had lost faith in her mother's assurances that all she wanted to do was to help her. Tamara felt, more strongly all the time, that her mother's interventions, or lack of them, have been part of the problem all along.

Her mom's persistent refusal to address Tamara's mental suffering through proven therapeutic practices had made its mark on Tamara in significant ways. Until she approached her tenth birthday, Tamara had little concept of what mental health was meant to be and so took her inner trauma as it came, with whatever help her parents could offer to soothe her. Then, following several life-threatening skirmishes with her inner demons, Tamara entered the fight at full tilt. The family began therapy with Dr. Samuelson, and one thing she demonstrated was that she had inherited her mom's gristle, her love for battle and her pride for the spoils. With every pit of darkness she crawled back out of, Tamara took it as proof that she could lick this. To her parent's grief, however, Tamara's violent counter-attacks were usually launched against them, because Tamara had nowhere else to aim the assaults born of her suffering.

But the fight was taking its toll, and Tamara's resistance to those demons had been waning. In those snake-eyes staring back at her, Tamara saw she needed another future. She wanted out of this reality, and she knew for sure she didn't want to fight her way out. She didn't have much fight left in her. But she also knew she was not going to let her demons win and drive her off the cliff into the valley of shadow and death anymore. To win this fight, however, she felt she had to seize the initiative from her mother whose persistence had driven her along this path for so long.

"Mom," said Tamara.

"What is it, honey?"

"I'm still wondering what baptism is all about. You and dad said we would talk with Dr. Samuelson about it, but we never seem to get there."

"You haven't brought it up," said Aimee.

"That's because ever since we got back from New Hampshire, you and dad have been trying to figure out what happened between you and him and the axe."

"Sorry. We have been preoccupied with that. Is there anything you'd like to talk about right now?"

"No," groaned Tamara, who felt their therapeutic hour was up. But her craving for a new beginning was intensifying, and while she wasn't sure how something like baptism fit in there, she sensed it should now.

"Well, next time we see Dr. Samuelson let's start with that."

"If nothing else comes up instead," answered her daughter.

That was always a big if since her life was far too unpredictable for her.

On several occasions, Tamara's mind had careened so far out of control she had come close to ending her own existence, but she managed to pull out of those attempts. Each time, she felt she had been handed back her life, but it was the same life as before, a life that continued down the same road toward the same frightful, deadly end. But that last time in New Hampshire, when she decided not to jump from the mountain ledge, she was given something new. Through the acceptance and faith of an old woman, Tamara began to realize what that something new might look like.

Though she was still a long way from understanding what was going on inside her head, as she lay in bed with her mom seated comfortably beside her, she knew that the fight no longer belonged to her mother or even to herself. There was another who had entered the field of battle to fight on her behalf.

Aimee leaned over and kissed her daughter on the forehead then told her to see if she could get a few more hours of sleep.

Rather than drift back to sleep and risk any further assaults on her mind, however, Tamara reached under her bed, found her sketch pad, and began to draw. With sharp angry strokes of her pen, she sought to purge her mind of the images still biting at her. She drew her tea-table surrounded by those stuffed animals that had come to embody the monstrous forces at work within her. They were all so oblivious to the deadly snake in their midst. But she couldn't quite capture the essence of stupid, so she concentrated on the fury of the snake which she reproduced all too well. She slammed the notebook shut and shoved it back under her bed.

2

THE INVITATION OF A LIFE-TIME

AIMEE COULDN'T WAIT TO GET home to share the news. The subway trip seemed longer than usual, but the familiar scenes faded as she dreamt through the possibilities percolating in her mind. She stopped along the way for filet mignon at the butchers, a bottle of red, and a bouquet of flowers for the table. She pushed through her front door in the mood to celebrate, but to her disappointment, she had come home to a quiet house. Her daughter had vacated to her room. When she remembered to turn on her personal phone and check her messages, she discovered Terrance would be working late again.

The stack of mail on the dining room table, topped with the note from Tamara's principle, sank Aimee's mood into the floor.

Aimee poured herself a glass of port and stared hard at three letters spread out on the table. The first letter was from the president of Singleton Investments offering Aimee a new position in their firm provided she represent them at an economic conference in Zurich. The second, a rather blunt note accompanying Tamara's fourth quarter mid-term report, informed the Baxters that their daughter was dangerously close to failing this year and recommended a summer session if she didn't want to repeat the grade. Failure would mean that Tamara's provisional acceptance into the Upton Academy of the Arts would be withdrawn. But the letter drawing all of Aimee's attention and draining her of her ability to focus on the other two, was a handwritten note, three pages long, from an old woman she barely knew. That letter was included with another, addressed to Tamara, inviting her to visit over summer vacation. Aimee hadn't shown that letter to her daughter yet since she felt she had to resolve the other two issues first.

The conference on global investment in Zurich had been offered to Aimee as the result of a new set of investment strategies she was promoting among the officers of her firm. Ever since she returned from their trip to New Hampshire earlier that spring, she had been growing restless as a trader on the floor of the New York Stock Exchange. Her personal powers had not been feeling challenged of late, and she had begun wishing for a change of venue. Her president, who was more interested in keeping Aimee on his team than keeping her on the floor of the Stock Exchange, offered to entertain her proposals. When the letter, along with the conference details, was delivered to her desk that afternoon she lost all consciousness of anything else going on around her. The letter consisted of three lines:

> I've given a lot of thought to your suggestions, and I agree. I also think the new position you have designed for our firm makes a lot of sense. After you return from Zurich we'll meet and discuss your new package.

After scanning the letter from the school principle once more, she let it drop from her hand and paced over to the window to look out onto the street which should have been bright with the light of spring but was overcast and waiting for rain.

On the wall by the window, a simply framed picture of a teenage girl struggling to get away from an elderly man drew her attention. *The Prodigal Daughter,* it was called. It had been given to her by her new friend, Barb, who still held forth on an old family farm in the White Mountains. Every time Aimee looked at it she saw something new: inspiration to continue the fight, a warning not to allow the fight to become the main thing, or dread as she realized there are some fights that may need to be lost if greater gains are to be made.

She needed a walk to clear her head of the tangle now forming in it. Dinner would be a while and it was beginning to look like an afternoon shower was on its way, so she'd best go if she was going at all.

"Tamara?" Aimee called up the steps then decided she would look in on her daughter. She found Tamara seated on the floor, her back to the wall, and her long legs pulled up under her chin.

"You okay?" asked her mom.

Tamara didn't look at her mother but answered back: "Yea. Guess so. You okay?"

Not so sure, thought Aimee, but she was touched by a question asked by a daughter who rarely said anything, much less inquired after her well-being. She was even more surprised by what came next.

"Sorry about that note," said Tamara, whose face was usually rigid, if not funereal, but was now softened by red, puffy eyes. There was defeat evident in every one of her features.

"I was just about to go for a walk. Want to stroll over to the park?" asked Aimee, already adjusting her plans.

Tamara slowly shook her head dislodging the puddle that had formed in her right eye. The wet streak on her daughter's cheek nearly drowned Aimee who knew better than to move toward her daughter or try to comfort her. Tamara's depressive moods walled her off from those around her, and her caustic responses to anyone who entered her personal space had them all trained to keep their distance.

Aimee risked it anyway. She stepped in and laid a gentle hand on the back of Tamara's head. Tamara responded immediately, seizing Aimee's hand and pulling it from her scalp. But instead of rejecting Aimee's touch, Tamara pressed her mother's palm against her own cheek. Aimee felt the heat of Tamara's tears. She crouched beside her daughter who turned and embraced her.

Years of psychotic rampage had broken this family in countless ways and prohibited any expressions of tenderness between them. But now, as if molten silver was being poured from its crucible into a new mold, a brief and brilliant moment of life, which neither of them saw coming, had just been forged. The embrace didn't last long, however, since the pressure mounting in Tamara's mind was causing her tremors. Her mother recognized all the signs. Aimee held her breath as her daughter massaged her temples then pressed in hard on her forehead.

"What is it? Can you tell me?" implored Aimee. But there was no need for an answer. Both of them knew what the letter from Tamara's school meant.

"It's going to work out, honey," whispered Aimee. "Trust me. Okay?"

She lingered to watch her daughter for a few moments and to enjoy this rare exchange between them. Then Aimee slipped out of Tamara's room allowing the brief moment of intimacy reassure her that Tamara was holding on to something she didn't want to let go of.

Aimee forgot about her walk and returned to the dining room. She drank the last sip of her port, took up the letter from New Hampshire and held it in her shaking hands. She wasn't sure if she had the fortitude to read it again. Aimee and Terrance had promised Tamara she could visit Barb over the summer if Tamara continued to do well in school. Aimee had selfishly hoped all would go well because she was as eager to continue getting to know this wondrous old woman who opened up so much of her heart and home to them under such terrible circumstances. But there were two other letters on the table that threatened to undo their plans. She hoped, if nothing else, that the wisdom so saturating Barb's letter would shine a bit of light on how she should handle the others. However, even as she began to read it through again, she realized that its gracious tone was only going to hurt all the more when she had to face other realities.

Dear Aimee,

Your kind note thanking me was so thoughtful. I confess I felt odd reading it. I had been composing my own letter of appreciation to _you_ for sharing your beautiful daughter with me. I can't tell you how much that meant. I think I saw so much of myself (and Sally Anne) in her that I got lost in those few hours and didn't realize all that was happening. So many old memories, and all of them still so fresh.

You are a very courageous woman to be raising your daughter as you are. Terrance and Tamara are both most blessed!

After you left, I spent much of the day roaming around this old house seeing it all again with such different eyes. Tamara's presence brought back spirits that once haunted me but now bring me a measure of peace as I consider them again. When Sally Anne took her own life, I had felt so forsaken. It took years to get over that. Or, I thought I had. I guess you never really do. Tamara's struggle helped me realize there are things in this life from which we never heal. Remember Paul's thorn in the flesh? He asked God to heal him over and over again, but the Lord simply replied, "My grace is sufficient for you, for my power is made perfect in weakness." I sensed a lot of grace at work in your family, Aimee. And that grace helped me see my own memories in a new way. There is a lot of pain still in my heart – in all of us, I know, but a great power was at work that weekend mining that pain for something new, which I still can't see yet, but trust it to come.

I can't stop praying for you, Tamara, and Terrance. The Lord has given you a rare gift. I know that you don't understand that. Few people could. But having been through all I've been through with my family, I see God accomplishing things in yours that can't be overlooked or taken for granted.

I can't begin to imagine all that you have been through. From the little that I witnessed, I know few families that could have endured the suffering Tamara's mind has caused you all. Forgive me for being so forthright, but you deserve honest talk, and I've been walking around with these thoughts for a couple of weeks now. My father's depression caused him to lash out at us, mine almost ended my life, and Sally Anne's did end hers. Tamara's mental struggles, however, seemed to give her power. She is a most remarkable young woman, and I feel deeply privileged to have spent those few hours with her. When I saw the suffering she clearly endures, and I saw the way she sought to steer a course through it, I felt a new kind of awe. God is reaching in to her young life, and I can't help but believe that God has great things in store for her.

When you showed up Saturday night, I knew it was an answer to prayer. I had been praying for Tamara ever since I dropped her off at Nanna's hoping I would have the chance to meet up with her again before you left. She reached in to my heart like no one ever has before. I felt a spiritual connection with her from the moment I sat down beside her on the river bank after the baptism. She has a searching heart, and there is little in this world that is going to satisfy it, I'm afraid. My guess is that her mind doesn't know how to erect boundaries between fact and fantasy, or between this world and others beyond, whether it be heaven or hell. In the same way, there are no boundaries between her and those in her life. She reaches right in, doesn't she! And, I have to be honest, when I felt her reaching in to me I wanted to shut her out at first. But something told me that wasn't the right thing to do. So, I opened the door, and in she came. She seems to have a genius for knowing right where you live!

After she went to bed, I prayed much of the rest of the night for God to heal her, ease her pain, and bring peace to your family. I pleaded with God to take this suffering from you. But, as God usually does, the more I prayed for what I thought was right, the more God turned the prayer around in my mind. That's when I was reminded of Paul's thorn, and that's when I felt some assurance that you have not been alone in any of this. There is great grace at work, Aimee, great grace indeed.

Please forgive the religiosity of an old woman! I know you and Terrance aren't "church folk," and I don't mean to preach. But there are those rare times when you realize you have been in the presence of the holy, and that is what I experienced the weekend you and your family came to our mountain. I know how much courage that took for you to bring her here. I could sense great struggles going on in all of you, and I have a feeling they have continued since you have been home. I pray for you every day.

After all this, I hope I don't have to say again how sincerely I hope your family will come and visit. I have no other plans for the summer, and there are no takers on the little farmhouse, so it's all yours. Also, I hope you won't be angry at me for over-extending my reach again, but I've enclosed a letter to Tamara with an open invitation to come see me anytime she wishes and to stay for as long as she can. She is growing up, as you know too well, and I want her to know that there are people out in the world beyond home that accept her, love her, and appreciate her for who she is.

I love you all, and pray daily that God will strengthen and supply you as you face your futures together. God bless you!

Sincerely,
Barb

A deepening silence, the likes of which Aimee had never known, washed through her cleansing her of any need to figure this out. She sat in that silence and allowed this strange peace to rumble through her. Closing her eyes, she pictured Barb and Tamara struggling to cook an omelet together the morning after a hike up the mountain to the overlook. There, atop that mountain, Aimee had watched her daughter's life drawing to a close on a precipice over which other lives had fallen. A vision of her and Terrance walking back down the mountain without Tamara thundered through her mind, and the sensation crushed her heart. Then, to remember the taste of the eggs Tamara had served them the day after slammed her with a fearful hope, and if she didn't do something soon, she felt she might collapse.

Terrance would be furious when he found she had made this decision without him, but the urgency rising within her to act displaced her caution. An alien inner voice was speaking to her, but it was to her own words that she was listening: "It's going to work out. Trust me. Okay?"

As she climbed the stairs to deliver Barb's letter to Tamara, Aimee heard the shattering of glass. She took the stairs two at a time and pushed hurriedly into Tamara's bedroom.

Since she was three years old, Tamara's bedroom had been arranged around a small tea-table where Tamara had hosted countless tea-parties with real and imaginary friends (and several fiendish intruders). As Aimee entered the room, Tamara was throwing the dishes, one by one, into her garbage can, smashing them as violently as she could. Aimee quickly grabbed up the last cup and saucer as Tamara lunged for them.

"Hey! I'd like to have these if you don't want them," shouted Aimee.

Tamara froze and stared at her mother.

"What gives?" asked Aimee.

"Done with them," said her daughter.

"Just like that?"

"Just like that."

"Can I help you with the table and chairs?" Aimee asked, hoping to save them from the wrecking ball.

"Do whatever you want. I just want them out of here."

So together, mother and daughter dismantled the set and carried it down to the cellar. When they returned to the room, they were struck by the change in atmosphere and how out of place Tamara's childhood decor now looked. Tamara took the teddy-bear clock off her wall and handed it to her mother, then she pulled down one picture after another opening up yards of bare wall space. Aimee found a few boxes for those things she wanted to hang on to, but much of it she would bundle up and discard. It was a cathartic experience for them, a purging they both felt and shared together. Lastly, Aimee picked up a set of children's books stacked on Tamara's dresser.

"Wait," said Tamara as she reclaimed an illustrated volume of *Watership Down*, placed it on her dressing table, and nodded to her mom that she could take the rest.

Aimee balanced the stack of books in one arm as she fished the letter out of her pocket and handed it to Tamara.

"What is it?"

"Just read it, and see," said her mom.

In her hand, Tamara held a pale green envelope with her name written on it. As her mom was about to leave, Tamara looked Aimee in the face. Her mom's eyes were glistening, but the expression seemed to describe pride, not frustration or fear, as it so often did when Tamara's actions or words had brought her mother to tears.

Tamara sat down on the bench by her dressing table and opened the letter.

Tamara, my dear, dear friend;

First of all, I wanted to let you know that the kittens we "hatched" have new homes! All but one, that is, and I named her Tam. She had the speckled face, remember? Also, I'm sorry to report that one of our hens is no longer with us. That's the way of the farm, however. God gives us these little creatures as a way of caring for us, and we care for them back. We feed them, and they feed us. You cooked some of her eggs, and you can be thankful that we all did our rightful duty by one another.

I so enjoyed your visit! I have missed you and want to remind you that you are always welcome to come and see me. I could sure use the extra help around here! The invitation stands, and the little farmhouse is ready for you and your family whenever you can talk them into coming.

Your visit was very special to me, Tamara. I don't mind saying it was also very hard. You are the first person I have talked to about my family in that way in many years. As you now know, life in my family, like life in yours, has been difficult. In many ways, we have been struggling with some of the very same things. Your struggle is very special, however, and I feel privileged that you chose to share it with me.

I've been thinking a lot about our conversation, especially the one about prayer. You asked me if I could teach you to pray, remember? And I had to confess I didn't know how to teach you. I'd like another opportunity if you'll give it to me. I pray for you and your family every day. I thank God for you, because I consider you to be a gift God brought into my life. And, I ask God to ease your struggles or to bring you strength when your struggles cause you pain. I also pray that you will learn from your struggles, and that God will teach you how you can strengthen others who suffer like you do.

You could not have realized it at the time (and I didn't, either), but that is what you were offering me when you came for lunch then stayed with me that evening. Your suffering brought me some peace. Or rather, I should say that your suffering helped me cope with my own in a new way. You were sensitive to my pain in ways no one else can be, because, I think, you feel pain in ways most other people can't. Then, when you asked me to teach you how to pray, I believe God was challenging me to pray in ways I've never prayed before. I actually think you helped God teach me how to pray my pain. Your suffering brought all my pain back to the surface, so I would have to talk to God about it in ways I've never talked to him before. Now, my pain includes yours. And I believe, that evening, your pain included mine in a way that was very healing for me.

Now, I would like to ask you to pray for me. As you know, I'm getting older all the time, and age brings with it challenges that young women like you can't even begin to imagine. One of those challenges is living with memories of those you've lost. So many of my loved ones are now gone. I have Tobias, my son, and I have my church. But so many of those who were most special to me are now deceased. I'd like to consider you a part of my family, Tamara. I would like you to thank God for the friendship he has created between us. And I would ask you to pray, that through our friendship, God would bring us both a little more peace of mind. Also, please pray with me for your parents. I pray for them every day. But they have such a big job raising you that it will take the both of us praying for them if they are ever to succeed!!! Thank God for them, Tamara. Please promise me you will. Your parents will do anything for you, and they have, and you are so blessed to have them. How I could have wished for parents like yours! Cherish them, or I'll spank you when I see you next!

You may be asking, "But how do I pray for all that?" Remember this, Tamara: God is already listening to you. I know he is. So just talk to him. And I know that you are already listening to him. So, listen. Listen with love, not with fear, and listen with hope, not despair. Trust that there is no darkness in him, only light. Listen to that light. I know you know what I mean when I say that. Then, speak back. Remember the Shepherd? The one who leads us through the valley of the shadow of death. He is leading us now, and he knows the way. Just talk to him. He has been through that valley many times and he is there with us now.

To be honest, I really can't imagine what your life is like in New York City, and by now you may have forgotten this old woman in the hills of New Hampshire, but I had to write and share my heart with you.

You are a beautiful young woman – beautiful in so many ways you can't begin to appreciate yet. And you are a suffering young woman. I know that. We don't have to hide that. In a mysterious way, your suffering is part of your beauty, and it always will be. It is refining you. And it will, one day, be the gift you give to others, just as it has been the gift you have given to me.

Come see me. If not this summer, then whenever you can. You will always find an open door and, no matter how old I get, there will always be chickens and, of course, eggs! I love you, Tamara. God bless you.

Sincerely,
Barb
Romans 8:18 (That's in the Bible I gave you.)

How hungry had she been to hear words like that? She never knew until that moment. No one had ever offered her true acceptance. No one. She has always been a problem to be solved, a dilemma in need of a solution. And, as much as she might wish someone might have found a solution to her pain by now, what hurt her most was an incurable loneliness that told her every day that she is alone in this world. New Hampshire began to change that. She felt her parents taking steps into her world in new ways. But no one came as close as Barb had come that night Tamara sought refuge in Barb's home after watching her own life plunge over that cliff at the top of the mountain.

Earlier that day, on a hike to an overlook on the mountain, Tamara felt the wind's ferocity blowing in over the valley and it convinced her that she could leap, and soar, and never be beaten down by her pain any more. She had approached the precipice with no intent of turning back from it. Below her stretched only the darkening shadow her life had become, stretching forever before her, and that shadow grew ferocious in its angering gloom. Any light escaping over the pinnacle behind her was lost before it descended into those depths. Yet out before her, on the far horizon, stretched that eternity of calm she so craved.

Whether it was a new and unseen grace at work in her, or another fiend simply wanting to draw out this season of torture, she was shown the plaque that honored Mark, Sally Anne, and their baby. It was fixed to a small wall separating her from her eternity. As she studied it, she saw her own name there, her own dates scrawled in the brass, and she was reminded again of just how easy it would be. It would be more peaceful to be her parent's memory than their constant source of anxious worry. How she longed to be free of the weight that pressed down on her head every day and crushed her hope that life could ever be anything more. All her desires were carrying her over that precipice – all but one, the one that dropped her to her knees in a final assault against the death that was waging war against her. As she thrashed around on the ground, trying to rip the skin on her arms and dig her way into the pain, all she saw were bright slashes of light searing her inner sight. But that lightning in her soul only intensified the darkness which rumbled loudly through her with thunderous intensity leaving her ravaged by despair.

Then, she saw two old eyes looking into her, eyes that understood, saw her for who she was, and loved her for it. She had needed to look into those eyes again to make sure they were real, to see if they still knew her as she felt they did.

As Tamara recalled the first time she met Barb, she lingered for a few more moments in the glistening darkness behind her eyelids, not wanting to open them but to stare deeply into Barb's face once again. Tamara's heart thundered in her chest, and the sound of the wind outside her window pulled her back to herself.

Her room felt barren to her, and the rain hitting her window accentuated her solitude. She reached for the light on her dressing table then chose the dark instead. Her spirit was retreating into one of those dim, cavernous spaces within her where dark felt best, and the quiet was good. A calm was building in her, so she sat very still to allow it room. She closed her eyes again just to wait it out, knowing it wouldn't last but cherishing every heart-pulse that reminded her time was passing without her demons thrashing about within her.

"Listen," wrote Barb, "listen with love and not with fear, with hope and not despair." So, she listened to the wind driving the rain against her window pelting it in waves, and she listened to the honking horns of drivers eager to be out of the afternoon deluge. She listened to the sounds of her home and how quiet it was within. She listened for what her mom might be doing downstairs, and then she trained her ears to listen for what her dad must be facing at his office. And all was quiet. She listened to the peace in that and wondered how she might feed that the next time her mind lashed out at her. Then, she wondered if her wondering was anything like prayer.

She opened her eyes. The space created by the lack of a table in the center of her bedroom made the room feel three sizes bigger than it once was. The four indentions created by the absent table legs marked out space that once was sacred to her. This was the place of her communion, the setting at which she kept company, though except for her stuffed animals few others ever returned to enjoy her hospitality.

In the center of her room, Tamara slowly circled and remembered the menagerie with whom she used to share her tea: a four-foot giraffe named Tabathina; Stamey and Jaunt, the two snappishly dressed bears; Heatherwhinney, the worrisome horse; Forlinda, a grim looking lioness; Terapauntia, the turtle; Swishmashish, the fish; and Thorafura, the snake.

How they all managed to take tea together at once was quite beyond Tamara who had to intervene far too many times. She remembered the night she had to end their quarrels, once and for all, with a long kitchen knife. But as she turned slowly about in her tight little circle even that frightening memory was being replaced. Other faces were joining her at her table, people for whom she had been asked to pray.

The letter laying on the dressing table passed again before her rotating eyes and it moved her deeply to think of Barb's concern for her. Then, remembering the notation after Barb's name, she grabbed the letter for another look: Romans 8:18 (That's in the Bible I gave you.)

The tattered old burgundy Bible Barb had given her was a chaotic mystery. Its language was foreign, its organization incomprehensible. She had given up trying to make any sense of it and had let it languish on her floor until it got kicked one morning under her bed. She had no idea what 'Romans 8:18' meant. She riffled through the pages, but the chapter titles made no sense, so she slammed it shut before figuring it out. She grabbed her smart phone and typed it in. Up flashed these words:

> [18] For I reckon that the sufferings of this present time
> are not worthy to be compared with the glory which
> shall be revealed in us.

She opened the book again and searched until she found the table of contents which gave her the page number for a chapter called Romans. She gradually figured out the numbering system and, armed with the quotation, found the corresponding verse: "For I reckon that the sufferings of this present time..." Though she struggled with the words, the more she read, the more she saw her story being told in this ancient book: a creation groaning in its suffering awaiting its freedom, then a Spirit who helps us in our weakness and teaches us how to pray when we don't know how. And then, this:

> [35] Who shall separate us from the love of Christ? shall
> tribulation, or distress, or persecution, or famine, or naked-
> ness, or peril, or sword?
>
> [36] As it is written, For thy sake we are killed all the day
> long; we are accounted as sheep for the slaughter.

[37] Nay, in all these things we are more than conquerors through him that loved us.

[38] For I am persuaded, that neither death, nor life, nor angels, nor principalities, nor powers, nor things present, nor things to come, [39] nor height, nor depth, nor any other creature, shall be able to separate us from the love of God, which is in Christ Jesus our Lord.

The words had been underlined by someone else. On impulse, she looked inside the front cover:

For Sally Anne,
our daughter in Christ,
on the day of your baptism.
July 21, 1924
Mom and Dad
Romans 6:3-4

Tamara ceased to breath. She closed her eyes and thought hard, back to that moment when Barb had given her the Bible. Her parents had returned to the car. Barb had placed it in her hands after hugging Tamara one last time. When she realized Barb had just given her a Bible, she felt embarrassed and successfully hid it from her parents until she could stuff it deep into her book-bag. She felt instantly ashamed to think how she had received Barb's gift, but that shame intensified when she remembered how she had tried to use it against her parents on the plane by parading it in front of them when she got bored, just to strike matches she knew would spark small bon-fires within them.

She closed the book and pressed it hard against her chest. Hugging it as she once hugged Stamey the bear on those horrifying nights when she was under siege, she hoped that her mind would explain to her what she was doing with Sally Anne's Bible. Spirits that should have been so long buried and left in the mountains of New Hampshire were whipping around her head and soaring among the demons so easily awakened in the cemetery of Tamara's soul. Her mental muscle memory told her to find her sketch pad and slash out the disorder now disorienting her.

Instead, she read the inscription again then navigated herself once more to Romans, this time to chapter 6, where she read:

> ³ Know ye not, that so many of us as were baptized into Jesus Christ were baptized into his death?
>
> ⁴ Therefore we are buried with him by baptism into death: that like as Christ was raised up from the dead by the glory of the Father, even so we also should walk in newness of life.

Tamara was once again seated on that river bank in New Hampshire, watching four young women being plunged to their spiritual deaths in a rapidly flowing stream. It was there where she had first met Barb, and it was that spot she was beginning to identify as the place of some new beginning she was experiencing. She had no thoughts that would coalesce around those impressions that could give them concrete shape, but that stillness she had so enjoyed a few moments ago was now deepening in spite of the emotional surges coursing through her.

As she listened to those memories and pondered the mysteries now washing through her like that mountain stream, she heard her parents' voices and became mindful of the trouble that lay open on the dining room table: the note from her principle and the threat it imposed. That jolt in her psyche spoke to the need she was experiencing now more than ever, to stand beside that stream once again, even enter it herself and start something new. To that, she listened intently, and from what she heard, she found fresh resolve.

"No," said Terrance, as Aimee sought to lay out her hopes, newly forged by the letters that had come from New Hampshire. He had been home only a few moments and was still drying off when he discovered the stack of correspondence and saw the perfect storm about to overtake him before dinner.

"Look, she knew the deal," he continued. "We applied to that school to firm up her foundation for college, and if a summer term can salvage that, then that's what has to happen. They are holding that spot, and we have to make a good faith effort to help her keep it."

"Look at her mid-term report, Terrance. She has been improving. And, look at *her*, honey. You know full well she's doubled down, especially since we came back from New Hampshire. This means too much to her."

"And – to you, too. Right?"

Aimee's face felt hot, and she couldn't look at her husband. It did mean a lot to her. The new school. And yes, the trip back to the mountain.

Aimee threw the filet mignon into the skillet filling the room with a flavor neither of them could appreciate in the moment.

"Besides, what about your trip to Zurich?" said Terrance. "You can't take any time off, not when you're about to begin a new career at the same time. It's too much, Aimee."

She set two wine goblets on the island in the middle of the kitchen and handed the bottle of red to Terrance.

"Please, let me sort out the job part of this," she pleaded. "Right now, I want us to sort out Tamara's trip to New Hampshire this summer." She handed him the cork-screw.

"Aimee, I'm having a hard time keeping up here," protested Terrance. "This new school was your idea, and now that we've got Tamara on board I really don't think we should change directions again. We need to follow through on this."

"I'm going to work this out," insisted Aimee. "I'll schedule another sit-down with the headmaster to go over her schoolwork and portfolio and see if they'll still take her on. They understood her situation, and they said they could offer some leeway for the first semester as she gets settled. Now, tell me truthfully, do you really feel summer school is the answer, or are you just resisting the idea of a trip?"

"Yes, and no. I would be glad for Tamara to visit Barb again. But if Tamara's tenure at this school is provisional upon her work the first semester, then I want her to have every advantage going in. I don't want to risk upending her again, starting her in a strange school only to have that yanked out from under her if she can't keep up sufficiently to stay."

Aimee stuck a meat thermometer in the steak and poured herself a glass of wine. She sat down on a bar stool to think this through.

"All right," she conceded. "I'll find out the summer school schedule and surely we can work in a long weekend somewhere."

"I'm not going to summer school," said Tamara, who was standing just outside the kitchen door. Aimee and Terrance both turned and stared at their daughter. They knew when she was throwing logs on the railroad track. She was the master of obstruction and refusal. They also knew to count to ten before trying to reason things out, but she spoke first.

"I don't want to change schools again," she said. "I can't." Her face was not displaying its usual obstinacy but was matter of fact. She had spoken truth, and it resonated in both parents.

Aimee's face flushed. She looked long into the red wine catching the light from the kitchen ceiling.

"Tamara," whispered her mom, but nothing else came.

"No," said Tamara, and that was that. She stuffed her hands in her jean pockets and pulled her arms in straight by her sides accentuating her height and lanky proportions. She looked her father in the eyes, but her mother had withdrawn from the conversation and sat staring toward the meat on the stove.

Terrance had been watching a tectonic shift take place. The fight in his wife, always held taught in reserve, had left Aimee. Tamara's quiet resolve held more authority in the room, and for the first time in a long time, Terrance was watching his wife yield.

Aimee turned the steak in the skillet, then she walked out of the kitchen.

Tamara and her father felt a gulf open up in the room, and both feared to cross it. Their relationship had been unclear since they returned from New Hampshire. A new respect had grown between them. It was not a respect that had flowered into much conversation, but it bore fruit in cautious expressions of mutual affirmation as they acted or spoke. They were listening to one another with new ears, saying more with their eyes than their words, and where toleration prevailed before, a comfortable acceptance resonated between them now. For the moment, however, they weren't sure what they were giving their common assent to. Neither one knew who should follow Aimee, and both felt awkward staying put.

It didn't matter. Aimee reappeared with a large shopping bag, which she placed on the floor in front of Tamara.

"I was saving these for your birthday, but I think you should have them now. I got them shortly after we got home from New Hampshire," she said.

Tamara felt awkward and looked hard at her father who displayed sincere ignorance.

She reached into the bag and pulled out a portable easel, a set of oil paints, two canvass boards, an assortment of brushes, and a pair of rubber barn boots.

Terrance was wrong in thinking his wife had surrendered her ground. He had completely miscalculated the direction her resolve had taken.

"Now, you are going to summer school," said Aimee, staring forthrightly into her daughter's eyes. "And Barb is going to be one of your teachers. We'll make all of this fit. You just need to follow through."

Their dinner, which was to be a celebration of Aimee's new professional prospects, passed quietly as everyone let the matters before them settle more deeply within, each tiptoeing through their minds seeking answers to whatever this decision was going to mean for them all.

3

THE CRUCIBLE WHERE ART IS FORGED

WITH HER BAG OF ART supplies in hand, Tamara slowly climbed the stairs to her room and paused after each few steps to look at the pieces she had produced over the years. All professionally framed by her mother to chart Tamara's artistic advances, her younger drawings began at the foot of the stairs. A crayon miasma of color anchored the collection; colored pencil tortoises lying on their backs came next. Then, a pastel forest of wintry trees and a watercolor sea of creatures no one had yet discovered led the climber to a series of dreamscapes rendered in acrylics. The oils she had in her bag were evidently meant to mark a new period of artistic maturity.

As she considered the collection, Tamara knew her mother could not have seen what the young artist saw when she rendered them. The body of work she had produced over her life-time had come roaring out of a creative center on fire with pain which her mother evidently chose to ignore when she selected these for display. Reaching the upper landing, Tamara surveyed the empty wall space beyond the last picture and wondered what the art supplies in her bag promised that would appeal to her maternal curator. It would be a while, she thought, before the creative morass in her mind birthed up anything acceptable.

Tamara unfolded her easel. She set her large sketch pad upon it and rummaged in her art chest for a nubbin of black charcoal. With the sharp edge of the charcoal, she made bold slashes at the base of the page. Then, in the negative space between the slashes, she laced airy gray strokes with the broad side of the coal. The picture resembled a smoldering bed of scorched logs and ashes. From the tube of red oil paint, she placed a small dab of color on the tip of her pinky and set red, glowing, incandescent coals among the black cinders on her paper. To that, she added a spark of yellow and ignited a fire.

As she felt that fire warming her insides, Tamara tore off the paper to start again. But first, she walked around the easel feeling a new image rise in her mind. She burrowed her consciousness into that figure now taking shape within her and tried to study the image, but it's fluidity wouldn't allow her to capture it in color. Her vision was lavender with swirls of deep maroon over which danced flecks of golden light. For a brief moment, the colors in her mind would coalesce into definable shapes but then quickly shed their form as if they were bleeding out essential fluids. Each time this cycle repeated, the colors grew darker, from lavender to a midnight purple, from red to darker shades of maroon then into black.

Walking around in a circle defined by the circumference of her old tea table, she passed behind the easel and was distracted by her reflection in the mirror. It was an awkward moment during which she didn't recognize what she saw. The walls she saw in her mirror were made of stone overgrown with thick vines bearing dark glossy leaves and tendrils made of gold. The tendrils were feeling their way across the stony expanse pulling the vine and thickening the mass of foliage. The vine, or so she thought, twined around her ankle and tightened its grip. She thrashed her feet which wouldn't budge and felt a scream which couldn't move up through her fast enough to escape. A gripping force had tightened around her throat and constricted both her movement and her mind.

A warm, moist voice whispered words in a language that made her head throb. The wispy murmurs turned to lament, sad and sorrowful, and invited her to lie down in the green and be warm. The moment the voice told her to be warm, however, she felt cold. The sultry lament frostbit her heart and dropped her into a deep remorse. She fell down a hole within a hole infested with a sinister carnivorous guilt that hissed through its teeth, sniffed at her soul, then bit her in the chest opening a wound from which a brackish sludge spilled, a liquid refuse drawn from the salt mines out of which her tears were dredged.

Tamara lashed out with what little strength she had left and swung at the easel which collapsed in a heap on the floor. She threw her body across her bed, doubled herself into a ball and beat on her body with her fists. She needed to make physical contact with her mind and pry out the shards of shattered soul that were irritating inner wounds that never heal. Like a raptor clutching its prey, she sunk her talons into her forearms and sought to draw blood to prove there was still life, but all she found was carnage and death leaving her feeling lifeless.

The snake was curling around her body and tightening its long singular grip as it looked for naked flesh to strike. The pressure building in Tamara's brain blinded her, and the scream she tried to push up from her gut was caught in her throat by a final spasm from the serpent choking out her last hope for help. Tamara relinquished any control she had and allowed all her fight to soak into the bedding beneath her. She tried to quiet the snakish voice in her head, but the energy that required was more than she had within her, so she relinquished her will and let it strike mercilessly where she was most vulnerable.

Tamara stared out into the space that filled her bedroom and no longer saw anything she knew or loved. She had emptied her room of so much that was familiar, purged it of memories which were now lost to her without the reminders hanging on her walls or scattered about on her floor. Her inner emptiness echoed out of her soul's cavernous hell.

A light knock on the door went unanswered, so her mom eased herself into the room and recognized the signs immediately. She sat on the edge of the bed and rested a gentle hand on Tamara's back then gently massaged her shoulders. If her daughter knew she was there she made no indication of it. Aimee took a deep breath and looked around, seeing again for herself just how much of Tamara's childhood had walked out of her room earlier that day. She saw Barb's letter on Tamara's dressing table.

"What did Barb have to say?" she asked.

No response – just wide and darkened eyes emptied of their humanity staring toward a fixed point in space.

But Tamara had heard the question, and the shape of it implanted a new point of contact around which her mind could re-focus. She had no capacity to speak and no energy or desire to formulate an answer. So, her mind began doing what it does quite well, it reduced all the verbiage, all the phrases, all the feelings and intentions into a singularity of darkness into which all consciousness fell.

It wasn't words she heard, nor was there new light, but the sensations of a different wisdom altogether found their way out of the dark and became impressed upon her soul: Pray, Barb had written. Pray.

She listened to that singular sensation and searched through it for a way forward. She then found she was listening to other sensations: to her mother's weight on the bed beside her and to the gentle pressure of her mother's hand on her back. She listened to the concern in the voice asking questions, and she listened to the silent presence of one who cared. She struggled to listen with love and not fear, with hope and not despair.

Her mom bent over, kissed her forehead, and Tamara heard: I love you. And: I hurt with you.

The inferno that was burning up her mind subsided, though her head continued to throb. While she was still in a great deal of pain, the intensity of her suffering was being borne by others, and she was listening to that too. She had never heard that before. She had known everyone's worry and had been wrung out by their feverish attempts to ease her pain in order to alleviate their own, but all she ever heard in that was darkness. If there was light in those concerns others expressed toward her, then it was absorbed by the black hole of her tortured psyche. She had never been able to listen in the way Barb told her she should listen. And now, she wasn't exactly sure what she was hearing, or what to do with it, but she could mark the difference, and that ought to mean something.

Aimee stroked her daughter's hair for a moment and suggested it was time for bed. Tamara heard that, too, and would have liked to close her eyes and sleep, but there was too much now awakening within her.

Something new was taking shape in her mind, and it was causing her a different kind of pain. Knowing that there was someone praying for her, someone concerned for her well-being, someone beyond her family, made her feel vulnerable in an uncomfortable way. Her suffering was no longer private but was being carried by someone she hardly knew. How did she deserve that? She didn't. It made no sense to her. Who would ever do that? The only other person maintaining an active interest in her mental health was being paid to do so: Dr. Samuelson. Twice a month he listened, asked questions, offered insights and, every so often, gave them some instructions for how to deal with new manifestations of Tamara's suffering. Mostly, he sought to keep her safe and her parents sane.

Unlike Dr. Samuelson, however, Barb walked into this on her own. And when she discovered what she had run into, not only did she stay, she wanted more. Instead of backing out, Barb ventured further into Tamara's darkened soul.

Weariness was intensifying the pain in her mind, but Tamara dreaded the sleep she knew awaited her, the sleep that would bring forth everything now stirring in her haunted sub-conscience. She rolled off her bed and on to her feet, but her legs felt weak beneath her. She stood, now outside the imaginary perimeter of her old table, looking across the expanse of her bedroom. The mirror framed her slender shape. The room around her was back to normal, except that normal would have shown her a picture of Alice, the Mad Hatter, and the faint but sinister smile of the Cheshire Cat hovering between them. Normal would have shown her the Jack-in-the-Box that sat beneath those pictures and a hanging depicting Pooh, Piglet, and Eeyore that covered the back side of her bedroom door. And normal would have shown her looking like a teenaged girl who could care less that she lived in a room fitted for a six-year-old. But now, there was a lot of emptiness framing her reflection. No color, just off-white walls, slender legs, a rather shapeless body, bony arms and straight black hair. Black, expressionless, eyes. No smile. The nose and chin of her mother, or so everyone said, and she could see it. It was true. She looked more like her mother in her face than her dad. Her slender, nimble, physique belonged to him.

On the dressing table, the letter lay opened and its reflection in the mirror caught Tamara's eye. Was she beautiful, as Barb had said in that letter? She certainly was not pretty. As she began to undress, she left her reflection alone and preferred not to look. There were ragged scars on her arms where she had ripped at her skin with her fingernails, razor-width scars behind her legs where she had cut herself, and a scar on her hand from the kitchen knife. In her navel were two small reminders of the piercing she had a friend perform on her, and there was a slight nub she could still feel in her tongue from the piercing he attempted there. Again, she looked in the mirror and more deeply into her eyes. She couldn't begin to number the scars there were in there.

She slipped beneath her covers then turned off her light. She quickly missed the little lamb-shaped night light that used to spread its reassurances around the room. The blackness of the dark's thick and heavy weight overwhelmed senses in her that weren't prepared for it. Involuntarily, she shut her eyes to the darkness as if that would shield her from whatever was outside her, even when she knew her eye-lids were powerless against a more violent darkness that lay within her. She fought sleep instead of yielding to it. The veil that lay between her waking mind and so many other frightening worlds which she inhabited was being disturbed by the winds of her imagination. She would love to capture beauty on canvas, but the passions that eviscerated her forced her to draw that which horrified her, instead.

Tamara slipped out of bed, collected the easel from the floor and situated it by the mirror. She had a mounting urge to paint her self-portrait. On her pallet, she placed globs of dull colored paints: black and white with which she could mix shades of gray, then blue and red, which, when tinted with black, made her favorite color. There would be lots of that in her painting.

Then, she stood before the mirror and studied what she saw. Her eyes, deep and dark, were absorbing all her attention. There was no light there, only intensity that drilled deep into places most people never wanted her to go. Why did she see those hidden regions of other souls? And when she looked within them, why did it so haunt her and those she loved? Involuntarily, she dabbed her brush in the black and made two colorless holes in the white canvass, holes that would draw the light from others into her painting. But as she applied the paint to the canvass, the eyes staring back out were a fluid blue that glistened more brilliantly each time she tried to correct the image.

She gave that up and filled her brush with more black paint and washed it over the canvass, painting long streaks of hair to frame her face. But as she lifted the brush, the hair curled slightly upwards. She slashed at it to correct the image, but then, not only did the hair curl again, it shortened, lightened, and contained streaks of white which slowly shaded into gray. Her own nose was slender and sharp, but she could not cut such definition into the canvass. That nose came out softer, making the eyes even more gentle than they were before.

The intensity she witnessed staring back at her from the mirror was heightened by her frustration for failing so miserably to capture what she saw. She intended a sharp horizontal mouth, pursed and full of tension, but the brush kept sweeping upward each time she lifted it from the painting leaving a pleasant, summery demeanor in the subject instead of the frosty face she intended.

Now, angry, she set out to destroy the portrait. She pressed her palm upon the pallet and smeared all the colors together, creating at first a brilliant rainbow, then a dense mortar-colored mess that became a dull black sludge in her palm. She scooped up a hand-full and slapped it on the canvass. Paint splashed across her room dropping rainbow colors all over the carpet while coal sludge filled the white space before her. She swiped her hand in a counter-clockwise motion pressing each successive circle more deeply into the surface, but the more firmly she pressed, the lighter the paint became which heightened her anger. She pushed and swirled with more ferocity hoping to reclaim the black, but white was all her hands were producing at this point. Exasperated and exhausted, she rested her arm and stepped back to discover that what she had painted was an egg.

From the other side of the egg, the gaping, fanged maw of a snake emerged, encircled the egg and swallowed it whole, leaving Thorafura's scorching eyes filling Tamara's entire field of vision.

Now, wide awake at twelve-forty-two, her insides were grinding with apprehension. Circular patterns of worry were carrying her deeper and deeper into her haunted, horrid self. The face she had seen in the mirror, the one she wanted to paint, was a face she loathed looking back at her because of what lay behind those eyes. Sensations of fear and anxieties about her world were mounting faster than she could answer them or reason them out. One thought pushed aside another, and each was worse than the one before it. She was failing in school. Her parent's marriage was collapsing because of her. She was sicker than anyone would admit. Barb needed her help on the farm, but she was powerless to be there. And these demons would soon rob her of her mind and leave her huddled in the corner of her room bleeding out from where she had cut herself to kill them.

Tamara got out of bed and started circling her empty room looking for something she recognized. Trying to resist the mirror, she was unable not to look at herself. She hated what she saw – the face she tried to paint in the dream. That angular, dreary, unsmiling face.

She started for her door but refrained from going downstairs. The knives were down there, and she had promised Barb. Her parent's medications were in the bathroom, but she kept circling her room, kept keeping the promise she had made. She walked faster in an ever-tightening circle hoping to exhaust herself, but it never worked. She hoped the dizziness would feel better than the pain, but she became nauseous. The exercise was only pumping her adrenalin and woke her up rather than tire her out. It never worked. Walking in circles. If her future resembled her past, she could be in for several nights of this. She would be up like this all night and on into the morning. Luckily, it would be a Saturday; no school. No failing at school tomorrow because of no sleep tonight.

The easel lay splayed on the floor and the stark emptiness of her room gave her the sensation of being in a foreign land. The ambient light from the street filtered through her drapes and cast a grim light over her bare walls. She had been walking around her easel, but now she shoved it aside, laid down on her floor, and looked at the ceiling.

Tamara wished Barb had taught her how to pray, but she was not in sufficient control of her ruminations to focus on praying even if she knew how. If only Shepherd Jesus could wield his staff and drive these demons from her mind. If it wasn't Thorafura filling her mind with venom, it was these granthyrs gnawing on her flesh from the inside out, snorting at her, laughing at her for being such easy prey. She thought of calling her mom, but her mom would hate her for it, hate her for being such a nuisance all the time with her head full of worry about nothing that meant anything to anyone else but her. She should do homework and succeed, but it was impossible for her to do anything but fail, so she kicked at the idea in her mind. She should draw something, anything at all, but she refused to turn on the light. She didn't want the light in her eyes or in her head or scraping against the insides of her body awakening anything that could still be asleep in there that might terrorize her. The drawing would just remind her later of all she was going through now. She hated drawing when she had to draw, hated studying her demons, hated giving them the benefit of line and definition on the page, hated others being able to see what her insides looked like.

All night she lay awake on her floor where her tea table used to be and those creatures of hers used to fight with her. But they were now dead. Thank God, they were dead. Then, why wouldn't they leave her alone? They kept sneaking back in to the party. But maybe now, since she had destroyed her tea set and removed her table, they would get a clue.

4

ALONE IN THE CITY

THE FAINT LIGHT OF DAWN found Tamara curled up in the corner of her bedroom. Her mood had sunk steadily over the course of the night depressing even her anxieties, leaving her in a dull state of apprehension. She studied the emptiness of her room and knew she had to assign herself a mission and drive herself forward. Otherwise, she was in for a day of dealing with her parents' tiresome worry over how she was doing. She pulled herself up off the floor, got dressed, then opened the small music box on her dresser from which she pulled several weeks' worth of allowance, about forty-five dollars, and stuffed that in her jeans pocket. She tiptoed downstairs and wrote a short note which she left on the kitchen counter ("Gone shopping"). Then, she slipped out the front door.

The moment the door latched behind her, Tamara realized she forgot her key. She tried the door, but it was locked. She had committed herself, perhaps, beyond what she was ready to endure. Still resting in the shadows of early dawn, the city was quiet which suited the fog in her brain. Her body felt like sludge poured into a mold that didn't want to congeal, but she needed to focus on something beyond her and make headway against the storm just over the horizon in her head. The sun had not warmed the masonry around her, so the world felt cooler than it probably was, and her solitude was deepened by being alone in a place where she was usually pressed and pushed by so many people.

She stepped down the four steps to the sidewalk that would take her, where? Usually at the side of her mother whenever she left the house, the sensation of autonomy was disorienting, and her indecision intensified as she stood at the corner and looked in four possible directions without a clear destination in mind. At almost fifteen years of age, Tamara should know her neighborhood pretty well, but Aimee's caution over Tamara's condition had kept her on too short a leash. And Tamara felt secure on that leash. She could find her own way to the subway each morning for school, and if she followed this street for several blocks it would bring her to Central Park. But there was no shopping to be done in the park. Still, that little bit of knowledge empowered her, so she crossed the street and headed in that direction.

It was only seven-forty-five on a Saturday morning, and the signs on all the stores told her that none of them would be open before ten. At the next intersection, Madison Avenue stretched northward before her, so at a casual pace she strolled past windows elegantly outfitted and beautifully designed, each one displaying nothing she could imagine for her room. Clothes she could not see herself in draped models as thin as she was, but their bodies were too shapely to be her own. There were handbags and accessories for a woman she never wanted to be, make-up for a face she never wanted to see in a mirror, and household elegancies that might look good in other parts of her home (she did recognize her parents' tastes here and there) but not in the room she wanted to inhabit.

She came to an art gallery, the marquee of which advertised a new show opening later in the day. A woman in brightly colored pants and a flowing top was fussing around in the tight space of the display window arranging paintings, the textures of which disturbed Tamara enough to hold her mind hostage. The colors had mass and dimension that lifted them off the plane of the canvasses. The vibrant textures forced their essence into Tamara's space and made her want to touch, if not grab hold, parts of the composition. Bronzes and magentas clashed then evolved into cubes and pyramids in one piece, while in another, turquoise and crimson collided like two trains erupting into flashes of light that shimmered and hovered above the wreckage below. As fascinated as Tamara was by the images, however, once she had taken them inside her they left her feeling icy.

Someone emerged from within and left the door ajar. No longer conscious of the time of the morning, Tamara slipped through the door curious about the rest of the display. The few people scurrying around took no notice of her. She drifted through an arched portal into a dimly lit room with dark portraits mounted on a wall illuminated by soft spot lights that brightened only the central space of the pictures. The portraits, such as they were, were not faces as one would recognize them, but each painting traced a range of human moods, a few of which Tamara could identify with rather well.

As she situated herself in the middle of the room, her periphery expanded as the muted tones and soft light evoked feelings that would not settle but became fluid within her as the artistic expressions of emotion washed across the surfaces of her awareness. Directly in front of her, a "face," highlighted with various shades of crimson and forest green, cracked across that plane where the eyes might have been. Searing points of gold flared into a fiery mass of light which lit up her mind with a metallic corona that illumined the fiends hidden within her. The face moved, searched the room for her, found her and punctured her mind with a savage burst of energy that filled her world with molten crimson. She felt her mind bleeding, growing dark. But that darkness was suddenly and fiercely effaced by a brilliant white light from above which flooded the room with a harsh neon glow.

"Who are you!" shouted a weasely looking character who had just turned on the light. "How did you get in here?" she squealed. It was the brightly clothed woman Tamara had seen in the window. But Tamara, already disoriented from the effects the paintings had on her, couldn't focus on the woman's face. Instead, she saw the emotions of the woman which flamed out at her as sharp slashes of gold and silver. Patches of blood-red sludge coursed across the floor and flowed toward Tamara then turned to a black bile which rose up around her until she felt herself drowning.

"Out of here, you street rat," the lady screamed, "or I'll call the police. And if I see you anywhere near here again, I will."

Tamara was powerless to move. She couldn't focus her will to respond or find any impulse within her to turn and walk out the door. The room around her had separated into a thousand pointillist pieces of pigment none of which were melding into any fathomable form. The fluid sensations of anger rushing around the room unbalanced her. There was no texture to her world in that moment and no coalescence or material shape for her to focus her eyes upon. She simply felt the atmosphere around her screaming. Then, physically, she was pushed. Her body was thrust around in a circle. Had her legs not reacted, she would have landed on her face, but there were steps being taken in the lower regions of her body which the upper stories couldn't account for. Her body knew it was being hurled through the space she inhabited, even if her mind didn't register it. As she turned, her visual range exploded, and she was swallowed into the vast regions of eternity and lost all sense of being.

Sounds of the street gathered in her ears and the array of hues ricocheting across her mind became a warm bath of consistent light. Sun light, now washing through the streets, was pushing other colors from her head and showed her standing at the edge of the street curb. Cars were lined up within inches of her waiting for the light to change. Nothing else was familiar to her. She could make little sense of her surroundings other than that this was the city in which she lived.

Was she about to cross the street? She didn't know. Where was her mother? Why was she here alone? She felt for her phone, but her back pocket was empty. She circled around hoping to gain her bearings and saw the art gallery. The paintings in the display window, the marquee that called her inside, they teased her memory and reminded her of her mission. She had needed to re-discover the world in which she wanted to live and bring home enough of it to create a space in which she could find some peace, free of her haunted childhood.

She had gone shopping.

Tamara thrust her hand into her pocket and was relieved she still had her money. Where was her phone? She looked around the sidewalk and felt panic slithering up her spine, whispering her name. She paced in front of the gallery, growing more agitated, she then rushed to the end of the block, following other impulses rising within her. She closed her eyes at the corner, took three deep breaths, and absorbed the warmth of the sun which was now high enough to shine into the valley forged by the mountainous buildings around her. Her ears were taking in the sounds of the city, but she was listening more intently to competing impressions whispering within her, one telling her to knock on the gallery door to see if her phone was in there, the other inviting her to let it go.

Tamara began to walk. The city was coming alive now, and a few shops were opening, though she no longer felt the urgency to buy anything. She was thinking of her easel lying on her floor and the empty walls in need of color, texture, and warmth.

In her periphery, a store display caught her attention. The window was filled with fabrics, weavings and other textiles, not the sort one would wear or drape from windows, but delicate, whispy fabrics of subtle hues that looked more like they should be a fragrance than anything material. These were hung near coarse, loosely woven pieces tinted in deep purples and dark greens. Others were heavy, earthy, dark, rich browns with a fertile feel as if you could drop a seed into them and something would sprout and grow. There were some with distinct images woven in to them, but mostly the effects of the collection left her feeling blanketed by warmth and love. So different from the harsh art she had been accosted by earlier that morning, these expressions moved her deeply. The swelling within her was not familiar to her. Sadness and remorse, she knew; they effectively produced the tears forming in her eyes, but that was not what she was feeling.

The sign on the door said the shop was closed until Monday with a number to call if she wanted to make an appointment. She took a deep breath and one long last look then moved along. Now, the bedroom walls she was seeing were hung with colors she could feel and smell and, if she wanted to, lay them on the floor and walk barefoot through them. As she pondered her room and her imagination moved through that space, she looked out her bedroom window and saw mountains instead of buildings, green trees instead of gray masonry. And she heard the sound of chickens instead of cars. The tears that had been forming were now rolling down her cheeks, and the swelling sensations evoked by the weavings she saw now swallowed her whole.

"Tamara Baxter?"

She heard her name but wasn't sure of the direction from which it came, and why should she trust what she heard after the morning she has had?

"Miss Baxter?" said the voice once again, and Tamara turned around. A police officer was calling to her from inside a car that had pulled alongside her.

Tamara wiped her eyes, stood still, and stared. The officer turned off the car and eased out of his door.

"Everything's okay," he assured her. "Don't be alarmed."

But she wasn't alarmed. It took a moment to adjust to hearing a strange person speak her name, but she had no impulse to run or be frightened.

"Are you Tamara?" he asked in a kind, calm voice.

She nodded.

The officer walked slowly around the vehicle but kept his distance from Tamara, easing into her space as delicately as he knew how.

"Your parents are worried about you," he said after studying her for a few moments.

Tamara remained still, feeling her heart beating faster than before.

"Do you mind if I call them?" he asked.

She didn't respond. A flash of anxiety shot through her mind, but as she considered the question what rose within her was relief.

"I could call them, if you want," added the police officer, "or you and I could just talk for a few moments." He was now close enough so she could see his face which had been shadowed under the visor of his cap. He was young, and the expression on his face was gentle.

"What are you up to?" he asked her.

She looked long into his face but didn't respond.

"Out doing a little shopping?" he continued.

Tamara nodded slightly.

"Find anything you like?" He was smiling.

She shook her head.

"I'm sorry about that," he lamented, and sounded as if he meant it.

"How about this. How about I call your mom and let her know you're safe, then I can take you home."

"You can call her," Tamara responded, "but I'll walk home." She looked down then turned to walk up the street toward Madison Avenue.

"Hold on." The officer swiped the face of his smart-phone. Tamara stopped but didn't turn around. She heard the policeman's muffled voice, and the longer he spoke, the calmer she felt herself becoming.

"Your mother says if you'll let me bring you home, then she'll take you shopping after lunch."

Tamara turned back toward the officer and halted by the passenger side of the car.

"I'm afraid there's too much equipment up here. Do you mind riding in the back? Let me be your chauffeur through the streets of this posh and glamorous city, young lady. Allow me." His gestures became grand, then humorous, as he swept his cap from his head and bowed in her direction. He swung open the door and beckoned her inside. As she buckled her seat belt, the policeman said, "I believe this might be yours." In his hand, he held her phone.

The look on Tamara's face was now pleading for answers, so the officer squatted down beside her.

"Your parents called the station a little over an hour ago quite concerned about you being out in the city on your own. Shortly after that, we got another call from a gallery a block over reporting a young woman who was up to some mischief. I assume that was you," he said, grinning at her. "I happened to get both calls. So, everything's going to be okay, right?"

He waited for an answer, but Tamara couldn't look him in the eye, and she felt no need to say anything.

"You okay?" Nothing. "Well, sit tight. It'll only be a few minutes."

He gently shut the door, took his place, and started the car.

Tamara's face was on fire. She pressed her palms to her cheeks and closed her eyes to soften the pressures mounting behind them. What must her mom have had to tell the police to convince them to go in search of a fourteen-year-old girl born in this city but unable to wander her own neighborhood alone? What was it that screeching woman in the gallery described to the officer? And what was going on in his mind to cause him to be so cautious as he approached her?

"I think this is your house, right? I'll just need to find a place to park," he said.

Tamara glanced out the window. Her mom was seated on the front steps talking on her cell-phone. As they drifted past her, Aimee waved and ended the call. When the cruiser came to a stop, Tamara tried to open her door, but the handle wasn't working from the inside.

"Allow me!" said the policeman, assuming his chaufferly demeanor again. He exited the car and scurried around to her door, swung it open and, as before, he removed his hat and swept it before him in a playful gesture.

"We have arrived, Miss Baxter. Your mum awaits you."

But it wasn't funny in the least, and Tamara worked exceedingly hard to keep her composure intact. She slipped awkwardly out of the car and left the thank-yous to her mother. Tamara hurried past her mother who was extending her hand to the officer. As they chatted, Tamara climbed the steps and disappeared inside.

The knock on her bedroom door came, as expected, a few minutes later. Aimee stood in the doorway for only a moment before taking a seat on Tamara's bed. Tamara had set her easel back upon its feet and it stood at attention in the center of the room awaiting its commands, but its commanding artist had taken a seat on the floor. She held a new paintbrush in her hand. Her gaze drifted through the space around her until it met the face of her mother. The connection didn't last because Tamara didn't want to deal with whatever anger or relief her mother was clearly expressing in those brilliant, watery eyes of hers. Tamara was as tired of her mother's emotional gyrations as she was of her own, so she looked back up at that annoying naked easel which she dearly wanted to address once she had some privacy. To her great relief, her mom stood and moved toward the door.

"Can I fix you some lunch?" Aimee asked.

Tamara took a deep breath. "In a little while?"

"Want to go shopping later?" asked Aimee.

Tamara never answered her.

"I'll be downstairs, whenever you're ready."

5

THE ART A CANVASS CAN'T CONTAIN

ONE OF THE CANVASS BOARDS Aimee had given Tamara
was waiting on the easel. Its stark white flatness irradiated her
mind with a piercing sensation she didn't like. It goaded her, and she
wanted to stab at it with something somber to soften its mood. Why
were artists forced to stare at something so harsh and unforgiving as a
flat white surface in those incubational moments of creation? The surface should be more fertile than this. Why not a soft earthy beige or a
pastel green like the paper on which Barb's letter was written?

And the walls of her room – they should be textured with a soily
brown that celebrated the fertility of spring, or a fallish mapley crim-
son-orange, or the shadowy rustling of a cool green canopy of summer
leaves.

"I want to wade through you," she said to the canvass. She studied
the tubes of color in her box. "As the trees begin to leaf out, and the
flowers start to bloom, I want to be able to smell their fragrance on the
wind blowing through those branches." She fingered the brush as she
continued her conversation with the canvass. "You should be something
I can hike through, climb to the top of, and feel the wind blowing in
my face as I look out over some hidden valley."

A forest full of green oozed from the tube onto her palette, then
a mountain's worth of ochre and black formed the quarry from which
she would mine her painting. She dipped her brush into the ochre and
filled in the bottom half of the space. The soil was blended with fertile
black to prepare it for planting the trees. She chiseled some stone out of

the black mass weighing down the lower right quadrant of the canvas so she would have a place to stand.

The green she had feathered into the upper half of the forest, however, refused to grow out into leafy trees, and the movement of the composition wouldn't let her eyes climb upward into the mountainous heights she felt rising within her. The wind she knew to be rushing through the painting couldn't move those treetops, and nothing could scamper through this forest's dense canopy. She had left herself no room for sky, so the painting was dark and suffocating and didn't resemble at all the little window she longed to create through which she could return to New Hampshire.

She didn't have inside her what she wanted to see on the canvass.

Tamara's head throbbed, and her tummy grumbled. Setting aside her paints, she slipped down to the kitchen and managed to spread peanut butter on some bread and slip back upstairs without being noticed. She had settled into the inner space she was inhabiting and didn't want to be yanked out of it by questions or observations from her parents. But the knock on the door came all the same.

"I see you got some lunch," said her mom, peeking in. "And I'm glad to see you're enjoying the paints." She cautiously moved into Tamara's room and sat down on the bed. She looked around the room and felt a chill in its sparse decor.

"Want to go shopping in a little while?" she asked Tamara.

Tamara never took her eyes off the colors in front of her and waited a while to respond. Then: "I'd rather go to the park."

"Okay. That would be nice – it's a beautiful day. Let me know when you're ready to go."

"I want to go by myself." Tamara picked up her brush and furrowed her eyebrows hoping to see her way into the forest in front of her.

"Well," said Aimee, trying to keep something audible in the atmosphere so the conversation didn't die there. She felt a knot growing in her chest. "About this morning, how did that go?"

"It was going just fine. Until I was hauled in by the police, thank you." The flushes of embarrassment and shame she felt earlier returned. She wanted to push her mother out of her room, but her angry words echoed back and slammed into her heart. She wanted, instantly, to haul those words back in, one by one.

"Sorry," said Tamara, looking at the misshapen rock formation she was trying to carve out of that flat, lifeless surface.

"May I barge in for a moment?" asked Terrance from the doorway.

"Please," answered Aimee.

Tamara, however, became rigid and withdrew into the world she had wanted to create before they crowded in.

Terrance saw his daughter's face flush and her eyes grow dark, so he improvised a quick invitation: "I was just craving an ice-cream float and was hoping the two of you would join me in one."

"I'm all in," said Aimee, who rose to her feet but waited to see if their daughter was going to budge. She didn't. She wasn't going to.

"I think you're going to want in on this, champ," said her father. His tone caught Tamara off guard, and the reassuring look on his face informed her this was not about the ice-cream.

As Terrance lined up bottles of soda and a selection of ice-creams, he said to Tamara, "Just so you know, it was my idea to rat you out and tip off the cops. Don't blame your mom. She was going to set out in search for you on her own."

Tamara absorbed that as Terrance scooped ice cream into glasses.

"So, I'm the one who needs to apologize for overreacting," he continued. "After we called the police, your mom and I had a long talk, and we both confessed we saw this coming. This was bound to happen at some point. It's been long overdue for someone your age, and we are both aware that you should be experiencing more independence. We want to help you do that – not stand in the way."

Everyone took sips simultaneously, though Tamara lingered much longer over hers than her parents, who were both eager for the conversation to continue.

"For starters, thank you for leaving the note," said her dad. "When we caught our breaths and gathered our wits, we realized you were being thoughtful, and responsible. But, laying all the cards on the table, you have to acknowledge that we had cause to be concerned. So, if you are to go shopping on your own, or go over to the park, then we, like any family, need to come to some understanding and take some meaningful precautions so we can all be sure that you're okay."

"I would really love to hear more about how your morning went," Aimee interjected, though she wasn't met with a willing reply.

Tamara, who was intuiting this should be for her benefit, was stuck in old familiar feelings of being cornered. Her impulse to shut down and tune them out was too well rehearsed for her to respond freely to her father's encouragement, or her mother's curiosity.

"I know, for instance, that you stopped into a gallery," ventured her mom, trying to nudge Tamara into the conversation, not realizing what she had just stepped in. Tamara recoiled as she felt again the harsh colors crash through her then dump her out onto the sidewalk without her phone.

"What did you see?" asked her dad.

The pigments mounting up in her brain were harsh shades of chartreus, aqua, harlequin green and lemon yellow, and they were screaming at her to get out of this conversation. She was watching the colors overtake her periphery. The pixels of color she saw in the gallery were closing off her visual focus as she remembered them. But as she considered her father's words, the colors coalesced into the soft inviting green that contained Barb's letter.

"The gallery wasn't open," Tamara confessed. "I shouldn't have gone in. I didn't realize." Her voice grew softer with each word.

"It's all okay," said her dad.

"And the officer said you looked fine when he spoke to you – a little intimidated being approached by a policeman, perhaps, but he said you handled yourself very well," continued Aimee. "I'm proud of you."

If her parents could have been on the emotional ride she went on, thought Tamara, they wouldn't be so reassuring. She saw herself coming conscious within inches of mid-town traffic, blind with panic over her phone, disoriented in a city she should know by heart by now, but doesn't.

"So, if you want to take a walk over to the park, I'm okay with that," she heard someone say, though the words felt far away and not very convincing to her. She wanted to go back to the mountain she was trying to paint in her bedroom. Then, she remembered why she needed to go to the park in the first place. She needed to feel a tree growing out of the soil and stand at its roots in her bare feet. She would climb on those massive boulders she never wanted to waste her energy on before. She wanted to lay down on one of them now warming in the sun and look through the canopy of trees toward the sky. She needed to build within her that expansive sensation she knew on the mountain above Barb's home, but which she never felt here in these cavernous streets of her own city. Looking out from atop a skyscraper wouldn't cut it. She'd done that plenty of times. Now, she wanted to see the majesty of the sky filtered through green leaves and let her consciousness empty out into eternity with nothing man-made interfering with her view. She yearned for the sensation of falling upward into life instead of hurling downward into death.

But every nerve in her was on edge and the thought of making the trip on her own filled her with the sludgy crud of anxiety.

"So how about this," said her dad. "You'll have your phone with you. Why don't you just call us after about an hour and check in, or before, if you need to."

"Call, don't just text, okay?" said her mom. "I want to hear your voice. I'm going to miss not taking this walk with you."

"It's twelve-forty, there-abouts," said her dad. "Why don't you plan on being home around four-thirty, and later we'll go up the street for noodles."

Then, before she comprehended how it all happened, she was standing on her front stoop, all alone. She didn't have to take another step, no one was forcing her, and for several long moments she held her emotional ground as she looked up and down her block.

When she heard the front door latch, Aimee listened for just a moment to the unwelcomed silence that slipped in past her daughter before Tamara closed the door on her way out. As Aimee watched Tamara linger on the porch, she paced and wondered what she was going to do for these next few hours to keep from following her daughter down the street. She decided to channel her agitation in another direction. She picked up her phone and let her finger hover over her contact list for just a moment before she poked it at Nanna's General Store. She exchanged a few pleasantries with Cindy Briggs and then asked her for Barb's phone number.

"She was just in," said Cindy. "She was on her way home from church. You just missed her, so you might give her a few minutes to get home."

"Oh, that's right," said Aimee. "I forgot they're Seventh-Day Baptists."

"You're not the only one that finds that inconvenient," Cindy grumbled.

"Still, it's a little late for church, isn't it?"

"Revival. Goes most all day, and they'll be back at it tonight." Aimee imagined Cindy rolling her eyes and ended the call.

She looked at the picture hanging on her wall, the one which Tamara said reminded her of Barb, the "Prodigal Daughter." Aimee remained cool to the picture, however, unable to appreciate the promise it contained for Barb and, evidently, for Tamara. The picture reminded her of something Barb had told Tamara: "There are those frightening things you should run from. There are those frightening things you should stand up to and defeat. And then, there are those frightening things you should let win." Aimee had thought through those words often since arriving home wondering what those victorious frightening things might be. She fretted she was about to find out, but she was willing to set her fears on hold for the moment as she tried the number Cindy had given her.

The route to the park was scored into Tamara's soul. She had walked it dozens of times with her mother. Four and a half blocks. Five streets to cross. Five little orange hands to tell her when to stand still; five little walking men telling her it was okay to cross. Connect the dots. But the sounds of the street were pummeling her concentration and the rapid pace of everything that went by disoriented her. When she did this earlier in the day, she had this neighborhood all to herself. There were no panhandlers or ladies walking dogs, no jack-hammers shaking the pavement beneath her or business-clad important people brushing past talking on their phones. She was pushed through one intersection by a tight mass of tourists following a loud woman wearing a bright orange vest and carrying a long stick with a small flag atop it. By the time she reached Lexington Avenue, her mind was in chaos.

The closer Tamara got to Park Avenue the busier her world became – and louder, much louder. There was an emergency of sorts up ahead and siren-driven vehicles were converging a little way down the avenue out of sight. The sidewalk was congested by hordes of people showing up but not being able to cross the street. Policemen directed the crowd to pass through the angry traffic snarl at the top of her street and use another crosswalk farther up the avenue.

Pushed out of her planned route, Tamara's agitation mounted, and she couldn't compute the adjustment. The crowd, now in more of a hurry than before, forced her farther up Park Avenue than she had intended. When they reached a crossable point, cars were stalled in the intersection despite the green light telling them they ought to be able to go. Through three lanes of north-bound cars, she wove a nervous path until she reached the median where she encountered three more lanes of south-bound traffic trying to make way for additional emergency vehicles. Sirens were slicing through her head as angry voices told them to keep moving. She was shoved out of the flowing crowd and pushed up against the post of a crossing light. There, she shut down.

How long she stood there, she could not have known, but the next thing she realized was that the traffic all around her had become unclogged and wasn't stopping for anything. Now, on all sides, there was movement sparking crisis in her brain. She couldn't remember which way she was going since all she saw were cars converging on this inter-section, and the vertical world was all masonry and towering heights that offered her no familiar land-mark by which to navigate. She had to sit down, so she strolled down the grassy median until she came to a cement planter out of which grew a small sapling tree. She sat down, put her head between her knees and pressed hard against her ears with the palms of her hands hoping to muffle the sounds of the city so she could think.

Humiliation plundered her mind and dredged up vivid proof that she was a loser, a fourteen-year old idiot without hope. A vicious voice screamed at her to go home as fast as she could. She screamed back at the diamond-shaped face taking shape in her mind and refused to allow it to enter her field of vision. She searched through her memories for sight of the Shepherd holding his great staff. If she could find this Shepherd and follow him, he promised to lead her to a green pasture, the park. But the park was so very far away, and her Shepherd was nowhere to be seen. Barb had written to her that this Shepherd was already listening to her, that she could speak to him and he would hear her, but her mind was crippled with distress, and any faith she had in that Shepherd of hers was being throttled dry. She was incapable of taking control of herself, and she wasn't going to voluntarily release control of herself into the hands of anyone she couldn't see.

Her inner darkness exploded into violent spasms of rage. Two words coalesced within her and intensified in her mind, their volume burst the eardrums of her soul. She dropped her head between her knees and wrapped her arms across her head and screamed: "Help me!"

The anxiety that had mounted in her all day now detonated, and the intensity of her terror choked her. She couldn't breathe. Her body shook as she wept into her hands. Unable to lift her face to the world around her, she filled her hands with liquid agitation and fear. She was trapped inside herself, and the chains confining her in there were tightening. Along with the tears, her body heaved out another plea for help. Involuntarily now, she was asking for direction, though there was no recipient of her pleas anywhere near her, only the inner audience of her own mind which screamed back, just as loudly, that she would have to sit there forever.

Tamara fought to refocus her senses in some other direction, but the cacophony of noise, the manic movement of the city around her, and the visual aura of terror in her head blended violently within her. She could sense nothing but the Author of her demise scolding her and telling her to remain dead still. So, she sat there, as alone as she could ever imagine herself being, isolated in her dread of the world now pushing its way deeply into her, and she couldn't force it back out.

Her arms began to tremble, and the physical agitation was forcing her to make some decision. She stared intently at the grass between her feet and knew she had to stand up and move in some direction, but her physical parts refused to respond to her mental stimuli. So, she closed her eyes and sought for whatever decision might be available to her to make. This is why she had asked Barb to teach her to pray, so that she might reach beyond her into that mysterious Somewhere and cradle in her arms the help no one else could give her.

Tamara tried to press her brain into service and remember the few hints Barb had offered in her letter. Just speak to him, Barb had written. But fighting against the roar in her head, Tamara wondered if such was possible. Listen with love, not with fear, wrote Barb. Listen with hope and not despair. But there were no murmurs of love and no whispers of hope that she could discern, only the snarls of granthyrs eating away at her soul and the serpent entwining herself around Tamara's torso so tightly she could scarcely breath.

But she did hear Barb's voice, faintly through the scorching hisses of Thorafura's scorn, and she let Barb's voice speak to the darkness: 'I will fear no evil,' she heard Barb say. "I will fear no evil," repeated Tamara, now staring into the face of the serpent. But the response from the dark was bitter and humiliating.

"She can't save you," said the snake. "And your silly little shepherd is lost in some alleyway uptown. Your parents, on the other hand, are realizing just what a mistake you are, so you should just keep walking. If you care at all for them, then you should just eliminate the problem you are to them."

But the snake's voice had a quickening effect on Tamara's mood. Instead of driving her more deeply into to despair, Thorafura's words evoked anger, then new resolve. To be reminded of her parents, and to remember they were behind her and awaiting her call, jolted Tamara. She snatched her phone from her back pocket. It was a good ten minutes past the time she was to check in with her parents. She so wanted that conversation to take place upon the rock formations where she should be relaxing by now. She was not going to call and report she was stranded on a traffic island on Park Avenue, and that small point of determination festered its way into initiative.

Tamara stood and started moving toward the end of the traffic island, but she had gotten turned around and wasn't sure of her path toward the park anymore. From which direction had she come? She closed her eyes and said it again: "Help me." Every one of her senses told her that, despite the thousands of people within eyesight, she was all by herself in this city with a problem she had to overcome on her own. Her soul still smoldered from her assault by the snake, but her imagination intervened and told her to trust in the proximity of the Shepherd Barb promised would guide her. She reached out with her imagination, but nothing within her range of sensate reality could offer her any assurance. She had no experience that would permit her to trust such a reality even if it had appeared, but she did trust Barb. And she did need direction.

There were three other people at the intersection waiting to cross the street. She could ask someone for directions, but then they were in motion. Without any further hesitation, she fell in with them and felt safer moving in their group. Half way across, she told herself she would keep moving in whatever direction that took her. She would walk that block and she would either be crossing Madison Avenue with the park almost in view, or she was on her way home which, as she pondered it, offered her mounting relief.

When she reached Madison, therefore, it was with mixed feelings. Emotions that were allowing her to settle back into her room at home were now in flux, and she needed to stoke her engine once again to carry her the last block to 5th Avenue, and then on to Central Park.

At the crosswalk, she felt the gravitational pull of the park and with little hesitation she hurried through the intersection and picked up her pace. She was growing uncomfortably aware now of her parents awaiting word from her. Their trust was meaning a lot to her in that moment, and she was eager to make contact.

As she awaited the change of light at 5th Avenue, she saw the wall that formed the perimeter of the park, her cornucopia of plenty with trees spilling upward over it. Strong and earthy, the wall was as wondrous for what it provided as it was for the beauty it simply contained within its wallish essence. It bordered, for her, a realm of quiet, another pace, and a deeper breath.

℘

The sun was too bright for Barb to be in the yard and her walk home from church was getting longer for her these days, so she ducked into the barn and balanced herself by her father's old work-bench for a

54

moment. She had left several chores unattended and was determined to see to them before she went in for the afternoon. She needed to fetch some feed to scatter for the chickens. But what did she do with that pail? A bright patch of light bathing the straw-covered floor darkened her mood. She would have to have that roof fixed, or worse would come.

The little kitten named Tam scampered toward Barb, twisted herself between Barb's feet and arched her back against Barb's ankles. Barb poked around among the long-abandoned stalls for a few moments noting her father's old milking stool and the hours he gave to keep them in cream, butter, and cheese. Barb collected the bucket she came for, then she turned toward the little shed where she kept the chicken-feed over by their coop. She saw an old hoe laying in one of the stalls and thought she'd best pick it up before the hired hand took another scolding from her father. After hanging it on the hook, she turned toward the door leading into the barnyard but felt like she was forgetting something. She turned back, then turned around again, hoping to remember what it was that had so suddenly caught her eye then so quickly slipped her mind. She heard a bell ringing faintly over in the house and wondered what time it must be. She'd best finish up here and hurry back inside to get breakfast, wake Tobias, and get him off to the school bus. As she scattered the chicken feed she was thinking it sure will be nice when he's old enough to help with some of these chores.

Tamara was not where she had planned to enter the park, so she headed north in search of a gate. As she passed within the park she took a few steps along the road and turned up a small path that led her to a large rock formation. There, she stepped into the grass, leaned against a large tree, and quickly called her mother.

"Sorry," she said before anything else. "There was an accident on Park Avenue and in the confusion it took me longer to get here. Sorry... Yes, I'm in the park... Fine. It was fine... I know. Four-thirty... Love you, too."

With her back against the tree, she slid down into a squatting position and wrapped her arms around her knees. A large mass of stone stood before her and her eyes ascended it. It wasn't all that high, but the strength of what she gazed upon lofted her spirits to heights beyond any she had experienced recently. The day had been climbing in this direction since she slipped out of her house early that morning. She took two deep breaths and closed her eyes. In the silence that now filled her, she became mindful of the last thing she had just said to her mother. She usually grunted back to her mom or ignored altogether the expressions of love that so routinely came her way. She had rarely reciprocated, but she was pleased with the sensations attached to it.

Tamara let her eyes climb up the nearest tree. She fixated on the dancing leaves then, following a bird, her gaze hopped from branch to branch. She relished the sparkles of light filtering through the tree's canopy and saw the sky which was missing from her painting. The sky was a soft blue. She felt the blue seep inside her where it glistened in those darker, inner places that rarely saw such things.

Then, as powerfully as the two words, "help me" had erupted from within her a short while ago, two other words were moving through her with as much intensity, pushing past the after-rumblings of anxiety into her conscious awareness. These new words crept through her like vagabonds in search of a host who would give them shelter. They were as alien to Tamara as her cry for help, and they wouldn't settle down within her. They needed out, and she needed to help them on their way. She had to verbalize them to someone who could hear them, or they would thrash about and fester in her soul until they were given their freedom. So, to the opening sky, she said right out loud: "Thank you!"

Tamara felt the sun's warmth radiating from the stone and she wanted to absorb it into herself, so she slipped off her shoes and tiptoed over to the foot of her mountain and set foot upon it. Gingerly, she climbed as gracefully as she could the few feet of altitude the stone cropping would offer her. She felt the stone's texture in the skin of her feet and her toes clung to small fissures as she ascended to its first peak. How was this to be painted? She marveled at the fine details which paint would never allow on a canvas, the subtleties of shading and shadowing, the sharpness of the stone cutting into her tender feet, all too wondrous to capture. Why would she even hope to think she could do this justice?

In her periphery, blocked by several trees, she saw the roof of a rough little hut made of tree-trunks and limbs. She inched her way toward it and studied its emerging form as she scaled the rock face. Her approach lent the diminutive house a bit of mystery as it revealed its shape and aspect little by little. When she was within reach to touch it, she drew her hand along one of the railings then gripped one of its sturdy posts. She could see the sky through its skeletal roof. The octagonal design was ringed with benches, so she sat down, enchanted to be in this space so ruggedly planted in a city so unlike it.

A small metal plaque was fixed to one of the posts: A Tree House for Dreaming, it said, and under it was etched a website.

A tree house for dreaming. She glanced about her with different eyes, now alert to the unseen mists of dreams that might be encircling her head. Dreams yet uncaptured by vagrants in need of inner sight loitered upon the air around her, if only those wayward wisps of vision would relent and relinquish themselves. It was not a cabin on a mountainside, but it could be. Here, in the midst of this strange city, it was a welcomed respite from all the concrete. And though it shielded her from none of the noises that bled into the park from the streets, its wooden texture muffled their intensity and made the city palatable. Sun and breeze filtered through the woven design, and the stone on which it was built provided foundation to its airy structure as it lent appropriate strength to something which was otherwise delightfully frail.

Tamara wanted the sensations of this place to trickle through her outer senses and inhabit her deeper regions, yet as she opened those regions to the wonder she felt, her perspective on the little hut darkened. Its association with dreaming conjured sensations of anticipation she did not welcome. The spritely fantasies she imagined just moments ago became soaring, swooping birds of prey, raptors come to snatch her up, or ravens come to pick at the carrion within her, and she no longer wanted to open herself to their influence. Tamara reached for her phone as a precaution, thinking she might listen to some music to filter out the crud washing up in her mind, but then she took a deep, cleansing breath and opted to investigate the web-site etched in the plaque.

Up launched a video commending a local art school. A flash of brilliant light revealed a young man in tights running across a stage then hovering in flight as he catapulted his sleek body through the air. A frenzy of cello players followed, then singers, actors, and visual artists, all with rapture upon their faces displaying passions previously unreleased yet now stirring them to zealous heights. Testimonies by students her age invited her to see this promised land for herself. If ever there was a video designed to inspire a nascent artist, it was this one. Yet, as she watched, Tamara grew small and contracted in her spirit. In not a single soul before her did she recognize herself, nor did she resonate with their aspirations. In their dreams, she discovered nothing she might call her own.

Going to art school was her mother's dream for her. It was the dream Tamara had been handed since she was a small child. She had no other aspirations for herself. Tamara had always needed to draw, manufacture, paint, and produce things with her hands. She had so much going on in that frantic mind of hers, her art had become one of those controlled psychic spaces in which she could push through those impulses driving her to do harm. She did plenty of harm, but her drawings channeled her impulses in directions her mother always interpreted as artistic passion.

The painting sitting on Tamara's easel was one of her first attempts to do something else. She had set out to touch, physically, another realm of creation, one that existed entirely outside of her, not one that eviscerated her from within. Yet, what she was feeling in that moment was not a desire to paint it but to live among it. She had come to the park to gather up some of this beauty, take it back home, and attach it to a flat surface where it didn't belong.

There, in the Tree House for Dreaming, she knew that the window opening upon whatever world awaited her was not going to be seen through one of her paintings. Her mom would have her believe that everything she saw in the video, and everything her new school offered, would help her realize just such a creational calling. But if that was what was required to be creative then there, in the tree house for dreaming, she felt it was time to let her mother's dream for her die.

But that flash of resolve turned into mounting agitation. Images of Thorafura's fury were now replaced in her mind by visions of her mother's, whose dreams for Tamara were a force against which she could not contend. She stood and felt driven to evacuate the little enclosure which, despite its open and airy construction, was now suffocating her. She picked herself up and started for the exit, but other inward impulses would not allow her to leave, as if she had unfinished business there. It was a Tree House for Dreaming, after all, and it seemed to be calling on her to wait, and watch, and see something new. But she had never produced anything out of her psyche from which she didn't want to run. Nothing ever emerged that suggested inspiration, only despair. She felt she should close her eyes, but she knew better. She sensed she was being drawn to look within herself but feared what might be staring back at her.

She sat back down, let her head droop, then she fixed her eyes on the woodwork before her. The structure was intertwined with vines and other plants growing through its loosely framed structure. She needed to articulate another reality for herself and dream a dream that wasn't pursuing her but one she could chase on her own.

The deep brown of the old gnarly tree trunk out of which the little shelter was built fascinated her. Her mind climbed the post as she followed the checks and cracks upwards. She felt in her mind the sharp edges of extruding remnants of cut limbs and knotholes and was tickled by the twining vines and weeds that laced themselves through the trellis-like walls.

A beetle descended along the post and captured her attention. It crawled around the edge of the post then into the brush beyond the shelter. She followed it as far as she could, but there was a sudden rustling in the grass and a small eruption. She saw the face of a bird lunge toward the beetle, consume it, then push through the brush onto the patio before her. It was a hen, in full majestic strut parading a brood of chicks across the gravelly yard then back through an opening in the barnboards. Tamara lept from her bench to follow them, then she grabbed hold of the post she had been studying hoping to shake herself free of where she was headed – into another delusional state. She was making every effort to remain within the little house and not take flight into an altered version of it, but she wasn't succeeding. The chickens were taking her precisely where she wanted to go, so she followed.

The posts and limbs which had become barn siding were now shaping themselves into a familiar old porch with a simple screen door that led her into a living room. An oval, woven rug, worn and faded, was spread before an open fire. She walked quietly into the room then eased herself into one of the large wing-backed chairs facing the fire.

"Speak to me," she heard Barb say softly, but Tamara heard the voice from regions deeper than familiarity, memory, or want. She was not reminiscing, nor was she hallucinating. She felt the breeze on her face as it filtered through the open gazebo. She knew herself to be present – not in faraway New Hampshire, but six blocks from home. She smiled, enjoying the quiet dark behind her closed eyelids, and she trusted the impulses to speak back into that calm. This, she thought, is why she needed to know how to pray, and this was the moment in which she would follow her old friend into that place of peace beside still waters trusting her words of encouragement. Whether it was prayer, or not, she recognized those feelings within her to be precisely what she walked those few blocks to discover.

"Shepherd Jesus?" she whispered. She was tickled inwardly, and unexpectedly, by the sensations forming around the words she had just shaped in her imagination. Baby Jesus, a storybook figure she associated only with Christmas, was all she knew until she had asked Barb to teach her to pray. Now, she was remembering the poem Barb read her from the Bible and the vision she had of a fierce, rod-wielding warrior savagely corralling the demons and ushering them out of those cavernous regions of darkness that so haunted her.

She worked to set aside the sensations of fear that accompanied her earlier approach to prayer and stopped trying to figure out this God about whom she knew so little. What she welcomed, instead, was the image of this shepherd. He had personified a strength which once filled her with fear, yet in the shaking of her soul, he had dislodged both fear and dread and replaced them with hope. Not a dream, and certainly not a vision for her life, but maybe something more essential. She could not name the hope, and now she sensed she didn't need to. Instead, she was feeling the hope hold on to her, whatever, or whoever, it was.

"Shepherd Jesus," she said again, lingering in the imagery now at work in her mind. "Did you bring me here?" The question wasn't the one she was needing to ask, but as she formed it in her mind she knew it was right. She had so many other concerns she had intended to bring to God's attention once she knew how, but this was another conversation altogether, and the moment she inquired, her heart craved an answer. Was she led here, to this Tree House for Dreaming? Why? So one dream could die in order to make way for another?

Tamara listened and heard the traffic a few yards away. She saw herself frozen in the midst of Park Avenue impaled upon her fear. Then, she remembered pushing back against Thorafura's wrath and the awakening resolve that pushed through her and got her here to this little spot in her neighborhood park. She saw herself curled up on her bed at home knowing she needed to create a new space for herself in this world and finding the determination to pursue it. She saw herself standing enchanted before the weavings in the store window and felt again the discovery of fresh texture and warmth swell within her as she envisioned the New Hampshire countryside. Then, she saw her portfolio, so cautiously compiled by her mom, leaning against the bookcase in their living room. She couldn't remember a single work of art contained within it. Her mom had pieced together the collection in hopes of convincing several preparatory schools with notable art departments to accept her. Only one school had considered taking the risk. But she was not going to go.

The thought brought a tremor of agitation she didn't want to let grow, so Tamara picked up her shoes and went to place her bare feet on the large massive front stoop in front of her little cottage. The sun had baked its brightness into the rock and she could feel the sun shining in her feet and soaking up through her legs until her whole torso warmed with the light it sent from so very far away.

A warm breeze jostled the trees and her eyes followed the bouncing gusts through the canopy. The treetops were caught in a game of catch between a couple of playful wind-giants who were tossing flurries of air from one side of the park to the other.

A squirrel, an unintended participant in the wind-giant's game, was trying to calculate the ever-changing distances between the swaying limb it was on and another branch that wouldn't halt its bouncing so the squirrel could take aim. The squirrel's tail waved wildly keeping its balance neatly in check against its vaulting center of gravity. Tamara felt her own center of gravity bound and swoon as her anticipation fused her to the squirrel's plight. She tried to imagine the lightning bolt of decision that would finally hurl the squirrel across those reaches of space now changing dimensions at an unforgiving pace. Was it waiting for the wind to cease, or for two fixed points in chaotic space to align for one mystical moment? And what would inform this little creature it was time to commit itself to flight? Would perseverance pay off or patience simply give out?

Then, without flinching or broadcasting its intent, the squirrel was airborne. Its gyrating tail and flailing legs pretended to direct its coarse but to no avail, for the wind-giant, in all its playful glee, yanked the limb from the squirrel's flight path and hoped to spank it in the fanny on its way past as it fell several squirrel stories through the tree.

Tamara's heart plummeted with the squirrel. But the limb the squirrel lost wasn't the only limb in the tree, and having missed its first target, it quickly fixated upon another. Not allowing the crisis of its fall to overwhelm it, the squirrel permitted gravity and trajectory to determine its destination as it prepared for impact, which it took in full stride and treated as the perfect landing it intended all along. The little creature continued its scurry down the trunk and across the lawn, grateful for the stability of the earth beneath it.

The squirrel urged Tamara to follow, so she wandered out across the greenspace. Her guide quickly vanished, but the swath of open lawn and the feel of the grass beneath her feet suited the mood she was in.

The winds brought clouds, so the sky grew overcast and shrouded the city's skyline with shadow. The jagged horizon of buildings which ringed around the park and overtopped the trees was now the grimy castle-keep of the wind-giants whose eyes were following her across the lawn. She grew small under their gaze. The wind was strong against her, a portentous force bringing her word of warning. Travel not this way, it said. So, she leaned in against the breeze and tried to pinpoint that fluid point in space toward which she would leap.

As she pushed forward against the wind, Tamara remembered the reason she had come to the park which was to study the landscape for the sake of her painting. Her easel, set in the middle of her room, held the small rectangular window through which she was trying to gain a glimpse of the mountains of New Hampshire, though her desire to complete it had been draining out of her all afternoon. What, then, was her new purpose in being there?

She heard a faint but chaotic sound that reminded her of the jack-in-the-box her grandmother had given her. Her grandmother would wind it up and let it play until its inner fiend erupted from its vault. Again and again her grandmother played the game, assured that eventually Tamara would find her delight in it. Tamara never thought it funny. Its grimacing face popped up in too many dreams without the warning of playful music to set a joyful mood.

Tamara would have walked away from the music, but she found it before she realized what it was; the park's carousel. Her distaste faded as she remembered numerous turns she had taken on it as a little girl. Her father always let her win the race by riding the horse just behind her, and he swore he rode it as hard as he could but never caught up. It was after one such ride that her grandmother bought her the stuffed horse, Heatherwhinny, to commemorate the experience.

Tamara still had her cash from her morning trek, so she fished out a ten and handed it to the attendant who counted back her change and topped it with a bright yellow ticket. The bell sounded, and the ride slowed as the ponies sought rest in their pasture while the jockeys changed places. One pony reminded her of Heatherwhinny, and she walked around to look at it up close. It had a creamy coat with reddish highlights and its saddle rested on a brightly spotted blanket, much like her old stuffed friend once had. She stepped up and sat herself in the saddle.

The bell told her to hang on for the ride of her life, but the slow pace out of the starting gate was underwhelming, and without her father behind her spurring her to ride faster, she felt awkward gliding up and down on a ride meant for children so much younger. A littler girl rounding the bend a few horses in front of her was screaming to get off as her parents took pictures and told her to sit still. The little girl's fears were as real as Tamara's ever were, but in that moment, her own fears had left her for a while. Instead, the placidness of the ride, with its steady, gliding pace, conspired to make her feel silly as she sat mounted on a large plastic horse going around in circles.

Tamara closed her eyes so she could focus on the movement of the horse and listen to the music, neither of which complimented the other, yet both now matched her mood rather well. The gentle rise and fall of the ponies reset the pace within her. Behind her eyes, she felt the world glide by, conscious of being too old for this herself, and knowing that was the right thing to feel.

Back out in the bright sunlight, Tamara sensed the tug toward home, so she checked her phone. It was a quarter to four and the reality of passing back out into the city haunted her. There was another thoroughfare just beyond the carousel, and she had little energy to resist it, so she turned toward 5th Avenue.

An ice-cream truck, parked just ahead, halted her, and the thirst in her throat talked her into an ice cream cone, strawberry with sprinkles. As she savored the cold flavor dripping down the back of her throat, she heard a sound: the long sorrowful moan of a heart that had forgotten where home was and could only imagine what home must be. A single note hanging on the breeze modulated hauntingly into a melody that gave voice to Tamara's ardent longings for peace. If her tears could be sung like that, they would wet the cheeks of everyone who listened. That is what she heard. The wind-giants, she imagined, had broken their hearts.

She walked a few steps and found a young boy seated on an over-turned bucket. His straight black hair framed an old expression on his face, though he must have been half her age. On his thigh he balanced a long, slender-necked instrument with just two strings, across which he was drawing a bow. From the top of the neck sprung two wings, or so they looked to Tamara. Above them, a dragon's head curled handsomely upward, its mouth opened as if it were the one voicing this mysterious music calling out to other dragons which would never come. The sound made by this little bow on this little instrument played by this little boy sounded unworldly, ancient, and if she could follow the waves of sound outward they would absorb the entire park in its mourning and render every soul as sorrowful as the young lad must surely be.

Tamara felt a cool sensation running over her hand and remembered her ice-cream cone. As she licked her hand it broke her reverie and the young boy's concentration. He looked at her, though without interrupting the phrase he was painting in the air around them. His expression did not change though the meeting of their eyes created another connection, one she couldn't sustain, so she looked down at his feet and saw a little green box, just as long and slender as the instrument it must contain. There were about thirty-five cents gathered in it. She tugged a dollar out of her pocket and placed it in the box. The boy nodded his appreciation but never let on that the music was capable of interruption.

On the inside of the lid was etched a stylized rabbit, leaping across an expanse of space.

"*Watership Down*," she said to the boy, who gave no indication that he understood but changed his expression to convey curiosity. Tamara pointed to the bunny, and he smiled. With an alternate stroke of his bow, the boy changed course in the tune. Out from its burrow scampered a rabbit, its melody hopping from place to place, slow and loping at first, but then it was joined by another bunny who inspired play between the two. Then there were many little creatures dashing through the meadow without a care among them. She licked her melting ice-cream and saw him watch her eat.

"Would you like one?" she asked. No comprehension, but also no refusal. So, Tamara raced back to the ice cream truck and ordered another. As she approached the boy, he seemed intimidated by the gesture and looked over his shoulder to an old man seated on the bench, hunched over, leaning on a stick. The man half closed his eyes and nodded. Only then did the boy allow his instrument to rest. He ate the ice cream with obvious relish, not hiding his satisfaction. Tamara felt a bit awkward watching him eat, knowing any other communication was beyond them.

The old man struggled to his feet and leaned heavily on the flimsy stick, which Tamara was afraid might break under him, though he was so slight of weight and height she changed her mind to think the stick had more to it than he. Each step was labored, but as he approached, the little boy broke his silence and spoke quickly, bringing a broadening smile to the man's face.

"He says you are nicest to him of all today," said the man. "His name is Li Jie; he's my young hero. What is your name?"

"Tamara," she said, feeling awkward in giving her name away.

"Thank you, Tamara, for your kindness to my grandson."

"No. I – " she wasn't sure how to articulate what she was feeling, so she pointed to his instrument. "It is so beautiful."

"It is called erhu, Chinese violin. Li Jie is now my hands," said the man, who extended one of his hands which was heavily deformed. The other resting on the cane was in no better shape.

"You taught him?" asked Tamara.

"He listened. Since a baby. Listened very well. Then he played."

Lie Jie interpreted from their signs that it was time to play again, so he began another melody. As he played, the man rocked back slightly and let the melody close his eyes. Tamara sensed the conversation wasn't over, it just now included Li Jie in the only way he could join in.

Tamara closed her eyes to hear what he was saying, and she heard long voyages, longer nights in faraway places, lonely days amid strange noises and even stranger people. She heard him telegraphing his longing across oceans and back through the ages, a yearning carried upon a tune inherited by his grandfather who heard it at the feet of some lonesome elder of his own, and has now bequeathed its loneliness to his grandson. And then, crashing through those beautiful waves of remorse, came the sounds of the city as his last note took flight and flew beyond her reach.

Tamara felt awkward now, not sure how this was supposed to continue, so she reached into her pocket and drew out another bill, a five, which she began to place in his box."

"No, Miss Tamara," implored the old man, looking wise and kind. "That was for you."

As she thanked them, then said good bye, the man said: "You are a beautiful young lady. I know your parents are very proud of you. You are their young hero, too." He turned to carry his bent body back to the bench.

As Tamara walked away, she let the new melody Li Jie commenced set her pace. The melody turned into flower petals taken up by the wind, glistening in the sun, lighting the air around her with sparkling wonder. She could smell their fragrance in the tones she heard and imagined the faraway garden from which they had been freed by those whimsical wind-giants who also knew a thing of beauty when they saw it.

At the edge of the park Tamara paused to listen for Li Jie's erhu, but the sounds of the city had now replaced melody with cacophony. A single note still sung within her, however, with just enough vibrato to sustain the wisp of joy she found there. She pulled her phone from her back pocket and quickly called her parents.

"I was just on my way home," she explained, acknowledging she should have been there fifteen minutes ago.

"Everything's great," she said with emphasis trying to convince her mom to put away the concerned tone in her voice.

"Can I just meet you at the noodle place?" she asked, then waited for her mom to discuss it with her dad.

"Okay. Five-thirty then, at the restaurant. Promise."

She pocketed her phone. A mournful voice from long away sung its song within her and it grieved for the solitude she so desperately needed and the peace she would lose in the streets. It was not just a simple seven block stroll for her to the restaurant. Every one of those blocks was mounting up resistance within her. But the little white man on the crossing sign said it was time, so she left the confines of her afternoon oases and pushed herself back into the city.

On the far side of 5th Avenue she turned back and took in the grand sweep of that miraculous expanse planted in the heart of the city. As she watched the wind giants having their way with it still, she couldn't escape the feeling that she was saying good-bye to something.

6

GRANTHYRS

"I HAD A LONG TALK WITH Barb this afternoon," said Aimee as they waited for their noodles to arrive. "She sounded tired. I may not have caught her at a good time, but we ended up having a great talk." Aimee watched Tamara for some response, but when her daughter didn't offer anything she continued: "She said how much she missed you and how much she could use some good help around the farm."

The arrival of their noodles gave them all a moment to retreat into their thoughts. Several decisions had been solidifying within Tamara over the course of the afternoon, so she listened for an opening in the conversation to lay them on the table. But Aimee plowed her way into the silence and never gave Tamara the opportunity.

"Barb said we were welcome to come at any time over the summer, so we have to look at the summer school schedule and see when the classes you need will be offered."

Tamara felt her temperature rising and looked down at her noodles, then she glanced over at her dad who remained neutral.

"On Monday, I plan to give the headmaster at Upton a call and set up an appointment," Aimee continued, then added: "And I thought you would like to come and sit in on that conversation."

The tone in Aimee's voice told Tamara this was more of a summons than an option and it irked her. She had no intention of going to an academy of the arts, but she wasn't ready to wade into that, not with her trip to New Hampshire at stake.

"I'll make the appointment, and you can let me know," continued Aimee.

Fine, thought Tamara.

"Now," said Aimee, a little unsure of this part still. "I haven't had a chance to tell you yet, but I've been offered a promotion that requires me to travel some this summer, and it may limit the time I have to go with you." Aimee's demeanor was dark and apologetic, but Tamara was hearing that as potential good news.

"But, like I said, it will all work out," Aimee reassured her.

"When do we meet with Dr. Samuelson again?" asked Tamara.

"Next Thursday," said Aimee.

Tamara nodded. She could wait until then.

As Tamara got undressed and prepared to turn out the light, she picked up Barb's letter and read it again. She heard the inflections in Barb's voice as she listened to the words on the page and heeded the assurances meant for her. It was time to take seriously all that Barb was promising her so, as she lay in bed, she considered everything else she had heard throughout the day. She wondered at the unheard whisper that had guided her steps when she was stranded in the median and so filled with doubt. She felt again the subtle push that purged her tortured mind of fear when she pleaded for help and brought her to some new place within herself. She had listened through her fear and heard love, and instead of dropping more deeply into despair, she had been lifted into hope. She had heard all of that. Now, it was long past time for her to speak.

As she considered what to say, she felt she had a duty to answer, one she wasn't terribly sure how to fulfill. Barb had asked Tamara to pray for her and for their friendship. She told Tamara to pray for her parents and give thanks for them. But words, Tamara found, weren't forthcoming.

What passed through Tamara's mind were vivid images of Barb's face. Her eyes were gentle, and the comfort they offered her when she looked into them settled her spirit into a quiet repose she rarely felt as she waited for sleep. They were old eyes, and Tamara wanted to see them again, soon. She wasn't used to carrying that sense of longing around within her. Primarily, she just existed as she moved through states of sorrow, anger, and fear.

But a new yearning was simmering within her, and she felt a mounting need to pursue it. She considered that if Shepherd Jesus could guide her through the afternoon she just had, then perhaps he could guide them all to discover a way to return to Barb's farm. She had simply asked for help before, so she simply asked for that help again.

Tamara thought of how old Barb was and how comfortable she was with that. She enjoyed being with someone who knew a lot about life, whose ways were slow and intentional, caring, and good. From her grandparents, she had experienced a lot of impulsive gifts, quick hugs, and insincere concern as they listened superficially to Tamara then moved swiftly on to the next thing.

She had never been with an elderly person whose whole heart was tuned to listen, understand, then treasure what she had said. Tamara had watched Barb move about the barn with such skill and purpose and interact with her environment with such fondness and care. But Barb wouldn't let Tamara just watch. Her hospitality expanded to include Tamara in her work and to share in her life as a partner. Well, as a pupil, but with grave respect. Barb never treated her as a child but as one who wanted to know how.

The images of warmth Tamara was seeing behind her closed eyelids becalmed her with sensations similar to those she felt on the carousel. They slowed the pace of her heartbeat, calmed her breathing, steadied the sensations of self-doubt and rested her imagination on a single image. The swell and release of her breathing modulated to match the rise and fall of the horse she had been riding. The music accompanying her vision, however, was drawn out with a bow by a small boy with a great soul. She imagined Barb, just now, catching the strains of the erhu on those breezes blowing through the New Hampshire hills, rustling the great maple tree in her front yard and settling the horses worries in their stalls.

The only light in the barnyard was cast by the lamps in Barb's kitchen filtered through lace curtains. The moon was hidden, or hadn't risen, or had forgotten how to shine deep in the valley surrounded by the mountains. Barb was at the kitchen door calling in the kittens to give them their milk before she locked the door for the night.

Tamara, with an arm full of oak logs, had just come from the wood pile by the barn. Barb held the door for her and told her they had time, maybe, for one more log on the fire and a cup of cocoa. Tamara held back her groaning protest hoping their first evening back together would go on all night. She was certainly not tired but felt refreshed by the night air and the opportunity to sit by the fire with her old friend and talk.

Barb lifted the kettle from the hearth and began to pour. Tamara rejoiced in the aroma of the cocoa and shut her eyes in delight. She was just about take a sip when a searing cry rang through the mountains, a howl as demonic as anything Tamara had ever scared up from within herself, but now it sounded as if the farmhouse was surrounded by unworldly fiends.

"Granthyrs," said Barb. Her face, just a moment ago so warm, was now deformed with wrath. She reached for one of the logs Tamara had just brought in and stormed out the door.

Tamara became disoriented as the night filled with screams – the wail of a horse in pain, under attack, being torn in its flesh. Next, she heard the chickens fleeing their roosts, scattering their feathers and their chicks to be picked off by those foul creatures.

Then, the shriek of a woman, a prolonged cry for help ripped through the valley. Tamara grabbed her own log and ran for the door but couldn't locate it. The entire barnyard was now in fury all around her, but she was trapped inside the house. She could go through the cellar, but it was locked, and she didn't know where to locate a key. With her piece of wood, she smashed a window and lept through it, but once she was out on the porch she couldn't see. The yard was suffocated by blankets of darkness.

She felt her way toward the barn hoping to sense her direction from the cries she heard, but they were all around her, disorienting her. A horse, its flight contorted by its wounds, staggered from the barn hoping to outrun the predatory granthyrs and keep its legs beneath it but failed. It slammed down upon its side and thrashed its legs, fruitlessly trying to right itself and fend off the teeth now buried in its flank.

As its cries echoed through the valley, she heard the sounds of sirens – help surely on its way.

Granthyrs, racing from the barn, saw Tamara and let the chickens scatter as they turned toward her. A car honked its horn, and a sharp pain in her foot stopped her up short. She swung around to take aim at the granthyr, but there was nothing there. She screamed for Barb but heard no response and couldn't move in any direction to find her.

The glare of the moon broke through as the blanket of clouds rolled back and the cries from the barn dissipated, but nothing was quiet. There was a hostile agitation in the air all around her and she strained against the lights now blinding her, coming at her, not yet realizing them to be the headlights of several cars that had stopped just in time.

Something was running toward her and the glare of the light gave it an inhuman shape. The silhouette of one of her demons was moving in on her. In her periphery, bright red staccato flashes distorted her vision and disoriented all her senses. She was aware of a voice, but her mind wouldn't gather the sounds into words she could process. Around her body she felt something warm being wrapped, a blanket, then firm arms across her shoulders were turning her, walking her, then standing with her.

"Where do you live?" were the first words that she recognized. But she didn't know what to say. As her eyes slowly focused she saw cars moving slowly past her.

"Can you tell me where you live?" said the voice from over her shoulder. A policewoman had both her hands firmly on Tamara's shoulders. Another officer, a man, was standing close by.

"Can you understand?" asked the policeman, who then spoke in another language Tamara did not understand at all.

"Where am I?" asked Tamara.

"We're at the corner of 61st and 2nd, Miss. Do you have an address?"

That, she knew, and was able to say. She sensed the gentle nudge from her shoulders and a few reassuring words in her right ear. Then, she began to walk, but her right foot was in terrible pain. She faltered and fell against the officer who helped Tamara over to a nearby stoop.

The two officers spoke in quiet voices, and the man walked on down the street. The woman lifted Tamara's foot to examine it and agreed they should sit there for a few minutes.

"Are you feeling any better?" the officer asked Tamara.

Tamara nodded, but she didn't speak. She struggled to make sense of where she was and felt the emotional crush of finding herself in the street with another police officer giving her aid.

"I want to go home," muttered Tamara, almost inaudibly.

"We're getting there," reassured the officer. "Can you tell me your name?" A few more questions later and the officer also knew Tamara's age, grade in school, and favorite foods, but not why Tamara was standing in the street a little after midnight. A few moments later, they were joined by Aimee and Terrance.

"Her foot appears swollen," said the female officer. "It could be broken, but more likely she sprained it, though it ought to be X-rayed. Once you get her home, you should put some ice on it."

"Thank you, officer, we'll do that," said Aimee.

"Officer DiSimone will go with you, Tamara. And could I speak with one of your parents for a moment?"

Terrance lingered as Aimee helped the policeman get Tamara back home, up the steps and into the house. Aimee made up an ice-pack and got a few blankets so Tamara could stretch out on the sofa rather than climb the stairs to her room.

Terrance slipped in and joined Aimee in the kitchen. As Tamara heard their muffled voices, filled with not-so-muffled worry, she put together another life-changing decision she needed to make. She began taking some initiative the moment her parents re-entered the room.

"I think we should try to meet with Dr. Samuelson before Thursday," said Tamara. Terrance looked quickly at Aimee.

"Your dad was just saying the same thing, and I agree. I'll call him first thing in the morning. Or, make that later today," said Aimee, looking at the clock on the mantle.

As Tamara settled in on the couch, Aimee got a blanket and got as comfortable as she could in the recliner. As each lay there, quite aware that neither of them was sleeping, Tamara said: "Barb told me she prays for you every day, and that I need to pray for you, because you have such a big job trying to raise me. Maybe we should pray for each other. I think we both need it."

The unfathomable riches of grace were moving among them. Glimpses of the holy, which Barb had seen at work in their family and Aimee had needed to behold, were winging their way from some unseen quarter. Aimee, who was trying to find a question to ask which might bring the light rather than deepen the darkness, relented in wonder and let Tamara have the last word as the night's quiet finally settled in: "Congratulations on your promotion, by the way."

7

ALL THE REPAIRS THAT NEED TO BE MADE

BARB AWOKE LATER THAN SHE wanted, but the barn would keep until after her morning prayers. God always got her full attention as soon as she set fresh kindling sticks on last night's coals, adjusted the damper, and let a new fire muster as she made up the coffee pot to set upon the wood stove. Her old Bible was resting by her wing-backed chair, and her dog-eared daily devotional was tucked into it at the chapter and verse where she left off the day before.

"Waiting upon God" was the focus for the day: her life was not to be a restless agitation over what may come, said her devotional guide, nor a fruitless effort to bring about what didn't belong to us. Time rested in God's hands, and its pace was his own business.

She loved the old verses from Habakkuk to which she turned:

> And the Lord answered me, and said, Write the vision, and make it plain upon tables, that he may run that readeth it. For the vision is yet for an appointed time, but at the end it shall speak, and not lie: though it tarry, wait for it; because it will surely come, it will not tarry. Behold, his soul which is lifted up is not upright in him: but the just shall live by his faith.

The just shall live by faith, she assented, and the faithful shall await their blessing, for it shall surely come.

The morning light was softened by the mountain rising near her house which held the dawn's brightest rays behind its massive girth, though it allowed the sun's promised radiance its full measure. It shall surely come, she whispered to herself. It shall surely come. Her devotional sent her to another of her favorites:

I believe that I shall look upon the goodness of the Lord in the
land of the living! sang the twenty-seventh psalm:
Wait for the Lord; be strong, and let your heart take courage;
wait for the Lord!

And though her devotional didn't tell her to look it up, her heart recited the promise from Isaiah she first heard at her mother's grave-side, intoned by a grim looking pastor who seemed to brighten with each word proclaimed:

But they that wait upon the Lord shall renew their strength;
they shall mount up with wings as eagles; they shall run, and
not be weary; and they shall walk, and not faint.

She cleared her mind of whatever worry might tarnish her mood and sat as still as she could. The rustling hens were alerting the rest of the barnyard that the sun was on its way, and the coffee pot was whispering that she should have a cup. She poured some fresh cow's milk (from Nazareth's farm down the road) in her mug and filled the rest with coffee. She set the mug on the stand beside her chair to cool a moment as she recalled the needs in her family and those voiced among the church members. She gleaned from the gossip she had heard yesterday the concerns beneath the concerns that really needing praying for. She sat with these for a few moments, offered the Lord all she couldn't understand, surrendered that which was beyond her reach, then sought input for what she should tend to as the day went on. Then, as the routine of her morning prayer played out and she took her first sip of coffee, she turned the dial in her heart and her mood grew serious. Now, for the heavy lifting.

There was a chamber in her soul that she kept under guard where that which was most precious was stored, yet rarely examined: experiences of her family's suffering, her sister's death, her husband's absence, her son's challenges growing up alone. And now, Tamara had moved in there, the one whose experiences were of most present concern. Tamara's presence in that little chamber cast a glare upon all that was contained in there, awakening the dead, stirring troubled spirits long thought to be at rest. Tamara's young life had brought this old woman back to that threshold of the past where, she began to think, she might glimpse a future other than the one she had come to imagine for herself. She had been so long alone, there in that wonderful house of her parents, now hers, but it would probably never be her son's. He was answering another call.

A farm needs a person, not a caretaker, she thought. It needs a person to give it its pulse and tend its heart. Each winged or hoofed soul that takes its fodder there needs a person who gives thanks for each egg that was laid then gathered into gentle hands. It needs a person who speaks quietly to the chickless hens that roam about nervously in need of reassurance. It needs a person who strokes the manes of those who bear their burdens and buries those whose burdens are now laid aside. A farm needs a person to scatter the feed then walk the fences with their rotting boards and shore them up. A farm's person knows the barn requires a nightly roaming if it is to breathe easy until morning. And the farm's person should meet the rising sun in the barnyard after the fresh milk has been refrigerated and the kittens are duly scolded for the mischief they no-doubt caused overnight.

Barb had kept the farm waiting too long. The day was bright, and she was late. Her coffee was cold, and she hadn't eaten anything, but she knew her duty and aimed to keep it.

Tamara's foot, and the events of the day coursing through her mind, kept her awake much of the night, though toward morning her thoughts turned northward. The throbbing in her foot had subsided, and she thought the swelling had gone down. At some point in the night her mom had given up the recliner and returned to her own bed, so Tamara was alone in the living room.

The day loitered in the gray moments of the morning at a time on a Sunday the Baxter family wouldn't be conscious of a new dawn. No work, no school, so the sun could do what it wanted, and those who had to get up and move the world along might be up and doing it, while the Baxters were just as glad to pay the bill for their share of it at the end of the month. They had worked hard all week to insure the capital basis for it all. Their job was done until the markets opened again on Monday and the banks along with them.

Tamara, wide awake, wondered if Barb was out gathering the morning's eggs and whether there were any in her own fridge. She tested her foot and found that she could manage if she hopped from couch to recliner to table to bathroom, then to the kitchen door, over to the counter, and finally to the refrigerator, where she found five eggs hidden behind the take-home cartons containing their noodles from the night before.

There weren't any peppers in the vegetable crisper, but there was some shredded cheese in the deli drawer and a few old mushrooms on the top shelf by the butter. She lined all her produce along the counter then pulled over a bar stool and perched herself upon it. The eggs were cracked into a bowl, the shells were fished out of the eggs, then they were beaten with a fork. She reached for a knife to slice the mushrooms and paused. She looked at the long scar in her hand and almost replaced the knife in its block, but then she grasped it firmly and slid it through the delicate mushrooms. She pushed the same knife through the butter which she placed in a small skillet.

It took her longer than it should have, however, to turn on the stove. The open flame excited memories of fire-filled rooms in which she became trapped and couldn't wake up in time, so as the stove roared to life she pushed back from it. But as the flames respected their boundaries, she slid the skillet onto the eye and laid in the butter, then the mushrooms. She had no idea how long to cook them, but when they turned dark, she scooped them out into a small bowl. Then, into the hot pan, she poured the eggs. She reached for her phone, called her mom, woke her up, and told her their breakfast was almost ready.

"I have a lunch appointment uptown on Monday," said Dr. Samuelson when Aimee called him. "I could stop in afterwards for a little while just to see what's up. We should go ahead and keep Thursday for a full session, though."

They agreed to the meeting, even though Terrance couldn't be there. Aimee and Tamara were taking the day off. They had a nine-thirty appointment to have Tamara's foot examined.

As Aimee fixed Dr. Samuelson a cup of tea, Tamara limped in to the dining room using a single crutch.

"It's sprained," she explained when he asked. "I'm supposed to stay off it for a day or two and keep ice on it." Her ankle was wrapped tightly in an ace bandage.

"So sorry to hear that," he said, hoping to sound sincere, but there was irony infused into every word. "Interesting it should happen just as you began to exercise a little independence. I wonder, what would Freud say about that?" He winked at her.

"If he were nice, he'd probably be glad it wasn't broken," answered Tamara.

Samuelson listened with great interest, showing little surprise, as Aimee and Tamara brought him up to date. He sounded most interested in the gutting of Tamara's room and the resulting impulse to leave the house three times.

"Only two of those times were intentional, though," said Aimee.

"Making the third one the most important to understand. I'll let the two of you talk more about that between now and Thursday. I'd like to hear your thoughts about why it happened, and I'll give it more thought, as well."

"In the meantime?" asked Aimee.

"In the meantime," continued Samuelson, "what sort of security features do you have on the house?"

"We have a house alarm," said Aimee.

"Which should have gone off if Tamara opened the door?"

"I guess she can – "

"Enter the code in her sleep." confirmed Samuelson.

"I guess so."

"Change it," he said. "Every night, and don't tell her. Text her the new code later the next day so she can get back in after school."

Aimee involuntarily looked at Tamara, who signaled her relief at the suggestion.

"So, you think this could happen again?" asked Aimee.

Samuelson nodded that he thought it could.

"And should we plan on keeping her in all the time?" wondered Aimee.

"It would be a good idea until the foot heals," he affirmed, smiling at Tamara. "But after that, here's my prescription: Every day, after school, you walk to the park and spend an hour there."

"Alone?" asked Tamara.

"Alone. Take your homework and do it there if you want. Walk around and discover something new whenever you go. But do this, take a new route each time and come home a different way than you went. Get to know your neighborhood. Doctor's orders!" he growled in Tamara's direction.

"Anything else?" he asked them.

Aimee saw all those letters lined up in her mind, and Tamara now had several life-changing decisions she needed to discuss. But neither wanted to talk about them without Terrance, so they shook their heads and thanked Dr. Samuelson for dropping by.

❧

Tobias was in his study at the church, hoping to finish some notes for the Bible study he was planning but was now preoccupied by a phone call from Pamela Nazareth, his mother's oldest and closest friend. She had assured the reverend too many times that she was sure there was nothing to worry about but sensed that Barb had been feeling poorly and was there anything she could do to be of help. He was stalled in his planning anyway, so he decided to pack it in for the afternoon and stroll over to the house and check in on her. He found Barb on the porch swing, gently rocking. She was clearly preoccupied but waved off any expression of concern and scurried in to fix him something cold to drink.

As he waited on the porch, Tobias scanned the barn-yard and noted the decay he was seeing more of these days. He would need to spend a couple of Sundays over here to shore up a few things that didn't look like they could wait much longer. Barb had been after him. The farm-hand's cottage was at the top of her list. No one had stayed in there for years.

He wasn't looking forward to what he might find in there, hoping at least the floor was still solid. He knew the roof was long overdue, but if it had been leaking…

Barb came back out with a pitcher of lemonade. They sipped, rocked, and took in the day. No one was in a hurry to speak.

"Tamara is coming this summer," she stated with little expression in her voice.

Tobias thought she spoke in those tones she usually reserved for impending storms. He had gathered enough about the Baxter's visit to know that his mom was eager to have them back, though he fully appreciated what it would require of her. She seemed, even now, to be gathering the spiritual reserves she would need.

"Are you okay with that? You're sure it's a good idea?" he asked as her expression grew increasingly dark.

"Oh, yes," she murmured. "Can't be helped."

"When is she coming?"

"Late June, probably. After school lets out. Best make ready. You finished the little house, haven't you?" she asked.

He looked hard at his mother and had no reason to think she didn't believe the job was done. She had only started pestering him about a week before last, and they had just been through their spring revival at the church which had taken everybody's last bit of spare time and energy. He was only now feeling somewhat revived himself in the aftermath and had promised to get to the little house as soon as he could.

"Let's walk down there now and look it over," he suggested, hoping a dose of reality might help them both.

Paint was the obvious priority, but he knew the real problems were going to be better hidden. The porch had been sagging for years, so there were joists beneath it that needed work. The front door creaked loudly in need of lubricant, a minor fix. A thick coating of dust covered everything they saw so he would need to bring his shop-vac to take off the top layer. The floor complained under them, reminding them both that it had been too long since it had been exercised by human traffic. But there was a lot of mildew, which meant there was a lot of moisture in the house, not a welcomed sign. Rot would follow, and he knew where to look for that. As he suspected, the bathroom floor was spongy, and the pipes showed a lot of rust. Barb was on her way to the stairs at the end of the hall to inspect the bedrooms, but Tobias halted her. Let him go first, he cautioned, to make sure the steps were sound. They were, up to the sixth step, which cracked beneath his weight.

"Come on, mom. I think we need to talk about this. Let's go back up to the house."

8

A Long and Lonely Walk

PAIN WAS ROCKETING THROUGH TAMARA'S leg by the time she had hobbled, with the help of her crutch, the two blocks from the subway to school. She had just made it through the front door as the bell rang but couldn't endure the hordes of students now hurrying in all directions to homeroom. Her head was hurting from another long night alone in her room and no sleep, so she gingerly maneuvered through the crowd to a bench and sat down. She fished her mother's note out of her book-bag and considered the route to the office, but she couldn't lift herself from her seat.

Her vision faded and everything she saw lost definition even as her hearing grew more acute. Strange sounds flooded the halls and echoed off the lockers lining the walls as her visual world pitched and rolled and caused her tummy to swell with apprehension. Car horns blared in her head and their burning headlights blinded her imagination. Tamara lay down on the bench and tried to push the memories out of her mind, but she couldn't flee the sensation that she was standing in the middle of traffic.

The hallway, mercifully, grew quiet, but in a few moments that bell was going to ring again, and if she hadn't reached the office with her note, then she would have to suffer the assault of those crowds. The anticipation of it curled her into a tight ball, and she made herself as small as she could. She closed her eyes and imagined a bright, moonlit night. Granthyrs don't come out in the moonlight, she knew, so if she could hold that image she should be fine.

The horse, however, was laying on its back, motionless, having been gored to death by the granthyrs. The slight breeze that whispered through the barnyard silenced her mind, though she knew there was nothing but death all around her. The moonlight was fading. She had to figure this out. How would she ever make it through this day? Still clutching her note, she grew terrifyingly conscious that her immediate destination, the school office, was growing farther away. She had to deliver her note. That was all she needed to do right now. Did the hens escape? And what of their chicks? She kept her eyes closed in order to keep some peace inside herself, but she was too aware of the long gray hallway between her and the office and the inevitable ringing of the bell.

Barb, she knew, could not have escaped the granthyrs, otherwise she would have emerged from the barn to rescue the horse. The note in her hand said Tamara had a slight accident over the weekend and required an X-ray on Monday and needed to be excused from gym, otherwise she should be fine if she took it easy.

The moonlight behind her eyelids was gone now, and the darkness was growing more severe. Somewhere, from over the mountain, she heard a bell ring, and then the granthyrs were all over her.

By Wednesday afternoon, Tamara could make her way with her crutch as long as she rested every so often. She needed to see more of her neighborhood and take three days' worth of scorching headaches for a walk. Her aim was Central Park, though whether she made it there or not, she needed to get as far as 61st and 2nd; the intersection where she awoke from her walking delusion.

The screams of granthyrs and the cries of distress had pulled her from her bed and pushed her out her front door. In her sleep, she had walked down her street and the whole width of the adjoining block to rescue Barb. She needed to retrace the illusional journey she had taken again and again in her mind and discover some new meaning from it. Unlike most of her dreams and delusions, this one required something of her.

Her halting pace kept her alert to subtler details she might have missed striding along on two able feet, but there was not much that captured her imagination or held her attention in a reassuring way.

Walking slowly meant there was more debris to distract her. As beautiful as she knew many of these homes to be on the inside, she had difficulty reconciling the street environment surrounding them. Like veins in the human body which carried away the body's refuse in the blood, the streets of her city joined poverty and wealth and provided those conduits through which everyone's waste traveled. The sanitary truck that passed with its "air of distinction" (her father's phrase) and the hearse followed by its funeral procession told her that these streets will eventually carry away everything we once loved and needed but can't hold on to forever. The man lying under the paper outside her neighbor's mansion, the policeman directing traffic, the chauffeur waiting by someone's car, the carry-out box with last-night's food strewn in the alley, they were all connected by this pavement she was walking with too much time to think. She had been this way late at night. Was the man under the newspaper awake then, watching her? Was that the cop, and would he recognize her?

She paused at the bottom of her street before turning right on 2nd Avenue. How could she have ventured so far in her sleep? What psychic forces drove her so furiously from her bed and her home? Slowly, she scanned the street and thought through her dream. A car horn ignited anxiety within her as it jolted violent sensations throughout her body. She couldn't remember anything of her nocturnal walk, but she could feel the hunt of the granthyrs resuming, and she felt like easy prey alone in the streets.

She was just turning for home when she saw an old man. He was hunched and lame in one leg and leaning heavily on his cane. The man had just stepped off the curb into the street, but Tamara knew he wasn't going to make it across the intersection before the countdown ran out and the lights changed. Tamara's heart latched on to him, and whatever anxieties she carried within her now raced after the old man. With four lanes of traffic aimed right at him, Tamara wanted to run, scoop him up and carry him to the other side. There were three seconds left on the clock and the man was hardly half way across. Then, the light was green.

The first lane of traffic took off without delay. The next lane paused a few moments then was free to go. But the third and fourth lanes became agitated and then openly hostile. She lost sight of the man, but she heard the wave of car horns traveling back through the pack. All the anxieties she had lent the man roared back and overwhelmed her. She could hear his heart scream in panic, and she felt his remorse over his inabilities as he cursed his age and condemned the circumstances that made him the brunt of heartless profanities shouted by people in too much of a hurry. She wished she could have met him on the other side, looked him in the face, and made sure everything was okay.

As she turned up 2nd Avenue, she was halted by the impulse that got her out of bed: Barb's screams, her cry from the barn when she discovered more granthyrs than she could master on her own. She should never have let Barb go out there alone. That old man should never have had to cross that street by himself. She wondered what Barb could be doing at 4:30 on a Wednesday afternoon. Thinking about dinner? What sort of chores needed doing on a farm before she could rest and eat? By herself. What if the granthyrs come back? And what else, beside her fantastical granthyrs, could be lurking around Barb's home that might attack one night?

Waves of loneliness washed through Tamara. She was half way down 2nd Avenue in one of the most crowded cities in the nation feeling acutely aware of how much loneliness there was in the world. Who was the old man going to see? To whom did he go at night? Who helped him? Who was helping Barb?

As Tamara approached the corner of 61st and 2nd Avenue she needed to rest her foot. The only bench was occupied by two animated hipsters smoking narrow, sweet-smelling cigars, talking over one another's sentences as their voices kept modulating from serious, to ironic, to just plain stupid, or so she thought. Her leg throbbed, and she wondered which front stoop the policewoman had used to look at her foot.

"Hey Miss, partner with the poor?" urged a voice which, when she looked at the man, told her of a rescue mission that needed her help. He had a stack of thin newspapers tucked under his arm and a small yellow bucket filled with loose change. She didn't have any money, but she took the paper. The lead article addressed the mental health of the homeless with a pledge to connect people with the help they needed. Financial assistance was available for medications and counselors were on hand especially for veterans suffering post-traumatic stress disorders. A young woman's face was pictured over a caption which read: "Tonya's illness kept her on the streets until Wayside ministries offered her the help she needed."

Tonya didn't look much older than Tamara. The article told Tamara that Tonya's parents weren't able to afford medications that might have controlled her delusions, and they couldn't control her, so they sent her to foster care and into the "system." The word was in quotation marks, indicating it stood for something Tamara ought to comprehend, but it was meaningless to her. However, that system couldn't contain Tonya either, so she wound up in the streets. She had been abused by a string of men and became addicted to heroin, a habit which she supported through prostitution. But God, through the work of the mission, had saved her and given her the promise of a new life.

The man who offered Tamara the paper had moved on across the street, and she wondered about him and whether he had suffered like Tonya had before the mission rescued him. How often had she passed people like Tonya while on outings with her mother? There was the man lying on the bench, sleeping under newspapers. Was he a victim of this "system?" The old man caught in traffic was still vivid in her mind. What would become of him in this hostile city?

And what of the young lady the policeman picked up Saturday morning after being reported twice to the authorities, or the girl standing in the middle of traffic later that night who didn't know where she was or why she was there?

Tamara looked down the street and wondered how far she might have walked Saturday night. Her foot was telling her she couldn't walk much longer without sitting down, but her mind was wandering down 2nd Avenue, moving her farther from home and from herself.

Her biggest questions weren't answered by the article: How did God save Tonya, and what role did the mission play? Who was God to each of the people, and how was God mixed up in any of their lives? She saw Li Jie and heard his erhu playing for those who were so lonely, inviting them home but never telling them where to find it. The article described services Tonya had received and the love she had discovered through the efforts of volunteers. Would Tamara like to be a volunteer? asked the article.

The emotional carousel she was on was racing ahead far too fast for her comfort, and the sights spilling through her brain were gaining on the frantic horse she was riding. There were granthyrs running down the hallway of her school just yesterday morning in broad daylight. And Thorafura, who shows little shame in her timing, keeps scorching Tamara with her snakish eyes and threatening her with her serpentine fangs.

The questions rushing through her mind were like flashpoints of lightning. They struck at her, and each one pierced her with indecision. How would she defend herself against the granthyrs if they should find her like this, so exposed in the city with no protection? Should she go and find this rescue mission? What if she disappeared in the city after being chased by her demons into the dark holes at the end of alleyways? Was that her carousel horse lying dead in the barnyard? Should she run and seek the help she needs but her parents won't allow? Why would God let this happen to her for so long if help was so close by?

Just before she heard the scream of sirens Saturday night, it was the fury of a dying horse that echoed through the valley. Was it the cry of God calling out to those in need? Barb's screams had brought her here, to this corner, and Tamara would have kept running if the car horns hadn't scolded her and kept her from her mission. Was God lost somewhere in the city, looking for all those who were just as lost and in need of a shepherd? She shifted on her crutch. Her heart held on to the old man now hobbling off in his own direction, and she wondered if Shepherd Jesus had found him yet.

Mercifully, the two hipsters vacated the bench and Tamara took their place. She wanted to go home but now needed to rest more than her foot. She was hurting for the security she knew awaited her on the inside of her front door, and her emotional fortitude was waning. Loneliness deepened within her, but she would rather nurse her loneliness alone at home, in her room, which was still so empty and barren of herself.

Tamara took out her phone and gauged that her mother would be coming home soon. She looked up and down the streets then decided she couldn't wait until their session with Dr. Samuelson, so she called her mother, told her where she was and asked if she could come and get her.

The mid-town, rush hour traffic, and the sidewalks now crowded with scores of people might have pushed Tamara further into her distress but knowing she could sit right there and let it go by gave her enormous relief. She didn't have to navigate her way through it alone. There, by the light of day, as her reason returned, she knew the granthyrs were hiding in their lairs gnawing on their own regrets, not hers.

"I got us a couple of hot-dogs," Aimee announced as she sat down. "Dad's coming home for dinner, but it will be a while. So, one all the way and a root beer." They ate in silence and watched the pedestrians as Aimee waited for her daughter to say something.

"Dr. Samuelson told us we were supposed to talk about why I left the other night," said Tamara. "I think I know."

Aimee felt quite sure she didn't want to hear this, since she had her own suspicions, none of which brought her any consolation. She felt agitated and would prefer to have this conversation on foot, walking toward something at a rapid pace, benefiting from the adrenalin now coursing through her. Her daughter's foot, however, meant they had to confront this face to face on a bench by 2nd Avenue, of all places.

"Go ahead," said Aimee, with all the caution she could muster.

"I need to go to Barb's."

"I know, honey," acknowledged Aimee. "And we're going to do all we can to take you to New Hampshire this summer. We've got an appointment with the headmaster at Upton on Monday – I tried to get one before we meet with Samuelson, but he didn't have an opening. And it looks like the third week in July is free as far as the summer school calendar is concerned, so we're shooting for that if I can squeeze in a long weekend from work."

"No, mom," Tamara pleaded.

"What?"

"I can't go to summer school. I have to go to Barb's." She took a long pause and then she said what the erhu had sung to her in the park and what the carousel had taught her as she bobbed up and down. She confessed what the granthyrs had ripped from her flesh in the hallway at school, and what the old man whispered to her as he walked off alone. She spoke to what echoed through her as she watched a suffering horse being disemboweled here at the corner of 61st and 2nd, and what Tonya confirmed for her just a few minutes ago.

"I can't live here anymore. Not like this."

Deep in her womb, Aimee felt her daughter kicking again warning her the time was coming when a life would emerge to which she would have to pay very close attention. As she had done more than fourteen years ago, Aimee had blanketed herself in the illusion of professional busyness, putting off the impending day of Tamara's delivery, though every indicator said it was getting close. Aimee was again so fully ensconced in her professional self that her daughter's tremors had become peripheral frustrations she could deal with as needed, yet she trusted they weren't going to derail her again.

But Aimee had been here too many times before. Their lives wouldn't sit still, and every time they lurched forward it resembled the pains of childbirth, which she evidently had never reconciled. So, she took her deep breath and hoped to bend this moment into something else, but the contractions in her womb wouldn't allow it. Aimee closed her eyes and listened for some wisdom to emerge. She was afraid of the answers she might hear to the questions mounting up in her mind, so the only wisdom to which she paid any attention was the voice which said she needed reinforcements.

"I'm listening," Aimee assured her. "But I want your father to hear what you have to say. Would you mind if we continued this tomorrow with Dr. Samuelson?"

Tamara looked down at the newspaper resting on the bench and saw Tonya's face, radiant with life in spite of the hell that had so eviscerated her. She nodded that she could wait.

9

THE SOUND OF SHATTERING DREAMS

CROWDED INTO DR. SAMUELSON'S OFFICE late Thursday afternoon, the Baxters talked through the details of their week beginning with the purging of Tamara's room and a fresh reading of the letters from Barb. Dr. Samuelson nodded severely when Tamara offered her interpretation of these events: that she had to go live with Barb and help her on the farm. He noted the frozen stares of her parents.

Terrance was the first one to brave any sort of response.

"Your mother and I have promised to take you for a visit, Tamara, but you can't be serious about living there for good. And I don't think that's what Barb had in mind, either."

Tamara had learned a useful debate tactic from her mother. She had set the bar higher than any of them could reach; now she had to help them build the step-ladder they would need to climb over their reservations. She knew she would have to lower her aim along the way, but not yet. Right now, she was moving in, permanently, with Barb. But her father wasn't finished.

"That said, however, I think you have something very important on your mind which you wanted to talk over with Dr. Samuelson that's related to why you want to go back," urged Terrance.

Samuelson gave Tamara his full attention, but the spotlight felt too intense and she withered in the moment.

"Go on, honey," said Aimee. "We're both behind you in this."

"I want to be baptized," Tamara whispered.

Dr. Samuelson rarely, if ever, felt shock over things he heard his patients say, so this was the exception.

"Please, say more," he urged her.

"That's why I need to go back," was all she said.

"So, this isn't just a vacation you want," he said with grave sympathy in his voice. "This is more of a pilgrimage for you."

Tamara wasn't quite sure what he meant, but Aimee lent her voice to urge this along.

"You know Barb, I take it?" she asked Dr. Samuelson.

"Oh, yes. Indeed, I do. Saint of a woman, and something of the community gadfly, as well – in the best sort of ways, I mean. I have long appreciated the wisdom that wonderful old woman carries in her soul."

"Tamara met her at a baptism by the river and then spent the night with her after that frightful hike we told you about."

"I think I've got the picture," reflected Samuelson as he sat back and drifted into thought. "Well, if you want both my professional and spiritual opinion, Tamara couldn't find a better mentor in the faith anywhere. And I can appreciate why she feels the urgency to return." Dr. Samuelson covered his mouth with his hand and returned to his ruminations. "Of course, I also appreciate that what she is seeking won't be realized on a weekend visit. So, clearly, we have some thinking to do about that. It's also one more piece we have to factor in to this growing puzzle we haven't yet figured how to put together. Where should we start?"

"Well, this Monday we have an appointment with the headmaster at Upton," said Aimee. "That may offer us some clarity on where that is headed. If we can firm up Tamara's chances, or even get a commitment from them, then it may be possible to negotiate with her current principle and see to it that her transcripts represent her in the best possible light."

Tamara shook her head and closed her eyes against what she was hearing. She bristled at the command her mom needed to take in every situation, and she paled at the thought of being the subject of those negotiations. So, she knew this was the moment. She saw herself seated in the Tree House for Dreaming and sought to muster once again the sensations that brought her to a new threshold in her life.

"Mom, I think we should cancel that appointment," she ventured.

"We are not canceling that appointment," said Aimee. "Honey, don't worry. We've all seen the artist you are becoming, and I don't want you to become discouraged by circumstances beyond your control. We are behind you all the way in this, so I hope you will trust that we are going to work this out."

"Mom," said Tamara, her voice rising. "Mom, no. I don't want to go. I can't go. You said yesterday that you were listening." There was a measure of defeat in her last statement.

"I'm sorry," said Aimee. "Go ahead."

"Mom, I can't help the art that I do. My illness forces me. I have to draw pictures of my demons to keep me from running into traffic. If I couldn't draw, I would cut myself or throw things through windows. I've never cared if the drawings were any good, only that I've gotten those images out of me. Drawing my dreams seems to keep me from falling back into them, but it has never brought me any happiness. Never. The one good thing is that it feels like I've made something instead of destroyed something, but every picture I've ever drawn means something is already broken and can't be fixed. All those drawings you want to show the headmaster are screams that no one ever seems to hear."

"But they are beautiful," said Aimee. "They really are. You have a gift, honey, and perhaps if you channeled that gift, learned how to draw things you love, instead, it would bring you some joy."

"How are they beautiful?" asked Tamara. "They can't be beautiful. I feel hideous every time I see them."

"We haven't experienced the pain that produces your drawings, Tamara. That's true," interjected Dr. Samuelson. "But they do show us something very important. And, I'm afraid I must agree with your mother on this point, not on everything yet, but at least on this point: the beauty you will make with your life will be like nothing else. The maelstrom out of which those drawings emerge conveys a reality that few people are going to find pretty, or pleasing to look at, but it may be something we need to see. If nothing else, what you draw challenges us to see something which, in a way, helps us define beauty, if only in contrast to the darkness you find so ugly. And it is ugly. Now, I know this sounds odd, but the way you do ugly is beautiful."

Samuelson reached for the note Barb had written to Tamara and read her words aloud:

You are a beautiful young woman – beautiful in so many ways you can't begin to appreciate yet. And you are a suffering young woman. I know that. We don't have to hide that. In a mysterious way, your suffering is part of your beauty, and it always will be. It is refining you. And it will, one day, be the gift you give to others, just as it has been the gift you have given to me.

"You can't walk away from who you are," pleaded her mom.

"And you can't run away from home," added her father.

"But you can move toward something new," said Dr. Samuelson. "Last Saturday, I believe, you set out to do just that. And we are going to walk with you. The question is, where are you headed, Tamara Baxter?"

This was the opening Tamara needed, but she felt herself shriveling. She drew her legs up into her seat and wrapped her arms around her knees. Her eyes became fixed on a small statue of St. Francis standing in the corner of Samuelson's office. In one of the saint's hands rested a bird.

"Please, don't make me go to Upton Academy," she said. "I'm fine where I am," though she knew she couldn't cover up the lie she had just uttered. She buried her face behind her knees and waited for the adults around her to figure out what to do with that.

"What if we pull out one of the links in this chain?" asked Dr. Samuelson as he watched Tamara brood. "Just for the sake of simplifying this for the moment, what if we took Upton out of the picture? What does that do for us here?"

No one moved. Aimee's face grew tense as she calculated the loss to her aspirations if they took Tamara's art career off the table.

But Tamara's brow softened, and her aspect brightened.

Samuelson gave them as long as they needed, but in that interim, Aimee's expression turned from agitation to hostility.

"Without Upton we wouldn't need to send her to summer school," whispered Aimee, unable to form her words without choking on them. "Is that what you're looking for?"

"And without summer school she is clear to go to New Hampshire, right?" asked Samuelson.

"Yes, but this new position in my firm is going to require a lot of me this summer. I just can't take a lot of time," protested Aimee. "Believe me, Tamara, there is nothing I would love more than to go back to see Barb, honey, but you know that just isn't feasible right now."

Tamara saw the conflict in her mother, and she knew why her mother drew vitality from such encounters when she was in a position of strength, but it gave Tamara no joy to realize just how far she had advanced against her mother in this conversation. Her mother hadn't reconciled all she had just learned, and she wasn't ready to move on to discussing New Hampshire. Tamara met her mother's gaze hoping to discover if there was any common ground between them. She held Aimee's eyes until her mother turned away. The tension among them had given way to emptiness, a sensation of emotional deprivation, and Tamara's mind began to ricochet around the room in search of a connection with someone, but no one took her in.

Dr. Samuelson watched the struggle between them, then, as gently as he could form the words, he said to Aimee and Terrance: "I think you need to listen very carefully to your daughter right now."

The air in the room seemed to freeze. Tamara searched their faces, but her parents presented themselves as empty shells. Their hardened exteriors seemed to be thickening and didn't allow any emotional residue to seep through. They were closed off to her, and she became panicky. Dr. Samuelson let them simmer for a few more moments, then he excused himself and stepped out of the room.

The horrors and blessings of that silence incubated within them. If there was any movement at all in the room, it was taking place in each of their minds. Though none of them realized it, in the collective soul of the family something new was being born. It didn't matter if they were ready for it.

"Where were we?" asked Dr. Samuelson when he came back in. But before anyone could speak, his phone buzzed. He picked up the receiver, thanked his secretary, and hung up.

"Pardon me for all of that," he said, "but I may have some good news here. I just asked Muriel to check on the availability of the cottages for June, and there are still a couple of weeks that are open at the end of the month." He held up his hand to capture their protests before they could utter them and continued.

"My wife and I are scheduled for the first two weeks of July, but here's an idea. What if we – my wife and I, I mean – what if we managed to get our reservations moved toward late June. We could drive up with Tamara and deliver her to Barb's, then you could work out a weekend later to pick her up. That way, I'm just up the hill if anything should happen down in the valley."

Tamara's heart soared, but she sat on her reaction a little too long. As joyous as she was to be gaining on two of her life-changing aims, to go to New Hampshire, and to be free of her mother's dream, there was still a third decision she had to lay on the table. Now that new realities were being presented to her, an old reality had to be met head on, not by her parents, but by herself.

Dr. Samuelson studied the parents, who were in an emotional stalemate from which they couldn't extricate themselves. Tamara, however, showed more complexity in her face. The doctor honed in, watched her shift into low gear and then stall out altogether. She had grown very serious, and as Terrance and Aimee followed Samuelson's gaze, they knew there must be more coming, and there was.

Tamara took a deep breath and looked at her mother. Panic was going toe to toe with resolve, and she needed some help getting her words out.

"Honey?" said Aimee.

But Tamara shut down instead. She had been prepared, until that moment, to state her third aim, but the gains she had made collapsed within her. Having her mother as an adversary had depleted her, and she wasn't sure she was ready for this. She knew her mother had abdicated nothing yet. No decisions had been made, and all could be lost if she pushed too far. But Dr. Samuelson committed her to it all the same.

"I think now it's time we listened to something else Tamara said a few minutes ago. I'm sure it probably escaped your notice, but I heard it loud and clear."

"What?" asked Terrance.

"Tamara used a word earlier I have never heard her say before. We adults have all fought over the word when she wasn't around, but at your insistence, Aimee, we've never used it in her presence."

After waiting a few moments, he turned to Tamara and asked her: "Do you remember the word, Tamara?"

Tamara turned her attention back to St. Francis. Her eyes grew puffy, and she nodded.

"Illness," she whispered.

"Illness," confirmed the doctor.

Aimee felt the word hit her in the chest. If she had been a weaker woman that would have folded her up, but she was a woman of power, and for nearly ten years she had been exercising the best of her personal power against what she saw unfolding before her now. She would have blinded Dr. Samuelson if the anger focused in her eyes had the force of hurling matter. She stood up and started toward the door.

"Honey?" said Terrance. Aimee stopped, she wrapped herself in her arms and squeezed herself with all the strength she had. There was no sound, but the intensity mounting up within her was unmistakable. Terrance turned to Dr. Samuelson and said he thought they needed a break.

"I agree," said the doctor. "Unfortunately, I have another session in a few minutes, so we'll have to wrap up shortly, and I'm not sure we should let this go yet. Aimee? We need to hear what's on your mind."

Aimee wheeled around and was in the doctor's face before anyone saw it coming.

"You son of a bitch – I cannot believe you let this happen. We had an agreement. I thought you affirmed the approach we were taking with her. I thought you supported the life aims we had been mapping out. Seems we were led down some therapeutic wind-tunnel, dumping us out right where we never meant to be. Everything fell apart this afternoon, and you let it happen. Yes, our daughter suffers challenges, everybody does, but we were sorting those out. And, yes, she is a very complicated young lady, most every artist is, but our daughter is not ill!"

Dr. Samuelson never flinched. He absorbed every syllable fired at him and each word sunk into his flesh. How long they locked their psychic horns was hard to tell, but it was Tamara who spoke next.

"You can't keep saying that, mom. I am. And I can't continue to live like this. I can't. And I'm not going to. I want Dr. Samuelson to prescribe me some medication that will help. If he won't, I know there are clinics that will."

There was a gentle knock on the door.

"Dr. Samuelson," said his secretary, "your next appointment is waiting."

"We should meet sooner than later," said Samuelson. "Ask Muriel for the earliest time next week."

As soon as they were settled in the subway, Tamara googled pilgrimage.

☙

The kettle announced it was time for tea, so Barb pulled the biscuits out of the oven and set them on the table, filled the teapot with steaming water and fetched the butter and jam.

"Sarah's back in the hospital, I'm afraid," Tobias told his mother.

"Poor soul," groaned Barb, "She has had her trials. Is it the cancer again?"

"Afraid so, and this time they don't think there's much they can do. I'm so sorry."

Barb nodded her head with understanding, her eyes glistening from the news. Another empty chair in her dwindling Sunday School class, and another friend passing on.

"I know you'll pray for her and be a comfort to her, as you always are," said her son, hoping to turn her mood, without success.

"Never took her off my prayer list. I've been praying for her healing for almost a year now," lamented Barb, taking stock of where her prayers had now brought her.

"Are you okay?" asked her son, though he knew she wasn't. He had seen the look of loneliness on his mother's face too many times. He could give each of her wrinkles its own name, starting with her sister, her parents, then a long procession of neighbors who had been like kin to her in this old, traditional, farming community. So few of them were left any more. Sometimes he wondered whether her hearty farm-woman physic really was the blessing she always said it was.

She sipped her tea and seemed to slip further away from him.

"I plan to be up tomorrow to work on the old cottage," he said, but she didn't register that she heard him. "For now, would you like me to give you a hand out in the barn before dinner?"

"I suppose there are eggs to be gathered. Never got to that this morning."

As they walked to the barn, Tobias noticed more impending decisions that would need to be made sooner than later. When they got to the hen house, he discovered that the chickens had been out of feed and water, he suspected, for a day or two. There was certainly more than a day's worth of eggs to be gathered. He glanced over at the farm-hand house and wondered if hiring a young family to come might be worth the effort or if the day was drawing near when they would need to sell the farm. His mother wouldn't hear of it, however, and his wife had flatly refused the idea of taking it on. There were no grandchildren on the horizon.

10

GREAT AUNT TAMARA

THE NEXT FEW DAYS IN the Baxter household were icy as the entire family dynamic became so fluid none of them knew how to navigate it. Relational lines were redrawn, confused again, then coalesced, only to fray once more. They were in what Dr. Samuelson called a 'therapeutic stalemate,' when the issues were best left alone until they could work on them together under supervision. Best not to move the pieces around on the board until we get back together, he used to coach them in earlier sessions. The pattern took hold, so that they often found themselves at loggerheads between appointments.

Terrance and Aimee sought to be as cautious around Tamara as they could be, though Tamara knew she had created more disruption to their lives in twenty minutes than she had for nearly fifteen years and felt just as cautious toward them.

Aimee kept the appointment with the headmaster at Upton, though she came away realizing that her dream for her daughter was on life support. Aimee was the only machine keeping that dream alive and it was time to pull the plug, though she didn't know how.

That same afternoon, Terrance knocked lightly on Tamara's door and eased himself into the room. She was seated at her dressing table thumbing through her old illustrated copy of *Watership Down*, the only one of her childhood books she held on to.

"Looks like we need to start building you a new library," observed her dad, eying the burgundy Bible on her bed which was the only other volume in the room.

"In the meantime," he continued, "I brought you this to hang on your wall – if you're interested, that is." Terrance handed Tamara a thin, rectangular parcel.

Tamara peeled back the brown wrapping paper. Looking back up at her was a middle-aged woman in casual dress leaning on a large, timber fireplace mantle with a warm and inviting smile on her face.

"Who is she?" asked Tamara.

"That is Tamara Esmeralda Cousins. She is your great, great aunt, and the woman for whom you were named. I'm sure you've heard us speaking about her, but not many pictures of her exist. As outgoing a soul as she was, she always dodged the camera. I found the picture in a stack of old stuff the other day at the bank and got it framed. I thought you should know more about who she was. If you don't want to hang it in here then we'll find a place downstairs, but I wanted to give you first refusal."

Tamara stared at the picture without saying anything, long enough to make Terrance think he had boxed his daughter into an uncomfortable corner. The moments that passed became increasingly awkward. Then, she stood and walked the photograph toward the wall directly opposite her dressing table and centered it at eye level.

"There. Now, no matter where I am, I can see her," said Tamara.

Terrance saw the reflection of his aunt in the mirror and couldn't imagine a more comforting thought than to have his great aunt forever watching over his daughter.

"One day, when I was a little younger than you, Aunt Tamara came and took me to the zoo over in the park to get me out of my parents' hair on a Saturday. I couldn't wait to see the tigers – they were my favorite. But Aunt Tamara wanted to visit the barnyard first. I thought she was silly. Anyone could see that stuff on a farm if they really wanted to, but no one could just drive out into the country and find tigers.

"As she stood looking at the lambs, I kept pulling at her telling her it was time to go. Know what she did? She made me touch one, feel its wool, with both hands. And I don't mean just pet it, she made me rub my hands over them and grab fistfuls of wool, then she told me to rub my hands together. I was amazed at how soft my hands felt all of a sudden. Then, she said, 'come look at this,' and she walked me over to the chickens. Well, my patience just left me, and I screamed, 'I want to see the tigers!' But she didn't flinch. She wasn't even paying attention to me. She was lost among the chickens."

Terrance sat quietly for a moment and then explained: "I had completely forgotten about that until I found this picture and showed it to my dad. He told me it had been taken at their uncle Wren's home. Turns out, her father's brother grew up on a farm not that far from Albany, and it seems Aunt Tamara used to spend large parts of her summers there with her cousin, Rosie. I never knew that until I showed my dad this photo, and now I can't help but think that so much of her sense and wisdom was born there on that farm."

Tamara looked even more closely at the portrait, wishing she could expand its frame and take in her aunt's surroundings.

"Tamara, I want you to know, I am so very proud of you for what you said the other day in Dr. Samuelson's office. That took more courage than I ever would have had at your age. Over these past few days, I have thought a lot about what you said, and I think I appreciate why you feel the farm is where you need to be. I have always admired my Aunt Tamara. She is the wisest woman I have ever known, and I don't have to guess what her advice would be for us on this occasion. She would have had you packed by now. She was not one to look back if a good adventure might benefit you in some way. So, even if I'm still unsure about all of this, I trust my Aunt Tamara! And, I want you to know, I also trust you, and I trust the decisions you are making now. Your mother, however, is still very confused about what to feel, and I just want you to give her some room. Be patient. Can you do that?"

Tamara nodded as she continued to look at the portrait, seeing just a hint of her grandfather in Aunt Tamara's face. She felt her dad's hand rest firmly across her shoulders and made a choice, not an easy one, to resist the impulse to pull away but to lean into him, instead.

Then, she asked: "Dad, do you think I'm ill?"

After only a brief pause, her father tightened his arm around her and said he did. "I've known for a long time, honey, and for a long time I've advocated for what you asked for last Thursday. But, I have to be honest with you. As frightful as it has been for all of us, and I know it has been more painful for you than any of us, in hindsight I'm not convinced that medication would have been the right thing to do. I just don't know."

"Why do you say that?" she asked.

"Your mother felt all along that medication would have smothered the person she felt you could be. She wanted you to fight, and not just to fight, but to win. Now, it seems the cost was just too high, and I am so very sorry for all that has put you through. I completely understand your desire to be free of this pain you feel every day. It is your right to pursue your own happiness and not be a slave to this. And it is our duty, as your parents, to help you find that. We've just struggled to know how."

"What do you think Aunt Tamara would say?" asked his daughter.

"Good question. I don't really know. She lived in such a different time. But if she could meet the young lady I know right now, I believe she would be very proud of you."

"Will you hang my picture for me?" she asked her dad.

"In a heartbeat!"

❧

As the days lengthened, Barb loved her front porch best after dinner. She buttoned her sweater against the chill still in the air and couldn't wait until summer when the warmth of the day would linger well into the evening. She thought of Tamara coming and of the fun they would have together.

Barb had been making a shopping list of supplies: small work gloves, an appropriate farm hat, a few bandanas, plenty of butter and cheese. She bought Tamara a hand-crafted, white oak egg-basket at the farmer's market a couple of days ago. They would go berry-picking and bake cobblers on the hearth in the evening. After worship last week, she asked Nora Jakes if she thought their horses might be suitable for inexperienced riders and received a positive response with a standing invitation to bring her over. Barb made a note to let Aimee know so they could pack suitable riding clothes.

As the swing moved with the breeze blowing through the porch, Barb remembered a barnyard bristling with productivity, but she had grown just as glad for the peace that had settled over the place these past few years. They had her son's wedding in the church, but the reception was held here in the yard. Natalie threw her bouquet off the porch and little Betsy Nazareth caught it. That was over twenty years ago. They're still awaiting Betsy's nuptials. Betsy just couldn't seem to keep a man, smiled Barb, and she knew why. Betsy's baby brother, eight years younger than she, had special needs. Betsy had taken over his care after their parents died in a car accident out on the Sledhill road one February evening coming home from North Conway. Tinder, they called him. He had been too slow for regular classes in school and too clumsy for farm work even though he loved sitting on the tractor and feeding the livestock. Barb was proud of the way Betsy took on both the farm and Tinder at only sixteen years of age. She couldn't wait to introduce them to Tamara.

As the chill of the evening crept into her bones and her sweater wouldn't help any more, she shut her eyes and offered her evening prayer: "Thanks be, dear Lord, thanks be. Yours is the splendor and yours is the glory, and this day has been blessed by both. Shine on, dear Jesus, shine on, and bring the light to those who face the darkness without you. Comfort all who are in your care, strengthen all who need your mercy. Gather your lambs, great Shepherd, gather your lambs. As we go to our rest, bless the night, and bring the peace. Let your children know you are near, and in their dreams, learn of your love. Amen."

11

THE PILGRIMAGE BEGINS

FOR DAYS, TAMARA STARED UP the street in the direction of Central Park but determined she was not going to complete her quest until she could do so without her crutch. She had been thinking about Dr. Samuelson's comment that it was more of a pilgrimage she was seeking than a vacation. She knew now that she had begun that pilgrimage, unintentionally, as she hobbled to the corner of 61st Street and 2nd Avenue in hopes of discovering the meaning of her dream. Now, with the state her family was in, she felt herself a lonely traveler with a destination that would be taken in short increments, and Central Park represented the next stop along her way. Her father's story about the zoo and the portrait of Aunt Tamara on uncle Wren's farm had suggested the destination for the day. She wanted to stand in the barnyard where her great-great aunt had so admired the lambs and to feel their wool herself. Then, she would go see the chickens that meant so much to her. A pilgrimage.

Tamara went to her bedroom to deposit her school books, and she looked once again at that face of Aunt Tamara, smiling with a light of genuine joy. What was she laughing at? What had she just been doing or thinking of there on her uncle Wren's farm? She wasn't dressed for work, but the work was in her, that was clear. This was a woman who would as easily shovel out a barn stall has hold conversation in the parlor. It was plain to see all over her face.

Then, a flash of remembrance sent Tamara to her closet. She had forgotten, until just then, the barn boots her mother had given her. They were still in the bag that had held her paint supplies. Tamara carried them to her chair and pulled off her school shoes.

The first boot slipped on perfectly well and covered her shins right up to her knee. She tucked in her jeans which snugged up the fit. The second boot, however, was harder going over her wounded foot. It must have been a little swollen from all her walking at school, so she grimaced as she pulled it on. Once it was on, the snug fit felt great on her foot and lent strength to the rest of her leg. She stood and walked around her room. The feel of the boots sent waves of vitality coursing through her. But as she glanced down at them she felt she would look strange walking through the city wearing barn boots on a bright sunny day. This was, however, a pilgrimage and not a sight-seeing venture, and she was going to the barnyard, not a tea-party.

Tamara paid the entrance fee at the zoo and the map told her the barnyard animals were in the children's area. She felt again those childish sensations she had on the carousel. But these would be live animals, and she was there to hear them grunt and squeal, smell real barnyard smells, and to touch the sheep if that was still allowed. She saw monkeys, penguins, bears, and ducks as she strolled toward the children's zoo, but she didn't pay much attention to them. She did, however, keep her eyes open for the tigers just to say hello for her dad.

As she entered the barnyard, Tamara had to remind herself not to be disappointed that it was not a real farm. The dozens of children poking and squealing at the animals were an instantaneous disenchantment. She would have to wade through a group of kids half her size to get close to the fence just to be near the animals. Her impulse to be annoyed, however, was tempered by a little guy who was too afraid to feed the goat poking its head through the bars. His mother, camera at the ready, was urging him on so she could take the shot, but he wasn't having any of it.

Tamara wasn't really thinking when she did it, but she squatted down on her haunches between the boy and the pen and held out her hand.

"Want me to feed him for you?" asked Tamara.

The boy became silent and stared at Tamara then backed away toward his mom. But his mom took some of the feed and handed it to Tamara. The wet nose of the goat, and the action of its mouth as it took the feed from her hand, made Tamara cringe, but the reaction on her face made the little boy giggle. He handed her more of his feed, and she repeated the action to more giggles. Then, again. It became a game. When the feed ran out, the mother thanked Tamara then moved on with her son.

Tamara sat there for a few moments then pulled herself to her feet to go in search of the lambs. She got there just a few moments after the same mother and son arrived, which was a bit awkward, but she didn't care. When she could get close enough to the fence, and when a lamb finally wandered in her direction, she reached in and laid her hand on its back. The wool had a coarse feel. It was not nearly as soft as she thought it ought to be. She brushed her hands back and forth then sunk her fingers as deeply into its coat as she could, grabbing fistfuls of wool.

Then, there were two little hands, beside her own, reaching for the lamb. The little boy she met earlier was pushing in right beside her hoping for a handful, but the lamb was just out of his reach. Tamara grabbed the sheep by the scruff of the neck and tugged it to the right. She was surprised at how docile it was and how easily it let itself be pulled. Then, she laid her hand on its rump and tugged it, bringing it parallel to the fence and within reach of the little boy who sunk his own hands into the lamb's wool.

"Now," said Tamara to the little boy, "let's see what our hands feel like." She rubbed her hands together. Her hands felt coated in lotion. They smelled rather bad, but the soft sensation was a revelation.

"That is so cool," said Tamara. The little boy giggled again.

"It's lanolin," said a familiar voice behind her. "It's used in some make-ups and hand creams." She turned to find her dad standing several feet away.

"I saw your note when I got home and hoped I'd find you here," he said. "Great boots!" he continued, laughing. "Watch it, or they'll hand you a shovel."

Tamara felt embarrassed and intimidated by her dad's presence. She had wanted this to be private, something she discovered for her own. Now, it was an experienced shared in a way that made her feel awkward. She felt crowded and wished she could watch the animals and think her own thoughts about her life. This was her pilgrimage, not an outing with her dad.

She felt his hand rest on her shoulder, and she took a deep breath.

"This is as close as I ever came to this part of my great Aunt Tamara's life," he said. "Now, I wish I'd had the chance to visit her uncle Wren's farm and see what it meant to her. But at that time of my life I was a pirate, or a Jedi-knight, or something too adventurous to be interested in farm animals."

Tamara was beginning to wither under his rambling. Her own ruminations interrupted, she wasn't really interested in his. She wished she had not left the note on the counter telling her parents where she had gone.

"Now, it's been long sold, probably to developers. Our bank may have even financed the houses built on it. No chance of ever going back." He sounded distant now, and sad.

Then, Tamara heard it in his voice. He was sharing in her pilgrimage, returning to find his aunt, and his daughter, both of whom had been lost to him for so long. Her life-long genius for burrowing deep into the psyches of those around her, that intuitive snake she unleashed which had done so much harm was still at work, sneaking into those darker regions of his soul where she could strike at will before he realized she was in there. She sensed herself slithering in, close to his inner heart, but now she felt some responsibility for being in there where he was vulnerable. She heard remorse in his tone and a softness in his words, just the target she had exploited before to her advantage. Now, however, the remorse was all hers for unleashing her venom when she had the upper hand. She listened closer, but his words had trailed off. He was watching the lamb, no doubt wishing his aunt could be with him again, so he could show her the respect she deserved rather than reject the wisdom she had for him so long ago.

Tamara reached in to feel the lamb again.

"Feel it," she said. And, he did. Together, they laid hands upon the lamb and let it soften their skin. Shepherd Jesus had brought them here, thought Tamara, and Shepherd Jesus must have a good reason.

12

SOMETHING HAS DIED

"FIRST OF ALL," SAID DR. Samuelson, as the family settled in to his office, "we are not here to plan anyone's funeral. No one has died, and no one is terminal, so why is everyone so grim?"

No one spoke, so Samuelson chose a topic at random.

"Art school. Where do we stand with that?"

"It's gone," whispered Aimee. The grief on her face was palpable.

"What happened?" asked the doctor.

"The headmaster told me that Tamara's grades were of real concern, and while her art demonstrated some aptitude, she had not developed sufficient technical skills expected of students to perform at her grade level in that school. He said he saw real passion in her work, but that raw passion let loose on the page wouldn't carry her very far if she was to mature as an artist. Hiring a teacher to work on her technique was an option, but he would need to see a fresh portfolio by mid-July when they would have to make the final decision. So, given what Tamara told us at the last session…"

"I'm sorry, Aimee," said Dr. Samuelson. He allowed a respectful silence and then asked about summer school.

"I called the school guidance counselor who took a fresh look at Tamara's records," said Aimee. "The guidance counselor said her grades were in trouble, but she also said it wasn't because Tamara had difficulty learning. The input she had received from her teachers indicated Tamara had the capacity to be a great student, but her anxiety issues were trampling all over her ability to succeed. She's having trouble coping with her surroundings – the pressures, the schedules, the deadlines, things like that."

"I think there's a lot of truth in that," replied Dr. Samuelson. "I've never noticed anything in Tamara to indicate low aptitude. She's bright, curious, extremely attentive – even when we don't think she's listening. And when she speaks, her insights hold a great deal of depth. What else did she say?"

"Well, I told her we were needing to make plans for the summer, that Tamara had an invitation to go stay on a farm in New Hampshire, and we were trying to sort out how essential summer school might be."

"And?" the doctor egged her on.

"And, she said she thought the trip would be more beneficial than putting Tamara through the pressures of school in an environment that seems so toxic for her."

"What do you make of all that?" Samuelson asked the group.

"All roads seem to be pointing in that direction," Terrance observed.

"I'm not sure you feel convinced, Aimee," Samuelson said.

"No, I am. I understand all that, and it adds up in my mind."

"But?"

"But – you said when we came in that no one has died, but that's what I've been feeling since our last session, that something has died," she lamented, looking at her hands.

"Your hopes for Tamara's art?" he asked.

Aimee' grief came to the surface, and she closed her eyes hoping to focus her thoughts. She opened her mouth several times wanting words to come out but sucked them all back in. Then, "It's not just her art. It's her life. I thought the art was going to be her way of sharing her life with others and making a life for herself."

"Not following in your or Terrance's footsteps?" asked Dr. Samuelson.

"Did you ever think about Tamara taking her place in the family enterprises somehow?"

"Good God, no," said Aimee. "She would suffocate and die."

Aimee became introspective. "When I saw she had an aptitude for art rather than numbers, I felt so glad for her. A part of me felt so alive again when I saw her drawing. And I thought, since I could never be an artist myself, why not my daughter? We could easily support her until she was ready to make a go of it on her own. We could become life-long partners in any endeavor she hoped to take up. So, something has died, and I don't know what to do with that."

Though she spoke of being in grief, Aimee's demeanor didn't match her words. She grew stronger as she spoke, though normally such emotions would have brought her to tears.

Those tears, however, were flowing from other eyes. Profuse tears streamed uncontrolled and unattended over Tamara's cheeks. She let them drip onto her shirt as she stared, without blinking, at her mother.

The moment required silence, and Samuelson let them sit in the solitude of their own reflections as he allowed them to see what they needed to see and hear what was being said in those deeply born words of remorse and consolation. They would learn more from one another in that silence, if given room.

Terrance grabbed a few tissues from the box on the table and handed them to Tamara, who took them but didn't use them. The act, however, was sufficient to dislodge the next thing on Aimee's mind.

"I also don't know what to do with Tamara's request for medication," she continued. "I've thought a lot about that – in fact, I can't get that off my mind, and I still cannot bring myself to agree. As many times as we've been through that, I'm still sure we made the right move. And for right now, until we work through some of these other matters, it's not something I care to reconsider." She was firm, and the look on her face defied anyone to broach the subject.

Dr. Samuelson, however, was not one to be bullied into a corner. "Tell us, then, what has so confirmed your position on this."

"First, as you said, all roads seem to be leading Tamara toward New Hampshire in a couple of months. I'm not sure how that will happen yet, but if it can, then I don't want this to stand in the way. I know enough about psychotropic medications to know that there is an experimental phase to this, and that different medications take time to begin working. Then, it's wait-and-see to confirm that they are producing the desired effect. We can't send her off under medication until we're certain she has the right combination of medicines at the right dosages, or we might be opening ourselves up to all sorts of new uncertainties."

"Do you have another option for us to consider?" asked Dr. Samuelson.

"Stay the course," she answered. "We've worked through this without medication so far. Now, Tamara has an opportunity to do something different, which may open up new possibilities for her. I want her to go into this without her having to contend with whatever medication may do to her. And, we don't know what that is, yet."

"I agree with that," said Terrance. "Though I want to hear from Tamara before we make up our minds."

"And, so do I," confirmed the doctor, now addressing his attention toward Tamara. "Commencing medication was your idea, Tamara, and we intend to hear what you have to say. I've given this a lot of thought, as well, and the thing I am most impressed with was the sincerity of your request. I think it took a lot of courage for you to say that. Knowing you, I know it was not an impulsive suggestion. Whether the three of us agree or not, doesn't matter right now. What matters is that we hear what you have to say, and we promise that we will listen and will consider it very carefully."

"Mom, don't you understand that I need to do this so I can go," explained Tamara, whose tears were still fresh on her face. "I can't do this to Barb, and I don't want to do this anymore to you and dad."

"Do what, honey?" asked her dad.

"Cause you so much pain."

"Cause us pain?" asked Aimee.

"Don't you think I can see, mom? I know what this has been doing to you and dad. I don't want to be the cause of that anymore."

"What about your own pain?" asked her father.

"That doesn't matter," she said.

"Now, Miss Baxter," said Dr. Samuelson in his professorial tone, "it's one thing to be noble and selfless, it's another thing to deny the truth. I've been watching you grow up with this pain, and I know it matters. The three of us have borne witness to a great deal of suffering in your life, and I can tell you what I believe to be the truth from my perspective. There have been so many times I felt you should have been medicated. I thought it was the right thing to do. Now, your mom persuaded me not to, but you convinced me that was the right decision."

Tamara was stunned by that insight and cocked her head wanting to hear more.

"Frankly, young lady, there were several times I feared we had lost you, but there is a force of life at work in you I rarely see in my patients. I know your parents may disagree with what I'm about to say, but I've seen you come back from the dead too many times to believe that it was simply by luck or personal determination. Each time you rallied, you came back stronger than before with more determination to bear your pain. I think you inherited a lot of that from your mother. But, and I want to be careful not to put words in your mouth, what I'm sensing is that you are tired of fighting it, and that worries me more than anything else. A person, any person, no matter how strong, can only take so much, and I don't want you to lose all you have gained."

"So, you are agreeing with Tamara?" asked Terrance.

"I don't think we're quite there, yet," said Samuelson. "I still think we need more of Tamara's input. So, Tamara, are you getting tired of this fight?"

Tamara saw Thorafura's fangs and recalled the sensations of defeat after her last tea-party dream in which the snake promised to pursue its campaign of terror as the flames consumed the room around her. She had never been able to outrun the granthyrs, and they seem to be growing in numbers and ferocity. And, she had overheard far too many late-night conversations between her parents.

So, Tamara nodded that she was tired. "I can't anymore."

"Tamara, look at me," said Dr. Samuelson. "Have you been thinking about suicide again?"

Aimee and Terrance felt the blunt force of the question and were horrified the doctor asked it so casually. As they watched Tamara, each felt their decade's old fear rush through them again.

Tamara, however, shook her head no, then she voiced it out loud: "No. I want to begin living and to stop running from these demons all the time."

"Yes. I thought so," said Dr. Samuelson. "I thought so."

"So, what are you recommending?" pressed Aimee, relieved at what she had just heard.

"Not so fast," said the doctor. "I'm not ready to recommend any-thing, yet. Tamara may well be right about all this, but I think we have been overlooking some other clues that are rather important."

"Such as?" asked Terrance.

"Tamara has been resorting to her art as a form of self-induced therapy. No one told her to do that. We've discussed meditation and adjustments to personal and interpersonal behavior to stem the intensity of her pain, and she took those principles and discovered that drawing brought her the relief she was craving. The mistake we made was want-ing to put her art in another category, independent of her illness, but art never is, is it?"

"If we brought health to her art, could it bring health to her mind?" asked Aimee. "If she were better trained, encouraged to consider other subjects, be around other artists – could that add up to better mental health?"

"Well, I can see how you might think that could work. But what I'm hearing is that she resorted to it out of desperation and discovered it worked for a while. But it may not be working as well as it once did, so she's moved on to something she feels will work better."

"The farm?" asked her dad.

"Or, some semblance of it," confirmed Dr. Samuelson.

"Tamara, once you finally got to the park that Saturday, did you have any more hallucinations or anxiety attacks?" asked the doctor.

She told them about seeing chickens in the Tree House for Dream-ing, but that it was different – not like one of her delusions. She felt refreshed after that one, not dead.

"But no others?"

She shook her head, no.

"When did your anxiety return?" he followed up.

"At dinner."

"When we were discussing the art academy?" asked Aimee.

Tamara nodded yes.

"If Tamara can no longer cope with the stresses of her daily life in the city," mused Samuelson, "then a temporary change in scenery and circumstances could offer us some valuable insights. It is not, however, all environmental. But Tamara's trip to New Hampshire may help us figure out which parts are triggered by her surroundings and which parts aren't. And, once we sort that out, we may know better how to target pharmaceuticals more effectively."

"That makes sending her to New Hampshire for two weeks just as dangerous an experiment as medications, though, doesn't it?" asked Aimee. "Is that fair to Barb and her family? We're making them participants in some mental health experiment that could go terribly wrong."

"Fair point," said Samuelson, "and we will have to talk this over with them. I don't mind calling Barb since I've known her for so long. Then, when she's sure she understands what she's taking on, and if she still wants to do it, you can call her and discuss some of the details. Remember, I'm going to be there the last two weeks of June, and we could take her then."

"I think I'd like to take her," said Terrance, who had grown increasingly pensive as he listened to their conversation.

"Ever since we returned from New Hampshire," Terrance continued, looking at his daughter, "I've been thinking about something Aunt Tamara tried to teach me. Somehow, I think it fits here for the both of us. My family had suffered a public embarrassment. A mishap in one of our banks spiraled out of control and became a major scandal. My father became a phantom in our home as he sought to reign in the trouble. I think I saw my father twice, both times he was on the evening news emerging from a court room! Anyway, Aunt Tamara said, 'Circumstances will grind you to a halt, young man. The unexpected event will stop you in your tracks. And you won't learn its lesson until it's all over. In the midst of a crisis, all you have is what you've been able to learn before. Those are the tools in your tool-chest.' Then, she said to me, 'A wise young man like yourself would do well to keep replacing his old tools with better ones every chance he gets. Because when trouble comes, that's what you'll have to work with. Once we're through with all this business,' said Aunt Tamara, 'you watch, and if I have my say, we're going to throw out a lot of old hardware.' I wondered at the time if by 'hardware' she meant my father," he laughed.

"My point is this," he continued. "I think Dr. Samuelson is right, Tamara. You have been developing tools that have helped you, and if I am hearing you, you are wanting to replace some of your old tools with new ones. We would be fools to stand in the way of that. And, frankly, I would be very interested in seeing what sort of gifts and strengths you have in you that you may not even be aware of yet. New Hampshire could teach us all a lot."

13

THE BIRTHDAY GIFT

AS HER CHURCH-SCHOOL CLASS GATHERED their belongings and drifted toward the sanctuary for worship, Barb remained seated and looked around the room. How many years had she been teaching these ladies, she wondered, and couldn't imagine the answer.

The organist had begun her prelude and her oldest friend, Pamela Nazareth, would be waiting in their pew for Barb to join her. Pamela had lost her son and daughter-in-law to a car accident, so the rest of the vacant pew, spanning out to her right, was always a reminder. Betsy, Pamela's grand-daughter, would slip in if she'd finished her work in the barn. Tinder would always sit alone in the back pew over by the wall.

Pamela was waiting, but Barb was having a hard time rising up out of her chair. The solitude was too rich. A gracious radiance filled her with calm and a deepening joy. She was fine right where she was, and that feeling of being fine didn't require a lot of hand-shaking and half hugs everyone gave each other in church.

She loved these ladies more than they could know. But she didn't know if she could continue to offer them what she felt they needed. For that matter, she was in need of it, too – someone to listen and to pray on her behalf. She was there to do that for them. They looked to her in that way. And her pastor was her son.

She had received a phone call from Stephen Samuelson last night and was putting off thinking about what it meant. She should talk it over with Tobias, but that would have to wait until the afternoon now.

She closed her eyes and whispered the words to the old hymn as Marianne played an arrangement of "How Great Thou Art," swelling as much as the little electric organ would swell: '*Then sings my soul, my Savior God, to Thee…*"

The ushers were greeting the worshipers, and her son would be pacing in the entryway. She thought it was nice that he still got a little nervous, even though he had stood before the same thirty-five to forty souls every week for – how many years? Again, she couldn't imagine.

She pictured her young friend, Tamara, and wondered why she was struggling so much that she felt she needed medication. 'Am I up for this?' Stephen had asked her.

The eight-member choir would now be in place, and Pamela would be craning around searching the room for her wondering if she was stuck in conversation. Then, not seeing her, Pamela would wonder if Barb had come to grief somewhere in the building, as unlikely as that might be.

'When Christ shall come,' she hummed in her heart, '*with shout of acclamation, and take me home, what joy shall fill my heart. Then I shall bow in humble adoration, and there proclaim, my God, how great thou art!*' She allowed the final 'Then sings my soul…' to lift her to her feet and carry her down the hall. Her son had taken his place on the chancel.

Barb's family of faith was now seated, row by row, all their heads were facing forward, all their hearts were trying to focus, and all their minds were struggling to follow their hearts. She slipped into her pew as the final chord sounded on the organ.

May Fortin, the worship leader for the morning, stood and called the people to come before the throne of grace and offer their souls to God in adoration, which they all did as they stood and turned in their hymnals to number forty-seven, '*O God, our help, in ages past, our hope for years to come, our shelter in the stormy blast, and our eternal home.*'

Barb allowed the assurances of the faith being sung all around her to settle under her skin and burrow deep into her heart. She left her hymnal in its rack and let the song speak to her rather than voice the assurances for others to hear. Midway through the hymn, she felt a touch on her right hand. Pamela gave Barb's hand a squeeze which Barb reciprocated.

Time, like an ever-rolling stream, bears all its years away,
they fly, forgotten, as a dream dies at the opening day.'

She felt older than she could remember feeling, less in her body than in her spirit. She was carrying more than she was used to this morning.

Her son offered the invocation and the congregation was seated so the two kids in the room could go forward for the children's sermon.

Where the rest of the service went, Barb didn't know. She had simply rested in the bosom of her church family for the morning. Without bringing her mind to a conscious decision, she knew that next week she should let her class know it was time for her to retire. She had to be up for whatever Tamara would require, and she knew she wasn't up for both. God was needing her for another mission.

As the last hymn ended, and the final Amen was sung, her son stretched his hands over the congregation and blessed them in the peace of the Lord. And she was blessed. She felt the blessing deeply and knew the peace of which he spoke, peace in her decision, peace in her direction, and peace from the Shepherd who was leading the way.

Aimee's silence over the next few days, and the emotional distance she kept from her daughter, was frightening to Tamara. They had been emotionally fused for so long Tamara felt a piece of her soul had been extracted. Aimee had chased her daughter through so many dark places, never able to catch up, just that far behind, but always there in pursuit. She had witnessed the ravages of Tamara's depressions, and Aimee had hoped to mop up the tears and dry out the psychological sludge left over after her daughter's psychotic rampages, but Tamara never let her near.

Now, Tamara felt her mother was backing out. Aimee wasn't cold to Tamara, but psychologically she was closed off to her. Her mom felt spectral. There was presence but no substance, a bodily image but no apparent soul. For several days following their session with Dr. Samuelson, Tamara felt her insides swell and get thick with remorse for all that had happened in that session to hurt her mother. It was too much at once, and Tamara considered how she might reel in some of the trouble she had caused.

These sensations became most acute in the afternoons as she took the subway from school back to her house. The weather had not permitted her walks to the park lately. The rainy afternoons meant she had to more time to brood as she waited for her mother to come home, and the more she brooded, the worse her ruminations became.

As the school bell rang Thursday afternoon, she went to collect her satchel. The noise in the hallway stoked her anxieties about going home on such a gray afternoon. She reached her locker but had a hard time focusing sufficiently to manage her combination lock. The thoughts smashing around in her head caused her to keep losing her place in the number sequence. Odd noises coming from within the locker didn't help. Then, she heard a watery whisper. A lispy recitation of three numbers dripped out from around the locker door: 'fourteen, sixty-seven, forty-two,' her combination. Tamara held her lock in her hand but hesitated to use the sequence. Her fingers felt cold and clumsy. The numbers wouldn't line up correctly. So, the voice spoke again, insisting that she complete the code and open the door, but again, she failed. Now, the voice was angry, and Tamara's eyes wouldn't focus on the numbers, but her shaking fingers managed the combination and the lock gave way. The inside of her locker was dark and wet. Her books were lying in a puddle of slime that reeked of decomposition and mold, and a thick layer of grime covered her satchel that hung from the hook. The back of her locker seemed to go on forever emptying into nowhere but more darkness.

"Thorafura," her mind warned her. "Reach in," said a force beyond her overwhelming her ability to resist. The longer she waited the more furious the voice became, until it was slashing at her like lightning bolts with teeth, hurting her for not obeying, intensifying its fury until she thrust her arm and grabbed her bag. The great snake snapped shut its mouth and held Tamara up to her shoulder, staring at her, eye to eye. Thorafura's diamond shaped pupils were ablaze with rage and scorched Tamara's face forcing her back, but she was held in place by the unrelenting bite of the serpent's fangs.

Tamara felt Thorafura's venom enter her bloodstream and her pounding heart was pushing it faster through her veins into her brain bringing the whispering assault to her conscious mind: "You have nowhere to go except with me. Your mother hates you now but not as much as you hate yourself, and your father hates your Shepherd. Look at what you've done to them and to all your friends. Can you even name your friends? Look at them gawking at you fearing who you are."

Tamara's head was gorged with blood-filled venom, saturated with hate, and ready to shatter from the shots of pain punching her behind her eyes. Thorafura held Tamara in her gaze until she was sure her victim appreciated once again just who she was dealing with, then the serpent released her and spit her to the floor.

Tamara climbed back to her feet, thankful to be clutching her satchel though acutely aware of the stares from those around her. Her biology book lay neatly upon her math book in a locker that bore no evidence of the battle that had just taken place within it. She grabbed her book as quickly as she could, stuffed it in her bag, and fled the building.

Later that evening, as Tamara was struggling with her homework, her mom knocked on the door, slipped into her room and apologized for bothering her.

"Can we catch an earlier subway in the morning?" asked Aimee, "I'm afraid I have an early meeting."

"Can I go later, by myself?" asked Tamara.

"Well," said her mom, "I know you've been walking the neighborhood, but rush hour on the subway? Even I find that stressful. Why don't we build toward that?"

"Okay," Tamara acquiesced. "What time do we need to leave?"

"Six-thirty?"

"You've got to be kidding," complained Tamara.

"Set your alarm, okay?"

Tamara found her smart-phone and did just that.

"Six o'clock," she grumbled.

Six o'clock was bad enough, but the next day was also Tamara's birthday, and no one had said anything about it since their session with Dr. Samuelson. They still couldn't face the changes she was putting them through, she thought, and they didn't know how to celebrate with her. Or, they had forgotten altogether, and it would go by unnoticed. She could only hope.

Tamara closed her history book and looked at herself in the mirror. "Happy birthday eve," she said.

Tamara awoke and then dressed, but she was still wiping the sleep out of her eyes as she headed for her bedroom door. Taped to the door was an envelope, on the front of which was written in highly stylized script:

Your presence is cordially requested…

Inside the envelope was a hand-lettered card which read:

Breakfast awaits you at
Testaroni's Pasticceria,
7:00 a.m.
You have a reservation.
Please present this at the door
to be shown to your table.

Tamara knew the place. Every morning she climbed the steps from her subway to walk the two blocks to her school, and the first thing she noticed was the aroma from the Italian bakery located just a few yards up the street. She often paused to admire the window display but had never been inside. There was usually a line out the door.

She walked downstairs and found her dad awaiting her at the bottom of the steps.

"What's going on?" she asked.

"Your car is ready, Miss," he said. Terrance opened the door and Tamara was greeted by a man she had only ever known as Steves, her grandparent's chauffeur. The roomy Rolls Royce was parked outside. Tamara had ridden in it only a few times during special family occasions. Steves opened the back door. It took a bit of coaxing by her dad, but in she crawled.

As the car moved through rush hour traffic, Tamara grew apprehensive. She had left her parents behind, which meant she was either dining alone or with her father's parents, who never failed to intimidate her. But she thought they were still in Florida.

The car was a womb of luscious quiet. Soft classical music filled the air around her. She was encased in elegance which shielded the soul from the troubles faced by others battling their way in to work, getting ready for school, or just glad to see the sunrise after a rough night in the street.

When she was formally escorted from the car to the front door of the Pasticceria, the chauffer spoke to the maître de who whisked Tamara to a table, where she found not her father's parents, but her mother's.

"Happy Birthday!" they said as they greeted her. Her seat was pulled from the table by the waiter who tucked her in to the table and handed her the menu, introduced himself, and then said with a heavy Italian accent, "We are pleased to share in this happiest of occasions with you, Miss Tamara Baxter. We have many specialties, but might I recommend the *Cornetto Ripieno*, a sweet, buttery, stuffed pastry. It is our chef's favorite, and he would love to make one for you."

"What is ripieno?" asked Tamara's grandmother.

"It means, the full orchestra!" said the waiter, with a flourish. "And that means it comes with sliced boiled egg, a superb prosciutto, and you may choose either mozzarella or asiago cheese. Might I suggest the asiago, which gives it that heavenly bight you deserve on a special day like today. We also have sautéed mushrooms, and some love it with roasted red peppers."

Tamara said yes, but without the peppers.

"Make that three," said her grandmother.

Tamara, still stunned by all that was unfolding around her, sat and stared at her grandparents.

As they were waiting for their order to arrive, her grandmother said, "I'm so glad your father set this up. We were hoping to spend your birthday with you. Fifteen years!" she said, proudly. "And we hear you will be spending part of your summer in New Hampshire. I think that is just so wonderful, Tamara!"

"We're very proud of you, Tamara," said her grandfather, who looked as if he had something prepared, though he was not sure how to say it.

Instead, he slid a small box across the table.

"When your mom told us part of the reason you were going, we wanted you to have this," he explained. The box was wrapped in green paper.

Tamara's discomfort was increasing. She wasn't all that close with any of her grandparents, so when important occasions called for sensations of intimacy, she felt awkward and usually sidelined herself. Now, she was sitting center stage in their efforts at affection, but not just affection, affection with some gravity attached to it. In their minds, her birthday had taken on a significance it clearly didn't have for herself. Slowly, therefore, to give herself time to catch up with them emotionally, she pulled at the ribbon, then carefully unwrapped the parcel. Inside she found a leather-bound book with a large cross on the front. A small card was taped to the cover which read: "For your pilgrimage, with love, Grandma and Grandpa Westbrook."

Tamara opened the cover and read the title: *The Book of Common Prayer and Administration of the Sacraments and other Rites and Ceremonies of the Church According to the use of the Protestant Episcopal Church in America.*

Tucked into the book was another small envelope with a gift card to L. L. Bean's.

"You may not know much about our religious traditions, Tamara," said her grandfather, "but we have always been members of the Episcopal Church. That's how we sought to raise your mother, and that's how your father was brought up early in his life, as well." With each sentence, his voice grew weaker as his conviction in what he was saying diminished.

"It became difficult," said her grandmother, trying to rescue him, "and we stopped going to church. But your mother said you were curious, and we thought you might like this, all the same."

"Thank you," said Tamara, as she thumbed through the pages, scanning the various prayers and instructions for worship. "Thank you, very much." She tried to catch their eyes, but they seemed embarrassed to look at her. They became more animated when she looked at the gift card.

"We thought you might have fun ordering a few things for your trip to the mountains," said her grandmother.

"I'm sure I will," acknowledged Tamara.

As Tamara finished her breakfast, she hugged her grandparents and tucked her gifts into her satchel. When she got to school, she still had a few minutes before the bell, so she found a quiet spot and opened up her prayer book. Like her Bible, it was incomprehensible to her, but as she scanned the text she was enraptured by the beauty of the prayers. Their soaring language and vaulted sense of the holy impressed her greatly. She whispered several sentences just to feel the words in her mouth, and she delighted in the resonances those words created deeper within her. This book would have a lot to teach her about prayer, she thought, and she grew more grateful for the thoughtfulness of her grandparents. She was disappointed when the bell rang and forced her to stuff her book back in her bag, but knowing it was close gave her a sensation of strength. She would try to return to it again, as she was able, throughout the day.

Just as Tamara was walking to the subway after school, she felt her phone buzz in her back pocket. It was her mom.

"Are you on the subway yet?" the text asked.

"No," texted Tamara.

Then: "Instead of going home, take the A to Cathedral Pkwy / 110th St. OK?"

"?????" Tamara texted back to her mom."

"Trust me," was the answer.

The subway took Tamara to the upper west side and let her out at the northwest corner of Central Park. When she got off the subway, there stood her mom and dad both of whom were wearing jeans and not looking much like themselves. Each of her parents had knapsacks slung over their shoulders. Terrance placed his arm around Tamara's neck and led her to a nearby deli, where she was told to order her favorite, chocolate cheesecake with strawberry topping.

After they had finished their cheesecake, Aimee pulled from her bag the hiking shoes Tamara had purchased in New Hampshire. They were going for a walk in the north woods, she explained.

"The north woods?" asked Tamara.

"Wait till you see it," said her dad. "You'll think you're hiking the highlands of New Hampshire right here in Central Park. Well, not really, but it's the best we can do without leaving town."

Tamara finished her cheesecake and swapped out her shoes. They walked south just a bit, then turned into the park. A short way in, Tamara was in awe of how densely forested the park was there. They hadn't walked very far before she was enclosed by the foliage. Birdsong replaced the cacophony of the street, and a sense of the wild crept through her. She felt the stresses of the day dissipate. Everyone grew quiet as they enjoyed the respite their surroundings offered them. They strolled at an easy pace along the paths which, while paved, were well naturalized by their setting.

"This is beautiful," said Tamara.

"I think so, too," said her mom.

"How do you feel?" asked her dad.

"Good," answered Tamara. "This has been a great day. Thank you."

She debated whether to tell her parents about the Book of Common Prayer in her knapsack, but she assumed they knew. Her parent's discomfort about their religion was a little frustrating to Tamara who thought this should be a good time to satisfy her curiosity about their early years in the church. She had a lot of questions. Their present state of rejection, however, told Tamara that all she would get from them would be negative which she could do without.

"Where are we going?" asked Tamara, after about thirty minutes of wandering to and fro through the north woods.

"Well, just beyond here we're going to stop for something to drink and a few more gifts," said her dad.

The trail they were on took a slight left and they crossed a small brook, along which they walked for several yards before coming to a waterfall that flooded the air around them with gurgles and splashes and the persistent undertones of moving water. Tamara stooped and put her hands in the icy stream.

"Aimee, if you want to fish out the juices, I need to make a quick call," said Terrance. "Go sit down, and I'll be there in just a moment."

As they sat on the grass by the stream sipping their drinks, Aimee and Tamara surveyed this portion of the park which neither one had been to before. The day was bright and cloudless and gave every indication that summer was well on its way.

"Sorry about that," said Terrance, who went back in to his satchel and pulled out a long, rectangular box. He handed it to Tamara. This was professionally wrapped and decorated in sterling silver paper. Where the ribbon joined in the upper corner, a crest was stuck to the box which bore a horse and rider.

Tamara gingerly loosened the ribbon, unfastened the stiff paper, then she opened the box. There, she found a pair of soft, dark brown leather riding boots.

"Those are from your grandparents. And this," he said handing her a square box, "is from your uncle Wesley."

That box, similarly wrapped, contained a riding helmet.

"Try them on," urged her mom, trying to circumvent the looks of perplexity on Tamara's face, who was mystified by the choice in gifts but complied awkwardly.

First, Tamara slipped on the boots which went on effortlessly and wrapped her entire lower leg, right up to her knees, in exquisite comfort. They were easy to wear, and where her barn boots gave her sufficient support to do hard work, these were clearly for the delight of the wearer who was going to allow the horse to do all the work. The helmet took a little adjusting, but soon it fit snug and comfortable as it sat lightly upon her head.

"Handsome!" remarked her dad. "And just in time." He pointed across the lawn. Down the path came four horses. One was ridden by a tall man in jet black pants, tall shiny black boots, a bright red riding coat, and a helmet similar to Tamara's. He was seated on a white horse guiding a black horse beside him on a lead. The other two horses were brown, led by a younger man, slight of build, wearing blue-jeans, a black shirt, and a gray woolen vest.

"I got a call from Barb the other day," said Aimee. "She has a neighbor who has several horses and said you can ride whenever you want, so she wanted to make sure you had suitable riding gear. We thought a little experience wouldn't hurt, either, so if you enjoy this, these horses belong to a stable that offers riding lessons."

Tamara remembered the gift card her grandparents had given her earlier and thought several pairs of jeans would be necessary. She was also pretty sure that formal riding gear wasn't what was called for in the mountains. As for the lessons, she was reserving judgment, for as the horses grew near their size took on new meaning for her. She had seen plenty of horses, most of which had been ridden by mounted policemen or pulled tourist carriages through the city, but she had never imagined herself riding one. As the horses stopped beside her, she was dwarfed by their height and girth.

The tall man dismounted and offered his hand to Tamara. He introduced himself as Jim.

"And this is Flint," he said, stroking the horse's broad forehead. "Here, offer her this," he said, handing Tamara a couple of carrots. "Keep your hand flat, just let her take them. She's very gentle." As she extended her hand, she remembered the funny sensation of feeding the goats at the zoo but noticed how small her hand was next to the great mouth now about to take something from her palm.

Jim offered her a few words of instruction, then he helped her mount and adjusted her stirrups. She felt her world jerking nervously beneath her. Jim told her, not the horse, to calm down, that the horse could sense her anxiety.

"Rub her, firmly, here," said Jim, as he stroked the horse along the side of its neck. The horse was solid black. Its hair glistened in the sun, and its mane fascinated Tamara as it lay neatly brushed down the right side of its neck where she stroked it. "Keep rubbing her until you feel comfortable touching her. That's it. And you won't need to pull hard on the reigns," he coached her. "Just hold them gently. You'll notice this is a western saddle – that's called a horn. You can also hold on to that if you like. Your parents are riding English saddles. See, no horn. In olden days, you and your mom would ride side-saddle, but today you're a cow-girl out on the range."

Jim turned his attention to Terrance and Aimee and instructed the stable hand to bring their horses. "This is Shantilla," he said to Aimee as she was presented her horse. "And this is Allegro," he said to Terrance.

"Allegro!" exclaimed Terrance. "I don't know much about music, but I think that means fast, does it not?"

"Not to worry, Mr. Baxter," laughed Jim. "He was bred for racing but suffered an injury, then he came to us. All the horses are trained for inexperienced riders, and here in the park we will only be walking at a nice, steady pace." He winked at Tamara, whose eyes were still a bit wide with worry as she felt Flint step restlessly to one side.

"And who is this beauty?" asked Aimee, who laid her hand on the white horse's shoulder.

"This is Ivory," he said, offering her a few carrots.

Tamara was surprised at how comfortable her parents were as they approached their horses then stepped up into the saddles. They had done this before. Terrance gave his horse a slight kick and moved over beside Tamara. Jim mounted Ivory and, without saying a word, urged his horse forward. He took a slight lead and the other horses fell in, one behind the other: Tamara, then Aimee, followed by Terrance in the rear.

"How do you like that?" asked her mom.

"It's great!" shouted Tamara without turning around. She was sitting ram-rod stiff in her saddle with a firm grip on her reigns. Her entire perspective on the world was different from her new vantage point riding atop this majestic animal of such strength and beauty.

Flint inhaled, filling her massive frame with air, then forced it out through her nostrils with explosive force reminding Tamara how alive the creature was beneath her. She had seen them gallop and jump and felt a powerful potential bound up inside Flint who could as easily break out and flee through the city. But as they loped forward down the asphalt pathway, Tamara was glad hers was a gentle ride that gave her the opportunity to look around and see the park in such a fresh way.

That changed, however, as they approached a busy street, and the cars soaring past them presented a harsh contrast to their current mode of transportation. Tamara was distracted then agitated by the action around her, and she became suddenly self-conscious seated atop a horse in such a modern place that had rendered these creatures obsolete for any meaningful work. She knew from school that the city was once crowded with horses pulling carts and carriages and filling the streets with their filth. And, she knew that her grand-parents were associated with people who had bred horses for show and for racing, people who lived much different lives than the livery classes of the past. She glanced over at her parents riding confidently in their English saddles and was reminded of which class she was expected to inhabit, and it wasn't the sort who would have depended on Flint for their daily paycheck.

As they waited to cross the street, she thought of the work she might be doing on the farm in New Hampshire and of where they might ride, up through the mountains. She wondered if another hat would be better than the elegant helmet on her head, which made her feel more like a jockey than a farmer.

Seated on the sidewalk, just a few feet beneath her, was an older woman with a small child. The woman held a sign: Homeless. Please help us.

From where she sat, they looked so far away. Like her grandfather's Rolls Royce, which carried her through the city earlier that morning, the horse acted as an insulator. The only people who looked at them did so out of curiosity, but they were shielded from the world by their mounts. Given their elevation, they had vivid visual access to all that was around them. They were closer to the leaves and branches of the trees, and their clip-clopping steps beneath them offered a sound sensation they would not have enjoyed otherwise. So, the horses joined them to their natural environment in wondrous ways. But Tamara remarked at how success-fully they also separated them from the other humans around them.

Tamara wanted to know what the woman was feeling behind the solemn stare she offered the world, but the woman never looked up. The child reminded her of Li Jie. She was small and slight, but her soul didn't look very musical. They both looked depleted. Tamara glanced back at the sign the woman was holding. She thought of Tonya and the rescue mission and wondered if the woman knew of such places. Then, Tamara considered how she might be of help, but their guide was crossing the street which meant her horse followed suit without any input from her.

As they crossed the crowded thoroughfare and took up the path by the reservoir, an unwelcomed sensation crept through Tamara. Across the water and over the trees the city skyline became prominent once again. The horse's hooves on the pavement were rhythmic and soothing, but the pace kept by the animals felt even more incongruent with the realities she faced. Her heart raced, and her horizon became fluid. She closed her eyes, leaned forward, and stroked Flint's neck hoping the feel of the horse's fur and flesh would steady her nerves and restore her own steady breathing, but the reverse occurred instead. Flint whinnied and leaped forward closing the distance between herself and Ivory. The jolt might have unseated Tamara had she not maintained such a sure grip on her saddle horn. Jim wheeled around and met them.

"There, there, girl," he said softly to the horse and offered her a few carrots. He extended his hand to Tamara and held hers lightly in his own. He looked her in the eyes.

"Flint tells me your anxious about something," he said. "Have you had enough? I can call Lenny and have him bring the trailer, or we can all dismount and walk the horses for a while until you're ready to ride again. What do you think?"

Tamara looked down at Flint and stroked her neck once again. Her parents had come alongside to form a tight cluster around her. Sensing all the horses so close she could reach them from where she sat steadied her, and she didn't want to part with the sensations of strength which the horse beneath her had lent her. So, she said she wanted to keep going.

The bridle path took them along the edge of the water and soon reminded Tamara they were not alone in their equestrian outing. They passed several other horses with mounted riders and countless horses pulling carriages filled with tourists. The sensation of being an oddity in the city left her, though her consciousness of the class status she inhabited kept reasserting itself as she encountered an increasing number of people she knew probably would never have the opportunity to enjoy such an outing as she was on. That became uncomfortably clear as the path gravitated toward Central Park West and took in more of the pedestrian traffic just off the street.

As they approached a small tunnel, through which they would have to pass, the sounds of some sort of demonstration became louder. A number of people wearing brightly colored clothing, and a few wearing very little clothing at all, were either angry or deeply engaged in expressing their feelings over something which Tamara couldn't interpret. Some were singing, others were chanting in a group. One lady, wearing a flowing garment and a wreath around her head, was twirling around on the edge of the bridge above them. Tamara looked back at her mom who nudged Shantilla forward and came up beside Tamara.

"This area is called Strawberry Fields," Aimee explained. "Just over there was where John Lennon was killed, and this was set up as a memorial for him."

"John, who?" asked Tamara.

"He was one of the Beatles," answered her mom, though its significance was lost on Tamara, and it didn't explain what all the fuss was about. But instead of dwelling on it, she reached forward and patted Flint on the shoulder and assured her everything was okay. Flint didn't seem concerned in the least. As they passed beneath the tunnel and left the revelers behind, Flint, her flesh and bones Rolls Royce, had done her job of insulating Tamara from that world.

Not many yards beyond Strawberry Fields, they came to another intersection of pathways over which they crossed into a small, open greenway. Jim pulled Ivory to a stop and dismounted. He walked his horse over to Tamara. Flint came to a halt, as did Shantilla and Allegro.

"Miss Baxter, you have arrived, and you did so in grand style, I must say. May I help you off your horse?"

The end had come a little too abruptly for Tamara, and she was uneasy about the embellished announcement of having "arrived." Arrived where, and for what? She didn't want to let go of her horse so soon. Her parents were now off their horses and standing beside Jim, thanking him for such a pleasant afternoon.

"Ready to dismount, honey?" asked Aimee.

"No!" said Tamara, though she acquiesced to reality and let Jim help her down. She had a hard time standing, and her legs felt awkward.

"That will pass," whispered her mother, smiling broadly at her daughter.

They left Jim to tend the horses and walked just a few feet to Tavern on the Green where they had a reservation for dinner.

As they were waiting for dessert, Terrance reached under the table and pulled out his knapsack. He pulled two more packages from it and handed them over to Tamara. One looked like another book; the other was a small square box.

She was encouraged to open the larger package first. Her heart initially fell as she saw it was an art book. Pangs of guilt for what she had done to her mother's dream surfaced along with frustration that her mother couldn't let it go. The title didn't help: *The Master Through the Masters' Eyes*. But she took a deep breath and sought to focus on what was in her hands. The subtitle gave her a sudden boost: *A Renaissance New Testament*.

She slowed down, turned a few pages, and lingered over some of the paintings: a graceful angel whispering to a bashful mother; then a barnyard filled with sheep, oxen, donkeys, and two prayerful parents, all gathered by a wooden box. Baby Jesus. Then, there was a painting of Jesus standing waist deep in a river being addressed by a scary looking ogre wearing a bear skin. Next, Jesus was arguing with a princely looking demon as scary as any she had encountered within herself. In fact, there were a lot of demons inhabiting this book, and a lot of broken people devastated by life, sorrowful and hungry, much like the woman and her daughter she had seen earlier that day. She also remembered Tonya, and the old man trying to cross the street. And among the poor stood Jesus. He was painted in rich, royal tones, awash in heavenly light. There were somber scenes of Jesus breaking bread and one of him praying in anguish. Then, she was horrified by what came next, as painting after painting depicted him being tortured, whipped, ridiculed, and nailed to a wooden cross. Each picture was more grotesque than the one before, each trying to outdo the other in capturing the essence of suffering, as if the earth's misery could be summed up and deposited in one place with its horrors gathered from all the world and painted onto one face.

She couldn't look anymore, and she didn't want to look her parents in the eyes, or even to thank them, though that is what she knew she should do. Tamara wanted to be alone with the book, not with them. She knew how they felt about religion, about this, and she couldn't navigate her way into what a conversation about this gift was supposed to be. Her heart was surging with gratitude, the likes of which she didn't know how to speak or show what she felt, so she simply nodded and said that it was beautiful.

Then, her dad handed her the small gift. It was simply wrapped in white paper with no bow or card. She unwrapped it and opened the little box inside. There, on scarlet velvet, lay a small, antique, silver cross. It hung from a delicate chain and was not quite as long as her pinky. The front of the cross was simple with a fine floral design around the edges. The back was engraved with the initials: T. E. C.

"Tamara Esmeralda Cousins," whispered Tamara.

"That's right," said her father. "That was her baptismal cross. It was given to her when she was a baby by some other relative on the day of her baptism, but her mother held on to it until Aunt Tamara got married. Then, as a wedding gift, her mother had it engraved with Tamara's new initials."

"It's lovely," she said, though she was troubled by its association with the images still burning in her mind of Jesus on the cross. All her life she had seen such images fly by her face without any notice: crucifixes on Catholic churches, stylized crosses fashioned into popular jewelry, and she was sure she must have seen artistic impressions of it. Yet she never associated the cross with herself, any member of her family, or with the Shepherd she imagined leading her around the city.

Her dad held out his hand, took the cross from Tamara and looked it over.

"Come here," he said, and she obliged him by walking around the table and turning her back to him as he put it on her neck and fastened it.

She could no longer see the cross, but she held it lightly between her fingers. Tamara struggled to join this delicate thing of beauty with the impressions of savagery and suffering she knew were being experienced by Jesus in those paintings.

"Let me see," said her mother. "You wear it well." Then, Aimee turned to Terrance. "How did this come to you?" she asked him.

Terrance became introspective, and Aimee knew that meant he was choosing his words with caution. She also appreciated that this was difficult, since he was such a committed atheist, and wondered what he had been telling himself as he prepared the gift and presented it to his daughter.

"When I found the picture of my great aunt the other day in the closet behind the board-room, I ended up having a long talk with my dad about the side of her I never knew, of her life outside family gatherings and the bank. Her life on the farm, for instance, was a complete surprise as was her commitment to her church. I never knew this, but evidently she served on the vestry of her church as a warden for a rather long time."

"What is that?" asked Tamara.

"The vestry is a board made of lay-leaders in an Episcopal church. The warden is selected to work closely with the rector, so she would have had numerous responsibilities around the church. Anyway, I told my dad that I was beginning to see some traits in you that I had always admired in her. After he patted me on the back and said he was sorry – he was joking, of course! – he said he thought there were still a number of her old things that his parents had accumulated and would have a look. One of the things he found was the cross. He checked with his cousin to make sure she didn't want it instead, then told me I should give it to you."

The evening was clear and warm, so they walked through the park and down the street instead of hailing a taxi. Tamara felt her cross several times and was eager to retire to her room and spend a quiet moment with the books she had been given. As she turned on the light in her room, she found a birthday card leaning against her mirror, inside of which contained a letter from Barb.

Happy Birthday, Tamara!

I hope you are having a wonderful day, and you can be sure that you are very close to my heart. I am now counting the days until you and your father arrive. I'm sorry your mother won't be with you on this trip. I was so looking forward to seeing her again, but I suppose I can wait a few more weeks until she joins us.

She tells me you love chocolate cheese cake, so I found a recipe and am going to try to bake one the day of your birthday and celebrate with you in Spirit. I've never made one, so it will be an experiment. If all goes well, we'll invite the neighbors and have a cheesecake party when you arrive.

You won't recognize your old room. Toby has come and finally moved out! I hope you like what I plan to do with it, but I'll keep you in suspense. Your dad will stay in the other room down the hall from you. I hope he will be comfortable. Toby tells me the little farm-hand house needs too much repair and won't be ready for your parents to use.

Spring is coming beautifully to the valley here. My neighbor, Betsy, told me her ewes just had their lambs and wondered if we'd like to keep a few while you're here. She said she could teach you all you needed to know to care for them. You could be a shepherd! Toby patched up the small pasture fence to hold them. You think about it, and when you get here, we'll go down to Betsy's farm and see them. Then you can decide. She also has cows and said you could help in the dairy if that interests you.

Now, I want us to be honest with one another. Dr. Samuelson called me the other day and told me you had requested he put you on medication because you were concerned for me. I deeply appreciate that. It is very loving of you. Of course, I can't advise you. You are fifteen years old and that is a decision you must pray about and decide with the help of Dr. Samuelson and your parents. It is a very adult decision, and I am proud of you for taking responsibility for your well-being. As I said, I can't tell you what to do. I just want you to know this: when I invited you, I invited you knowing who you are. I knew there would be challenges, and I expected we might have some difficult times. I am an old woman, Tamara, and there is very little I haven't faced with those I love, so I hope you will trust that I am ready for whatever might happen while you are here. I asked Dr. Samuelson a lot of questions and nothing he told me changed my mind about you. I will be praying for you, and

I will support whatever you decide to do. I am ready to face whatever we need to face together. I only want you to feel confident in your decision.

Tamara paused there before reading the rest of the note. Barb had reminded her of unfinished business, her need for medication to alleviate her anxieties and stem the warfare in her mind. But now she wasn't as certain having listened to her parents and considered Dr. Samuelson's input. She glanced at the other gifts she had been given throughout the day, the Book of Common Prayer, her riding gear, the illustrated New Testament. She fingered the cross hanging around her neck. The next few weeks might be difficult as they sort out what her summer will bring. But these gifts said, at last, that her family was listening. Whether they understood or not, Tamara couldn't have said, and perhaps that didn't matter. She had been given a nod, and a nudge, by those who love her.

She continued reading:

The other day I was coming in from church when I saw a deer out in the pasture. It was a young doe, I think, and they aren't usually out alone, so I looked for others but didn't find them. We stared at one another for a long time and I was reminded of a birthday party I had as a young woman.

I think I was about twelve years old. I was a handful, but not the troublemaker I would become later! Anyway, several of my mother's friends at church offered to host a surprise party. They all had children, and they all took turns doing those sorts of things for one another. Of course, since it was a surprise no one told me about it! So, I went off deer stalking instead. I had been reading about that in one of my school books. On my way home from school that afternoon, I saw a deer by the edge of the forest, a young buck with a small set of antlers. He looked rugged and beautiful. I crouched down real low and began inching my way towards him silently as I could. I saw him sniffing the wind and looking around. Then, our eyes met, and he bolted for the trees. I ran after him. I could still see his eyes in my mind, and I just had to get close to him again.

Once I had run a fair ways into the woods, I halted, sat down next to a tree and waited. And I knew I could wait all afternoon, if I had too, just to get another look into that young buck's eyes. My waiting paid off. The buck didn't return, but two does wandered by. I sat as still as I could, without a sound. I never concentrated as hard on being still as I did that day. They came within four feet of me. I was sure they could hear my heart pounding in my chest, and I was surprised they didn't smell me (deer have a very keen sense of smell, so the wind must have been just right). Then, the older of the two glanced in my direction and we stared at one another. I saw her muscles get tense, and she began her own waiting game wondering if she should move or remain frozen. The younger deer read her body language and froze as well. There we were, the three of us, locked in one three-way eternal stare. They were better at the waiting game than I was, however, because the itch on my nose couldn't wait any longer! As soon as I moved to scratch it, they were off in different directions, dashing, then leaping in these great majestic arcs. They launched into the air and seemed to float in forward motion as they dodged limbs and bolted to and fro through the trees. Their white tails were standing straight up like signal flags. It was one of the best birthdays I ever had until my mother and the other church ladies found me a few hours later!

The woods and streams are waiting for you, Tamara. They are filled with wildlife and wildflowers!

And, there is the trail up the mountain. I have one very special dream which I hope, perhaps, you will help me fulfill. I'd like to hike up that trail one more time. As old as I am, I think I can make it, and I would love to look out over that valley with you and thank God for the life he has given us both. Each year, I find that life becomes more precious all the time. I hope you do, especially now that you are a year older. You have such a life ahead of you! I pray that as you begin your sixteenth year you will discover more of what God is promising to offer you, forever.

With much love,
Barb.

Tamara had rarely ended a birthday on a glad note. For all her parents' efforts each year, the emotional disasters were usually heightened by their hope that all should go well just because it was her birthday. She had a wealthy family, so her gifts were always beautiful and well-intentioned but usually adorned those who gave them better than they reflected Tamara's sense of who she was.

Tamara looked at herself in the mirror and admired again Aunt Tamara's cross. She turned to examine the photograph to see if it was worn by its original owner, but it wasn't. Still, she studied the face and sought to trace some lines of personality back through her father and grandfather. She thought she could imagine a fair approximate of Aunt Tamara's character after subtracting the business and adding the farm. The honesty of the smile said more about her than the cut of her dress, and the rustic fire-place mantle she leaned against said where she felt home ought to be.

Tamara's father had told her that she was beginning to manifest traits he recognized in his great-aunt. Not that smile, however. Where did that come from? That was not a smile for soirées or board rooms. It was a smile at home in the world of animals and children and people who love the little they have. Li Jie's grandfather. That's where she had seen that smile before, on the face of an old man as he listened to his grandson share the music of his soul. What was Aunt Tamara laughing at? Who was with her? What was the occasion? What did that smile feel like?

Tamara wondered if there were any family photograph in which she was captured smiling. None that she knew. The only face her friends and family had ever seen was formed by nights fleeing granthyrs and days fending off Thorafura's sneak attacks. Taught and grim was the shape her muscles gave her mouth and eyes. Her brow was frozen, furrowed and foreboding, and her hair hung around her face casting her in perpetual shadow.

The cross around her neck was the only sparkle about her, which was an irony to her when she considered the menacing portrayal of Jesus' crucifixion in the book her mother had just given her.

Tamara looked long at her face in the mirror. Her face was chiseled out of just the right stuff to bear the pain Jesus must have felt. She identified with what every single one of his nerve endings must have endured as the nails were driven and he was lurched heavenward to hang in public view to suffer such public shame. If Jesus can hear prayers, Tamara wondered, had he heard the silent prayers of those who stared at him, the prayers of those who watched him die and thanked God it wasn't them?

Tamara saw Jesus' suffering staring back at her in the mirror, and she considered the traces her pain had left on her face. She felt the nails pushing through her brain, and she heard the howling granthyrs mock her shame.

Where did Aunt Tamara learn that smile?

There was a light knock on her door.

"Come in," she said. Her dad slipped in and sat on her bed.

"Saying goodnight to Aunt Tamara?" he asked.

Tamara nodded and hung the picture back on the wall.

"She was a beautiful woman. Seeing you on the horse this afternoon jogged another memory about her. The family had come to our house to celebrate my father's birthday. When he opened Aunt Tamara's gift, all there was inside was an old horse-shoe. My dad held it up acknowledging the practical joke it must have been. Everyone laughed. But I guess it wasn't a joke. 'That belonged to Nellydame,' she said, 'a beautiful, brown quarter horse, and the wisest woman I ever met.' Then, she explained the gift: 'The old custom is to hang it over a door with the open end up, so it will catch good luck. In your case, I'm hoping it will catch you a little more horse-sense.'"

Tamara looked back at the picture for a moment then turned to her dad.

"I've come to say good night and to give you one more birthday present, though it's not one you can unwrap." He looked down at the gifts arranged on her dressing table, considered the deeply religious nature of most of them, and took a deep breath.

"I want to give you my blessing, Tamara. I want you to know that I love you, and that I love what you are doing now. If a farmer is what you want to be for the summer, then a farmer you shall be. And, if your time with Barb leads you to be baptized and even leads you into the church, you have my blessing there as well. Whatever any of that means for your future, I have no doubt that this experience will instruct you and strengthen you in all the best of ways. This could be one of the most important summers of your life."

Tamara's mind didn't have those crevices through which assurances seep in and trickle down and become absorbed in the soul. Her mind was a well-fortified citadel against the intrusions of her parents, especially emotional or psychological intrusions. But the story about her great-great Aunt Tamara had opened up a fissure, and the one word, blessing, became a molten ore that began to move through her being. Blessing. She felt a brightening within her and it burned like liquid fire. Her mind explained to her that this would be an appropriate occasion for that smile she was admiring on her forebear's face, and her heart was listening, but her face didn't know how those muscles worked. Still, she made the effort. Her eyes followed through even if her lips and cheeks couldn't.

Tamara felt the emotional distance between her and her father diminishing, though she felt powerless to move closer to him. She knew she was going to need her parents' blessing if she was to take any significant new steps in her life, but the maternal half of that blessing was still absent. She pictured her mother stewing in the den unable to offer her affirmation.

The molten movement through her core became cool, then solidified. Why wasn't her mother seated there with her father?

As wonderful as the day had been, Tamara was feeling the tremors of a long night ahead. No one in her condition gets a day off, she thought, and if the day offers respite and release, the night will usually take it all back.

As Barb prepared for bed, she kept remembering little chores that needed doing like adjusting the dampers on the wood stove so it wouldn't go out overnight, sorting the silver-ware drawer, and hanging up a blouse to prevent it from wrinkling. Each little task reminded her of two others. Twice she yelled up to Toby's room to tell him to come dry the dinner dishes, and twice he had ignored her. She was not going to climb those steps again, tired as she was. After she dried the dishes herself and hung up her towel, she felt she could retire, though her mind was racing with a thousand things that still ought to be done. It didn't help that she was now so frustrated with Toby.

As she laid her nightgown across the foot of her bed, her eye caught the picture of her husband, the only one she had of him. The browns and greens were faded, but he looked sharp in his uniform with his cap set at the precise angle and his expression conveying the appropriate amount of pride to be serving his country.

"And you," she said to the picture, "I wish you'd hurry up and get home and help me raise this son of yours."

14

The Other Half of the Blessing

"**M**ISS! YOU LEFT THIS," SHOUTED an old man as Tamara hurried for the subway door. It was her science book which wouldn't fit in her over-stuffed knapsack.

He held the book in two trembling hands. Tamara nodded to him as she received it then stepped onto the station platform. She turned to look at the man as the train made its way slowly forward, but he was lost to view.

"Thanks," she said to him, as the train left the station. "But no thanks," she called out to the cavernous dark that followed the train into the tunnel. She held the book suspended over the tracks then recanted.

"It will all be over soon," she whispered, then she closed her eyes. The platform was quiet for the moment, and if it weren't for the pungent air, she might have lingered.

Exams were coming soon, so Tamara's backpack was heavier than usual, and she lamented her decision to exit the subway and head for the park before going home to unload. An outcropping of stone at the edge of a small grove of trees gave her a nice vantage-point to watch people and be alone with her thoughts. She set her bookbag down and took off her shoes.

"Hello Nutplunder," she said to the squirrel perched on the limb above her. It snapped its tail and chippered loudly at her. "Sorry, but I have a reservation."

Promenading beneath her stony perch, horses were gracing the bridle path. She dangled her feet off the small ledge and watched two young women canter by. The horses enthralled her, so she mounted her imagination and rode off after them.

"Did you see us ride through here the other day?" she asked the squirrel. "That should be me and my mom," she lamented as she watched the two women. She imagined herself and her mom riding to the overlook above Barb's home, where they might envision a new beginning for their family in a place where horses really belonged.

As the two horses clip-clopped out of sight, Tamara's mood turned dark. She was still in possession of only half a blessing. Aimee had made no further advances toward Tamara, and that morning her mother was as distant as she had been before her birthday.

She rummaged for her sketch-pad, but she didn't have it with her. Tamara closed her eyes to marshal some strength and hoped to refocus the dark thoughts soaking through her. But her mother's resistance to her decisions kept pushing Tamara further down the well into those conflicted depths where she never knew who she was, or who she was meant to be.

"You'll never see the light of day again," she reminded the images searing her consciousness. "I shredded your only portal into this world and I'm not going to open that door again."

Overhead, a pair of ducks quacked their way northward. New images formed in her imagination, and she followed their flight path up the greenway.

"Give that brood of yours my best," she whispered. Then, "Sorry, I can't come today."

She looked at the bulging book bag and felt her emotions cascade over the precipice into the yawning darkness of her remorse. Thirty pounds of failure. Each book represented its own reason for her mother's disappointment. No wonder her mother was backing away. No wonder she held only half a blessing in her darkening heart.

"I need that blessing," she said to the squirrel, who was hanging upside down on the tree, waiting for a handout.

"Is that all you care about?" she asked. "Very well."

She pulled out the crumpled remains of her lunch bag and broke a piece of bread from her uneaten sandwich and threw it over the ledge.

Nutplunder lept for the crumb and ran off with it leaving Tamara alone and desolate.

And in that emptiness, she brooded. Yet there, in those shadowy depths of her inner mind, she saw a way into the blessing she craved.

Tamara packed up her school books and headed for home.

As Tamara approached her house, her mom was seated on the stoop with her head in her hands. In one hand, she gripped a letter. The strength, usually so evident in her mother's frame, and the air of purpose always on her face, was gone, leaving her looking lost and small. Her eyes conveyed fear, though her aspect was already admitting defeat. She never looked at Tamara but kept her eyes fixed on the pavement at the bottom of the steps.

Tamara sat down beside her and waited, but her mom remained rigid.

"I think I know that feeling," whispered Tamara.

Her mom became incredulous.

"I really don't think you do," said Aimee.

"Is there a snake wrapped around you constricting the breath out of you, its eyes within inches of your face about to strike?"

Aimee's eyes became scarlet red, whether with anger or grief, Tamara couldn't decide, but the residue of both was evident and the combination seared her.

Her mother nodded.

"Yes," she whispered. "That's exactly what it feels like."

Tamara gently freed the note from her mother's fingers, waited for her mother's objections and, hearing none, read the letter.

Dear Ms. Baxter;

Our affiliate in Brussels is in jeopardy of financial collapse and in need of immediate intervention. After discussing the situation with Sarah Carlton, their CFO, I forwarded her a copy of the proposals you recently presented to our board, and she is requesting your temporary transfer to their office for a few weeks. Our board agrees that you have the talents they require. I would like you to modify the proposal you have prepared for Zurich and begin its implementation in Brussels, instead, at the earliest possible date. You will need to be there by the 19th of June if not before. You will report to Ms. Carlton. She is assembling a team that will be at your disposal. My secretary will supply you with her contact information, and I suggest you be in touch as soon as you can. Over the next few days, you will begin receiving their reports and other relevant financial data. Once you have looked over the materials, please contact my secretary and schedule an appointment with me so we may discuss this personally.

Regards,

Tony Singleton

"Congratulations? Or, not?" asked Tamara.

Aimee's eyes remained fixed on the curb for a while longer, then she shook her head as tears streamed down her cheeks. Turning to focus for the first time on her daughter, Aimee discovered that in addition to her backpack, Tamara was carrying two grocery bags.

"What have you got there?" whispered Aimee.

"I thought we should go on a picnic tomorrow," said Tamara. "Just you and me."

Aimee said nothing more of the letter or its implications. Their evening together was stark, and they all went to their separate corners early.

Tamara spent another sleepless night as she sought to rescue the blessing she sensed was in such jeopardy. As she rehearsed her plan once more in her mind, a shadow moved through her ruminations and darkened her prospects.

Sensations of shame replaced her aspirations, and Tamara regretted her intentions of pushing her mother to grant a blessing she seemed incapable of giving. Her father's blessing had been given freely, and the strength of the gift came in its surprise. Its gracious nature was what gave it power. Having tasted that blessing, however, she had been coveting another and had set her mind to securing it. Now, whatever aspirations

Tamara had for claiming her mother's blessing, she knew she had to let them go.

As that reality passed through her mind, Tamara felt she had walked through a door into an unfamiliar room.

Aside from passing through the kitchen Saturday morning to get a cup of coffee, Aimee avoided Tamara as her daughter put together their picnic. Aimee looked haggard. She and Terrance had spent much of the night talking in bed. Tamara couldn't make out what they were saying, but she could tell from the intensity of their voices that it wasn't good.

Tamara and Aimee left the house mid-morning. Tamara carried their lunch in a knapsack slung over her shoulder, and their slow walk to the park became a grim reminder of all she was hoping to overcome as Aimee kept drifting deeper into thought.

Now, as her mother's guide for the morning, Tamara felt herself in possession of a great responsibility. Her mother was in pain and probably was only humoring Tamara by tagging along on their childish outing. Nevertheless, her mom had entrusted herself to Tamara who began identifying with Shepherd Jesus in a profound way. As he had led her through that horrifying afternoon on Park Avenue to that place of peace within herself, so she was leading her mother. As they paused before crossing 5th Avenue, Tamara closed her eyes and imagined Shepherd Jesus standing on the opposite corner waiting for them. She quietly asked him to lead the way.

When they entered the park, Tamara followed a fresh impulse and turned north. Though it wasn't on her itinerary, Tamara led her mom to the Tree House for Dreaming. There, they sat quietly without talking. Tamara took out of her backpack two bottles of juice and a small plastic bag containing slices of smoked gouda cheese and crackers. As she prepared their snack, Tamara was feeling conflicted over being back in the spot where her mother's dream for her had died. She had lost her nerve for broaching that subject.

"A Tree House for Dreaming," said Aimee, as she studied the enclosure. "It's beautiful. Do you come here often?"

"No. Just once," answered Tamara.

"I've seen this from the path over there," said her mom, "but I've never come up close, and I never knew what it was."

For just a moment, an air of peace enveloped Aimee and it seemed to offer her some relief, but as they nibbled on cheese and crackers, Tamara sensed her mother's discomfort returning. Tamara wanted to ask her mother about her letter, and why it was so upsetting, but her mom spoke first.

"I learned a long time ago that dreams aren't just fantasies we hope will come true. They generate an essential locomotion that drives our lives. I remember when my childhood dreams had to give way and become adult dreams."

Aimee paused and looked through the skeletal roof. Her eyes were growing red again.

"And now, I'm realizing that adult dreams need to change, as well. This city has been my dream. Financial markets have been my dream. That letter I received yesterday should have been all the confirmation I needed that all my dreams are coming true."

Aimee fell silent.

"You weren't the only one affected by our trip to New Hampshire," Aimee whispered. "Ever since we've returned my heart has been changing, and my priorities are shifting faster than I can catch up with them. One afternoon, as I was racing around the floor of the Stock Exchange, I hit an emotional wall. I looked around me and I felt like a stranger there. I didn't know who I was anymore. I stood there looking at the purchase orders in my hand, and I just wanted to walk away. For three more weeks, I fought those feelings, but nothing helped. Then, I became scared, and I felt trapped. When I finally mentioned it to your father, he thought it meant I was bored and needed a fresh challenge, so I requested a change in my responsibilities which was granted. But the further I pursued that new role, the emptier I became. Evidently, I was doing it pretty well, but when that letter came yesterday, all I heard in my gut was a voice screaming at me telling me, no."

"You're not going, then?" asked Tamara.

"I have to go."

"What is your new dream?" asked Tamara, curious about what goes into the making – or changing – of a dream.

Aimee's look of emptiness turned to complete depletion and she became white.

"I don't know, anymore," whispered Aimee, "except for the most essential dreams I've always had. Your father is my dream husband, and seeing you grow up into the woman you are becoming is the most important dream of all. But, I'm afraid so many of your dreams have been nightmares. Do you have any dreams that bring you hope?" Her voice pleaded for a positive response, but then she felt the topic might be raw for her daughter.

"I'm not sure I know how to dream," said Tamara.

Aimee stared at her daughter, then nodded gently as she reflected on how much energy Tamara must expend just to remain ahead of her anxieties. Dreaming requires leisure and calm. One's mind needs a measure of tranquility for dreams to ripen beyond flights of fancy and to deepen into one's personal vision for life.

"Can I help in any way?" asked Aimee.

Tamara considered the question but didn't know how to reply, so she shrugged her shoulders. Aimee saw the struggle in her daughter and felt bad that she had pressed her into such an uncomfortable corner.

Tamara had intended to have their picnic at the outcropping of stone by the bridle path where she spent most of her afternoons doing homework and sorting out her world. But her intuition was telling her to remain where they were, so she spread out a small blanket on the bench beside her and began opening containers of food: rolls, slices of salami, ham, roast-beef, hard cheese, mustard, pickles, lettuce and tomato, pretzels and dip.

"There are chocolate-chip cookies for dessert," she said.

"Tamara, this is beautiful," said her mother. As she assembled a sandwich, her cell phone rang. "Damnit to hell," she whispered as she saw the caller ID then stood and walked a few paces away to take the call. When she returned and sat back down, the ashen expression had returned to her face and her mood was shattered.

"I'm sorry," she said, looking at Tamara. "This is not the picnic you expected, I'm sure."

"Who was that?" asked Tamara.

"It was my boss," said Aimee, fighting back tears. "He wants me to step up the pace for my proposal and be on a plane by Tuesday morning. So, I'm going to have to get back home soon, I'm afraid, honey."

Tamara handed her mother her sandwich then lifted her juice bottle in a toast: "To Brussels, then."

"To Brussels," said her mom. Then, Aimee closed up, withdrew completely into herself and couldn't speak.

Tamara was not far behind. She had exhausted enormous internal resources just getting her mother there, and now she could sense the granthyrs on the prowl sniffing around to see what else they could snatch from her. She was used to her mother being her source of support. However unwelcomed her mother's intrusions might be, they were essential to the little emotional stability Tamara was able to maintain. Attempting to take on that role for her mother was a lot harder than she thought it would be.

Tamara looked around and searched her mind for something positive that would dislodge the thorn now piercing her psyche. She let the wooden frames of the Treehouse help her restructure herself inwardly. Their simple, natural beauty refreshed her and gave her the strength she needed to follow through and fulfill her purpose for this outing. This is where the art dream died, but it died so that something else might live.

Blowing through the trees and into their small structure came the memory of one of her earlier birthdays. There were no other children since it had been a difficult spring for them all, and Tamara's emotions had been fraying. But there was clearly a theme. That birthday was one of the first moments Tamara could remember that her parents began targeting her artistic tendencies. Her parents gave her a huge box of crayons, a large tablet of paper, and modeling clay. On the kitchen walls her mom taped large pieces of paper, set out several trays of finger paints and told Tamara to paint anything she wanted. Tamara stared at the large, intimidating surfaces, then she lashed out at them throwing paint and slamming color against the wall. Her mother mistook that for artistic passion and never saw the hell on full display. Every year thereafter, Tamara would unwrap a different medium and face a renewed set of family expectations. So, each year, her eviscerated soul found expression in more sophisticated ways as her mother pushed her to create, when all Tamara wanted was to purge herself of the monsters that inhabited the swamp inside her.

The memories confirmed for Tamara the truth of her mother's displaced aspirations, and her mother's inner conflict told Tamara it was time for her to act.

As her mother finished her sandwich, Tamara took one more item out of her back-pack, a small flat box in a simple wrapping with blue ribbon tied around it.

Aimee unwrapped the gift and discovered Tamara's well-used sketchbook and ink pen, the new set she had given Tamara for Christmas. The pad's pages were all clean and white, though it bore evidence that many had been torn from it.

As Aimee pondered what she held in her hands, Tamara said, "That was always one of your dreams, wasn't it? And you tried to give it to me, instead. I think it's time for you to take it back."

Aimee thumbed through the white pages, looking for something in them to help her grasp what her daughter was trying to say, but the emptiness on all those pages was mounting up inside her mind.

"What do you mean?"

"That has always belonged to you, not me," answered her daughter. "I've been holding on to it for you, but it's not mine."

"No. Of course it's yours. You keep it, honey." Aimee tried to hand the pad and pen back to Tamara.

Tamara stood up and shoved her hands into her pockets then drew in her long proportions so she could stand as tall and straight as possible. Her sketchbook hovered between them as Aimee's imploring eyes searched for understanding. But Tamara shook her head and closed her eyes so her mother's gaze wouldn't derail her. Her words were soft but brimmed with conviction: "Mom, I want to give you my blessing to be the artist in the family."

Aimee's mind seized up with paralysis. Her daughter's genius for burrowing too deep for comfort had overwhelmed her once again. Tamara watched as the last morsel of strength left her mother. The pad of drawing paper slipped from Aimee's hands and fell to the stone floor of the little wooden cottage.

Tamara picked it up and handed it back, then she walked to the other side of the Tree House for Dreaming. She turned around to face her mother, but her mother wouldn't look at her.

"Remember what Barb once said: 'There are some frightening things you should run from, and there are some frightening things you should stand up to and defeat.'"

Her mom nodded then realized Tamara was waiting for her to finish the saying.

"And there are some frightening things you should let win," whispered Aimee.

"Let it win," said Tamara.

As Aimee looked down at the sketch pad resting on her lap, her daughter walked over and stood beside her.

"Mom, art should come from those whose hope would die if they couldn't paint their visions for others to see. My hope died every time I saw my visions etched out in front of me on those pages. I'm going to do something else with them now. But you have visions and dreams that have never found the proper medium, and if you don't discover what that is, you are going to die."

The words hammered Aimee and she withered under the truth her daughter was speaking to her. But the blessing Tamara had bestowed upon her would do its work, and already Aimee was feeling the shackles of her bondage begin to loosen.

"So, you haven't been drawing?" asked Aimee.

Tamara shook her head. "No. When we decided I shouldn't attempt medication until after New Hampshire, I became frightened, and my dreams became worse. One morning, on my way to school on the subway, I took out my pad to try to get those images out of my head before school. But as I stared at the book, I decided I wasn't going to relive them long enough to give them existence on the page, and I certainly didn't want to open the notebook and see them all staring back at me. So, that afternoon, over on the other side of the park where I do my homework, I ripped them out, shredded them up, and threw them to the wind."

"What are you doing, instead?" asked Aimee.

"I've found things to do here in the park each afternoon."

"Like what?"

"Want to see?"

"I'd love to," said Aimee.

"Do you have time?"

"Honey, Brussels can wait for this."

"Okay."

Tamara packed the picnic supplies back into her bag, then she said, "Follow me."

The two headed north along a pathway that meandered through the park. The noon-day sun was warm, and their pace wasn't rushed. As they rounded a bend and saw the Jaqueline Onassis Reservoir stretch out before them, Tamara approached a bench which caused Aimee another mild emotional set-back.

Aimee recalled a day several years ago when she was at her lowest ebb with Tamara. They had set out for a walk to escape the atmosphere of oppression that had settled upon their home and to gain some fresh perspective, but Aimee's inner strength had given out, and on the very bench Tamara had just sat down upon, Aimee had come close to having a breakdown.

Tamara set her back-pack on the bench and from it she pulled the bag of Kaiser rolls. She handed one to her mother then proceeded over to the wrought-iron fence. Aimee followed, enthralled by her daughter's confidence.

There were five ducks swimming not far from the shore about thirty yards from where they stood. Tamara picked up a small stick and lightly struck the fence.

"You'll frighten them," corrected Aimee. But to her astonishment, the ducks responded by making a bee-line for their position. The one in the lead was making a fuss about something.

"That's Quackamarack," said Tamara. "He's the loud-mouthed daddy duck. And that's Puddleponderer, the mom. She's the quiet, thoughtful one. Those are their three ducklings, Waddles, Loper, and Lumpkin. They've grown a lot over the past few weeks." She tossed several pieces of bread into the water.

"Most days I bring a piece of bread from my lunch," explained Tamara.

"You do this every day?" asked Aimee.

Tamara nodded then pointed toward the shore. "The nest was over there. I saw the ducklings the first day they came out on the water."

As Aimee watched the ducks, then her daughter, she saw something in Tamara she had so rarely glimpsed: delight. Her face was as placid as ever, and there was no smile replacing the earnest expression she usually wore, but her aspect had brightened. The gray tones around her eyes were gone, and the attentiveness she showed the ducks spoke of wonder, even joy.

"Barb was right, honey," said Aimee. "You are such a beautiful young woman, and I haven't told you that often enough, Tamara. Until she pointed out what is now so obvious, that your beauty has been shaped by your struggles, I never realized how selfish I have been. I always thought I was the one who was going to protect you and manage your emotional health. I was the one who was going to polish your life by encouraging your art career. But Barb is right, there is another grace at work in you, Tamara, one I haven't fully appreciated. God has been shaping something truly beautiful in there. And, I think you know that now, don't you?"

Tamara felt her face grow warm, and her eyes were losing their focus for the tears brimming in them. She looked at the ducks who had lost interest since the bread had run out, then she closed her eyes and nodded.

"Shepherd Jesus," whispered Tamara. She became self-conscious and then embarrassed for naming him. Knowing her parents' views on religion, she feared her mom would consider it another form of madness. Then, she felt her mother's arm across her shoulders. The embrace was firm and filled with all the authority and power she always attributed to her mother. There was nothing tentative in the love her mother was expressing to her now. Tamara felt it deeply within herself and, as never before, she was rejoicing.

As her mother held her, Aimee whispered in Tamara's ear: "Thank you for the blessing you have given me, Tamara, and for the new life challenge."

Tamara look up at her mother.

"I have no idea where my life is headed now," Aimee continued. "It's nice to imagine that I could be the artist you think I am. But more importantly, Tamara, I would simply like to think that I could be half the person you have become and face life as bravely as you have. Whether I ever pursue my old dreams or not, you are the real blessing in my life."

"We should go," said Tamara, now feeling overly self-conscious. "You have to get ready for your trip."

"I do, I'm afraid," conceded Aimee. "But, I've got a new reason to go now," she said with lightness of heart. She held up the sketch book Tamara gave her. "I can draw Brussels!"

Early Tuesday morning, Aimee said good-bye knowing that when she returned Tamara will have departed for New Hampshire.

On the first Saturday after school let out for the summer, Terrance and Tamara loaded up the Porsche and headed north. They stopped for lunch in Rhode Island and were climbing up into the White Mountains by sun-down.

The trip to Brussels would prove to be a crowning moment in Aimee's career, and it would be her last. Upon returning, Aimee tendered her resignation and began making plans to join her daughter.

PART TWO

15

ARE YOU READY FOR THIS?

BARB HAD DINNER WAITING FOR Terrance and Tamara: a slow-cooked roast, sweet corn from the Nazareth farm, candied sweet-potatoes, and fresh bread. Pamela Nazareth had baked a chocolate pie for Tamara and sent it over that afternoon. There was a fresh stack of wood near the porch (courtesy of her son), a fire going in the great room, and their bedrooms were ready.

Tamara paid little attention to the food in front of her. As wonderful as it smelled and tasted, it was her surroundings that were feeding her. So unlike her own home, this was an atmosphere that proved more nourishing than the roast.

Barb noticed Tamara fidgeting and invited her to find the pie on the shelf over the stove.

Relieved to have a purpose, Tamara slipped into the kitchen and stood there alone taking inventory of what she remembered and of what it felt like to be back. It took a few peeks through several drawers to locate a knife, but she took note of what occupied those spaces for the future.

The pie was still warm. As she cut the first slice, its chocolaty essence drew Tamara further into the mystery opening before her. There was a neighbor, somewhere in this village, that baked this and brought it over for her to enjoy. There was no packaging, no caterer's logo, and no one was tipped when it was delivered. When she had sliced three pieces and placed them on plates, she licked the knife and tasted so much more than chocolate. She closed her eyes and heard the sounds of the mountainside creeping through the open kitchen window.

Barb and Terrance talked quietly at the table, and their conversation held Tamara in the kitchen. She imagined herself making such a pie, even delivering one to someone else, and what a marvel it was to consider that people might do such a thing. She scanned the kitchen and its wares certain that such a pie could emerge from this kitchen, as it did from Pamela Nazareth's, perhaps one even better. Tamara glanced over to the table, pondered Barb's profile, and wondered at the life-experience gathered up inside that small but sturdy woman.

She carried the plates to the table and set them before the others.

"There's fresh milk that came over with the pie," said Barb, moving to get up.

"Let me," said Tamara, now feeling a growing urgency to be of use. She found three cups in the cupboard and the pitcher of cow's milk on the top shelf in the fridge. The milk was thick and had a bold smell. As she delivered it to the table she felt herself being woven into some other fabric. Each new awareness pricked at her mind and told her to pay close attention.

The night was fresh, and the two travelers were stiff from being in the car all day, so Barb suggested they take an after-dinner stroll. The evening was cool as a brisk breeze moved through the valley, and the graying evening settled their moods into a contemplative silence. Barb led them out the farm road and in towards town. Nanna's General was closed, and there was little activity on Main Street, but the evening peace was what they needed. The deepening quiet wasn't awkward to any of them as they strolled without talking. Bonds were forming where the bonds needed forming, and it was just fine that they took their time about it.

"It must seem such a small place to you, Terrance," said Barb, as she scanned the few houses and businesses along the road, glad to share her home with him, though conscious of him being so out of place.

"I was just thinking of the contrast, myself," he mused.

"Think you could ever get used to it?" she asked.

"I don't know. The city may have ruined me!" he chuckled. "I was just thinking what a contrast this is going to be for Tamara and how grateful I am to you for inviting her to experience this. It means more to me and Aimee than you can ever know."

Barb slowed her pace and then halted. She turned so she could address Terrance directly.

"I have given this a lot of thought and a lot of prayer. I know this was meant to be – for all of us. We are going to have a good time," she said as she smiled at Tamara. "And we are going to work hard, because that's what you do on a farm. So, this is no vacation, young lady!"

Barb laid her hand on Tamara's shoulder. Then, she cupped her palm to the side of Tamara's face and looked her in the eyes.

"Are you ready for this?" Barb asked.

"Yes," responded Tamara. "Yes, I am."

After a cup of hot cocoa and more conversation in front of the fire, Barb showed her guests to their rooms. Terrance's room was once Sally Anne's bedroom. It had been converted into a den with a hide-a-bed which Barb promised would be comfortable.

A few paces beyond the den, Barb opened the door to the room which Tamara had slept in before. It had been remarkably transformed. Out had gone all the knick-knacks and bric-a-brac of a young adult male, and in had come the library and artifacts of Barb's former classroom. A lifetime of spiritual reflection, expressions of her faith, and the tools of her teaching career were now reflected in every crevice of the small room.

"I hope you don't feel this is too cluttered," said Barb.

Tamara was transfixed and couldn't take it all in at once, but she felt the warmth and grace at work in it immediately. The contrast to her stark room at home was immediate and gratifying.

"Oh, no. It's wonderful," said Tamara.

"It's almost like taking a pilgrimage and never leaving home. I come up here sometimes and just get lost. Well, you get settled in, and I hope you sleep well. Tomorrow we're going down to the Nazareth's farm to see those lambs after we do a little work around here. Would you like to sleep in like your dad or get up with me and the sun and go to work in the morning?"

"With the sun!" said Tamara.

Her new surroundings sparked every one of her emotional sensors and she felt electrified within herself. The shelves were crammed with ornaments, statues, artifacts, and trinkets of every sort. There were collections of crosses, pictures, and books. Some of the pictures were life-like while others were stylized two-dimensional faces surrounded by strange symbols. From out of her bag she took her picture of Aunt Tamara and set it among the other small portraits, the subjects of which looked much more religious than Aunt Tamara, though she seemed to hold her own. Over the upper corner of the frame, she draped Aunt Tamara's cross.

The writing desk, which was now situated over by the window, contained a rack that held several small books on prayer: *The Way of a Pilgrim, The Cloud of Unknowing, The Imitation of Jesus, The Practice of the Presence of God*. She set her illustrated *New Testament and Book of Common Prayer* among them.

She pulled Sally Anne's Bible from her satchel and searched for a place where it might rest with honor. She put it on the nightstand by her bed.

Tamara looked around her new room and knew she wasn't ready for bed. The mysterious signs, symbols, and images which, for her, had no meaning yet, drew her in and captivated her mind. She wasn't naïve. Before her night was over, her fascinations would become corrupted and the images that so enthralled her waking moments would slash at the soft part of her soul once she had gone to sleep. She would rather spend the night conscious of the good surrounding her.

But the quiet of the room, the stillness of the world around her, and the darkness so evident outside her window pressed in upon her. She remembered the darkness of the dream that brought the granthyrs to the barn and pulled her from her bed to go rescue Barb. She wondered how far she might have walked through these hills, with no cars to awaken her before she walked off the ledge.

Tomorrow, Tamara decided, once her father had left for home, she would give Barb that second chance she requested for another lesson in prayer. For now, she would unpack and explore her new room.

She closed her door, and there hung a brightly colored poster of one she recognized as St. Francis from the statue in Dr. Samuelson's office. This picture showed the saint in a meadow; he was surrounded by deer and birds. Down alongside his image was printed the words of a prayer:

Lord, make me an instrument of your peace;
where there is hatred, let me sow love;
where there is injury, pardon;
where there is doubt, faith;
where there is despair, hope;
where there is darkness, light;
where there is sadness, joy.

O Divine Master,
grant that I may not so much seek to be consoled as to console;
to be understood as to understand;
to be loved as to love.
For it is in giving that we receive;
it is in pardoning that we are pardoned;
and it is in dying that we are born to eternal life.

As Tamara was reading the prayer a second time, there came a light tap on her door. Her father slipped in to see if she was okay and felt he had been there before. He recognized the décor from Barb's classroom and recalled the claustrophobic sensations he felt then.

"What do you think?" he asked.

Tamara shrugged. "I think it's great," she said.

"You're sure you want to do this?"

"Yes. I need to do this," she declared. There was an earnestness in her voice that gained her father's instant, and enormous, respect.

Terrance looked long at his daughter, and Tamara sensed he was finding it difficult to leave.

"I brought Aunt Tamara with me," she said.

Terrance smiled an ironic smile to see the company she was keeping.

"Saint Tamara, you mean?"

"Saint Tamara," she agreed.

"May she keep you well," he said as he backed out the door.

16

IN THE BEGINNING

THE MORNING DIDN'T COME NEARLY as early as Tamara thought it would. She managed to pass the night better than she had hoped and was awake at first light. The house was quiet, and she was afraid she had missed Barb who must have already slipped out to the barn.

Tamara dressed in a new pair of jeans and a work shirt, care of her grandparents and their L. L. Bean gift card. She pulled on her barn boots and headed downstairs. There was no sign that anyone had stirred. The kitchen door was still latched.

Tamara quietly let herself out the door and stood on the porch, glad to see the farm by morning light. A heavy dew glistened upon everything in sight, though there wasn't much sparkle to the dawn yet since the sun was still behind the mountain. The morning light was gray, but it promised so much more. She breathed in the dewy air and heard the muffled clucking of the chickens.

The hens didn't seem overly surprised to see a stranger standing by their pen. 'Don't let them out,' she remembered Barb instructing her. 'Just shoo them gently away and slip in.' Tamara looked around and found the bucket she had used to feed them, and she remembered where the feed was kept, so she scooped the right amount and stepped inside the coop. The hens dispersed quickly on their own, but Tamara crouched down to see if she could coax them to come. She scattered a handful of feed then studied their halting motions as they ate. They would need some water, she noted. But first, the eggs. She finished spreading the feed then went over to the shelf where the hen's boxes were lined along the wall. Seven fresh eggs. Certainly, enough for breakfast.

With her bucket in hand, she wandered for a while around the barnyard hoping to see her namesake, Tam the kitten, but she was not to be found.

Tamara's tour brought her around to the back door, so she entered the kitchen and was going to wash the eggs.

Barb was startled as Tamara entered the darkened room. "Tobias?" she said.

"It's Tamara."

"What?" responded Barb, not yet recognizing who had just spoken. She fumbled to find her glasses in the pocket of her dressing gown and put them on, then she stared at Tamara until recognition returned.

"Oh, my Lord, of course! Good morning." Barb strode across the room and embraced Tamara then looked deeply into her eyes.

"Forgive me, I wasn't quite awake, and sometimes Tobias passes through on his way to the church. How did you sleep?"

"Actually, better than I thought I would," admitted Tamara.

"You're up early."

"With the sun."

"Yes, well, we did say that, didn't we?" Barb laughed. "I was just about to stoke the fire in the stove and have my morning prayer. Why don't you work on the fire, and I'll make us some coffee. Or, do you prefer tea in the morning?"

"Coffee," said Tamara, though she had never had any.

Tamara opened the fire-box on the wood stove and began to insert a log.

"Here," said Barb. "Start with these." She showed Tamara some smaller kindling. "Start small, then lay on the larger stuff as it gets going."

Tamara set some small sticks on the coals and watched them smolder until they burst into life and invited more fuel.

"I see you've already earned your breakfast, Miss Baxter," Barb said, admiring the eggs.

"Is there anything else I can do?" she asked.

"Yes, there is." Barb beckoned her to sit down in one of the chairs by the stove.

Barb's kitchen, always the heart of her home, was as much living room and den when there were just a few friends in. Barb liked a fire in the living room, but lately her kitchen was large enough for her, and it was becoming homier to her all the time.

"The farm always waits on God, and God always supplies the farm, so before we do anything else, we let God wake us up and prepare us for the day."

Tamara sat down and felt the old chair absorb most of her body. Barb walk over to an old hutch, from which she took a small package, simply wrapped in brown paper.

Tamara received it awkwardly and hesitated to open it. When she did, she found a black, leather bound Bible. Her heart raced, and she was unsure what to say beyond thank you.

"But, Sally Anne's Bible…" Tamara struggled to articulate the question she wanted to ask.

"That's right. I wanted you to have that for several reasons. But you probably realized how hard it was to read."

Tamara was embarrassed to nod her head, though she did so, anyway.

"This one is written in modern English. It should be much easier for you to read. And, it has notes at the bottom of the page that will help you understand what each passage is about. So, while our coffee is brewing, and the sun is still rising, let's read and pray and let God get to work in us, so we can get to work for God."

With that, Barb left Tamara to fumble through her new Bible as she tended to her usual devotional routine. Tamara kept a keen eye on what Barb was doing, but she wasn't sure where to begin herself. It soon came to her that, perhaps, the right place to begin was where it said, "In the beginning, God created…"

She read of the birthing of creation and of the garden God had made, and she felt she was in just the place God made for her to be. The soft, dawning light through the window quickened her spirits. She felt an impulse, an invitation pulling her into the morning air gently rising from the valley bed as it warmed and stirred the mists gathered in the hollows of the land around her. She agreed with God: It was good. Very good, indeed.

Barb's eyes were closed, though her face had an air of attentiveness about it which Tamara found fascinating. What was she thinking? Or asking? Or, was she simply listening?

Tamara closed her eyes and wasn't sure how to start her own prayer, so she thought through what she could remember of the prayer of St. Francis posted behind her door. She thought how unlikely it was that she could ever be an instrument of peace for anyone, much less sow the seeds of love, pardon, and faith, all of which she consumed from others and depleted, daily, in herself. The hope Francis requested had always seemed beyond her reach, and there was no light in her. And joy? From which star in the heavens does that fall? Yet, as she pondered the prayer, it dawned on her that perhaps Francis felt the same. After all, why ask for something you already have? Isn't prayer the asking for something you need, not for something you already possess? 'Lord, make me…' she thought.

She imagined Francis roaming around the garden she had just read about, calling out the creature's names that Adam had given them, letting the birds rest in his hands as he strolled among the deer. 'Chicken,' she thought. 'Horse, kitten, and lamb,' the simple names of simple creatures God had placed in his garden for them to enjoy. She saw herself, barefoot, walking through the cool morning grass in a garden where everything is freshly made. 'Lord, make me…' she thought again, and wondered what it would be like to be newly made. A new creation. Fresh, from the beginning. Her restlessness became unbearable. She had to move, be outside, and not miss a moment of this spectacle unfolding all around her.

Tamara heard her father move from his room into the bathroom and knew he would be down soon. She became self-conscious and didn't want him to find them at prayer. She succumbed to her agitation and set her Bible aside. As she was about to rise from her chair, she felt Barb's hand rest upon hers.

"Thank you, Lord," said Barb, her eyes still closed, "for my dear friend Tamara, for her safe arrival, and restful sleep. Now awaken us to your will and show us the way through this day which we offer now to you, in Jesus' name. Amen."

Tamara felt humbled by the woman's faith and intimidated by her father's unbelief, but Barb's warmth helped her relax into her own place somewhere between the two.

Barb said, "Let's go see what we need to do before we fix your father his breakfast." She rose up and charged toward the counter where the bucket of eggs lay.

"Well, that will never do," said Barb, and Tamara felt pinched emotionally, wondering what she had gotten wrong. Barb disappeared into the pantry and came out with a box from which she pulled a basket with a most interesting shape, woven of thin strips of wood.

"There, young lady. A proper egg-gathering basket. Don't let me catch you bringing that old bucket into my kitchen again." Barb's smile was broad and proud.

"Yes ma'am," said Tamara, in her most dutiful voice.

"And you'll be needing these," said Barb, as she laid upon the table a pair of work gloves, a few bandannas, and a straw hat.

"Well, put 'em on," said a fresh voice, her father's, from just outside the kitchen. "Let's get to work. The farm won't wait."

"Already gathered the eggs while you were sleeping away the day," she said.

Tamara tried on the gloves and hat, and Barb and Terrance exchanged the usual morning pleasantries as they both filled their coffee cups. They all took their warm cups and stepped out onto the porch to greet the morning.

After a few moments of quiet, Barb said they ought to go get breakfast, and Terrance acknowledge he would have to start back home soon.

"What's on your schedule for the day?" he asked.

"We're going to go get sheep today," Tamara said to her dad. "I'm going to be a shepherd."

"Well, we're going over to look at the lambs," Barb corrected her. "They're still a bit young to move over here yet, but Betsy said she'd teach you what you need to know to care for them, and in a few days, well, then, perhaps. We've also got a garden to plant. Tobias came and tilled it late last week, and I picked up some plants yesterday, so we're going begin putting those in. It's a little late for the spinach and other cold crops, but I'm primarily planning on tomatoes, cucumbers, and beans.

As Terrance drove away, Tamara sensed a different kind of emptiness emerge within her. She had been so eager to be on her own with Barb she hadn't prepared herself adequately for what that might feel like.

"Let's sit on the porch-swing for a moment," said Barb, "and plan our day."

Barb let the swing rock gently. She was in no hurry to push Tamara into chores.

"Betsy's expecting us late morning. Her farm is just beyond the church, an easy walk, so once you get your lesson with the lambs you can go check on them whenever you need to. It's still too wet to work in the garden, so I thought we'd walk the fences around the pasture where we might keep the lambs to make sure they're tight. So, why don't you go get your gloves and hat, and I have a little box of tools we'll take with us."

Barb set a slow, purposeful pace as they traced the perimeter of the pasture. She told Tamara it was just as important to watch the field for wildlife as it was to study the fence for breaks in it.

"And every once in a while, be sure to look up," said Barb, as she directed Tamara's gaze toward the mountainous heights that enclosed them in the little valley.

The graceful lines made by the sloping hills were textured by the evergreens, birches, and maples shadowed by the dawning light. The lay of the land drew her vision upward and a sense of majesty settled into her psyche. The ridge was brightened by the sun now cresting over it. Tamara recalled the description of the garden in her Bible and scanned the pasture for signs that God's creative work was still in progress. The landscape flourished with wildflowers and small scrub bushes. There was a stark and unpolished beauty to everything she saw.

The grass was tall and wet, and as Tamara stepped through it she was missing her mother who had the forethought to give her these wonderful boots on her feet. She felt again the emptiness she experienced as her father drove away, and she regretted how hard she had pushed her parents out of this experience, coveting it for her own. Her mother would love this, thought Tamara.

"It'll be good to have some sheep in the pasture," said Barb. "They'll help us put it back in order."

The pasture, clearly, had not been used by domesticated farm animals for some time, but the wildlife must love it, thought Tamara. The fence, on the other hand, seemed in fair shape, thanks to Toby's efforts, and Barb pronounced the second span of fence to be fit.

As they rounded the far corner and began their survey of the third side of the pasture, Tamara could hear the faint sounds of the river. Her heart raced as she listened intently to the movement of the stream by which she had witnessed the baptisms and had met Barb. The farther they walked, the more pronounced her memories became as the sound of flowing water reminded her of the pilgrimage she was on.

Soon, they had reached the trail that ran beside the stream. Tamara had lost all sight of the errand they were on. She paused by the fence post and looked across the little path to see if she could see the water.

"Over here," pointed Barb, who turned up the path and walked several yards to a bench situated on the bank overlooking the stream.

"I had Tobias put this in last week, so we could come and enjoy the stream whenever we want and not have to sit on the ground! I should have done this years ago," she said as they sat down.

There was no talk between them, yet there sat two souls fully enraptured by their environment, answering the only call that mattered, to be still and allow their spirits to be refreshed by the glisten and sparkle of moving water. The choruses sung by the river recapitulated those ancient refrains of God: Let there be, and there was, and it was good. Very good.

'Lord, make me an instrument of your peace,' remembered Tamara, 'this peace,' she thought. She glanced sideways at Barb, whose eyes, again, were closed.

17

THE NEW SHEPHERD

JUST BEFORE THE SEVENTH DAY Baptist Church, on the left, was the narrow dirt road that took them to the Nazareth's farm. Unlike Barb's place, which still had scarcely awakened, Betsy's farm was vibrant with activity at ten-forty-five that Sunday morning. A tractor was harrowing the field out beyond the barn and several large brown cows stood sentry by the fence leading into the barnyard. The sturdy, deep red barn was much larger than Barb's. It's massive sliding doors were wide open and there were several people bustling around inside.

"Come, look," said Barb, as she led Tamara up a walkway beside the house where, Tamara figured, the owner must live. They turned back behind another small building to find a pasture with thirteen large sheep at the far end, and seven small lambs.

"Morning," shouted a woman behind them.

Approaching them was a strong-looking woman in overalls and work boots. She removed her hat, wiped her forehead, and extended her hand to Tamara. Her grip was firm, and as she held Tamara's hand she looked long into her eyes. Her dirty blond hair was uncombed, and there was a smudge on her left cheek.

"Welcome," she said. "I'm Betsy, and you must be our new shepherd. Come on in," she directed, as she threw back the latch on the gate and ushered them inside the pasture.

Betsy placed her fingers between her lips and whistled a whistle Tamara felt sure her parents could have heard back in the city.

Tamara's periphery went wild as two black and white creatures darted past her. One of them brushed her legs in its haste. Three more whistles from Betsy and they were racing one another toward the flock. The two dogs circled round the sheep, drew them together into a tight group and then marched every one of them toward Betsy. Silent as wraiths, the dogs briskly answered their whistled commands as the sheep complained loudly – the ewes in deep tones and the lambs with high pitched squeals. As the sheep complied, they soon became a small huddle gathered around the legs of the onlookers. The dogs made one more tight circle then sat themselves directly in front of Betsy who gave them each a pat on the head and dismissed them back out of the gate which she shut and latched.

Tamara took her first breath since Betsy whistled and looked in awe at the lambs by her feet.

For the next hour, Betsy introduced Tamara to the sheep then gave her a tour of the farm while Barb sat on Betsy's swing and took in the morning. As the farm-hands began to break for lunch, Betsy led Tamara back to the house then in through the mud-room off the kitchen.

"Kick off your boots," said Betsy. "There are some clogs there that might fit you, then come in and wash up while I get us some lunch."

As Tamara was taking off her boots, a young man startled her as he came bounding through the door then froze when he saw her. He looked embarrassed to have met a stranger, and Tamara felt herself seize up in response.

"Tamara, this is my brother, Tinder. Tinder, this is Tamara. She's staying with Barb for a while. You remember me telling you, right?"

He nodded but didn't speak. He looked trapped and unsure of the way forward.

"Shake her hand, Tinder," instructed Betsy. Tinder nodded, tentatively, and extended his hand as instructed, but the moment it was shook he charged past Tamara and disappeared.

"Your boots, Tinder!" shouted Betsy. She rolled her eyes and looked exasperated with him.

Tamara heard the boots hit the floor somewhere down the hall.

"Tinder takes a little while to warm up to people. He's always been deathly shy of others."

Tamara didn't want to let on, but she was just as glad to avoid the awkward social realities of meeting someone else her own age.

Lunch consisted of salad made with greens from the garden and chicken sandwiches. Though he was invited to join them on the porch, Tinder chose to eat in the kitchen.

"Well, we have a garden to plant," said Barb, as they finished their lunch.

"What time, tonight?" asked Betsy.

"Oh, will five do?"

"That should be fine."

"See if Tinder won't come," said Barb.

"I'll see what I can do," she answered, shaking her head.

Tamara waited to see if anyone would enlighten her, but no one cared to fill her in on whatever plans were being made.

Their first afternoon in the garden reminded Tamara of her morning in the kitchen during their visit back in the spring. Could she ever be any more out of her element, she wondered. As Barb had so patiently coached her through her first omelet, she was now taking great pains to talk Tamara through the gentle handling of the plants and how to tuck them into the soil at the right distance from one another. Tamara's legs and back were beginning to complain from the constant bending and squatting. She got the tomatoes planted and half of the peppers before Barb told her they would have to come back to it tomorrow.

"Would you like one more small chore before we quit?" asked Barb.

Tamara's energy, along with her emotional fortitude, had been ebbing, but she didn't want to say no, so she nodded that she would. Barb led her to the barn and showed her a large bundle of long sticks. She pulled one from the stack and held it up.

"We need to sort through these and find twelve that are about this long for the tomatoes," she said, "and then around eighteen that are longer, like this one, for the beans." She stood the two sticks side-by-side for Tamara to compare.

"We'll use three of the longer poles and construct a tripod for each hill of beans for them to grown on. Do you mind doing that while I go fix us some lemonade? When you're done, just come to the porch and we'll have a rest."

There was no light on, though the crevices between the barn siding gave Tamara enough ambient light to see. The stakes were covered in dust and cobwebs as was most everything around her. She sorted the stakes into piles and let her mind wander around the barn. Shadows of anger, and the lingering despair that dripped down through the generations, crept through the crevices of her psyche. A milking stool, a coil of rope – unfinished legends were being retold, one of which was her story of how she came to be here. She felt the irrepressible sensation that she was inheriting something. Whether it was the family curse or one of its precious heirlooms, she couldn't tell, but she sensed she was the recipient of some mysterious bequest handed down through this family, and she was the last of the line.

She heard a rustling in the stall just beyond her. Startled out of her ruminations, she went to see. Amidst piles of old musty hay, she saw Tam, the tabby cat. Tam's back was arched. She was hissing and groaning from deep inside her being. Tamara tip-toed closer to see around the stall and found she was facing a great, long, gray snake, its body shaped in a tight zig-zag pattern with its neck slightly raised. Its mouth was opened, and its fangs were menacing.

Tamara felt her sight become confused and her head pulsed with pain as her entire body recognized the presence of the snake. She became unstable and lost her balance then dropped to her knees. Her chest seized up with fear as her mind readied her for the attack she was certain would come. Fierce, striking sensations pierced her psyche as she drew the attention of the snake whose eyes were now fully focused on her.

Tam spat at the snake which reared back, something Tamara didn't expect. The snake remained in place, however, and Tamara slowly regained her focus enough to shift her concern away from herself and offer it to Tam. For all Tam's protesting, however, the snake didn't appear to be on the attack. It seemed cornered and might have fled, but evidently it didn't want to turn its back on its intruders. Beside the snake lay a dead rat which, Tamara surmised, it didn't want to abandon to the likes of that cat.

Tamara picked up one of the long bean poles. She slowly reached in with it, set the point of it under the rat and pushed it beyond the snake under the boards of the partition into the next stall. The snake turned and disappeared in search of its rat, and Tam scampered off before Tamara could greet her. Tamara backed slowly away from the stall mindful that the snake was hidden somewhere in the barn.

She found Tam over by the workbench arching its back against the leg of a stool. Tamara bent down to pet her, and the kitten leaned into Tamara's leg. She scooped up the kitten and held it in her arms. Its fur tickled her chin. She buried her cheek into Tam's soft side, and Tam remained docile until they were disturbed by another person in the barn. The cat sunk her claws into Tamara's arm and scratched her way free of Tamara's embrace leaving her bare skin punctured in several places.

"Well, I wondered what was keeping you," said Barb, who then apologized for startling them and getting Tamara scratched. "I'm glad you met Tam, though. Looks like you're going to be good friends. And you got the sticks sorted I see. Well, almost. That's okay, you can finish tomorrow."

"There was a snake," said Tamara, by way of explanation for why she didn't get finished.

"Oh. Don't be frightened," said Barb, laying a hand on Tamara's shoulder. "We have several. Was it a large gray snake?"

Tamara nodded.

"You should give it a name. I used to name them all. They're good for a barn. They keep the rats at bay, and they're harmless. They're usually long gone before you get near them, and they're not poisonous. Here, come look."

Barb took Tamara to one of the far stalls. Tacked to the barn wall were several long crisp things that looked like dried out sacks of flesh discarded by ghosts that had long since flown free of them.

"As the snakes grow, they shed the old skin, explained Barb. "You'll find them all the time around the barn."

18

A Hard Lesson in Lambing

A LITTLE AFTER FIVE-O'CLOCK PEOPLE STARTED to arrive. No one knocked. They all walked right in as if they lived there, and everyone brought food. The smells that filled the house enthralled Tamara, though the swell of strangers was taking its toll. Her insides were feeling crowded, and it had already been a full day. Worse, they had come to meet her, which meant a lot of questions she didn't want to answer and a lot of small talk she didn't want to endure.

Betsy, without Tinder, was the first to arrive. She was followed by Betsy's grandmother, Pamela, and another neighbor, Nora Jakes, who owned the horses Tamara was invited to ride. Cindy Briggs, from the General, came in with Tobias and his wife, Natalie.

"Tobias," Barb called, "would you lay up a fire for us?"

"Sure," he responded and headed for the door.

Tamara followed and offered to help carry in some wood.

Alone on the porch, Toby extended his hand.

"Tamara, it is very good to properly make your acquaintance. I got to know your parents a little, but I missed meeting you. I'm glad you are here with us."

Tamara wasn't sure how to respond, so she quickly shook his hand then headed for the wood pile.

"You've had a full day" he said, sensing some heaviness about her.

She nodded her affirmation.

"A little overwhelming, I'll bet. Here, come sit down. The fire can wait a minute."

They each took a seat on the porch and spent a few moments looking out over the yard. Tamara's mind raced back to the river bank where she first encountered this man and watched him baptize four women, all a little younger than herself. She felt intimidated by all he represented though he represented all she felt she needed. If she was on a pilgrimage, as Dr. Samuelson had suggested, then Pastor Toby ought to be one of her guides. Her mind, however, was not up to conversation at the moment, so she remained tightly curled up within herself. She would ease into this, and Barb would help her take those steps she needed to take.

"Mom already considers you part of the family," he said.

Tobias had inherited Barb's gift of the long pause, that ability to say a lot in few words then let it trickle in to the consciousness of the listener. Tamara also appreciated that none of his sentences ended with question marks.

"She's also been looking forward to having some help around here. I think she's been growing despondent to see the old place go fallow."

Tamara hadn't been looking at her surroundings with anything but a grateful eye, though during Toby's latest long pause, she studied her new setting through another lens and could see what he meant. She hadn't drawn a comparison with Betsy's farm except to share Barb's gratitude that it was quiet without a lot of activity, but now she appreciated what it needed.

"She says you're going to be tending a few of Betsy's lambs, and there might be some horse-riding in the plans. It's a beautiful place to roam around in. Be sure to get out and hike around some."

Tamara's mind climbed back up the trail from which she thought she never wanted to come back down, were it not for Barb. She wasn't sure she wanted to make the climb again, but she was eager to explore the valley a little more.

"One of my favorite walks – just beyond the church – is a little path that will take you to an old, historic cemetery. It's surrounded by a rock wall and filled with many of this area's first settlers. Mom, and many of the other ladies, have planted azaleas and rhododendrons back there that are in bloom now. And if you keep going out the dirt road beyond Nazareth's farm, there are meadows filled with wild-flowers. Wait till you see the lupines. They'll take your breath away."

They were interrupted by Barb, who came to investigate where her fire-starters had wandered off to. There would be blessings that needed saying, she reminded her son, once they were through lazing around on the porch.

With a stack of firewood in her arms, Tamara felt shielded from the wall of conversation she walked into as she re-entered Barb's living room. Learning how to build the fire gave her purpose, and she was glad for the attention the fire would need from her if it were to grow steadily into the blaze they wanted.

The table was now laden with food from every farm in the valley. Barb gathered them all around it. At Toby's invitation, they joined hands, and he offered a prayer that thanked God for Tamara's safe arrival and sought his blessing on her time with them. He then thanked God for the beauty of creation, the sustenance offered by the meal, the warmth of love around the table, and the presence of Christ among them. Everyone sang out, "Amen," as he finished.

As Tamara listened to the conversations around her she was moved by their deep familiarity with one another and the ease with which they involved themselves in each other's lives, an experience she could not identify with any of her own family gatherings. And, there was no small talk. They were rummaging around in one another's depths before a single dish had been passed. Tamara was drawn quickly into the sincerity of concern she heard expressed for what was going on in their lives, on their farms, with their livestock, and families.

Barb interjected a few explanations as the dishes were passed and pointed out the produce harvested by those around her. When Barb indicated the meat on the platter was roasted lamb prepared by Betsy, however, Tamara's face became pale, and she hesitated to take any.

The room grew quiet.

"Tamara," said Betsy in a near whisper. "I can remember the first time I realized I was eating one of my momma's lambs. I had always been allowed to play with them, name them, and later, help shear the ones who grew old enough for breeding. But until I was five years old, I never realized what happened to some of them. I thought momma gave them away. Then, one day, I asked her where Fornie was. She was one of my favorite lambs. That's when she sat me down and explained some of the hard parts about living life on a farm. From then on, she always let me say good-bye. I'm sorry, I probably shouldn't have brought that. You won't hurt my feelings if you don't want to eat it. But I can promise you this, we raise our lambs with a lot of love. We enjoy them, give them a good life, and we make sure that when their end comes, it comes with care and with a lot of appreciation for what God gives us."

Tamara held the platter in her hand and hoped Betsy's words would find a comfortable place within her, but nothing she said would settle. Tamara nodded her understanding and placed a slice onto her plate, but she hadn't committed to eating it yet. Her facial aspect grew dark, and she was conflicted now in the role she might be playing by tending some of Betsy's lambs.

She felt Barb's hand upon her back. No words, just a welcomed touch of empathy, then the table conversation moved on to whether the season was going to be as dry this year as it was last year. Back home, Tamara noted, that would have been the sort of small talk that drove her crazy. Here, she could appreciate just how much it mattered.

"Leave your plates and we'll tend to those later. Let's go into the living room," instructed Barb. She asked Tamara to put another log on the fire while she went and got their dessert.

The fire calmed the conversation as everyone found their place in the great-room and watched the logs burn. Barb reentered and passed out plates of her second chocolate cheesecake, which everyone seemed to love. Tamara thought it was a little dry, but she couldn't recall a cheesecake tasting as good as that one, served there by Barb's fire.

The flames, and the light they cast around the room, settled the weariness in her soul, but the rich cheesecake lingering on her tongue made her lonesome for her parents. She was so far from home, and as the evening began to wind down for all of these early-to-bed-early-risers, her loneliness became acute. Soon, she would climb the steps, close her bedroom door, and face a long night in a very dark valley.

As everyone left, each person made physical contact with Tamara, something for which she was not prepared. Pamela Nazareth embraced Tamara warmly and thanked her for coming to be with her oldest and dearest friend. Her long gaze into Tamara's eyes meant something more to Pamela than Tamara could fathom. Cindy, Toby, and Natalie each shook Tamara's hand, and Nora Jakes laid her hand on Tamara's shoulder as she said good-bye and reminded her to come and ride soon. Betsy gave Tamara a firm slap on the back and held her hand there as she asked Tamara what time she might expect her in the morning for her third lesson in being a shepherd.

"Third?" asked Tamara.

"Lesson one: you met them today and made their acquaintance. Sheep form attachments, so you began that this morning and did very well. And, I'm afraid your second, and hardest lesson, is over there on your plate. I don't blame you for not eating it," she assured Tamara as she pulled her close and gave her a one-armed hug.

Tamara felt a little lost as Betsy closed the door behind her. Barb had begun cleaning up the dining room, and Tamara felt she ought to lend a hand, but she hadn't any energy left. Her mind was aching for solitude.

"It's a beautiful evening," said Barb, as she watched her young friend trying to find her place. "I really enjoy the porch swing at this time of day. Go on out and sit for a while. I'll join you in a few minutes."

Tamara wanted to go to her room, but she didn't have the strength to resist Barb's suggestion. However, once she sensed the soft movement of the swing and the quiet of the evening, she was grateful for an old woman's wisdom. The moon had not yet appeared over the mountain behind them, so the dusk felt somber. A light breeze blowing through the valley gave the air a crisp sensation that enlivened Tamara's senses once again. Her distracted mind began to settle as images of the day sifted through her.

Barb joined Tamara without a word and slipped into her own ruminations as the swing found its pace once again.

"There's the barn owl," whispered Barb, as she pointed up toward the lone tree over by the pasture. Tamara, however, wasn't sure she could absorb any more that day.

"Doing okay?" asked Barb.

Tamara nodded.

"You'd tell if you weren't, wouldn't you?"

Tamara looked her in the eyes and nodded again. "Yes," she said. "Yes, I would."

Barb took Tamara's hand and gently squeezed it.

"This is my favorite time of day," said Barb, and the look on her face confirmed it as she searched across the pastures, gazed up over the far ridge, closed her eyes, and took a long, deep breath.

Tamara had just been thinking the opposite, that with the setting of the sun and the quieting of the house her haunts usually began to emerge. Left alone with her thoughts and insufficient energy to distract herself, she plummeted too easily into morose ruminations and darkening apprehensions which, if they weren't checked, led to delusional visions or self-destructive impulses. She hated the evening.

"I call this porch my summer prayer-room," said Barb, "and I probably feel as close to God right here as anywhere else in this world." Barb noted the interest that sparked in her young friend and cautiously continued.

"As familiar as I have been with that view all my life, I never fail to discover something new God has made, or done, to keep his creation flourishing. I was just now thanking God for your company here with me, and for the help you have given me today. That garden over there probably would not be getting planted this year if you hadn't come. And I can't wait for the lambs! That pasture is going to be so beautiful with them at work in it."

Tamara tensed. Again, the long, deepening pauses between Barb's thoughts were having their effect on Tamara, this time for the worse.

Barb squeezed Tamara's hand more firmly.

"I honestly think you have everything it takes to be a great shepherd, Tamara," said Barb in a near whisper. The old woman was now looking toward the ground. Her face had become solemn, and the hold she still maintained on Tamara's hand became a tight grip.

"I saw how quickly you became attached to the lambs and how eager you were to have them come. Do you still want to do that?"

Tamara didn't know how to answer. She hadn't resolved her conflict over raising them for potential slaughter, and she didn't want to disappoint anyone, especially Barb, who seemed so eager for them to come.

"Let's wait a day before we decide for sure," said Barb. "There's no rush. You can pray about it and let Betsy know in a day or two. In the meantime, there's no reason you can't go over and enjoy them anytime you wish."

"She's expecting me in the morning," said Tamara.

"Then you should keep your commitments. Just take it a little at a time."

As Tamara reflected on what that visit might mean for her, she thought how differently Barb approached such matters. Her mom would have told Tamara to 'think' about it, then tell her what she thought about it and expect her daughter to follow through in like manner. Barb simply told her to 'pray' about it, as if that were as normal as thinking about something, and then left it entirely up to Tamara. The sensation was a little disorienting. She would have been relieved for some clear direction from this wise old woman. Instead, Barb's wisdom consisted of simply holding her hand and entrusting her to God.

Tamara had, on several occasions now, thought about Shepherd Jesus and the guidance he might offer her. She had asked, even pleaded with him on a few occasions, for help. But those were moments when she was utterly alone and falling deeper down a well in which she had drowned far too many times. She hurt for the insights of her new friend and was feeling short-changed. Now might be the time to press Barb for a real lesson in prayer, she thought. But before she could say anything, Barb offered a brief benediction.

"Yours is the day, O God, and yours, also, is the night, and we thank you for the beauty of it all," she prayed as she gazed toward the far ridge across the fields, her eyes wide open. Then, she closed her eyes for the rest: "We bless you for the beauty of your creation and ask from you now the rest we need, so we may rise to greet you in the morning and offer you our lives afresh. Grant us your peace and keep a watchful eye upon us. In Jesus' name, we pray. Amen."

With one more squeeze of Tamara's hand, Barb pulled herself up out of the swing.

"Feel free to stay and enjoy the evening, but I think it's time for this old body to go to bed."

Tamara didn't think about that long before she followed Barb through the door. Flashbacks to the dream she had of the horse being attacked by granthyrs in that very yard didn't entice her to remain out there alone. She would rather face the end of her day, or her long waking night, in her own room.

Tamara turned on the small desk lamp and searched about for something focus her mind. As captivated as she was by her new room and the endless avenues for exploration to be found there, she was drawn inwardly by Barb's encouragement to pray about the lambs. Who better than another shepherd to guide her, she thought.

She reached for the illustrated New Testament her mom had given her and opened it, careful to avoid the grotesque pictures of Jesus' death in the back of the book. She didn't have to look at them. Too many of those images had been scorched into her mind and they flashed through her consciousness as she thumbed through the pages.

'In the beginning,' she remembered from her morning reflections. Go back to the beginning. She turned to the front of the book and rested her eyes upon the soft glow of painted light filtering through barn boards, shining upon a baby being adored by such humble looking people. She was in awe to discover that some of the onlookers were shepherds. There, among the angels filling the night sky, were shepherds with their sheep, alone on the hillside. As she read, she learned that shepherds were some of the first to see baby Jesus. She felt again the deep privilege of what she had been offered, to tend some lambs. Why, she wondered, were shepherds offered such a gift? To be invited by angels to be the first to visit Jesus seemed absurd, and yet it humbled her to feel herself part of the story in some wondrous way.

Tamara took that image to bed with her and resolved that she could go over to Betsy's to see the lambs once more before she made up her mind about them.

Sleep came rather easily, but it didn't last.

Tamara was awakened by a disturbance downstairs. Something heavy had hit the floor and she heard voices, or at least one voice, though its modulations made it sound like a conversation. Already suspicious of her own mind, she struggled over what to trust and how to act, but as her mind clarified she was sure the voice was Barb's, and there was trouble.

Tamara dressed quickly and eased down the steps. The great room was dark. The only light came from the little lamp over the kitchen sink. Barb, in silhouette, was moving rapidly around the kitchen, agitated about something and scolding someone named Thomas.

"Barb?" said Tamara, but Barb didn't hear her as she went into the mud-room off the kitchen and began rummaging through one of the drawers.

Tamara went to her and laid a hand gently on Barb's shoulder.

Barb was jolted by the intrusion and looked threatened when she saw Tamara, but she quickly calmed and pressed her hand to her face.

"Barb?" whispered Tamara, but Barb didn't indicate she recognized Tamara at first.

Slowly, light began to dawn in Barb's face and she rubbed her hand across her brow.

"I've woken you. I'm so sorry. Forgive me. I didn't mean to be so loud." Barb was still a bit disoriented, but she ushered Tamara back into the kitchen and encouraged her to climb the stairs to bed.

Tamara lingered, however, and looked into Barb's eyes where she thought she detected traces of fear.

"Are you okay?" asked Tamara.

"Yes, yes. Everything is fine. Just a little trouble sleeping, so I thought I might tend to a few odds and ends rather than lying in bed."

Tamara wasn't convinced, but she didn't feel it was her place to be forward and press Barb any further.

"I'll try to be quieter," said Barb.

"Do you need help with anything?" asked Tamara.

"Nothing I can't tend to," she said, quietly. "I'm going back to bed, myself."

Tamara made her way back to her room, though now she was wide awake and didn't look for sleep to come again. She closed her bedroom door. By the ambient light from the moon coming in her window, she could make out the profile of St. Francis in the poster.

'Lord, make me an instrument of your peace,' thought Tamara as she climbed back under the covers and pondered what she saw in Barb's eyes.

19

WEANING THE LAMBS

"THANK YOU FOR STARTING THE fire," said Barb, as Tamara came in with her basket of eggs. "It was nice coming in to a warm kitchen."

"You should teach me how to make the coffee," said Tamara as she rinsed the eggs and put them away. But Barb had slipped back into her morning prayer, so Tamara joined her.

Tamara hefted her Bible into her lap and took up where she left off in her reading about the garden. The first words of the third chapter slammed into her chest with considerable force: "Now the serpent was more crafty than any other beast of the field that the Lord God had made."

As she read, her psyche began to seethe with empathy for the predicament in which Eve suddenly found herself. Tamara knew full well just how merciless the serpent could be – and just how sly. She felt her fury mounting at the way the serpent twisted God's words, and she was glad to see how thoroughly God had cursed the snake. But she was heart-sick over the punishment God gave Adam and Eve for falling under the influence of the fiend. She felt enormous compassion for the two garden-dwellers and knew just how perilous it was to resist the snake.

Thorafura had tortured her relentlessly. Her attacks were most venomous whenever Tamara thought she could outrun her tempter, tester, and tormenter. She usually found the only way to get relief from the attack was to relent and surrender to the assault she was under. Just let it happen, and it would pass. But God had sent Adam and Eve from the garden and set a guard at the gate, an angel with a flaming sword, to prevent their return. How long would God punish them before letting them back in, Tamara wondered, but she had little interest in reading any further.

Barb's eyes were shut in prayer, but Tamara wasn't about to shut hers. She felt no peace, and the agitation created by the story reignited her inner conflict about the lambs. She wanted to get up and pace but didn't want to disturb Barb, so she sat there as the snarls in her mind became grimacing and fowl. She fixated on the snake in the barn as the physical manifestation of her spiritual suffering and wanted to hunt it down, stomp it to death and nail the beast – not its empty skin – to the barn wall. Then, she would run to Betsy's, free the lambs, and find a place where she and her lambs could hide somewhere far from the garden.

But Thorafura followed her everywhere. There was no hiding from that serpent. The image of the gray snake in the stall morphed into a more sinister shape in her mind. She saw the snake strike Tam in the face then encircle the kitten's small body and begin to squeeze as it dared Tamara to come any closer. Then, as it slithered through the barn door, she knew it was headed for the lambs. Nothing was safe.

Before she could think it through, she was out the kitchen door and in full stride toward the barn. She snatched one of the bean poles and began poking it into corners, shoving patches of hay aside and stabbing into the darker crevices of the barn, to no avail. Then, unsure if snakes could climb, she swung the pole wildly at the rafters aiming her wrath in every direction.

Tamara heard her name but rejected the summons. She had had enough of Thorafura and wasn't going to submit to her any longer. The serpent could disguise her voice all she wanted and fake all the concern she could muster, but Tamara knew her subtleties too well. She could be anywhere.

A worn door to an old cupboard wasn't fully latched. Tamara threw it open and out fell a large knife which bounced on the counter and landed near Tamara's foot. As she stooped to grab it, another hand grabbed hold of hers. She wrenched her hand free and wheeled around with the knife. A large post interrupted her swing and she hit her hand sending the knife across the barn where it landed in a stall.

Tamara's eyes met Barb's, and she wasn't sure yet who she was looking at, still sensing the presence of the snake all through her.

"Thora - who?" asked Barb.

"What?" said Tamara, who was struggling to connect.

"Who were you screaming at, honey?"

Tamara stared at Barb and held her breath. She had never mentioned the serpent's name to anyone, not wanting to give credence to its existence or allow it life anywhere outside of her. It likes those dark crevices inside her, and so long as it stays hidden, Tamara was glad to let it lie. When the serpent attacked, however, she had always been powerless to fend it off. So, she resisted the mention of its name for fear of summoning it from its hiding place. But, she had chosen to entrust her life and new faith to Barb, so she chose to shape the word in her mouth and give it voice.

"Thorafura," she whispered.

"And who is Thorafura?"

Tamara closed her eyes and felt herself trembling within. She wouldn't say anymore, but Barb seemed satisfied and didn't press any further for which Tamara was grateful. Tamara didn't possess the emotional triggers that would have permitted her to reach out to Barb, but she was hoping Barb would embrace her, and she did. With Barb's arm still around her shoulders, Tamara allowed herself to be guided back into the kitchen for breakfast.

Barb felt it to be a good morning for ham biscuits which she remembered Tamara really enjoyed.

The taste of the biscuits grounded Tamara once again, and her surroundings began to soften the residue of fear still vibrating within her.

"Would you rather just take it easy today?" asked Barb. "We may have overdone it on our first day."

"I need to go see the lambs," said Tamara.

"Betsy would understand, honey."

That's just what Tamara didn't want, another person to practice such 'understanding' toward her. She had come to the farm to face down her apprehensions about life and to try something new where all her old efforts had failed her. 'There are some frightening things you should stand up to and defeat,' she repeated to herself.

"I'll be okay," insisted Tamara.

"Well, life starts pretty early over there, so if you're going, you'd best get a move on," Barb said, patting Tamara's hand then picking up her breakfast plate.

"Are you coming?" asked Tamara.

"I could, but it's probably best you go on your own. If you feel up to it, that is."

Tamara nodded that she did. This was all still so new to her, and the residue from her most recent joust with Thorafura had reignited many of her old anxieties. It had taken her seven or eight trips to Central Park before she could relax the apprehensions that rushed through her as she approached each intersection. This would be a short walk with little traffic.

The fifteen minutes it took Tamara to walk the dirt roads to Betsy's farm proved more refreshing than she had anticipated. She savored the morning air in her lungs and paid close attention to the vegetation along the roads thankful it wasn't the refuse that blew about the streets in the city. The quiet of the countryside wouldn't let her go. She wished the walk were longer as she saw the gates appearing and decided she should take Toby up on his suggestion to venture out past the farm and see what lay beyond it.

Despite Barb's suspicion that the farm was already a hive of activity, it was relatively quiet. There were a few people in the barn, but no one spoke to her, so she wound her way back to the pasture where the sheep were grazing. She leaned against the fence and watched the mist rise from the meadow. The lambs were by their mothers; several were nudging in close and pushing up into the underbellies of the older sheep, who kept walking away from them. Two of the lambs looked lost and whined for whoever might come to their aid.

"Morning, Tamara," said Betsy, who had just come from the house. She laid a book on the picnic table then extended her hand to Tamara.

"You don't look like you got much sleep," Betsy observed.

Tamara felt invaded and didn't like the way Betsy read her so quickly.

"Well, you and me, both," Betsy said as she wrapped a firm arm around Tamara's shoulders.

"We've begun weaning the lambs, and they don't like it much, so they kept us awake last night. It'll take a few days, then they're all yours, if you still want them."

That's what she had come to figure out.

"Come over and sit down for a minute," said Betsy.

Tamara joined Betsy at the picnic table and discovered the book laying there was Betsy's Bible.

"When my momma had that talk with me about the lambs, she read me a few passages about Jesus." Betsy was flipping through the pages of a very worn Bible.

"Here we go: Jesus once said, 'I am the good shepherd. I know my own and my own know me, just as the Father knows me and I know the Father; and I lay down my life for the sheep…' He also said, 'the sheep hear his voice, and he calls his own sheep by name and leads them out. When he has brought out all his own, he goes before them, and the sheep follow him, for they know his voice.'

"My mother explained that the relationship we have with our animals ought to look like that in some way. We shouldn't stop caring for them just because we know their lives may be short, but we should remember that the little life they have is a gift from God, so the care we give them ought to honor God for entrusting their little lives to us.

"That's where lesson three begins," continued Betsy. "The ewes' milk is drying up, so we are beginning to shift the lambs to other food. They haven't been fed yet this morning, so they're agitated. I was hoping you would spend the morning with the lambs, comforting them. Listen to them."

Tamara was already intensely aware of their distress and had begun to embody it in herself.

"Their feed is in the little shed. Grab a bucket, fill it about half-full, and go see what you can do. Let them get to know you so they'll trust you're the one taking care of them. Now, you see that small enclosure on the other side of the shed? That's called a creep. There's a little door.

It's too small for the ewes, but the lambs can get through. It'll be much easier to feed them in there without their mommas butting in."

Tamara let her sense of duty carry her forward, but she wasn't feeling any positive internal motivation now. This was not the zoo, and she had wrestled with the realities now facing her most of the night. But with her bucket of grain, Tamara let herself into the pasture.

At first, the lambs were spooked, and they scattered, so getting close enough became her first challenge. One ewe proved protective, so Tamara's sense of caution was peaked, and she felt intimidated by her diminishing prospects. There were two lambs, separated from the rest of the flock, which looked rather lost, so her heart rested with those. She walked gingerly over to them, but they began to lament her approach rather loudly. She stopped, scooped a bit of grain in her hand, and flung it toward them. They startled but remained focused on Tamara. She put a little more in her palm, crouched, and held out her hand. They didn't come any closer, so she poured out a cup-full into a small pile on the ground then backed up three paces and sat down. They all stared at one another across the pile of feed. Then, Tamara began to speak to them coaxing them to come.

It didn't take long before Tamara felt herself wanting to take that next step she knew she was consciously avoiding, giving them names. She had given all her stuffed animals names. She had named her family of ducks in Central Park. Barb had told her to name the snakes, of all things. And her reading of the Bible yesterday morning told her that is what you do in God's garden, you name the creatures. Jesus knew the names of all his sheep, and they knew his voice. He must have spoken to them frequently.

"Lanolander," she said to the smallest, wanting to rub her hands in its wool. "And Woolimittens," she said to the other. Then, she explained a few facts of life to them, that their mothers couldn't feed them anymore, and they shouldn't be afraid. They would be well taken care of. Still, neither budged in her direction.

So, she picked herself up, grabbed her pail and walked toward the creep. Tamara squeezed through the little gate, dumped the rest of the grain in the trough then started to climb out over the fence. But a second thought halted her. She climbed back down, turned the bucket over on the ground, and sat down upon it.

Every eye in the pasture had followed her into the creep. From the other group of lambs that had clustered together, the largest of them stepped out and trotted toward the enclosure, pressed its way through the small gate, sniffed the trough, then buried its face in the grain. Fluffermore would be its name. Woolimittens came next, followed by the rest in turn. Sheerborne, Lamblitten, Lupinore, and Gentleomen all found their names and their places at the trough.

When, at last, Lanolander pushed its way in among them, Tamara grabbed the lamb by the flanks and rubbed her hands through its woolen hide. It protested minimally but found its feed.

"Fine work," said Betsy, over her shoulder. "What do you think?"

Tamara nodded her head and patted Gentleomen's back.

The two of them lingered with the lambs for a little while. Then, as they finished their feed, the lambs let themselves out of the creep and rejoined the ewes.

"Lesson number four," said Betsy, as Tamara climbed over the fence. "As much as you will enjoy this, and as much as you would like them to depend upon you, they are not pets."

Betsy laid a hand on Tamara's shoulder as they turned toward the house.

"We walk a different sort of road, we shepherds," Betsy continued, squeezing Tamara's shoulder. "Cherishing the life God places in our hands, enjoying the beauty of his creation, we work side by side with our creator, realizing all the while that God has given this for our well-being. Our appreciation for what God has given increases, I believe, when we then have to face the sacrifice that his creatures make for our livelihood."

Tamara felt her face grow warm as she struggled to make room for Betsy's words of wisdom and accept the role she was being offered. She had never had pets and never knew the experience of losing one. The only death she had ever faced was her own, and that, many times. She never grieved the prospect of losing her own life, though she had come to appreciate the responsibility contained within that reality. Barb had made her promise, and her parents had devoted their lives to keeping her safe. But these little lives were being placed into her care, and they were nestling their way into her heart. This was an answer to much of the longing she had been experiencing. Now, the rewards of that longing were going to cost her more than she bargained for.

They paused to watch the lambs in the pasture. When, Tamara wondered, would it happen for them? And would she have to be here when they were taken from her? She didn't have the courage to ask.

"Once they are fully weaned," said Betsy, "they will spend their time as a flock in the pasture. Barb's pasture isn't quite large enough for seven lambs, however, so you'll need to feed them some fresh hay each day which we'll bring over from our farm. Watching their water is also important. This afternoon, I thought we'd go back to Barb's together and look at the little stable just off the barn. We'll clean it out, put in some fresh hay, and see what kind of trough it has for water."

As they were eating a quiet lunch on the porch, Tinder came over from the barn to tell Betsy she was needed.

"Sarah Bell's down again," he said.

"Bless her heart," groaned Betsy. "Does Earl think it's time?"

"He wants you to make the decision," said Tinder.

Tamara's heart was pounding. Betsy's face had turned red and the look of pain on her face informed Tamara there were serious decisions about to be made. She felt out of place – and in the way.

"Okay," said Betsy, as she put her face in her hands and breathed deeply.

"Tell Earl I'm on my way."

Betsy looked Tamara in the eyes.

"Sarah Bell's been around here since I was a kid. She's been one of the best cows we've ever had, but she's suffering. We never should have let her get so old. Just couldn't let her go, I guess. Now, looks like we have to."

Betsy stood up and started into the house.

"You can wait here if you want or go on home. I wouldn't expect you to be around for this. I'll come over later and we'll look at the stable. How about that?"

But Tamara looked hard at Betsy, read the pain she felt, and in an odd way, it reassured Tamara. It also called from Tamara something new. 'Lord, make me an instrument of peace,' she heard her heart say in that moment. And she knew that peace would come at a price.

So, Tamara stood and said she wanted to come.

Betsy looked long and deep into Tamara's eyes and nodded her head. She stepped into the house then came back out with a rifle.

Together, they walked toward the barn. Betsy introduced Tamara to an older man, with whom she conferred quietly for a few moments. They followed Earl through the barn, out another door, and across the field.

The old cow lay on its side straining to breathe. Her eyes were fixed, but she struggled to regain her legs.

Betsy handed Earl the gun then went and knelt down beside her old friend. She stroked the cow's strong neck, then she bent over, gave the cow a gentle kiss on the forehead and laid her hand upon its head. With her eyes closed, she began to speak. Earl quickly took off his hat.

"Good Lord, we praise you for Sarah Bell and for the burdens she bore. They were our burdens, Lord, and she carried them well. Now, dear Lord, we pray you ease her suffering and grant her peace. We give her back to you in thanksgiving, Lord, for the life you offered her."

Earl handed Betsy the gun. She aimed and fired.

The pain that slammed Tamara in the chest was unlike any that she could imagine. As they stood respectfully beside the dead cow, an ache overtook Tamara which felt so noticeably real in a way her other distresses felt so empty, meaningless, and false. She leaned into the pain and let it roar through her. There was an authenticity to this pain. It held meaning, and because of that it was elevated beyond the suffering she endured on a daily basis. And to the degree that it held such meaning, Tamara knew a measure of calm that was inexplicable to her. This pain didn't curl her up into a ball, it expanded through her and drew her to Betsy, and she obeyed the impulse.

Tamara walked to Betsy and placed her hand on Betsy's shoulder. The emotions that then coursed through her were explosive. Betsy only turned slightly and looked at Tamara to acknowledge the gesture, but the human connection she felt allowed Tamara a moment to set this new pain in its rightful place. Tamara closed her eyes, as she had seen Barb do on so many occasions, and quietly asked Shepherd Jesus to shepherd them both.

Then, Tamara remembered: 'Where there is sorrow, let me sow joy.' She had never imagined it within her reach to sow seeds of joy in another person's life, since she had no supply of joy stored up in her own being to give away. Her soul had been broken with sorrow more than she could fathom. Now, evidently, she sensed seeds had been sown where they were most needed. Something new had taken root within Tamara, something she would not have thought possible: pain that could become a blessing to offer others, even a source of new joy. It seemed a miracle to her. She pressed her hand more firmly upon Betsy's back, and Betsy turned into the embrace.

Betsy handed Earl the rifle then wrapped both her arms around Tamara.

The stable was going to need some work, but by mid-afternoon Betsy, Tamara, and Barb had stored the debris in one of the old cow stalls, so the stable was ready for fresh hay. Betsy would send Earl over for some repairs, but she thought the lambs would be ready for delivery on Wednesday.

After that, it was back to planting whatever Barb and Tamara thought they could get in the ground before dinner or their energy gave out. For Tamara, it was clearly the latter. Her lingering sensation of grief, and the awareness that brought her, supplied a new sort of aftermath to this emotional experience. She was now grieving a real loss, which was so different from being wrenched through sensations of remorse born of fruitless rumination and inexplicable despair over figments let loose in her mind. A life had ended before her eyes, and seven little lives might possibly see their end while under her care. So, the beans Tamara tried to plant were suffering under her lack of attention, and Barb took notice.

"I'm going to go fix us some lemonade. Why don't you stroll down to bench by the river, and I'll bring it to you."

"Let me help," said Tamara, though her voice betrayed her weariness.

"No. You go sit by the stream."

Tamara set her trowel in the wheelbarrow, dusted herself off, and wandered down the path. As much as she was coveting the solitude, she wasn't convinced she should be alone. Her insides were in shambles now, and she was craving Barb's wisdom.

Betsy had given Barb a run-down of their morning, and in her old farm-woman way Barb was letting those experiences lie fallow for a while in Tamara. But instead of fallowing in respite, Tamara's cognitive processes did what they do best after years of practice, they festered into something putrid. Her mind had an insidious way of turning such humble human experiences into cause for self-loathing. Granthyrs gnawed at what should be a life-transforming moment and reduced it to emotional carnage. This was when she used to grab her drawing pad. Now? Her hands were empty, and her heart was roaring with regret.

She found the bench and sought to build some positive thoughts around her day with the help of her surroundings. She forced her memory to push back to her first visit, but that was now old. She needed something new to fixate upon before the well she was now falling into swallowed her completely.

"Is this seat taken?" said a man, behind Tamara.

Tamara's state of mind wasn't to be trusted, and she didn't give the question credence, but she also knew the voice was real. Turning swiftly around she disbelieved what she saw at first, a familiar face in very unfamiliar clothing.

"I just stopped by the house, and Barb sent me down here with this," said Dr. Samuelson, making himself comfortable on the bench beside Tamara.

Tamara could only stare.

Dr. Samuelson laughed. "Did you forget that I was going to be here this week?"

Tamara had, but permitted her memory a moment to catch up to her visual reality and allow it to make sense in her mind.

"Lemonade?" he asked.

Tamara accepted the cup, but the shock to her emotions, let alone being seated beside her therapist all of a sudden, left her more withered within herself than she was just the moment before.

"I heard you had quite a morning," he said, but Tamara withdrew further and didn't respond.

"This is where you met Barb," he observed, not needing to ask.

Tamara pointed to a tree several yards downstream.

"By the baptismal?"

Tamara nodded.

"How does Barb seem to be doing, by the way?" the doctor asked, with some worry in his voice.

Tamara said, well, she thought. "Why?"

"No reason. Just wondered," he answered.

"And that's where you want to be baptized," he continued.

Tamara felt her face flush, but she nodded then looked down the bank into the stream.

Dr. Samuelson drew in a deep breath, became even more introspective, then looked Tamara full in the eyes.

"I really hope you will," he said. "It's a mighty big step, but one I believe you should take. I've been praying for you ever since you told me."

He looked at her in a new way, and the voice was now that of an old friend. He had shed his professional mannerism along with his professional attire and replaced them both with cargo shorts, a green t-shirt, sandals, a straw hat, and a more companionable demeanor.

"You might be surprised at this, but that's where I was baptized," he said. "I was twenty," he continued, "and just beginning college. I was so full of myself! I had already decided I was going to heal the world of all its psychotic disorders and couldn't imagine what faith or religion could have to do with that. My parents had a small cabin not far from here and had gotten to know the Nazareth's somehow. Anyway, they kept carting me off to the church over there. On Saturdays! Well, the pastor at that time was a Dr. Sturbridge and he had a thing for Carl Jung, which caught my attention, and for the mystics, which intrigued me enough to start asking questions. I think the only one who could hang in there with all my questions and objections was Barb. So, we ended up discussing the sermons afterwards and before long, like you, I found her to be a very sensitive and persuasive guide. She helped me a long ways down my own spiritual path and right into those waters over there. She has so much to teach. Have you ever seen her library? I used to borrow books from her when I came home on vacation."

"May I join you?" Barb asked.

Dr. Samuelson rose and gave his seat to Barb.

"It's nice of you to join us, Stephen," she said patting him on the shoulder.

"Well, I had to welcome our new neighbor!" he said. "And I'm sorry we couldn't make the gathering last night. Our son came down just for the day, so we had him up for dinner."

"How is Patrick?" Barb inquired in a knowing way.

"Doing much better for the moment, thank you, though he's got a long way to go. He's going to give school another try in the fall. We'll see."

"Bless his heart," she said. "I hope things work out better for him this year."

"We all do," confirmed the doctor.

Tamara knew that look she saw on his face. The coloring of his aspect had changed, and the worry in his voice was too familiar for her not to know its origins. That wasn't the look of a therapist, but the look of a parent who had been harboring his own worries about his own child. Before Tamara was prepared for it, Dr. Samuelson looked into her eyes. His face bore the distress he carried for his son and she knew, in that instant, that she had never just been a patient of his, but that he, like Barb, had been carrying her in ways she never appreciated. And now the three of them were gathered by the waters of new life, each captured by the hope those ancient streams evoke for pilgrims in search of a way forward.

"We'll be praying for Patrick, Stephen," said Barb, and Tamara knew that 'we' was meant for her.

"Thank you, both of you. That means more than you can know," he whispered. "Now, if you two ladies will excuse me, I think I'll hike back up the hill. If you need anything, just call."

As he climbed the trail by the stream, the sounds of the water replaced the conversation and the two women relaxed into their silence.

"Oh," said Barb. "I nearly forgot. Your father called a few moments ago. That's what took me so long. He asked how you were doing."

Barb paused to consider her words. "I told him you had a very hard day."

Tamara looked at Barb, whose face was etched with concern. Then she looked down at the water.

"I told him how proud I am of you," Barb said. "And how well you are handling the challenges you are facing."

A long silence ensued as they each thought back over the morning.

"Betsy told me how much it meant to have you there when she had to put Sarah Bell down. With all the men around the place, she feels she needs to be strong, and she is. Betsy is a strong woman. But, she said she sensed a different kind of strength in you she needed just then. She said you were the Lord's servant in her life this morning."

Tamara didn't know what to do with that except to feel awkward and unworthy. If Betsy felt strength, she must have consumed all there was in Tamara, because all Tamara felt afterwards was depletion. The elation she experienced in that moment was short-lived, and she wasn't sure where those seeds of joy ended up being planted, but evidently not in her. She felt the day's strain in her mind, and nothing that had taken place since she came to this peaceful bench by the baptismal stream had brought her any relief.

The river flowed, the breezes sifted through the canopy above, and the holy danced among them. Tamara's ability to understand any of this was beyond her reach, but to be enveloped by such a mystery was having its effect. Words weren't nearly as important to her mind now as peace might be, but there was an agitation at work within her. What she heard inside herself was the cries of the little lambs, their squeals of disappointment at their mothers for denying them. She heard their expressions of anguish and the loss each lamb felt: disorientation, uncertainty, fear, abandonment. But she, their shepherd, knew better. They were simply being weaned. Their distress was a consequence of growing up, so their suffering also had meaning, even purpose, of which they weren't yet aware.

Tamara became acutely empathetic, and she felt a kinship with the lambs. No longer just their shepherd, she was also one among them, just as scared, just as lonely for her mother, just as hungry for the milk she supplied. She saw her own emptiness puddling up in Lanolander's eyes, reflected back to her as the lamb squealed for help and none could reach it.

"Are you getting hungry?" asked Barb.

Tamara wasn't ready to engage in conversation, so she said yes on impulse.

"Sit here as long as you like. I'll get dinner started, and it'll keep until you're ready." Barb rose and started off.

Tamara considered for only a moment just how silly she thought little Lanolander and Woolimittens were for not recognizing a good thing right in front of their faces, and for not following their new shepherd right into the creep.

"Coming," she said. "I want to help."

20

THE STING OF DEATH

THE NEXT FEW DAYS WERE all about Tamara finding the rhythm of the farm and her place in the web of interlacing relationships and responsibilities. With the sun came the fire in the stove, making the coffee, collecting the eggs, then morning prayer and breakfast. The lambs came next and the tending of the new shepherd along with them. The afternoon was for the garden and walks along the river. Dinner, and their evening reflections on the porch, gave them the opportunity to listen again to the pulse of God's creation and make slight adjustments for the day ahead.

With the new rhythm of Tamara's life came new and different struggles, all of which introduced her to fresh sensations of soul. Faith and prayer, the very topics she sought to master on her pilgrimage, were never the subject of outright instruction, but she found them becoming available to her, harvested, as it were, from the very soil of the life they were living together there in that little valley.

By Wednesday evening, Tamara and Barb could sit on their swing and watch the lambs by moonlight as they loitered around their stable. Later, with her bedroom window open, Tamara could hear them missing their mothers. Loneliness, long a familiar haunt of hers, was now a shared experience, and she couldn't sleep for worry about them. But, she thought, what a relief it was to be worried over something else for a change.

Thursday was as near perfect a day as any Tamara could remember having. Her lambs were acclimating well, and the garden was fully planted. Their evening on the porch was celebrational and Tamara sensed again the effervescence of joy, though her mind wouldn't allow her to trust it. Still, she climbed the steps with resolve to go to bed grateful. Slumber snuck up on Tamara as she listened for sounds of the lambs; the other evening noises, the frogs and crickets and the occasional owl, sung her to sleep.

Barb woke her up. Her voice was clear and angry. She was scolding someone, several people in fact, but there were no reciprocating voices.

Tamara crept back downstairs and listened.

Barb's words were forthright and stern but cracked repeatedly with apparent remorse. As Tamara stepped into the kitchen, Barb turned toward her, and Tamara took the brunt of Barb's rant.

"You were told NOT to go with him," said Barb, looking straight at Tamara. "And now look at where that's gotten you. And all of us. I've had it with you, Sally Anne. You really should be ashamed of yourself."

Though Barb spoke in Tamara's direction, her eyes weren't fixed upon Tamara but looked through her at the face she knew to belong to Barb's older sister.

Tamara didn't speak, but she watched Barb, knowing too well from her own experience that nothing she said to Barb would mean anything, and it might make Barb angrier. Tamara stepped back and gave her room, but Barb said nothing more.

"Barb," whispered Tamara. "It's okay. Come, sit down."

Tamara beckoned Barb to join her in front of the fireplace. She led Barb to her old wingback chair. Barb walked as if she didn't know the way. Once she was seated, Tamara reached in for the only connection she thought might work.

"Barb, I think we should pray. Will you pray for us?"

Barb sat quietly for a moment then gently took Tamara's hand.

"No, honey, I think you should."

Tamara was not prepared for that. Her face burned, and her mind was overwhelmed with doubt, but the sensations reminded her of being stranded in the middle of Park Avenue and triggered the one impulsive prayer she knew to be just what they required.

"Shepherd Jesus. Help us now. We need you." Tamara's prayer, just a few words separated by long pauses, was all she could muster. But the familiarity of it went deep, and she then knew the moment Barb had taught her to pray, several months ago, when their roles were reversed, and Tamara had just had the mental thrashing of her life. The old woman had ventured into Tamara's soul, and her soul had learned something new which lay dormant until now.

"Comfort us. Guide us. Tend your lambs." Short, impulsive petitions, stripped of any unnecessary verbiage, saturated in silence.

"And bless this new under-shepherd of yours," whispered Barb, whose grip on Tamara's hand was growing firm once again. She grabbed Tamara by the back of the neck and pulled her face close to her cheek.

"I'm so, so sorry," she said. "I think I was over tired and couldn't sleep. I woke you again. I'll finish up here and go back to bed, myself. Head on back upstairs. A farmer needs her sleep."

But Tamara didn't move. She looked into Barb's eyes, which glistened in the dim light. Apparently, the intensity of Tamara's gaze was too much for Barb, who looked down at her hands.

"Who is Thomas?" asked Tamara.

"What?" asked Barb, jolted by the question.

"Thomas. You were speaking his name when I came down the steps."

Barb looked away, wiped her eyes, then stood and walked into her bedroom. She came back with a framed photograph of a man wearing an Army uniform which she placed into Tamara's hands.

"Thomas Fletcher. We went to high-school together," she said. "He was several years ahead of me. We didn't fall in love until after we had graduated and both of us had gone on with our lives – but that's too long a story for tonight. That was during the war – World War two. Thomas was drafted into the Army. So, he decided we should marry before he shipped out, and I thought that was a grand idea. Well, you remember what a fool I told you I was back then! He was on a transport ship, on his way over, and they were attacked. All were lost. I didn't know, until shortly after that, that I was pregnant. Of course, he never knew."

"Reverend Toby," whispered Tamara.

"My mother helped me raise him. I wasn't fit to be much of a mother for a while, I'm afraid. But then she got sick, and she was sick for quite some time. I had to learn. Toby never was much for the farm. For a long time, he wanted to go complete his father's adventures and talked about enlisting in the service. But then, he heard another calling. It took him a while but..."

Barb was halted by a loud clattering in the stable and the squeals of lambs. Tamara's heart roared after them. Every one of her faculties came alert to the dangers that the little lambs might be facing.

"Granthyrs," she muttered, then looked at Barb to see if there might be guidance forthcoming, but Barb looked as stunned as Tamara was.

"Could be a coyote," said Barb.

Tamara didn't need to think this through. She had already rehearsed it again and again every time she ruminated on her dream of the granthyr attack in the barnyard. She pulled on her boots, grabbed a fire-log, and headed for the door. Barb called after her, but Tamara didn't hear, or care.

As Tamara passed by the gate to the garden she discarded the log for the hoe leaning against the fence, then she entered the pasture and headed for the stable. Two lambs ran free from the stable to join four others waiting in the yard, but one still inside was in severe distress. It was dark, and she didn't want to corner something that might attack her, so she whacked the side of the stable with her hoe which stilled the tumult for only a moment. She held the hoe in front of her as she entered the stable and saw something gray, about the size of a dog, crouched over the lamb in the middle of the stable. Tamara held out the hoe like a lance as she circled the animal. Then, she swung the hoe and connected with its head. It growled and shied from her, then it ran from the stable as Tamara charged toward it again.

The little lamb, however, was dead. Lanolander's neck was matted with blood. Tamara dropped to her knees to see if there was any life in it. Only the lingering warmth of the little creature, so well insulated by its immature coating of wool, gave evidence that life had thrived there just moments ago.

Tamara buried her face in its side and screamed. She rolled over onto the ground with it, covered her face with her hands, and curled into as tight a ball as she could. Waves of remorse coursed through her and she loathed herself for the loss of the lamb. Two deaths in one week, and one of them belonged to her, but both had reamed out her soul and left her in a vicious desolation. This was hers, and it was not a delusion, it was much worse. From this there would be no waking. She could not sketch this image to exorcise it out of her head.

She felt a hand on her shoulder, but she was not ready to face anyone. She was ashamed to look at Barb, who was now gently shaking her and speaking her name, yet that only deepened Tamara's agitation and remorse.

Tamara grabbed fist-fulls of her hair and began wrenching at her scalp, but that didn't hurt enough, so she dug her fingernails into her cheeks. Her hands were wrenched from her face, so she thrashed with every other part of her body. But Barb held on and rode the thrashing until Tamara stopped fighting. All her vital internal resources seemed to expire beneath Barb's weight. Tamara was gasping for air, heaving in vast sums of oxygen to fuel her sorrow which now silently trembled within her.

When Tamara's sobbing ebbed, she freed herself from Barb and went in search of the other lambs. As she called their names and sought to reassure them, they answered and followed her back into the stable. There, Tamara sat down, her back against the wall, with the hoe laid by her side. She refused to go back in to the house.

Barb left, then returned a few minutes later with a picnic blanket, a large woolen afghan, and an old towel. Barb covered Lanolander with the towel, spread the blanket for them to sit on, then wrapped the afghan around them.

In silence, they dozed off and on as Tamara watched over her sheep.

As the day dawned and Tamara stirred fully awake, she saw the little bundle a few feet away. She wished for the daylight to cleanse the image from her mind but knew too well how real it was. She wanted to approach it, but she was too numb to act.

Then, Tamara saw Betsy walking up the drive and wanted to hide. She felt raw and angry at herself, and she dreaded seeing the woman who had so graciously taken such a chance on her. But Betsy was on her way to the stable with Barb.

"God bless her," said Betsy, as they stepped through the door.

Tamara had turned her back to them, and she didn't want to turn around.

Betsy knelt down, laid her arm around the young woman, and pressed her cheek against Tamara's, but she had mercy enough not to say anything.

"I'm sorry," whispered Tamara. Her face was wet, and her eyes were still red. She became rigid at Betsy's touch, but Betsy didn't take the cue to cut her lose.

"I'm very proud of you, young lady," said Betsy, as she squeezed even tighter. "But you are lucky not to have been attacked yourself. So, we're going to clean out a few of the stalls in the barn, and I'm going to send Earl over to put some gates across them, so your lambs can spend their nights inside for all our sakes.

"First, though, we're going to bury your lamb, then we're going to walk the fence line again to see if we can figure out how that coyote got in here. Okay?"

Betsy wrapped Lanolander in the towel and handed the lamb to Tamara, who wasn't given the option of holding it. Barb went for a shovel.

A simple service, with prayer offered by Betsy for the goodness of God and the short but good life of the lamb, was held by an old apple tree in the corner of the pasture.

The walk around the perimeter revealed a shallow dip in the ground, masked by the tall grass, that bore evidence of possible entry. Betsy tied her bandanna to the fence to mark the spot and told Tamara how she could repair that later.

They explored the barn and assessed the possibilities for the lambs, then they cleaned out two stalls that could be converted into pens for the sheep. The overhead tracks for the large sliding barn doors, however, were quite sluggish. Tamara volunteered to climb the ladder to oil them.

"Now," Betsy instructed her, "you can lead them in every evening and secure them. Then, you have to turn them over to God for the night and ask him to keep them safe. You can't spend the whole night worrying over them."

Tamara spent the rest of the afternoon filling in the low place beneath the fence, spreading fresh hay in the stalls, and introducing the lambs to their new enclosure. She gave them an extra measure of grain to help them feel safe in their new home.

Tamara slid the great barn door shut and turned toward Barb's house. The day's work had given her focus, but as she made her way toward the porch her insides began to tremble again. Lanolander's body lay prostrate across her mind, and the image of him lying deep in the earth, at the bottom of the hole they had dug, left her feeling desolate. She hurt for the loneliness of the little lamb, barely weaned from its mother, then failed by the one who had promised to keep it safe. Tamara had not been able to eat much all day, so she was feeling depleted physically but wasn't sure she would eat dinner.

Tamara turned and looked upward toward the mountain ridge. The last traces of color from the sunset had faded. Gray now shrouded the valley and cast a veil over her heart. The little bare patch of earth by the apple tree stoked her grief and ignited new flames of self-loathing within her.

Barb watched Tamara from the porch but waited patiently for the young woman to find her way in. There was no use rushing this, and no point in trying to make it go away.

Tamara ate little and said she would prefer to go to her room instead of sit on the porch after dinner. She hoped to sleep since she had so little the night before but knew that wasn't likely. With each step up the stairs, she accused herself again for endangering her lambs. Were they safe? She thought they were last night. And could she trust Jesus to watch over them? What kind of a shepherd was he, really?

Tamara sat at her desk and watched the last of the light leave the valley, then she opened the illustrated New Testament her mother had given her. She turned the pages to find the shepherds with their sheep the night baby Jesus was born, and it wasn't lost to her that the baby was every bit as vulnerable as the lambs were. And while Jesus was safe that night, surrounded by onlookers watching out for him – even angels – the granthyrs would one day win. How is it, she wondered, that Jesus could be confused with God? And why should she seek the counsel and guidance of a shepherd who, in the end, wound up little better than Lanolander?

She turned the page, then another. A rugged hermit-like man was standing with two men, and the hermit was pointing to another walking by. The caption read: "Behold, the lamb of God, who takes away the sins of the world." John the Baptist, explained the text, was directing his disciples toward Jesus.

Tamara's head was hurting too much to sort out the mystery that the Shepherd was also a lamb who could take away sins. She closed the book, but the images of his crucifixion were now forcing their way into her mind, and she rejected the impulse to look at those paintings.

The memory of her bloodied lamb was disemboweling her soul all over again, and the temptation to do herself harm was mounting within her to punish herself and to hurt on behalf of the lamb who should still be alive. Her mind became inflamed, and she knew Thorafura was close by. The seething, slender wraith that haunted her psyche promised never to leave her alone, and tonight the serpent had come and brought the granthyrs with her.

Tamara turned through the pages in search of Jesus' agony. She had promised not to hurt herself, physically, so now she sought to inflict emotional pain upon herself. She wanted to stare into Jesus' eyes as he suffered, to feel the cruelty launched against him, and to claim that ridicule in herself. If Betsy wouldn't shame her, then let the crowds that shamed Jesus inflict their rightful disdain upon her. She deserved every bit of it.

Holes, savagely punctured in Jesus' flesh, poured fresh blood upon Tamara's perforated psyche. She knew how those thorns felt as shards of hatred tore at her scalp and pierced deeply into her mind.

But as she stared and invited the pain that she saw depicted so ferociously on the page, what she received instead was a deepening loneliness. The anger toward herself ran steadily out of steam as a cancerous sense of alienation began to eat through her soul. As alone as Jesus was when he died, so alone did she feel as she watched him. She envied the death that would soon relieve him, and when she turned the page, that is what she saw. Still rendered in somber shades, there was a break in the clouds and a ray of light was shining upon a man who was now still. His head rested against his chest, his eyes were closed, his body was relaxed.

Tamara's loneliness became insufferable. She closed her book, turned out her light, tip-toed down the stairs and out into the night.

21

THE LAMB OF GOD

WHEN BARB CAME INTO THE kitchen Saturday morning, there was no fire, no coffee, no eggs, and when she tapped lightly on Tamara's door, there was no Tamara. The house was empty of her.

Barb stepped onto the porch and scanned the fields. By the old apple tree knelt Tamara, keeping vigil.

Barb dressed quickly and walked quietly through the pasture. She knelt beside her young friend. There was hay in Tamara's hair, and she was shivering from the morning air, so Barb came close and put her arm around Tamara's shoulder.

"Tell me how I can help," said Barb, whose tone was commanding. She wasn't speaking out of sympathy. The old, practical farmer in her knew that problems were for solving, and this was one area for which her life had prepared her.

But Tamara only shivered and stared at the lamb's grave.

"It's time to let the lambs into the pasture so they can have their breakfast," said Barb, "and then it will be time for ours. I'll go and get the eggs while you tend the sheep. Do you hear me?"

Tamara nodded and slowly climbed to her feet. As out of step as her life had become, it would be the rhythm of the farm that would help reset her pace. The act of duty was momentarily cleansing. She had developed a routine, and her routine began to govern her mind once again. To see the lambs grazing in the morning light gave her some solace from the horrid images that haunted her all night. She watched for a while, then she went inside.

Barb was finishing her preparations. The table was set, and beside her place lay her opened Bible.

"Since we missed our morning prayer, I thought I'd read a portion of Psalm 103 as part of our blessing:

Bless the LORD, O my soul:
and all that is within me, bless his holy name.
Bless the LORD, O my soul, and forget not all his benefits:
Who forgives all your sins; who heals all your diseases;
Who redeems your life from destruction;
who crowns you with loving-kindness and tender mercies;
Who satisfies your mouth with good things;
so that your youth is renewed like the eagle's.

Tamara scarcely heard Barb's prayer. Her mind had latched onto several phrases from the psalm which lay at the heart of her emotional pain and spiritual confusion.

Barb saw Tamara's concentration furrowed in her brow.

"What is it, Tamara? What is on your mind?" Barb's queries were spoken in earnest. "I can tell God is working overtime in you right now. I wonder if you can tell me what he's doing?" Again, these were not the gentle words of a supportive friend, but those of a woman now determined to go to work in Tamara's soul. If she was nothing else, Barb was a gifted spiritual guide and had honed her ministry over years of tending cattle and caring for the souls of her Sabbath School ladies, not to mention supplementing all that was lacking in her son's seminary education.

Tamara wasn't used to such blunt commands to reveal herself. Dr. Samuelson had therapeutic tactics which Tamara had deciphered long ago and learned to navigate, but Barb's straightforward, all-farmer, no-nonsense way about her struck a new chord in Tamara, to which her spirit responded with mounting confidence.

"Sin," whispered Tamara. "Have I …?" asked Tamara. She wasn't sure how to frame her question, or even knew all that the word sin meant. But she knew that her neglect hurt God's creature and must have angered God, made Barb ashamed of her, and damaged Betsy's faith in her. So much was severed within her, and her desolation confirmed just how far from God she must be. So, she had no sense that God could be doing anything within her, save punishment.

Barb prayed quietly for inspiration then said, "Yes. You sinned. Truth is, Tamara, sin infects all that we do. And where your lamb is concerned, I could try to reassure you that it wasn't your fault, or that you just made a mistake, but it's not that simple, is it? You wouldn't believe me. So, let's be honest about it."

Barb's words were not harsh or filled with judgment as Tamara's self-inflicted doubt felt she deserved, but they were saturated with the tones of her love-born wisdom. Tamara leaned into what Barb was saying and listened for the truth meant for her.

"And you sinned, I think, not because the coyote snuck in and killed the lamb you were responsible for, but because you thought it was all up to you, that you were totally responsible for the life of the lamb and that you could take all the blame. God doesn't give us that much power over life and death. God created the coyote to hunt, and he created lambs for wool and for food. He made one aggressive, the other, passive. One is ferocious, the other is gentle. Now, because God made the lamb gentle, he also gave the lambs their shepherd to watch over them, feed them, and keep them safe. But when we fail, as we so often do, he promises to forgive us. The Shepherd who watches over us is also the shepherd who looks after our loneliness and grief. He pardons us when we go astray so we can return to our work in his pastures."

"John the Baptist said, 'Behold the lamb of God who takes away the sins of the world," whispered Tamara.

"That's right," confirmed Barb.

"How is the powerful shepherd also such a feeble lamb? And how can the Shepherd forgive us if he is dead?"

The question jolted Barb, and it led her into that territory where her practiced, church-school theology always ran smack into a wall of utter mystery. But as she stared at her young friend, she saw new light under her own veil of uncertainty.

"Why are you feeling so horrible over the death of one little lamb?" asked Barb, but the question was more rhetorical than a request for a response. "Think about that for a moment. Betsy told me how personally you took on the task of weaning the lambs. She said she could sense how you felt for them as they struggled to make sense of their new lives. You took that very personally, didn't you?"

Tamara's face was darkening, and her eyes were growing red again. She nodded but couldn't look at Barb any longer.

"Yes, I know you did. And when they hurt, you hurt. When they cried, I think you were crying with them, am I right?"

Tears formed in Tamara's eyes.

"You became a better shepherd because you couldn't help identifying with the lambs," continued Barb. "The other night, you were prepared to do anything for the sake of your lambs."

"A shepherd lays down her life for the sheep," Tamara whispered.

"Yes. Jesus said that about himself, though, and it is his life that he has given so that we may live our lives in peace knowing that he has shouldered the greater burdens we would otherwise have to carry ourselves."

Tamara was getting lost, so Barb tempered the explanation she was hoping to offer.

"Think about it this way. Jesus loves you so much, and he takes it personally when you hurt. And when we sin, it also hurts him. But he feels that hurt in himself because he doesn't want anything to come between us. Sin saddens him, and he wants to heal us of it. When he died on the cross, much of the pain he felt was your pain, and all of the sin you will ever commit he died for, so that we can be forgiven. He died for us, so that we don't have to do all that dying all by ourselves."

"No, he did not," countered Tamara who was acutely aware of the suffering still suffocating her, and of the sin, her sin which caused the death of the lamb, a death which she has died over and over within herself.

"And how does any of that matter if Jesus is dead?" Tamara shouted, rising to her feet. Images of the crucifixion slashed through her head. And little Lanolander was still just as dead because Tamara had not trusted Jesus to shepherd them but thought she could meet all the lamb's needs by herself.

"Tamara, honey. That's not the end of the story," said Barb, who realized some of the blockages within Tamara's faith that would have to be addressed if she were to see beyond this.

"The cross was not the end of the story," Barb said softly. "That's not the end, at all." As urgently as the rest of the story needed to be told, however, Barb intuited that her young disciple was experiencing theological overload and more information might not be what is required. Later, Tamara would be able to absorb the resurrection, ascension, and reign of Christ. But not now.

Barb simply said: "Death was not strong enough to hold Jesus for long." She let those words resonate for a while between them, and she listened afresh to them again, herself. Then she whispered, "And your sin is not hateful enough to keep him from forgiving you. Jesus wants to forgive you. You should let him."

Tamara walked toward the stairs.

"Tamara," said Barb, halting her. "Worship starts in a little over an hour, and I am planning to go. I would completely understand if you didn't feel like going, but I also want you to know how glad I would be if you came."

Tamara nodded her affirmation of the invitation but didn't commit herself one way or the other.

"I'll leave around 9:30, so if you want to walk over with me, just meet me down here, otherwise, I'll see you at lunchtime. Okay?"

Okay, nodded Tamara.

Tamara climbed the stairs and laid down on her bed. Her body was exhausted, but her mind was agitated and wouldn't release her.

Not the end of the story, she heard Barb say again. She reached for her illustrated Bible, which was still opened to the dead Jesus now at peace, though the cruelty of his death lingered in the open wounds throughout his body.

Tamara turned the page. There were several paintings, rendered in deep shadow, of women visibly grieving the loss of their loved one. Then, a painting of women on their way somewhere bearing lanterns and jars of something. The caption said they were going to Jesus' tomb to anoint his body with oils and spices. On the following page, they stood bereft, at the tomb, with a massive stone blocking their entrance.

Their pain made perfect sense to Tamara. She had wanted to clean the blood off Lanolander before burying him. Barb and Betsy were eager to do their duty to bury the lamb, but little more. Tamara would have soothed him longer hoping to convey into its dead psyche a reassurance that it wasn't alone or forgotten. But she had had to drop the lamb, rather abruptly, into the hole then cover it with dirt. So, she knew the impulse that drove the women to go to Jesus' tomb. She had joined them in spirit and stood with them in their grief as she lingered at Lanolander's grave, yet she too was prevented from seeing the lamb by two feet of soil.

Tamara heard Barb downstairs and knew it was time for her to go, but her head thundered from her sleepless night and the mysteries at work in her. She did not feel right about carrying her doubts through the door of the church, and she couldn't cope with all the new faces and hands that would need shaking.

Tamara heard the door close, and her heart hurt for the disappointment Barb must feel towards her. She knew she should try to sleep a bit, but that was beyond her now. Perhaps, she could just walk down to the river, sit by herself for a while, and let the sound of the water do what it does best.

Her body refused to follow her desire, however. The pain in her mind had sapped her strength, so she relented and simply lay still. Her thoughts became fluid and wouldn't meld though one stream of awareness kept delivering a question to her mind. How does the story of Jesus' life end if not with his death? She had not looked any further since it didn't make any sense for her to do so. The pictures just kept delivering up evidence of death and all its aftermath. She had enough of that on her own.

But the question persisted, so Tamara turned the page, and there was an eruption of light. The massive stone that prevented the women from entering was now rolled away, and the figures were bathed in a brilliance which emerged from the tomb. Then, a parade of canvasses showed Jesus saturated with glory, standing before the tomb as all who watched were now huddled in fear or adoration. In most of the pictures,

Jesus' arms were raised in triumph, and his eyes were fixed on heaven. In some paintings, there were angels hovering in the glow that Jesus cast from himself. His wounds, his gaping bleeding wounds, however, were still just as visible, though the rest of him defied the reality that he had been so savagely killed.

Tamara' mind collapsed in on itself. Already weary, her sense of reality wouldn't allow for what she was seeing. Her father's skepticism was operating at full throttle despite her desire to accept what she knew he had so firmly rejected.

Tired as she was, the conflict raging within her brought her to her feet and she paced the length and width of her room, but the room wasn't large enough to contain her agitation.

Tamara started for the door, and as she opened it, she glanced at the photo of her dad's Aunt Tamara. Saint Tamara, her father had called her. She, evidently, had believed. And Barb believed. Betsy believed. Three strong women whose horse sense Tamara would never question held to a faith that drove them, completed them, and seemed to satisfy them when nothing else on earth possibly could. Such a hope could not be satisfied by one who had simply died. Where would be the promise in such cruelty if it wasn't answered by God with something new beyond the dying?

Tamara found herself on another sort of precipice looking out over an expanse of endless brilliance. If Jesus were not dead, then what other boundaries had he surpassed? What other impossibilities had he overcome? What darknesses had he fathomed so he could bring light where it once refused to shine? Into whose graves could he descend, or whose hells could he plumb? Was he, even now, comforting Lanolander with his Shepherding presence? Her heart, inexplicably, told her, yes.

By the time Tamara had walked to the church the service had started, and the congregation was at prayer. A kindly lady handed her a folded piece of paper with the picture of the church on the cover and a lot of words printed on the inside. The lady asked Tamara to wait just a moment, and when they started singing, she could go in. As the organ introduced the hymn, the lady escorted Tamara to a seat near the back.

At the other end of the bench, near the wall, sat Tinder. He looked briefly at Tamara then looked away.

Tamara was lost, however, and had no conception of what was going on, so she simply listened to a rather triumphant song about crowning Jesus lord of all. Several others, like her, weren't singing or even pretending to try. A few, like Tinder, looked miles away. But there was a group of ladies on either side of the aisle, toward the front, whose voices were clear and joyful. Among them, she identified most of the guests from their dinner her first night in town.

Tobias, standing in the front facing the congregation, saw Tamara come in. An instantaneous expression of gladness lept to his face and it embarrassed her.

Following the song, Reverend Toby opened his Bible, and read a story of Jesus casting out an unclean spirit from a man in a setting much like their own, a place of worship.

Toby invited everyone there to name their demons and to identify what they would ask Jesus to cast out of them. What had they brought into worship they wanted to leave there after Jesus had freed them?

Tamara felt he had nailed her to her seat, and she sensed her insides on full display for everyone there to see. She could name a great many of her demons, though most of them were faceless, shameless, and had personalities that never coalesced into any identifiable form. Thorafura and the granthyrs, however, lept foremost to mind as Toby probed the quarries of her madness. She resented him for prying so deep inside her, and if she could have extracted herself from there that moment, she would have. But in the silences Toby gave them for pondering, Tamara noticed that his words reverberate amongst them all.

Tamara witnessed affirmation in many of those around her, some of them were in tears, others nodding their assent to what he was saying to them. He was speaking to each person in the room, and each person there, in some fashion, was confessing their need. She glanced over at Tinder who was enthralled by Toby's voice. There was no movement in Tinder's face, but his eyes conveyed he wanted terribly what Toby said Jesus could offer him. The same sense of familiarity and intimacy, which Tamara had felt at the dinner table when so many of them had come to meet her, she felt again as these people had let down all pretense and had come before God in their need.

Then, Tamara heard what she sensed must be the end of the story. Toby explained that while this was Jesus' first public healing, it certainly wasn't his last, and that all of Jesus' miracles allowed us the hope of such healing for ourselves, possibly now, but if not, then certainly on the day of his appearing, when all our graves would be opened and every malady, every sadness, every injustice would be swept from the earth. Christ's own would rise up to greet him, be healed of their death, and serve by his side forever more. Either way, we wait in faith, he said, and in that faith, we know we are healed of what is most harmful, our alienation from God. Reunited with God, we are given what is most needful, his compassion and care. For with God sustaining us, the insurmountable can be overcome, the grief can be weathered, the illness can be accepted, and even death can be endured, since death will never again have the final say now that Jesus lives and reigns over all creation as King of kings, Lord of lords, and our Prince of peace.

"That," said Tobias, "is the good news of the Gospel. Let all who believe in it say, Amen."

And all said "Amen," loudly, and joyously.

"I invite you to accept the grace of the Lord Jesus," Tobias then said. "Should you wish to follow him in faith and baptism, then I invite you to come forward as we sing or speak with me following the worship."

Tamara ceased to breath and wondered if he really meant for her to walk down that center aisle in front of everyone and openly acknowledge what her heart has been driving her to do for months now. She opted for the second choice, and decided she would speak to him, if not today, then soon.

22

THE WORK OF THE SABBATH

"NORA ASKED ME IF YOU would like to go riding this afternoon," said Barb as they left the church and walked back to
the house. I told her I would ask you, but I said the lambs have been
keeping you up and that you might need to rest, which I think would
be a very good idea."

Tamara nodded that she agreed, but then asked, "Don't we need
to finish staking the garden?" That task had been started, but it was
repeatedly interrupted by other matters.

"Not today. Today is the Sabbath, a day of reflection and rest,"
explained Barb.

"I thought churches meet on Sundays," observed Tamara.

"True. That's true. Every other church around here does. And promise me you won't say anything to Tobias, but I think they're right. But
our people have been Seventh Day Baptists for generations. Remember,
after the six days on which God created the earth God rested, and then
he commanded his people to rest with him. So, we do."

"Why do other churches worship on Sunday, then?" asked Tamara.

"Sunday is the first day of the week, and on the first day God said,
'Let there be light,' then also on the first day Jesus rose from the dead."

Tamara saw the light from the paintings flash in her mind, and Jesus'
triumphant presence before the mouth of the tomb lit up before her.

"That's also when Jesus sent the Holy Spirit on the day of Pentecost,"
continued Barb.

Tamara hadn't gotten that far in the story yet, and she decided not
to get in to it now. She had more than enough to absorb for one day.

So, rest and reflection sounded perfect to her. After lunch she excused herself and said she wanted to walk down to the stream.

"Do you want to go alone?" asked Barb.

Tamara hesitated then nodded that she did.

Barb smiled and honored Tamara's honesty with a hug and her blessing.

Tamara scanned the barnyard on her way to the river and was halted by several things that caught her attention. She saw tools in disrepair, rot in the barn boards, fences bordering other pastures that needed mending. The chicken-coop looked particularly decrepit given the amount of use that one working part of the farm endured. It needed cleaning in an awful way. She stepped into the barn to find a shovel but decided to honor their mandate for the afternoon: rest and reflection.

She took those new concerns to the little bench by the stream where she considered just how full her life had become with other people's troubles and other creature's needs. Her tendency was to remain burrowed in her own anxieties, but she had been placed in circumstances that didn't allow her to remain there for long. She couldn't think of a time when she felt she was needed around her home. And, she couldn't recall a time when she was challenged to care for anything, or anyone, beyond her own critical needs. The farm regimen was exhausting her, but it was cleansing, and she wanted to lean in to those new sensations.

The stream helped to relax Tamara's mind and encouraged it to wander. She had not allowed herself to think too much about those strange, late night episodes with Barb, but those events resurfaced and linked themselves to several inquiries concerning Barb's wellbeing. She only now recalled the brief exchange she had with Betsy as they walked the fence-row together after Lanolander died. Tamara had been in such a daze that Betsy's comment didn't even register, but now it replayed vividly in Tamara's mind.

"My grandma's been worried about Barb," Betsy had said. "How does she seem to you?" It was the same question Dr. Samuelson put to Tamara. But Betsy had gone further. Pamela felt Barb had been increasingly distracted lately, even disoriented, and was concerned enough to tell Tobias on more than one occasion.

Tamara had brushed off Betsy's observation and didn't let it interfere with her own self-reproach as they charged back in from the field to clean out the barn stalls. But now, it moved to the front of her mind, and it gave Tamara considerable concern. She knew only of her own brand of mental torment, but she had seen vivid traces of it at work in Barb. Had Tamara's behavior, or moods, triggered those episodes? she wondered. Had Barb taken on more worry than she could contend with?

Tamara listened to the gurgles of the stream and heeded the stirrings of her soul. She closed her eyes and saw her Shepherd, now bathed in brilliance standing on the other side of hell, and she decided that if he could find his way through death, then he was capable of leading them through life, no matter how hellish it became.

When Tamara walked back up the path to the house, Barb was sitting on the porch. Tamara sat down beside her.

"Guess who called while you were out," said Barb.

"Dad?" said Tamara.

"Close."

"Mom? Is she home?"

"She asked that you call when you can," affirmed Barb.

Tamara retrieved her phone from her room and had to walk up toward the General before she got enough signal to call home.

Tamara refrained from offering details about the challenges she had faced but assured her mom that she was where she needed to be and that, no, she was in no hurry to come home.

Aimee took that all in, then she said, "I can't wait to show you some of the drawings I did. I didn't have much time, so they're just thumbnail sketches, but I am so grateful for your encouragement."

Then, after a lengthy pause, Aimee continued with a great deal of hesitation which placed Tamara on alert: "I talked with Barb a little while ago. She told me how much it has meant to her to have you with her and, if you wanted to stay longer, then, well..." Aimee struggled to finish that sentence, so she started a fresh one: "I have a lot I want to discuss with you, Tamara. Brussels gave me a lot of time to think."

Aimee's long pauses betrayed the struggle she was having articulating what was on her mind.

"I shared a few things with Barb," Aimee continued, "and she wondered if your dad and I would like to come up this week. Unfortunately, your dad can't get away until the weekend, but I could come up in the meantime. How would you feel about that?"

Tamara felt suddenly crowded and her initial impulse, as usual, was to push her mom out of her experiences. But her second impulse felt more genuine which was to explain the responsibilities she had taken on, and that if her mom wanted to help, she thought that would be great.

"Or," said Tamara, acting on a third impulse. "You could spend some time drawing around the farm."

"I thought we'd eat out here on the porch," said Barb, as she set the table for dinner. Then, after she had offered their blessing for the meal, she asked: "Is your mom going to visit us?"

"She said you invited her," said Tamara, looking down at her plate.

"I did. Perhaps I should have discussed it with you first," said Barb, after studying Tamara's face.

Tamara shrugged. "No. It's okay. I think she will really love it here." Tamara brightened slightly as she scanned the grounds now seeing them as she hoped her mom would.

"Did she say when she'd like to come?" queried Barb.

But Tamara kept her focus on the pasture and tried to let this line of conversation die.

"How about a horse ride tomorrow?" asked Barb, after a long pause. "Nora called to see how you were doing, and we both agreed that a ride through the valley was long overdue if you are going to make the most of your time here. And, it might re-charge your spirits."

Tamara recalled how eager she was to be back on a horse and renew those sensations she felt on her birthday, and then she thought that would be something else she and her mother could do when she came.

"What time?" asked Tamara, also considering the chores she had assigned herself for the next day.

"Well, let's think this through. Betsy said she wanted to come visit in the morning, and I know you have your lambing chores to tend to, so if we ate an early lunch we could go over in the afternoon. Would that work?"

"The chicken coop needs cleaning, and I want to arrange the barn a little better," said Tamara, as much to herself, as to inform Barb.

"Goodness!" exclaimed Barb. "In another week we won't recognize the place," she chuckled. "You were supposed to be resting," she said good naturedly, as she nudged Tamara.

"And reflecting," responded Tamara.

"Yes, you're right, we do need to tend those things, and so many of them are long overdue." Barb began to withdraw into her own regrets as she tried to resist scanning the barnyard but couldn't.

"Farm work works best when it is purposeful and planned," said Barb. So, let's do this. After you tend your lambs in the morning, let's do a survey of what we'd like to do. We'll make a list of supplies we need and plan them into our days for the coming week, okay?"

Tamara nodded.

"Now,' said Barb, "let's set aside our reflections on all the work there is to do and spend these next few moments reflecting on what an extraordinary artist God is to be painting such glorious sunset for us to enjoy."

23

FINDING HOME

ON SUNDAY MORNING, BETSY FOUND Tamara out in the field with her lambs.

"I've got some good news for you," announced Betsy, "but it comes with a little bad news mixed with it, I'm afraid. Earl and I have been talking about expanding the flock, so the good news is that we're going to be keeping most all of the lambs. The bad news is that I already promised one of them to an old friend. He and his wife will be celebrating their fiftieth wedding anniversary later this year and I had promised him one of the lambs for their party."

Betsy spoke matter-of-factly and gave Tamara plenty of room, but the reaction was not as bad as Betsy had thought it might be.

Tamara fell into deep thought as they strolled through the fields, and her face told Betsy she was feeling relieved for most of the flock, but then the inevitable darkness settled over Tamara's brow.

"How do we choose?" asked Tamara, who choked a little as she spoke.

Betsy notice Tamara's body brace for the answer as she halted and looked over at the tiny flock.

"You have four females over there," said Betsy, and we'll keep all of those. We only need one new ram, and he should be the strongest. So, by process of elimination..."

"Gentleomen," whispered Tamara, whose face became solemn, but remained strong.

"When?" she asked.

"Not until the fall, but I felt it right to let you know."

Tamara nodded and said nothing more.

With her new riding boots on her feet, and her helmet under her arm, Tamara and Barb walked past the General then down Main Street a ways before turning into Nora Jakes's drive. The horses were in the small pasture behind the humble farm house. A small barn, closer in vintage to Betsy's than Barb's, was set off to the right.

Nora, a slight but vibrant woman, met them at the door and welcomed them in to her home. She was considerably younger than Barb, though not as young as Betsy, and Tamara wondered if all these women were without true age the way they addressed themselves to the life they led. For Nora, that was horses. She had eight, two of which belonged to her daughter. Her husband began raising them after he retired from cattle, but he died a few years later. Their daughter had taken over the operation, but then she went off to school to study nursing. Nora had sold one horse, and she was thinking about selling all but her daughter's now that it was just her looking after them.

Tamara found all that out as they strolled to the paddock and began getting the horses ready.

After Barb was confident Tamara was settled into good hands, she said she'd see Tamara when she got back home.

"Now, saddle up, and have a great time!" said Barb, as she turned toward the gate.

The horse Tamara was offered wasn't quite as tall as Flint, her mount in Central Park, so after some awkward trial and error and a bit of coaching by Nora, Tamara climbed up into the saddle on her own. Sarasota was its name, a reddish-brown horse with a little more spirit than Flint.

Nora led Tamara into a small oval pasture that had numerous short, free-standing fences and other obstacles built of white boards. She was brisk in her instructions. After explaining how to sit correctly in the saddle, Nora showed Tamara how to start, slow, and stop the horse, then turn it in one direction or the other. She asked Tamara to spend some time walking around the perimeter.

"Don't let her run in here," said Nora. "If she feels like she wants to take off, pull back slightly. She's pretty steady. So just walk her a bit. See if you can take her once around."

Sarasota's walk was a little fast for Tamara, but it was either that or stop, so Tamara held her breath a lot and spent most of her effort just holding on. When she got to the far end, the horse halted, and it took a bit of nudging and pulling on the reigns from Tamara to get the horse to turn and start back.

"Not bad," said Nora. Why don't you walk her around a bit more while I go get my horse ready."

Nora conveyed more confidence in Tamara than Tamara felt in herself, but Tamara's concentration was acute, and her respect for the massive creature tempered any impulse to let her mind wander. She leaned forward, stroked Sarasota's neck, then explained to her that they were going to walk all the way around again and come back without stopping this time. Once she felt she had made herself perfectly clear, Tamara nudged the horse forward. Perhaps, she thought, she wasn't clear enough. More nudging, then a bit swifter kick, caused Sarasota to leap forward into a trot, faster than Tamara had intended and far bouncier than she was able to contend with. She clutched the horn of her saddle but was bouncing fiercely and realized she needed to reign in with both hands as she approached the far fence much faster than she anticipated. With both hands on the reigns now, instead of pulling to a stop, she pulled to the left and leaned slightly into the turn. Sarasota made a nice broad arc, then she trotted toward where they began.

Tamara saw Nora, seated on her horse, watching from the other side of the gate and turned straight toward her.

"Nice work," said Nora as Tamara approached then came to a halt just inside the gate. "But you need to sit forward a little more, and don't squeeze with your knees. Pull in toward the horse with your feet."

Tamara's next turn around the paddock was slightly less painful, but Nora said it would take time and practice to smooth out her ride.

They let their horses walk out a small dirt road that led away from Main Street through a wooded grove behind Nora's home. This joined a well-traveled gravel road where they turned right. Nora gave Tamara another short primer on trotting, then she picked up the pace.

The road they were on took them along the back side of Betsy's farm. Nora turned into the lane that led them toward the barn from which Betsy was emerging with a large jug.

"Afternoon!" said Betsy. "Don't tell Earl you caught me robbing the dairy," she said to them. "Would you like a taste of homegrown milk?" she asked Tamara. "Fresh squeezed this morning."

Betsy fetched a mug from the barn.

"You look mighty sharp up in that saddle," Betsy said to Tamara, handing her the milk.

"We're off to see the lupines," said Nora.

"Been meaning to walk down there, myself," said Betsy. "You should take her out by way of the cemetery. I hear there are a few things still in bloom there, as well."

Tamara handed Betsy the mug.

"How's the hay holding out?" asked Betsy.

"I think we'll need some by Tuesday," said Tamara after doing a little calculation.

"I'll get some up there tomorrow," said Betsy as she headed toward the house with her milk jug.

Tamara and Nora turned their horses about and headed down the lane then onto the dirt road. Several yards later, Nora took them into a small grove of trees in the midst of which was a perfectly square stone enclosure, about thirty yards on a side. A wrought iron gate was set permanently open in the middle of one side. Throughout the area, several azaleas and a few rhododendrons were just past bloom, the evidence of which lay more around their feet than on their branches.

Nora dismounted and held Sarasota while Tamara did the same. Tamara's legs were tender beneath her; it was good to be on her feet after their trot.

Nora led Tamara through the gate and gave her a brief tour.

"Right up that little path is the church, so most of the folk buried here are families from the congregation. My family is right here, and over there are Barb's parents and grandparents. As they got closer to those headstones, Tamara saw a flat stone with a bronze plaque that read:

> Pvt. Thomas Fletcher
> April 13, 1923 - October 27, 1942
> U. S. Army, World War II
> Lost at sea.

By the plaque was posted a small American flag.

"Ready to go see the lupines?" asked Nora, as she watched Tamara begin to descend more deeply into herself.

But Tamara didn't hear her. She had been absorbed into the ancient atmosphere of this small space. The inscriptions carved in some of the stones bore witness to generations of life and loss, memory and hope. Love, even in death, characterized the eternal solitude marked out by each small plot governed by its headstone.

Tamara had never been in a cemetery, and her spirit was softened by the garden-like quality to its design and purpose. Rev. Toby had said Jesus would appear and open these graves. Did she believe that? She didn't know, but she saw that many of those lying there did, as their inscriptions bore witness to the hope they took with them to their graves. Tamara's own brushes with death gave her an affinity with those lying beneath the ground. At one time she might have felt envy, but on that day, with their horses tied to trees awaiting them, Tamara marked that she was glad to be alive.

Nora strolled quietly over and stood by Tamara as she read one of the older stones, a tall obelisk with a cross prominently engraved in the upper quarter.

"Reverend Jeremiah Stover. He was the founder of the church," said Nora. "This spot was once part of their family farm, all back over there and up that side of the mountain. Rev. Stover left the farm early in life to go to the mission field somewhere in Africa, but he had to come home due to illness. When he recovered, and the doctor told him he couldn't travel anymore, he looked around and saw this valley as his new mission field. He gathered some neighbors to start the church. His grandfather let them build a small meeting house then later deeded them the land for a new church; the one over there now."

Tamara had difficulty pulling herself away and knew she would need to return. She paused once more at the gate to look around.

"It's beautiful," said Tamara. "Thank you."

"Lupines?" prodded Nora.

"Lupines," affirmed Tamara.

They climbed into their saddles and walked the horses through the grove of trees until they met the road once more which led them into an open meadow that consisted of sparse bramble and small scrub bushes. The landscape was coarse, and at another time of the year it might look desolate and haunting, but at the onset of summer it was brilliant green, dotted with wildflowers. The road became pockmarked with holes and grew more rugged the deeper they went through the meadow.

Nora pointed toward the west. A doe and two young fawns were grazing by the edge of the forest. A little further, she halted her horse.

"The ground is a little rough, so let's go slow and keep our eyes open for anything that might trip us up."

The horses threaded their way along a narrow path through the thigh-deep thicket. Then, as they rounded a small grove of trees, they met a better trail that took them slightly upwards.

"If you ever want to walk here," explained Nora, "This little footpath will take you back by Betsy's farm."

They came to the crest of a hill, crossed over the ridge, and were overlooking another expanse of the valley. The brilliance of the pinks and purples that lay before them was stunning. Lupines, by the thousands, quilted the countryside. Tall, spikey flowers, as majestic as any Tamara had ever seen, ignited her senses with awe. A steady breeze kept the lupines dancing in waves that heightened the hypnotic sensation she felt as she gazed over the field.

Tamara had not been conscious of keeping a list of things she wanted to show her mother, but as she realized she had just added this view of the lupine meadow to that list she became mindful that something significant had shifted within her. Or, it had been shifting over the course of the week but was now firm. She had a life that was now her own. It was only a few days old, but it was hers. She would be sharing it with her mother, not as a tourist, but as her mother's host.

The people of this little town had made room for her, given her work to do, offered her a way of contributing to the community. And, she had begun reshaping her life with abilities that were foreign to her city-born existence. Most importantly, she recognized herself there. She saw herself belonging among these people who accepted her as someone with a reason for being, a purpose for existing.

Sarasota shifted her footing beneath her, and as Tamara adjusted her balance her impulse to reach down and stroke the horse's neck confirmed her musings. This is where horses belong, she thought, not in Central Park. Tamara scanned the bowl-shaped contours of the meadow, lifted her eyes to ridges that climbed high in the sky beyond them, and she felt at home.

"Tamara, honey," said Nora, siding her horse over to draw nearer. "Are you okay?"

Tamara nodded, as her eyes brimmed over. The complexity of her emotions would not let her settle into any particular attitude. As joyful as she intuited she should be, her ever-present low-grade depression always tempered her mood and rarely gave her permission to rise into spheres of gladness. But impressions of meaning moved her deeply, and as she discovered new regions of being within her, even pain-filled regions, she was compelled to draw out from them substance that might give her life significance. When she could let down her many barriers and finally invite someone inside, it reassured her that she was not alone which was a rare sensation. Even better, when she realized someone else had invited her into their life, as scary as her life was, and she could believe that her life might have meaning for them, then she became overwhelmed within and had a hard time withholding her tears.

In that moment, the beauty of the landscape before her reminded her of what she had given up trying to paint and had proposed to live. And, there she was, with yet another woman who had welcomed Tamara into her life, not because she was sick or in need, but because Barb had adopted her into this community. She felt herself deeply humbled by the grandeur all around her and rising up within.

Some loose ends to her mind-scattered life were finally merging within her, but too many remained frayed and disconnected. She was in the midst of a pilgrimage, she reminded herself, but she had considered that to be leading her toward baptism. Now, she sensed it was leading her home. Her soul had been telling her for months that home had to be somewhere else.

Home, she thought, as she remembered the little cemetery, is where you bury your loved ones and continue to live among them, feel they are near, and carry forward that life you inherited. She had nothing in New York City she wanted to carry forward. But here she had buried one she loved. And there were Lanolander's flock-mates, Barb's chickens, Sally Anne's memory, and the commitment Tobias should be able to make to the farm, but for some reason, he can't. In New York, all she had to carry forward was the daily slog of her solitude. Here, a community had given her purpose and had already entrusted her to fulfill it.

She felt at home, but she knew she wasn't there quite yet. So, as they slogged back through the thicket, Tamara knew it was time for a long talk with Barb.

As they came to the road and began their trot home, Nora said, "Now, let me show you something I think you'll enjoy even more; it's called, cantering."

After supper, Barb and Tamara took their dessert out to the porch and sat in the swing. Tamara wasn't sure how to broach the subject of where her home was meant to be, however. It felt too big and too sudden. So, she decided she should stick to her primary reason for coming to the farm in the first place, her spiritual pilgrimage.

"Should I talk to Pastor Toby about being baptized?"

Barb had sunk into her own ruminations, so it took a moment for the question to register.

"Say that again," said Barb, wanting to make sure she heard Tamara correctly.

As she repeated her question, it dawned upon Tamara that she had discussed baptism with her parents and with Dr. Samuelson, but amidst all that had overtaken them since she arrived, she had not mentioned to Barb the one prevailing purpose behind her pilgrimage to the farm.

"I've been thinking a lot about baptism since last time," said Tamara, visualizing once again the service she witnessed by the river a few months ago. "Yesterday, Pastor Toby said if anyone wanted to be baptized they should speak with him."

"I see," said Barb, with a faint smile. "Yes, that would be an excellent idea. He would be glad to discuss that with you. As would I, if you wanted to talk more about it now."

"Could I be baptized here?" asked Tamara.

"Oh, wouldn't that be wonderful!" exclaimed Barb, who then became a bit more thoughtful. "Truth is, honey, it would be best for you to be baptized in the church you plan to enter."

As Barb paused, the force of Tamara's unresolved questions of home paralyzed her with doubt over where she was meant to be.

"When a person is baptized," Barb continued, "they are baptized into the church, and we become part of Christ's family." Confusion was painted all over Tamara's face. "It is important to belong to a congregation where you can grow in your faith and serve in those ways Christ calls you to serve," said Barb, trying to be clear, though Tamara's composure became more doubtful.

"Christ?" asked Tamara, who had heard the word, but didn't understand its significance.

"Christ means, 'anointed one' in Greek, which was the language spoken then. In Hebrew, the word is messiah. For us it means that he is our savior and Lord. When a person comes to that point in their lives when they realize who Jesus is, and experiences his calling to follow in faith, then baptism becomes an important step.

"When you realized that you were in need of Jesus' help and you began to reach out to him, you were acting on a faith you probably didn't realize you had yet. Now that you are getting to know him as your shepherd and want to follow him, your baptism becomes a celebration of your new faith and a sign of your commitment to follow Jesus. Just as importantly, Tamara, baptism is God's sign of the promises he is making to you, to continue the grace now at work in you and guide you through his Spirit. It's like a pledge Christ is making – to keep you and preserve you as God's child, forever."

"So, I can only be baptized here if I'm going to live here," said Tamara, hoping to move the conversation in a direction that might open new possibilities for her future.

It was now Barb that looked conflicted and became introspective.

"Dr. Samuelson said he was baptized in the river," reflected Tamara.

"Stephen is a member of our church, that's true," confirmed Barb. "Of course, he lives in New York, but he and Shelly are often in town for the weekend, and he considers our church his spiritual home. They took over Stephen's parent's cabin down the road after his father died and vacationed there for a while, but I think they got tired of the maintenance, so they just use the lodges when they are available."

Tamara furrowed her brow, and Barb realized she had reached the end of her current usefulness in this matter.

"So, yes, I still think you should talk with Tobias. Who knows, honey, where the Lord is leading any of us these days!" said Barb, throwing up her arms and casting her eyes heavenward.

"In the meantime," Barb continued, resuming her more serious tone, "I am going to be praying about this and how we can prepare you for that moment. You are right to be considering it. If you like, I'll call Tobias in a little while and see when you can meet. Or, he'll be at the church tomorrow, you could just walk over."

As the swing set the pace of their reflections, Tamara tried to imagine being part of a church in the city and couldn't place herself there. Then, the images of Tonya from the rescue mission, the old man crossing the street, and the woman with her daughter begging for help tugged at her, and for the moment, she felt conflicted about where she belonged. She fought the sensations struggling within her as the images of the city triggered anxieties she knew she had come here to escape. What if she wasn't meant to escape them? What if following Shepherd Jesus meant following him back into the city?

Barb saw the consternation on Tamara's face, placed her hand on Tamara's, then she gave her hand a gentle squeeze.

"I have been watching the Lord do some wonderful work in you this week," said Barb. "I think the farm is agreeing with you, also."

But Tamara's mind was busy watching the old man cross mid-town traffic against the assaults of old age and impatient drivers, and she felt again the impulse to guide him across. Whatever following Shepherd Jesus might mean, she was now having her doubts. Managing her own assaults from Thorafura and her horde of granthyrs brought Tamara misery enough. Following Jesus into the misery of others was crippling her desire to follow him in baptism.

"You look frightened," said Barb. "What is it?"

Tamara shook her head and shrugged her shoulders.

"I don't know," said Tamara. "Maybe I'm not ready."

"Nobody is ever really ready," said Barb. "Baptism is like birth. You come to it new and inexperienced in the life that awaits you. There are some things you should understand about faith. You should be aware of the commitment Jesus wants you to make to him, but it's also important to trust that Jesus will prepare you, lead you, and support you in the life to which he calls you."

Barb paused, then she added: "I was scared to death of what Jesus had in store for me, what with my past and with the questions I carried into the waters with me. At first, I was afraid it might mean the mission field, somewhere far from home. But in the end, this is where Jesus wanted me to serve him, just as he might want you to serve him in your own neighborhood."

The suggestion re-confirmed for Tamara the dangers of saying yes to Jesus, and her eyes grew wide with the prospect. Her afternoon on the horse had persuaded her that she was now where home should be for her. But suddenly, she felt like an exile in both places, unsettled. She feared going home, and she worried that staying on the farm might be unfaithful if Jesus wanted her there, instead of here, in this valley, among these gracious people.

"My mother used to tell me," mused Barb, "'There are some frightening things you should run from, and there are some frightening things you should stand up to and defeat. Then, there are some frightening things you should let win.'"

As Tamara listened, she wondered if Barb had forgotten that she had told her that before. She looked at Barb. A distant expression of longing had appeared on her old face, as if the light within her had dimmed and she was searching for it someplace else. Tamara followed Barb into that memory.

"When did she say that?" asked Tamara.

"When did she say that?" repeated Barb, with little focus. "Just before I married Thomas," she reflected.

"You were afraid of marrying him?" asked Tamara.

"I was afraid of marriage. My parents, Sally Anne and Mark. It wasn't good…" Barb's voice became too quiet to be heard, then she slipped into silence altogether.

Those silences that speak more than they intend engulfed the two women, and Tamara didn't need to hear the rest in order to understand.

"I'm sorry, what were we talking about?" asked Barb.

"We were talking about baptism, then…"

"I was baptized just over there, in the river. I remember it like it was this morning." Barb's voice trailed off, then she became quiet again.

Tamara felt alone in the swing. Her emotional connection with Barb had been severed, and she experienced sensations of desolation instead. Barb's hand still rested on hers, but the grip had loosened, and Barb's attention had been drawn far, far away.

Tamara slipped her hand from underneath and rested it atop Barb's. She took hold of the old woman's hand and gripped it firmly. There was little response. Tamara wondered if Barb was now walking down the bank of the river for her baptism so long ago, chasing deer through the forest, or doing chores around the hen house with her mother as a younger woman. They shared a world, thought Tamara, in more ways than anyone else might appreciate, and Tamara had a strengthening sense that she understood what was going on in Barb's mind right now.

The swing had ceased its gentle movement, and the sun had now set beyond the far ridge. The breeze was a little cooler that evening, so Tamara suggested they go back inside, but Barb didn't answer her. She stepped inside, got Barb's woolen afghan, and wrapped it over Barb's shoulders.

'There are some frightening things you should let win,' Tamara heard Barb say again. Whether or not Barb forgot telling her, the words were well placed, all the same. Tomorrow, thought Tamara, after tending the lambs, she would walk over to Betsy's, then possibly go knock on the church door to see Rev. Toby.

24

QUESTIONS THAT NEED ANSWERS

EARLY MONDAY MORNING, AS THEY sat by the wood-stove finishing their morning prayer, Tamara felt her thoughts from the night before strengthen into resolve.

"After I finish with the lambs, I need to go over to Betsy's and help her load up some hay for them," said Tamara.

"She called last night to say she would be doing that right after lunch. But she didn't say she needed your help loading. Earl can help her do that."

"I'd like to, though," insisted Tamara.

"Shall we have lunch before, or after?" asked Barb. "I need to go over to the General for a few things."

"Do you want me to pick them up on my way back?" asked Tamara.

"Thank you, honey, but I've got some laundry to do and I need a few essentials before I can do much today, so I'll go a little later in the morning."

"Then let's have lunch after we get back with the hay. Is that okay?" said Tamara. "I may go for a walk after I feed the lambs."

"That sounds like a good way to spend your morning," affirmed Barb.

"Then, after lunch, I'll work on the hen-house," said Tamara.

Tamara spent the next hour roaming the pasture with her lambs, filling their crib with hay, cleaning out their stalls in the barn, and filling their water. She looked over the hen-house to see what would be involved with that and thought it would take several afternoons. It needed a thorough shoveling out, general cleaning, and the walls sorely needed scraping and painting.

Barb had left for the General, so Tamara cleaned up a little then headed out the lane toward Main Street. She walked in the direction of the church. As it came into view, she slowed her pace and considered what Barb had said about being baptized into the church. Could this be her church? Or, was it her church already? She could see a portion of the congregation in her mind and had spent much of her week with some of them. She had seen four of them be baptized, and she knew many of them had been praying for her.

Tamara walked around behind the church and found the little gravel path she assumed would take her to the cemetery. As she passed beneath the canopy of trees, and the sunlight became filtered and soft, she felt herself walking back in time. Seeing the dates and names of the generations lying there, she wondered what it must be like for those who still remembered the departed to approach the stone enclosure then pass into this old, old garden.

The only thing she could associate her sensations with was viewing the gallery of ancestors in her grandfather Baxter's home. Those old portraits, however, were far more intimidating than the earth and headstones she found herself among in the cemetery. Here, there were no facial expressions permanently cast for all to see freezing the viewer's remembrances. Instead, she sensed the wisps of ancestry, now refined of its permanent pain and remorse. Ancient loves and animosities, softened by the years, had settled among the azaleas that had also lost their blooms but not their vitality. Here, still, there was life pushing up from roots sunk deep in the soil of this valley, now branching out amongst the living, bearing fruit as these heirs of an ancient fortune faced the challenges that now beckoned their best.

Tamara felt that vitality of life in spite of the apparent evidence of so much death. If these people had produced the souls that now lived alongside her, then the pains they shared and the hopes they realized together had been the grist of something wondrously nourishing and good.

Tamara gazed long and hard at Barb's parents' marker and wondered how two people, so different in temperament, could have ever been married. But she felt grateful that they were and that such a crucible as their home had been had forged such a woman as Barb. She lingered by Thomas Fletcher's marker and found she had a piece of her mind she wanted to offer to him as well. She told him not to worry. Barb's going to be fine, she assured him.

"I promise."

Exiting the gate, she turned toward the grove of trees through which they walked their horses. She found she could follow their hoof marks out to the road, but where they turned right, she turned left toward Betsy's farm.

"My grandmother is afraid it's 'old-timer's' disease," said Betsy, as they leaned against the pasture fence. "That's her way of pronouncing Alzheimer's." She laid a hand on Tamara's shoulder as they walked in from the field to the barn where the hay was stored. They sat down on a couple of bales.

"My grandma has been seeing some of the same things in Barb," continued Betsy, "and she's spoken to Toby about it, so I think they all have their suspicions. They've tried to get Barb to go see her doctor, but of course Barb doesn't see what others see."

"But," continued Betsy, "my grandma said she feels Barb has greatly improved since you came. Maybe some of it is just living all by herself in that big old place with no help and companionship. A body's mind can get awful tired and dull when you're lonely and just going through the motions. But there's been a new spark to Barb lately, which I think you have a lot to do with."

Tamara had been worried that her moods and attitudes might have been taxing Barb.

"Do you feel okay being there with her?" asked Betsy, now cautioned by Tamara's facial expression.

Tamara nodded, but her face grew more serious.

"Is she okay with me there?" asked Tamara.

"Oh, honey. She's probably more than okay," Betsy reassured Tamara. "Tell you the truth, I think a lot of people around here are relieved you are with her. But if anything should really worry you, you need to tell one of us, okay?"

"Is there anything I should do?" asked Tamara.

"Pray for her," said Betsy. "And keep an eye on her. She is really enjoying having you here, so spend as much time with her as you can. She still wants to work – that's in her bones and blood – so don't hesitate to let her do whatever she wants to do. Keep her as active as she wants to be."

Tamara pictured the hen-house project waiting for her, which she had determined she would do by herself to save Barb the trouble. Acknowledging how beneficial the week's work had been to her own frame of mind, and considering how the same could be true for Barb, Tamara re-envisioned the project and nodded her affirmation. That made perfect sense. In fact, thought Tamara, she could do one better.

"Want some lunch?" asked Betsy, after they had loaded her truck with several bales of hay.

"Barb's waiting until we unload, then we were going to eat," explained Tamara.

"Well, I'm famished," said Betsy, "We got a very early start around here this morning, so do you mind if I grab a bite first?"

Tamara shook her head. "No. I'll walk home. There's something I want to do on the way."

Tamara left Betsy and walked directly to the church. The side door, labeled, 'Office,' was unlocked, so she walked in and found Rev. Toby in his study.

"Tamara!" he said. "Welcome. Please, come in." He showed her to a seat and sat across from her.

"How are you getting along?" he asked, in a thoughtful, caring way. He really seemed to want to know.

Tamara nodded that she was doing well, then she got right down to business.

"I need to get baptized," she said, softly, but with conviction filling out every word.

Tobias cocked his head but considered deeply what he just heard before responding.

"You need to get baptized?" he asked. Then, he chuckled. "I've heard young couples say they need to get married, but I don't believe I've ever heard anyone express the need to be baptized with such urgency. I'm delighted, of course, but tell me, why do you need to get baptized? And, how soon do you feel that needs to happen?"

There were too many questions now applied to what Tamara felt was a simple statement of intent, so she froze up as she sought to wrestle her way through to an explanation.

Tobias witnessed the consternation on Tamara's face then assured her she didn't need to answer all at once and asked her if they could make some time to discuss it.

"Baptism isn't something we should rush into," he said. "It will take some preparation and, depending on how long you will be staying – "

"Could Barb prepare me?" she asked, interrupting him.

Tobias smiled broadly.

"Oh, by all means," he said, nodding his affirmation. "That would be splendid. You'll never find a better teacher," he assured her. "Present company included! You let her know that we spoke and that I said I approved whole-heartedly! And, if you feel you want to be baptized here, you'll let me know, and then you and I will talk some more."

"She said I need to be baptized into the church that will be my church family," Tamara said, speaking to the floor, unable to look at Tobias.

"Well. There, you see what I mean. And, she is right," acknowledged Tobias, tempering his enthusiasm over Tamara's decision, now appreciating some of the complications.

"Still, no matter where you are baptized, she will prepare you well," he encouraged her.

Tamara considered hard her next statement then laid it before Tobias.

"I think Jesus has led me to belong to this church family," she said, closing her eyes to avoid seeing Toby's reaction. But with her eyes closed, she could make out at least three new faces she felt sure she wanted to call family, though what that meant, she wasn't sure. She still had to sort that out, and she had a few days before her mother arrived to come to some conclusion.

"I see," said Tobias. He stared long and hard at the young woman seated across from him. He went to a filing cabinet and pulled out a little booklet.

"Do you remember the questions I asked during the baptism you watched a few months ago?" he asked Tamara.

"I'm not sure if I do," she confessed.

"Do you renounce Satan and all his ways? is the first question I ask. Then, do you confess Jesus Christ to be your only Lord and Savior? Do you believe that he died on the cross to save you from your sins? Do you believe that he rose again from the dead and that you, too, shall join him in new and everlasting life?

"My hope is that as you are baptized, you will have come to some reasonable understanding of what you are committing your life to as you answer those questions.

"It's the last question we need to sort out," he continued after a long pause. "The question goes, 'By the power and guidance of God's Holy Word and Spirit, are you ready to become a communing member of the body of Christ, the church?'"

He handed Tamara the booklet. "I prepared this for those desiring baptism. Each section addresses those questions and suggests Scriptures to read along with them. I hope you'll read through it and pray about how you will answer those questions, not just while you're standing in the water, but for the rest of your life."

Tamara felt the weight of his words, and the seriousness with which he said them left an impression that would linger with her. She thanked Tobias for the booklet which she thought looked a little like the dog-eared guide Barb used every morning during their morning prayers.

"Are you headed back to the farm now?" he asked her.

When Tamara nodded, he offered to walk with her.

"Look who stopped by and invited me to lunch," said Tobias, as Barb watched him and Tamara walk up the drive.

"Oh, splendid," replied his mother, as they exchanged what Tamara thought to be a knowing glance filled with insider information.

The three of them ate ham-salad sandwiches on the porch and watched the lambs graze in the pasture.

"That's a beautiful sight," said Tobias. "You've really livened up the ranch," he said to Tamara.

Tamara had been feeling awkward, unsure if she was supposed to mention she had spoken with Toby about baptism, or if he was going to bring it up which, so far, he had not.

"She's got me cleaning out the hen-house after lunch," Barb said to her son.

"Thank God! It's about time someone exercised some managerial oversight around here," he laughed. "Long overdue," he continued to rib his mother.

As Tobias left and Tamara was excusing herself to go down to the hen-house, Barb asked Tamara if she had stopped by to ask him about baptism.

"I asked him if you can prepare me. He said, yes, then you would let him know when you think I'm ready."

All of that came out faster than Tamara had intended which made her blush and look down at her hands.

"Would you?" whispered Tamara.

"Honey," said Barb, "I'm not sure how much more I can prepare you," chuckled Barb, becoming introspective. "Jesus has been doing a pretty good job of preparing you, already," she continued.

Tamara's glance urged Barb to explain.

"I think you gave yourself to Jesus a few months ago over there on the bank. You may not have realized it then, but I've seen his grace at work in you, and I've seen you growing in that grace in some beautiful ways. He's been guiding you ever since. Without a lot of help from anybody else, you have been figuring out how to follow him on your own. He has been teaching you how to pray and how to care for others.

And, even more important, he has been putting your suffering to work on his behalf.

"So," Barb continued, "the question is not whether you are ready. I think you are. But we need to keep praying about where. That's what we don't want to rush, okay? You could get baptized here. Tobias could immerse you in the river. But when you climb back up on the river bank, it ought to be your church family that welcomes you in. You can't be baptized then just continue to live your faith by yourself. Jesus calls us to live in community for all the right reasons."

They both grew quiet, and thoughtful.

"Now, in the great, mystical sense," continued Barb, "you will be baptized into the universal church. Jesus' church is much bigger than this little group of people here. But it is the local expression of that bigger church which offers you the love, guidance, and support you need. And, in that church family, Jesus also shows you the needs he wants you to help him meet."

Tamara said she thought she understood as she turned to take her plate back to the kitchen.

"I'll join you in just a few moments," said Barb. "You go get us organized, then I'll come down and provide the cheap labor!"

As Tamara stepped off the porch, a harsh reality wrapped itself around her, something she heard in Barb's words that unsettled her. Tamara had stopped thinking of herself as a guest in Barb's home and saw herself as a resident in this community, but that was a presumption she had no right to make.

The work Tamara had taken on, the schedule she was keeping, the life she had adopted had served as a bulwark against the world she so wanted to leave behind: the streets she walked, the subway she took to school, the hordes of kids that tormented her all day long, and the numerous tensions in her home. They were not just irritations but sources of her mental suffering, triggers that drove her into those dark crevices of her psyche.

Since she had come to Barb's home, she had found herself on the terra firma of another world. She still contended with ferocious strikes from Thorafura. And the other night, the granthyrs mercilessly tracked her through her dreams, but with each new dawn she could push her mind in directions which, by breakfast, had allowed her to set aside the haunts of the darkness and take in the promise of the day.

Tamara found a hoe in the barn and entered the hen-house. Working gingerly around the chickens, she started to rake the floor.

"Let me get you a bin and a shovel," said Barb, behind her. "We'll scatter that on the garden later – it'll make great fertilizer for our vegetables."

As they worked together, Barb offered additional lessons in raising chickens and how she wished she could expand that part of the farm.

"The hens were the first thing my father turned over to me. He told me I had to make it work or he was going to get rid of them. He was all about the cows, and he didn't like the distractions the chickens created or all the time they took.

"My first decision was to let them out! I hated seeing them cooped up in here and, frankly, at that time I didn't know any better. I didn't really care much for them, either, or anything about the farm. To tell you the truth, I was thinking about leaving. I hated it here.

"But then one morning, I was standing over there when I heard a hawk squeal, and from out of that tree it flew down, scooped up one of the hens, and carried it up toward the ridge. The poor hen squawked and thrashed the whole way. Well, it took a while to coax them back into the hen-house, but that's where they've been ever since. It was these hens, or their great-grandparents, that finally taught me how to be a farmer just like your lambs are teaching you."

The boarding in the hen-house walls was still rather sound, but the paint had completely failed inside and out, and the flooring was growing soft. Barb said it would have to be replaced if she was going to continue keeping the hens for much longer.

"We should have poured a concrete floor in here a long time ago, but wood was cheaper and more plentiful. Now…" Barb scanned the structure with new eyes. "Now, I'm not sure how much more effort I can really give it. Still, as long as these ladies are offering us their eggs, we'll do right by them," she said with new resolve.

"What can I do?" said Tamara.

"Bless you, child," said Barb. "You're doing it. There's always more than can be done on a farm. More paint, new roofs, cleaning stalls and coops, weeding gardens, mending fences, feeding, bedding, tending. You're doing it, and you're doing a fine job of it."

But Tamara wasn't satisfied. Even she could see that all was not well in this little corner of the farm. The only tools she had ever held in her hands were pencils, pens, pastels and paint brushes. If Barb wouldn't help satisfy Tamara's desire to make some further contribution, then when Betsy delivered the hay she would get another opinion. In the meantime, she asked Barb if she could paint the coop.

Barb stepped back and studied the siding.

"It'd be a big job, to do it right," she said, mostly to herself. "And we ought to do a good job if we're going to do it at all," she coached Tamara.

Tamara nodded her agreement.

"The walls will need to be scraped of all that loose paint," Barb explained. "We'll need brushes and primer. Then you can pick out the new color!"

"When do we start?" asked Tamara.

"Gracious!" exclaimed Barb. "Well, we could check with Cindy to see if she has any paint supplies or if she can order them."

Tamara said she'd walk over there now.

"Let's take this to the compost first," said Barb, indicating the bin full of debris.

"I thought we scatter it on the garden," said Tamara.

"It's best to let it rest a little before its ready," explained Barb.

"I've got paint scrapers, a few brushes, and I think this will work well enough for a primer," said Cindy, as they scanned the shelves at the General. "It's not the best paint, but for that little coop of Barb's, it should be fine. You'll also need some paint thinner. That, and the paint, I'll have to order for you."

Tamara nodded, though she felt disappointed she couldn't get all she needed.

"We're not really a hardware store like we used to be," Cindy said, reading Tamara's expression. "Betsy's is the only fully productive farm here in the valley, so we stopped stocking a lot of farm and building supplies. But this should get you started. What color paint would you like?"

"Red. Just like it is now," Tamara said.

"Red it is. It should be in in a day or two. You'll have plenty to keep you busy in the meantime."

"Barb said to put this on her bill," said Tamara.

Cindy pursed her lips and shook her head slightly but then nodded as she rang up the supplies.

Aimee would arrive on Wednesday, Barb told Tamara when she came back with her supplies.

"She just called," said Barb. "I told her she better pack plenty of work clothes, that you had taken over the farm and had conscripted us into forced labor!"

Tamara noted the sparkle in Barb's eyes and considered what Betsy had told her about keeping Barb as active as she wanted to be.

"I bought two scrapers," said Tamara. "Want one?"

Barb smiled broadly and said, "Sure. But I don't do ladders anymore!"

"I'll have to take that out of your pay," said Tamara, who felt awkward making a joke, something she had no practice at, but when she saw Barb laugh she was grateful for the nudge Betsy had given her. And she was very glad she wasn't going to be tending to the chicken coop by herself.

As they were cleaning up from a late supper, Tamara remembered the little booklet on baptism which she had stuffed in her back pocket and thought she would take it up to her room and begin reading. Then, on second thought, she was tired and wanted to be fresh when she considered the questions she was to answer with the whole of her life, so she laid the booklet on top of her Bible and would build those reflections into her morning prayer and conversation with Barb.

25

The Place of New Beginnings

TAMARA WAS AT THE FAR end of the pasture late Wednesday morning with the lambs when a bright red rental car pulled in by the house, and Aimee stepped out. Barb came out onto the porch to welcome her, and they embraced warmly.

"Look at her out there," said Aimee.

"She's quite the shepherd," Barb exclaimed. "She sure loves those lambs."

Tamara started in from the field when she saw her mom. Two of the lambs followed behind her. Barb and Aimee strolled over to the gate, let themselves in, and went to meet Tamara midway. The lambs halted when the other two women approached.

Tamara felt a little crowded with her mom in her pasture, but she was proud to be able to welcome Aimee into a place that she had made her own.

"This is Woolimittens and Gentleomen. Over there is Fluffermore, Sheerborne, Lamblitten, and Lupinore. Then, she added in more serious tones, "Under the apple tree is Lanolander."

"That was a hard night," Barb said, looking Aimee in the eye. "But we are all very proud of Tamara."

"Let me look at you!" exclaimed Aimee.

Tamara felt invaded and self-conscious as her mother grabbed both her shoulders and looked her over.

"This has been good for you," said Aimee, shaking her head. "You've put on some weight. I can tell you've been working hard."

"She has been working very hard," said Barb. "I can't get her to stop some days. Over here is the garden she planted."

They walked over to the adjacent lot to admire the plants arranged in neat rows which, Tamara noted, were in need of weeding.

"There is a lot to do," observed Tamara.

"Well, I'm here to help," said Aimee. "So, put me to work."

"After lunch we can either paint the coop or weed the garden," said Tamara. "I've got to walk over to the General, though, and get the paint," she informed Barb. "Cindy said it should be in by lunchtime."

"Why don't you show your mom around while I get lunch," said Barb. "Take your time. We'll eat on the porch whenever you're ready."

"How was Brussels?" asked Tamara as they strolled slowly toward the barn.

Aimee didn't answer for a while but then said, "That's a long conversation I hope we have some time for over the next few days. From a business standpoint, it went great. One of the best experiences of my professional career. But..." Aimee waved off the rest of that sentence, not really wanting to finish it.

"But?" prodded Tamara.

"Well," Aimee struggled, "it made me realize that that profession is over for me."

Tamara didn't want to pry but wished her mom would continue, so she stopped walking and turned to look at her.

"Each evening after dinner, I took the sketch book and walked around the city looking for things to draw. There was a little pond not far from our hotel. And, there was a pair of ducks..."

Aimee's speech became halted, and she had difficulty continuing with the story.

Tamara felt awkward and unsure of what to do, so she turned toward the barn, letting her mom follow at her own pace. Tamara led Aimee through the barn to show her the stalls they had secured for the lambs.

Tam appeared without notice and rubbed herself against Tamara's leg nearly tripping her. Tamara scooped up the kitten and laid it over her shoulder where she rested lazily for the remainder of the tour. As they exited a small door at the far end, Tamara let the cat down to scurry off in another direction.

Mother and daughter emerged from the barn onto the small path that led alongside the fence bordering the lamb's pasture. Tamara pointed out the small stable where Lanolander died.

Very little had been said between mother and daughter, though so much had been communicated. There was an ease between them that had never existed before. Tamara's confidence in what she had been doing had given her a strength which introduced a new dynamic into their relationship.

They strolled the path to the river where Tamara offered her mother a seat on the bench. She noted her mother's immediate recognition of the location and felt joined to her in a powerful way. Both women were recalling the way their lives had begun to change there.

Tamara felt her mother's hand rest on hers and, for the first time in her life, Tamara removed her hand in order to take her mother's instead. She held her mother's hand firmly then let it go so she could wrap her arm around her mother's shoulder.

Aimee was weeping uncontrollably.

Tamara closed her eyes and silently asked Shepherd Jesus to meet them there on the bank again, as he had met them there before, and teach them the next steps they were supposed to take in their lives. The prayer came effortlessly and rode up through her soul as she released herself, and her mother, into God's care.

This was not all up to her, or to her mother, she thought. Lanolander's death was still instructing her to allow God his portion of responsibility even as he showed them theirs. And right now, Tamara's duty was to listen.

"You were telling me about the ducks," said Tamara.

Aimee sought to compose herself, and as she did so she found it hard to curb the laughter that was fighting its way now up through her lingering sobs. If nothing else, it provided Aimee with the cathartic cleansing she needed.

"Oh. I think that cry has been coming for some time," said Aimee, as she felt herself growing quiet again. "It was waiting for just this moment, and just this spot."

Aimee let the rushing song of the water wash through her for a few more moments before she resumed her story.

"There was nothing special about the ducks, of course, except that it was while I was drawing them, and remembering our last outing before we all left, that a new sense of clarity for my life overcame me.

"I think I had known for a while that my life in finance was coming to a close. I just couldn't see it or accept what that might mean. All I had been working for felt increasingly empty. Drawing those ducks – that felt amazingly real. And when that felt more real than the financial crisis I was supposed to be addressing, then my whole world came unglued. I became very frightened, and I felt so far away from you and your dad.

"If it hadn't been for that pearl of wisdom you reminded me of, allowing those frightening things to win, I think I would have had some sort of breakdown. But your words –"

"Barb's words," whispered Tamara.

"They may have been Barb's words, honey, but I heard them in your voice, and with your conviction. And that, Tamara, is what gave me hope in that moment. I knew that you believed them, even if I couldn't. And I thought of you coming here, and of the courage you have to start something new..."

Aimee's composure collapsed again.

"You have faced more frightening things then I can fathom," Aimee continued, "so mine ought to be small by comparison, but..."

The stream filled their silences with the perfect accompaniment for their reflections.

"What are your most frightening things?" asked Tamara.

Aimee was moved by the wisdom of the question, and she wanted to sort out an answer to honor it.

"By far, my most frightening thing has always been losing you," said Aimee. "I've lost you more times than you know, and so often I wondered if I would ever have you back."

"Were you afraid of that in Brussels?" asked her daughter.

"No," said her mom, "and, yes. Look at you in those farm clothes. When I saw you with those lambs, I wondered whose daughter you really are. And, when I told myself, 'that's my daughter,' I felt so proud. But I didn't raise you to do this. This is all yours, and from all I've heard, you seem to be right where you belong."

"What else?" pursued Tamara.

"No career," said her mom. "That's pretty frightening! And, of course, your dad's opinion and his family's estimation of me. But your dad was far more understanding than I imagined he would be. We haven't told his folks yet," she added softly.

"What do you think?" Aimee asked Tamara.

Tamara shrugged and wasn't prepared to say. So, she asked, "How did the ducks turn out?"

"I'll leave that for you to decide, but I really don't think an art profession is in the cards. Maybe as a hobby. I really enjoyed it, but even as much as I love it, I never had the passion I saw in you, and I think that counts when you are pursuing your life calling."

"What comes next, then?" asked Tamara, after a long pause in the conversation.

"What comes next? I don't know," Aimee answered. "Your dad is hoping to come Saturday afternoon, then he and I, at least, are going home on Sunday. In the meantime, we have to discuss your plans."

A darkness fell over Tamara at the hint that her time on the farm was in question. She was far from ready to consider that. She had dug her soul into the soil around her. Part of it was buried under the apple tree, and she wasn't of a mind to uproot it.

"Barb must think we've gotten lost," said Aimee. "We should head back to the house."

They stood and meandered back to the barnyard.

"So, this is our project after lunch?" said Aimee, admiring the work Tamara had been doing to restore the coop as they passed it on their way to the porch.

Tamara nodded.

As they strolled toward the porch, Aimee paused and looked out over the pasture and admired the sheep again.

"I'd love to meet Betsy if that could be worked out." asked Aimee. "Barb has told me a lot about her."

"She's coming to dinner," said Tamara.

Lunch consisted of roast-beef sandwiches, chicken soup, and a lot of stories told by Barb about Tamara's accomplishments over the last week and a half.

Tamara remained quiet for most of the conversation. Her mind had turned back to the chicken coop. All the attention that had been focused on her had made her increasingly uncomfortable, and her mind was beginning to feel the tedium of too much conversation.

Tamara had learned to lose herself in the solitude of work. It focused her and gave her body the opportunity to exercise her anxieties before they got the better of her. The same intensity she used to pour into her drawings she now vented into her efforts with her lambs or the chickens. Now, staring back at her were glimpses of life flourishing under her care, not the hideous remnants of her psychic explosions. She was eager to get going now, so she excused herself.

"I'm going to the General to get the paint," announced Tamara, as Barb refilled Aimee's glass with tea.

"Oh," said Barb, halting Tamara. "We should start getting ready for supper around four, if that's okay with you."

Tamara nodded. She gathered her plate and glass then disappeared into the house.

With three paint brushes at work, they managed to get the coop painted in a couple of hours.

Aimee saw the satisfaction in her daughter as they looked it over.

"I think it's time to start a new portfolio of your most recent work, young lady," Aimee announced. "That is a masterpiece."

"It hasn't looked that good in years," acknowledged Barb.

"Betsy said she would ask some guy named Skate, I think, about lumber for a new floor," said Tamara.

"Skate Matthews," said Barb. "He runs a lumber mill a few miles from here. But, that may have to wait a while, I'm afraid," said Barb. "Anyway, why don't we all go get cleaned up and get ready for company."

Aimee looked quizzically at Barb.

"Tamara wanted to throw you a welcome party, and she volunteered to cook," Barb said, raising her eyebrows back at Aimee. "We marinated a roast all morning and put it in just before you came."

"Should I check that?" asked Tamara.

"You should also check the temperature in the oven and add a little more wood if need be."

"And the bread?"

"Yes. We should start the dough so it has plenty of time to rise," confirmed Barb.

"You've been learning to cook?" inquired Aimee.

Tamara shrugged and nodded and shook her head all at once.

"She does help a lot in the kitchen," said Barb. "But this is her first big effort."

The same cohort of guests that welcomed Tamara on her first night there started to arrive around five-thirty. Tamara greeted them and took their dishes as she introduced them to her mother.

"Are you sure about this?" asked Betsy, as she handed Tamara a jug of cow's milk and a large plate covered with foil. "Barb said you were making a roast. You don't need this, too."

Tamara nodded but didn't say anything as she laid the plate on the table. She introduced Betsy to her mother then kept a watch on them out of the corner of her eye as they fell into a rather deep conversation from the start.

Betsy and Aimee were soon joined by Nora, and the group of them retired to the cluster of chairs in front of the fireplace.

"The chicken coop turned out well," Tobias said, as Tamara was uncovering the roast and preparing to slice it.

Tamara nodded, glad that he noticed.

"Mom got here just in time to help paint it," Tamara told him.

"Your mother seems right at home," he said, watching the women talking as if they had known each other for some time.

The cozy dynamic was interrupted, however, as Dr. Samuelson and his wife, Shelly, came through the door. Tamara noted the surprise in her mother and realized she might have warned her.

The color in Aimee's face washed away for a moment, and the warmth that had so characterized her demeanor with the other women tempered then cooled altogether.

Tamara welcomed the Samuelsons, and everyone greeted them warmly.

Aimee stood and politely extended her hand.

"Aimee, I'd like you to meet my wife, Shelly. Shelly, this is Tamara's mother, Aimee."

"I'm pleased to meet you after all these years," said Aimee. "Dr. Samuelson has spoken of you often."

"Please, Aimee, you can call me Stephen," said Samuelson. "Everyone else does. I'm not anybody's doctor tonight. Besides, you are all practically family around here."

"You're still our doctor, though, and I think we have a lot to talk about," whispered Aimee.

"But tonight, we're all here to celebrate with you. And, we have a lot to celebrate, I think," he said, with a glint in his eye and a nudge for the sake of encouragement.

Barb called everyone to the table and asked Tobias if he would offer the blessing.

"I would be glad to, but tonight I'm going to defer to our young friend here," said Tobias, nodding in Tamara's direction.

Tamara blushed slightly and looked as if she had taken on the challenge of her life, but she nodded at Toby in confirmation.

Barb, seated to Tamara's right, looked elated and took the young woman's hand. Tamara gripped Barb's hand and held on to her. She quietly thanked them all for coming then bowed her head.

"Shepherd Jesus, we thank you for bringing us together, here in this home, for providing this food, and for watching over us in our need. Amen."

Everyone at the table rendered their own, loud, amens.

As the dishes were passed, all eyes followed Betsy's dish as it made its way around to Tamara, and all conversation halted when it was handed to her. She scooped a portion onto her plate then explained to her mother that this was one of Betsy's lambs.

Aimee, not fully appreciating the gravity of the moment, exclaimed how much she loved lamb and thanked Betsy for it.

Tamara blushed and studied her plate, but with her knife and fork cut a piece and put a taste of lamb in her mouth. She wasn't conscious of everyone watching, but she closed her eyes and concentrated on the flavor. Then, as full as she could fill her heart with appreciation, she gave thanks for the lamb that had given that to her. She remembered Lanolander and grieved for Gentleomen, but she allowed those sensations of heart find their rightful place within her as she swallowed.

Aimee glanced from Tamara then to Betsy and wondered at the tears in their eyes.

Following all that dinner conversation, Tamara preferred the solitude of washing the dishes over more talk on the porch, so after their guests left she offered to clean up while Barb and Aimee went and sat on the swing.

"I hardly know that woman in there," whispered Aimee, as she stood by the screen door watching Tamara clear the table and put the food away like it was her own home.

"Barb, how did you – "

But Barb halted Aimee before she could say anymore.

"Before you get carried away, I worry, and I think you do too, that this is going to cost her. I've noticed that Tamara has to work so hard to stay focused, and that focus keeps her moving forward, but she'll reach her limit and then the little girl that breaks our heart is right there, shattered and out of control. She turns her intensity into purposeful thought and action, but what she is struggling to learn is to discipline her work and moderate her expectations of herself."

"Well, she couldn't find a better place or teacher, for that," affirmed Aimee, with a sigh of self-reproach. "She certainly never learned that from us."

"God is teaching her with the help of those lambs over there," Barb responded. "He is working overtime in her. We've all been noticing that."

"That group of women is amazing!" exclaimed Aimee.

"Yes, they are, and they think the world of your Tamara. She has found a real place in their hearts," Barb assured her.

"I saw that. But in talking with Nora and Betsy there was something else," said Aimee, fishing for what that something else was.

"It's respect," said Barb. "That's what I think it is. It might surprise you, but Tamara has gained some stature in this community. They quickly saw she was no tourist in for the week. The way she comforted Betsy when they had to put down her cow, then took on those lambs and protected them, went to work on the chicken coop, learned to ride a horse. And, her prayer at dinner tonight. She's been talking with Tobias about baptism. Those sorts of things might not light much of a fire in anybody in New York, but this is a small farming community, and those are the qualities that people look for in one another. And truly respect."

Aimee became quiet and introspective.

"That sense of community is very strong," whispered Aimee.

"And very healing," said Barb.

"Yes. Yes, it is."

Tamara stepped out onto the porch to say that she was going to bed.

"Betsy and Earl may come by tomorrow to see about building that creep around the old stable," said Tamara, "so I want to get an early start."

Barb stared at Tamara with no recognition of what she was talking about.

"A creep?" Barb asked.

"She said she had spoken with you about it," said Tamara, though her words trailed off as she realized Barb may not have recalled, and Tamara didn't want to apply undue pressure.

"What is a creep?" inquired Aimee.

"It's a small enclosure for weaning the lambs. Just in case," answered Tamara.

"Just in case?"

"It's best not to keep young rams with the older ones, so Betsy wants to keep Sheerborne here with the other ewes," explained Tamara. "And chances are, in the fall they may breed."

As Barb brought her hand to her brow, Tamara knew the older woman was struggling to remember a conversation she now realizes she must have had. And as her mom's expression turned dark, Tamara considered that she had indicated more about her own hopes too quickly without giving her mom ample warning. So, she said good-night, and walked upstairs.

Tamara heard the muffled conversation downstairs and hoped that Barb might be of some guidance to her mother. The various relational pressures she found herself navigating throughout the day were now taking their toll on her mind. Weariness overtook her, which meant she didn't have the mental energy to force her darker thoughts to the periphery, so her mind raced as she sought to sort out the many scenarios slamming around in her head concerning her future.

She had thought too often in recent days that if she had to go back to the city, then she would die. As long as she was alone with Barb and had plenty of purpose, she had been able to maintain the illusion that she was making a new life for herself. She had lambs who were becoming sheep, a garden she would harvest, chickens that needed better quarters, and a friend who needed someone with her.

Tamara heard muffled bleating from the barn, but by now she had learned their various tones and inflections and knew they were just arranging themselves for the night. She reflected on her morning with the lambs and the conversation she had with Tobias.

Shortly after filling the manger with fresh hay that morning, Tamara had sat down with her back to a fence post to watch the lambs. Lamblitten came over to her while the others were grazing, and Tamara softened up her hands in the lamb's wool. They were getting big and looking more like the mature sheep they were becoming, so Lamblitten was a handful and Tamara felt respect for the lamb's strength.

Tobias strode across the field and surprised Tamara who couldn't see him for the lamb standing in front of her.

"I had an appointment cancel out from under me, and it was too nice a day to sit in my office, so I thought I'd come see the lambs," he said.

Tamara stood, brushed herself off, and reintroduced him to the flock.

As they strolled around the pasture, Tobias came to the real reason for his visit: "Tamara, you said you feel Jesus has led you to be a member of this church family," he said. "Would you like to talk more about that?"

Though the conversation was stilted at first, over the next hour the two of them grew comfortable with one another, and Tamara found it easy to talk with him about matters of life and faith. He acknowledged several times how grateful he was that Tamara was able to devote so much time and attention to his mother.

The one thing both mother and son seemed to share, much to Tamara's dissatisfaction, was that neither one would offer her much direction. Tobias listened and nodded a lot, but he was not inclined to encourage, or discourage, Tamara's insinuations about remaining on the farm with Barb. 'Pray about it,' was as much guidance as she was given. She was not used to people granting her so much latitude or giving her the responsibility for such big decisions. Tobias and Barb were listeners, not talkers, and they were certainly not inclined to exercise their authority over the autonomy of another. They also respected that prayer was to be the substance of one's decisions, and should Tamara's decision be the genuine fruit of that prayer, would that be sufficient for them?

Tamara pulled the Book of Common Prayer from the shelf on her desk and thumbed through it wondering if there was such a prayer for the kind of guidance she needed. She found one titled "For Vocation in Daily Work."

Almighty God our heavenly Father, you declare your glory and show forth your handiwork in the heavens and in the earth: Deliver us in our various occupations from the service of self alone, that we may do the work you give us to do in truth and beauty and for the common good; for the sake of him who came among us as one who serves, your Son Jesus Christ our Lord, who lives and reigns with you and the Holy Spirit, one God, for ever and ever. Amen.

Tamara thought of the life flourishing under her care, and she felt healing – or at least some personal relief – had come by pushing her mind out of her own head and tending the needs of her lambs, the vegetables in the garden, the chicken coop, and especially the help she was giving Barb. Taxing as it was, emotionally and physically, it was purifying to deny room to the darkness that wanted to creep back in when she let down her guard. Doing the work she was given to do 'in truth and beauty for the common good' lent dignity and power to her efforts. More importantly, the prayer assured her she was not laboring for the sake of the work itself, but for the sake of Jesus who had been shepherding her through these experiences. He had been saturating her efforts with purpose and her life with new meaning.

As she idly turned the pages of the book while ruminating on that prayer, a second prayer, 'For Joy in God's Creation,' sang a new song in her heart:

O heavenly Father, who has filled the world with beauty: Open our eyes to behold your gracious hand in all your works; that, rejoicing in your whole creation, we may learn to serve you with gladness; for the sake of him through whom all things were made, your Son Jesus Christ our Lord. Amen.

Tired as her mind was, she pushed it to memorize the prayer so she could take it with her into the field in the morning. She heard her mother say goodnight to Barb, climb the stairs, then close her bedroom door.

Now, thought Tamara, what will the night bring? If she was right, it wouldn't be long before Barb began her nightly bumping about. Tamara had stopped being surprised, and on some nights she waited up for it. Thankfully, most of the time it was a matter of saying goodnight again and gently reminding Barb it was time to rest as she nudged her toward her bedroom. Barb was just born and bred to work, but there were evenings when her mind didn't know to tell her she was tired and it was time to go to bed.

Night brought out old agitations which Tamara understood. The dark, mingled with the quiet of the house, gave the soul the opportunity it needed to flush out all that the conscious mind refused to pay attention to when the day was light, busy, and filled with purpose.

She didn't have to wait long. Tamara heard the porch door slam, then she heard Barb's voice, but this time it came from out in the yard.

Tamara dressed as quickly as she could and raced down the stairs in pursuit. She saw Barb disappear into the barn, then she heard a metallic clatter, the sound of tools being knocked over. As she approached the barn, Tamara heard Barb calling her father's name. It was time for dinner and they had been waiting long enough.

Tamara grabbed the pull chain and turned on a small light over the work bench just in time to see Barb enter one of the stalls and excite the lambs. Lupinore scampered out. Tamara halted the lamb and turned her back into the stall, but Barb was turning in circles, dismayed over the presence of sheep when she thought she'd find her father doing the nightly milking.

Matters became worse when Barb refused to recognize Tamara.

Tamara halted when she saw how agitated Barb was, confronted by a stranger in her own barn. Tamara kneeled beside Fluffermore.

"Want to pet the lamb?" Tamara asked Barb. But it didn't work. Barb seized up. Her inability to sort out the unfamiliar stimuli flooding her mind proved too much.

Where was her father? she wanted to know.

"He must have gone back to the house," said Tamara, though she felt saddened to have to lie. However, that dislodged Barb, who nodded with some recognition and turned toward the stall door.

Tamara stood and took hold of Barb's elbow to guide her back toward the house. Aimee was standing on the porch as they approached, but Tamara hardly acknowledged her until she had escorted Barb back to her bedroom.

Tamara sat with Barb on the side of her bed, talking gently with her like she talked with the lambs, reassuring her that they had had a very productive day on the farm. All their work was done, dinner was splendid, the dishes were put away, and now it was time for bed.

As Tamara started to rise, Barb reminded her they had not had their evening prayer. Tamara took a deep breath, but as she was figuring out what she ought to say, Barb began the prayer on their behalf.

"Yours is the day, O Lord, and yours is the night. Ours are the blessings of your love. Grant thy peace and watch over your tender lambs. Then bring the dawn of that new morning, forever promised your children. Amen."

"My mother taught me that," whispered Barb. She looked at Tamara with growing recognition, though with little realization of what had transpired. Did this seem normal to Barb, Tamara wondered, for them to be seated on Barb's bed together? Barb treated it as the continuation of an earlier conversation they had been having.

Tamara stood and started to leave, but Barb rose, as well, and embraced Tamara, thanked her, and gave her a kiss on the cheek.

Tamara met her mother in the hallway. When their eyes met, and Tamara saw the recognition in Aimee's expression of what had just happened, her strength left her, and she collapsed against her mother. Her mind folded in on itself, and she felt the ravages of the granthyrs gnawing at the fleshy part of her soul.

Aimee, dazed by what she had been witnessing, wasn't prepared to catch the weight of her daughter but sought to steady Tamara and get her to the kitchen table.

Tamara put her head down on her folded arms and started to sob. All her possibilities were collapsing around her. She had not intended to tell her mother. She had determined to carry Barb as far as she could. Tamara's own lucid moments had been increasing, her mind had been clearer these past few days than she could remember. And throughout the day, Barb's mind was as focused and as sharp as ever. Tamara had herself convinced that if they could get through the night and on to the next morning, everything ought to brighten. They would figure this out, and they would soldier on together.

Illusions, however, are easier to maintain without others looking on, and Aimee's presence shattered the fantasy Tamara was building in her mind.

"Here," said Aimee, as she placed a cup of warm milk on the table. "I hear it was fresh squeezed this morning."

It was not her mom's levity that jolted Tamara, but the reminder that the milk came from the neighboring farm that momentarily refocused Tamara's heart. As she took a sip and noted the richness of the flavor, she remembered her prayer book lying open on her desk and the prayer for creation she was trying to learn. She couldn't remember the words, but she trusted in the sensations those words instilled within her, sensations of the rightness of what she was doing, and the necessity to fight for it if it was to continue.

Tamara placed her glass on the table and looked her mother in the eyes. She didn't say anything but let her gaze convey the conviction of what her soul was telling her, that this is where she belonged. Shepherd Jesus had called her to be part of this family, this community, and this church. She had only attended the church once, but she had seen it at work for two weeks, and she had found herself nestled close to its heart from the moment she came. Jesus had prepared her for them, and he had prepared them for her. It would be unfaithful for her to leave.

Tamara braced herself as she watched Aimee trying to figure out what to say, but she sensed what was coming. She was prepared to fight for her new life now. But she was about to discover that she didn't need to.

"How can I help?" was what came out of her mother.

Tamara looked down at her milk and thought for a few moments.

"We need to talk to Tobias," said Tamara. Trusting that her mother intended to be part of a solution rather than a source of obstruction, Tamara opened up about Barb's nightly roaming and her occasional lapses of memory.

Aimee listened with little comment. The only concern she vocalized was whether Tamara and Barb could be safe together if both were struggling.

"What would you be doing right now, if I weren't here, and we weren't able to talk about this?" pressed Aimee.

Tamara knew she would be curled up tight on her bed, railing against the granthyrs who would be feasting on the little confidence she had left. She would be fending off deadly strikes from Thorafura as her mind shattered into shards of remorse for the slow decline of her dearest friend. But even as she saw herself alone on her bed, she knew herself to be surrounded by others. She would tell Betsy in the morning, who would tell her grandmother, who would tell Tobias, who would look in on them. Nora and the other women in the church would drop by. They would be prayed for by the church family. Tamara would find strength when she needed it, and Barb would still offer wisdom and selfless love, even if her mind strayed off course from time to time.

Tamara let her mother's question linger for a few more moments, then shrugged, and said it would be okay.

"You'll talk to Tobias?" asked Aimee. "Would you like me to be with you?"

Tamara shook her head and said she thought she should do it herself. "Betsy and Earl are coming in the morning," Tamara reminded her mom.

"So, it'll have to wait until after lunch."

"I was going to take a walk around the village while you worked with Betsy in the morning. I had thought about stopping in to see Rev. Toby, just to say hi. I didn't get to talk with him much this evening, and since he was so kind the last time we were here, I'd like to renew the acquaintance. Would you mind? I won't mention any of this, if you prefer to tell him yourself."

Tamara nodded her affirmation.

"Think you can sleep now?" asked Aimee.

No, thought Tamara, though she agreed it was time to go back to bed. Tomorrow could be a big day.

26

RENEWING OLD VOWS

WHEN BETSY ARRIVED THE NEXT morning to consider the creep, Tamara took her aside and said they needed to talk this over with Barb again, and why.

"Oh me," said Betsy. "Dear old soul. Do you think we should push this with the lambs?"

Tamara was conflicted, but she wanted to trust Betsy's earlier words of wisdom.

"She really loves having them here," said Tamara.

"We need to talk honestly now, Tamara," said Betsy. She laid a hand on Tamara's shoulder and looked out over the pasture. "The sheep are here because you are here. Barb can't tend them once you're gone. I know what you want to do, honey, but could it be that we're letting our dreams get ahead of us? Especially now, with Barb, I mean."

Tamara felt her face get hot, and her soul grew cold. A scream was climbing up through her, but she looked Betsy in the face and shook her head.

"I have to stay," she whispered. Her eyes went from conviction to pleading, and Betsy read every degree of need in between.

"Have you talked with your friend?" asked Tamara.

Betsy looked away and shook her head. "Look, we at least need to discuss that with your mother. But even before that, have you asked Barb about staying and going to school here?"

"I thought we should know if it was possible to enroll first," said Tamara. "If I can't, I can't," she whispered, but to utter the words was painful.

"Okay," said Betsy, honoring Tamara's interest even if she felt they were treading into dangerous territory. "I'll call Melinda later on today and ask her to check with the guidance counselor. Remember, she only teaches science, so she doesn't have any pull. They're all out on vacation now, anyway, so it may take a while to find out if it's even possible. But, pretty soon, we really need to discuss this with Barb and your parents. I love dreaming with you, and it would be fabulous having you here, but this is getting very serious and some of it may be out of our hands. Do you realize that?"

Tamara stood frozen in a reality she didn't want to accept but had enough presence of mind to trust Betsy's horse sense about all of this, so she looked down and offered a single nod. She turned away as tears flooded her eyes.

"Hey," said Betsy. "If you've got something to cry about it's only polite to share. I shared with you the other day, so fair's fair. Right?"

Tamara turned around, right into the embrace Betsy had prepared for her.

Earl, Betsy, and Tamara decided together that the creep would work, and if the lambs were to mature in the pasture and stay for the fall then there was plenty of time to build it. First things first, however, and they agreed to take whatever steps each thought best to encourage Barb to visit her doctor. Tamara said she planned to go talk with Tobias, but Betsy told her to wait. She wanted to discuss it with her grandmother and that maybe the three of them could talk with Toby together.

"Grandma knows her better than her own son," Betsy assured her. "And she'll know how to persuade Toby and Barb to follow through. I think you're right, Tamara, Barb won't think she needs a doctor. She's not stubborn like a lot of New Englanders can be, but she's never been one to complain about her health. And, if she doesn't realize she has a problem, forget it. She weathers things she can't fix, and if they won't be weathered, well, I'm not really sure she's met much she can't weather. So, this will be a test for all our sakes."

"Will the creep work?" asked Barb, who was standing on the porch as the others walked across the yard.

Betsy's and Tamara's eyes met, and both shared a look of surprise.

"Could," said Betsy. "What do you think about that now?" she asked, cautiously.

"It is exciting to think of God bringing births back to this tired old place," Barb said. Her eyes radiated delight in all directions. "It even made me think, maybe we should get a rooster and let some of those eggs hatch, too. Got a spanking new roost for him to rule, right Tamara!"

"Right," said Tamara.

"God's wonders never cease," whispered Betsy, to which Earl grunted, "Amen, to that."

As Betsy and Earl walked toward the road, Tamara caught up with them.

"About the lumber for the floor in the chicken coop," said Tamara.

"Yes?" said Betsy.

"We need to talk more about that, too."

Aimee, returning from her morning walk, met Tamara at the end of the farm lane, and they walked together in silence to the porch. Both had more on their minds than the short walk would allow them.

"Nora called a short while ago to see if the two of you would like to go riding after lunch," Barb said as mother and daughter approached the house.

"It is a beautiful day. I'd love to if Tamara can get out of work early," joked Aimee.

But Tamara froze. "I'm not sure if I can," she said, feeling caught between opposing forces.

"Well you two work that out. I'll get our sandwiches," said Barb, leaving Aimee and Tamara on the porch.

"I just told Betsy I would come work with her this afternoon. I'm sorry," said Tamara.

"What's the matter?" asked Aimee.

Tamara stewed in her thoughts then spoked very quietly. "Mom, I don't think Barb can afford the lumber for the chicken coop. So, I asked Betsy if I could work it off at her farm, and she said I could come help clean stalls this afternoon. But you should go riding with Nora. You'll love it."

"Tamara Baxter," said Aimee, but that was as far as she got. Words wouldn't emerge, so she just stared at the young woman seated across from her, wondering where she had come from.

"I had a nice visit with pastor Toby," whispered Aimee, hoping to relieve Tamara of the conflict still so evident on her face. "He asked me how long you are planning to stay with Barb, but I wasn't sure what to tell him. He said he had asked Barb the same question, but all he got from her was, 'I'm going to keep her as long as I can.' I asked him if he had any concerns about that and he said, quite the contrary, that he hasn't seen his mom this happy in a long time. He expressed genuine gratitude for all you are doing here, and he said that as far as he was concerned it was a win-win situation. But, Tamara, I have to be honest, what happened last night – "

Aimee was interrupted by Barb's return to the porch. Tamara searched her mother's face for some sign of reassurance, but Aimee turned her full attention to Barb. Tamara began to sink, and she labored over every bite on her plate then gave it up altogether.

After lunch, the three women walked to the end of Barb's road then went in different directions at Main Street. Barb escorted Aimee to Nora's for an afternoon on a horse, and Tamara, already wearing a day's worth of farm dirt, was off to lend her labor elsewhere.

Aimee and Nora ventured by Betsy's barn to find Tamara pushing a wheelbarrow toward a large composting area.

"I gotta say," announced Aimee, as she dismounted, "you look like you've been doing that all your life. If I didn't know you were born and raised in Mid-town Manhattan, I would swear you crawled out from the cabbage patch."

"Are you making fun of the help, ma'am?" shouted Betsy, who followed Tamara out of the barn carrying two large buckets. "I'll have you know there's a bidding war on for her. All the farms in the county are after her."

Aimee beamed to see her daughter being appreciated, and to know Tamara had commitments to keep and was keeping them so well. She patted Tamara on the shoulder, told her she'd see her at dinner, got back in her saddle, and trotted off with Nora to see the lupines.

After her mom and Nora turned the bend, Tamara let the wheelbarrow rest and fell deep into thought. She looked at her dirty jeans, her now well-worn barn boots and caught a whiff of the fragrance she was sporting. She tried to put her Mid-town Manhattan self back into the picture, but she couldn't see it anymore. She pulled her bandanna out of her pocket and, as she was wiping her face, she pictured her great-great Aunt Tamara leaning against an old weathered mantelpiece, grinning for the love of life. Why was she smiling? wondered Tamara. If, by chance, Aunt Tamara happened to be looking out a window, then she would be looking at something like this; a valley flourishing with life and love, quiet and care, populated by people who made it worth living there.

She asked Betsy if she could use her phone.

"There's one just inside the milk room. Everything okay?" asked Betsy.

Tamara nodded then said, "I want to call Dr. Samuelson."

Betsy grew concerned as she watched Tamara enter the barn.

"Do you have his number?" asked Betsy.

"He made me memorize it," said Tamara. "Just in case."

Tamara felt awkward walking into the General looking (and smelling) like she did and was glad to see Dr. Samuelson waiting for her on the porch with two bottles of root-beer in his hand. They decided on a stroll to the old cemetery.

Though Tamara had called this meeting, she was unsure how to begin it. Samuelson, however, was a master at reading silences.

"I've been hearing what a good farm-hand you are, Miss Baxter," he said. "And, word has gotten around about the change that has come over Barb since you've arrived. Actually, make that changes," Samuelson added in lower tones.

Tamara's heart beat faster and her face flushed, driving her more deeply into her fears for both her future and for Barb's.

"Fact is," said Dr. Samuelson, reading the concern in her face, "people have been worried about Barb for quite some time."

He laid a hand on Tamara's shoulder then continued: "Tobias wasn't sure if your coming was a good idea given some of the difficulties he's seen. And Pamela Nazareth was even more insistent. But both have seen a change in her that neither expected, and they attribute that to your company and encouragement."

He stopped and turned toward Tamara to address her directly.

"That doesn't mean there aren't still problems to address. Thanks to you being so alert, there is now a full court press at work in the village. Everybody is conspiring to get Barb to a doctor."

He turned, and they resumed their slow stroll.

"Pamela called a little while ago to see if I knew of anyone. I made a few calls and found someone in North Conway who said she could do a basic neurological screening tomorrow, but that we might have to go to Concord depending on what she finds. Getting Barb there, however, is going to take some work. What we need is an accomplished shepherd. Know of one?" he asked as he winked at Tamara.

As they entered the iron gate of the cemetery, Samuelson drifted to the far corner and pointed to a headstone. The names of Frederick and Natasha Samuelson, along with their dates, were engraved in to it.

"I did a lot of my growing up around here," he told her. "I was born in the city, like you were, the last of six kids. My parents were a lot older when I came along, so they retired early in my life and we came here. I was fourteen. My folks had been worn out by city life, but I resented the move and couldn't wait to get back to New York."

He let a respectful silence settle between them which Tamara appreciated. Her body was tired from a long day of heavy work, but her ruminations never let her rest, and she was working hard to fit this man into these surroundings. But then Dr. Samuelson insinuated himself into their quiet.

"This has been good for you, hasn't it?" he asked, once again assuming the therapeutic demeanor he had shed just a few moments before.

What Tamara then saw in his eyes reignited the conviction to which he clung. He was nodding gently, encouraging her to claim what he evidently saw to be true. So, she said, "Yes. This is good for me." She looked away to avoid anything in his expression that might rob her of what she had just said. But Samuelson's arm around her shoulder answered instead.

Their walk back to Main Street was quiet. As Tamara turned up Barb's road Samuelson said, "Have your mom get in touch with me when she can. We're going to be here through Sunday. So, if anything comes up and you need to call me again, feel free, okay?"

Tamara nodded as she waved him good-bye.

Tobias and Aimee were sitting on the porch with Barb as Tamara approached the house and, from the looks of it, were in earnest conversation together. Mostly, her mom and Toby were talking to Barb who was putting up some resistance. Tamara hesitated to intrude, but once everyone took notice of her she felt the gravitational pull of their looks. She stepped up onto the porch and took the empty chair across from Barb.

Barb's eyes met Tamara's and clung to her searching for answers. At first, they were eyes of accusation: she had been betrayed by those she loved. But then, they were eyes pleading for solace from anyone who would take her in.

Tamara leaned toward Barb, scooped up her hand, then closed her eyes. It was a posture that Barb responded to immediately. Tamara's prayer lay in silence upon her own heart, but as she focused her hopes on Barb's behalf she felt the old hand release its tension as the old soul across from her became calm.

Tamara opened her eyes and stood. She was aware of the uncertain looks surrounding her, but she squeezed Barb's hand and pulled her to her feet.

"We should go for a walk," said Tamara. Then, without saying anything further, Tamara followed the impulse within her to guide Barb off the porch. In silence, they walked across the yard then along the little path beside the lamb's pasture. Aimee and Tobias followed tentatively, as if they weren't sure whether they were invited.

As they approached the river, and its gurgles sang to them like an old familiar hymn, Barb squeezed Tamara's hand and pulled her close. When they reached the river bank, instead of turning toward the bench, Tamara guided them leftward, down river, toward the baptismal pool.

They let the rushing stream speak for itself. Tamara, who had no plan beyond offering some respite from the pressures of decision-making, searched for something to say because all eyes were still on her. And all those eyes said they expected some explanation for why they were there. But as she held Barb's hand and looked down the bank where, earlier in the spring she had watched Tobias baptize several young women, all that came to mind were the questions she had been exploring during her morning prayer. So, as awkward as it felt, she ventured in:

"Barb, "Do you renounce Satan and all his ways?"

Surprised by the question, Barb looked hard at Tamara, but quietly said, "Of course I do. Why – "

"Do you confess Jesus Christ to be your only Lord and Savior?" Tamara asked, closing her eyes to Barb's protest.

Barb hesitated a moment, but with a sense of recognition in her voice, said, "Yes, yes I do."

"Do you believe that he died on the cross to save you from your sins?" continued Tamara, now looking Barb in the eyes.

"I most certainly do."

"Do you believe that he rose again from the dead and that you, too, shall join him in new and everlasting life?"

Barb squeezed Tamara's hand and said with considerable rejoicing. "O thank you, Jesus, I do!"

"And by the power and guidance of God's Holy Word and Spirit, are you ready to become a communing member of the body of Christ, the church?"

Barb became thoughtful again, then said much more quietly, though with firm conviction: "Yes, and I am so thankful that I have."

"Your church wants you to do this," said Tamara.

"Tamara's right, mom," said Tobias, "and you've said it more than I've ever said it myself, that to be a member of the Body of Christ means that we must be as ready to accept the care of others as eagerly as we offer it."

"And I've only known you for a short while," said Aimee, "but my guess is that it's easy for you to say it, because you're so eager to offer care to others and want it to be accepted. Now, we hope you will accept it from us."

Tamara had grown quiet and had stepped back from the conversation, not wanting to contribute any more intensity to what Barb must be feeling from them. She was glad Tobias had taken charge again. But Tamara's retreating posture only drew everyone's attention in her direction and she felt the crush of their expectation, which she thought was horribly misplaced now.

But as she looked hard at Barb, the older, wiser woman came to her aid once again.

"This is the place of new beginnings, if ever there was one," Barb reflected. "A place of dying and rising to new life," she whispered to herself. "We never really leave these waters behind, do we?" she asked her son.

"No, mom. We do not. It's time to live into your baptism once more, knowing that you are embraced in the arms of the church family who hold you close to the heart of your Lord."

"When is the appointment?" asked Barb.

"Tomorrow at one-thirty, in North Conway," answered her son.

"And I'm going to drive you down there," said Aimee.

"I'm afraid I have a grave-side service tomorrow afternoon," said Tobias.

"And I promised Betsy I would help her in the afternoon," said Tamara. "But we will be praying for you," she assured her old friend.

"Then, I suppose we all have our duty to keep," Barb acknowledged as she took her son's hand. She looked back down into the waters and got lost in her gratitude.

After dinner, Aimee told Barb and Tamara she wanted to walk into the village in hopes of getting some cell-phone signal to check in with Terrance.

"Oh. I forgot to tell you. Dr. Samuelson wants you to call him," said Tamara.

"I only have his cell-phone number, and he probably won't have a signal," said Aimee.

"I have the number for his cottage," said Barb.

Aimee walked down the lane toward Main Street and breathed in the evening air fully appreciating what Tamara found so beautiful there. The height of the mountains around her were having a familiar effect on her. Like the skyscrapers in the city, they swamped her with awe, but unlike those megaliths of pride and power, the heights toward which she now looked were humbling her in purifying ways. Aimee was glad she didn't have to choose between them. For the moment, she was thankful she could relish them both as part of her existence, though she surmised she might be seeing a lot more of this little valley in the weeks and months (and years?) to come.

She had to walk a ways before she found sufficient signal and connected with Terrance just as he had gotten home from the office. After catching him up on her flight, she leaned in to the situation she discovered when she arrived.

"I just spoke with Dr. Samuelson who's here until Sunday morning. He said he'd be glad to meet with us. But from the conversation I had with him, I have a feeling I know what he's going to say, and I wasn't sure we wanted to take the little time you're going to have here for a session. I think it would be better just for you to get your own feel for it all. Then, if anything, I think we should meet with Tobias instead of Samuelson. I could meet with Samuelson tomorrow, if that's okay with you, just to get his impressions but not make any decisions."

Terrance consented to Aimee's meeting with Samuelson, but he wondered why they should meet with Tobias.

"I have a feeling they are running out of time with the farm. I know that finances are of concern – at least that is Tamara's sense – and to look at the farm, I'm sure she's right. The little cottage Barb offered us will probably have to be condemned, and Tamara is taking it on herself to do maintenance and repairs around the farm. I sensed from Tobias that he's not sure how much longer they can keep the farm going. His wife is a city girl herself, and she's tired of rural life. So, they're thinking about retiring and moving closer to Philadelphia, where she's from. His mom, of course, would never leave the farm, but they can't afford to keep it up. I suspect that lays at the heart of Barb's deepest worries. And, Tobias' too, if I read him right. I sense he is under a lot of pressure from his mom right now and is caught between her and his wife."

Terrance reminded her that these were people who had been dealing with matters like this for generations, and that there was little reason to believe that relative newcomers, such as they were, would suddenly become indispensable to their cause.

"And yet, I'm beginning to believe that, maybe, we are," she responded. "Terrance, you should see the respect the other farmers have for Tamara already, especially Betsy, the woman who lent Tamara the use of the lambs for the summer. They have grown quite close. Tamara has never had a friend like that before. Betsy treats her like a sister, and Tamara is learning so much from her. And they are all seeing how important Tamara has become to Barb, including pastor Toby. So, whether we want to be part of this, or not, whatever began back in the spring has only deepened over these past two weeks and pulled us further in."

Terrance continued to apply the brakes and insisted that this was not going to rest on the shoulders of a fifteen-year old girl from Manhattan who just arrived two weeks ago.

"Until last week, no one has been keeping the farm going. But now, Tamara is here and the whole community has been watching what these two have been doing."

Terrance asked Aimee if she was entertaining notions – he used the word delusions – that they would be buying the farm.

"I made the mistake of asking him if they were thinking about selling it, and I'm afraid he got a little threatened. He said his mother wouldn't hear of it, and I assured him we weren't hunting for property in New England."

Terrance asked Aimee if she knew if Barb had some sort of pension. If the farm wasn't productive, how did she live there at all? Tobias couldn't be supporting her also, not on a pastor's salary.

"Evidently, they get some income from the cabins, enough to maintain Barb's home, at least."

"Don't those belong to the outing club?" asked Terrance.

"Not really," said Aimee. "Here's what I've been able to piece together from my conversations with Tobias and Dr. Samuelson, and this is fascinating. You know Barb owns practically the whole mountain, don't you? Remember the story? Two thirds of the mountain behind Barb's farm used to belong to the Stovers, and Mark got it as a present when he married Barb's sister. But he deeded it over to Barb's dad during the depression. They've owned it ever since. Then, several years ago, there was an interesting confluence of events. Dr. Samuelson was struggling to keep up his parent's house while living in the city, but he didn't want to lose his connection to the village. He also had heard that Barb was struggling to keep the farm going all by herself. So, he met with Tobias and together they hatched this plan. It was Samuelson who started the outing club with a couple of his buddies from the city. They put together a non-profit land management group and agreed to lease the land from Barb. They built two cabins the first year then the other three the next. Two thirds of the rent is used for upkeep and land-management. The rest has been going into a trust to maintain the farm and provide a small income for Barb, though it barely keeps up, especially as things deteriorate faster than they can maintain them now."

They wound up their conversation, then Aimee called and left Dr. Samuelson a message to invite him to the farm in the morning before she and Barb left for North Conway.

As she was walking back up Main Street, her phone rang. It was Terrance, calling to say that he had checked his calendar and was able to rearrange a work session he had scheduled with his father and a few of the officers, so he could come on Friday now. To his surprise, his father offered the corporate jet for the trip up.

"How did you rate that?" she asked with surprise, knowing her father-in-law had not been overly supportive of his son's family situation.

Terrance laughed and said he didn't know, but he thought it might be his angelic Aunt Tamara sitting on his dad's shoulder giving him a piece of her mind.

Aimee agreed to pick him up at the airport after Barb's appointment, and he would need to see if there was a seat on the flight home with her since the jet would have to return to the city for his dad's use over the weekend.

Aimee found Tamara sitting on the stoop and Barb swinging on the porch. The evening was quiet, and everyone had pulled much more deeply into themselves. But Tamara decided she couldn't take the uncertain futures that lay littered all over the porch. So, she pulled herself to her feet and stepped off the porch.

"Earl asked me to phone him the measurements so they could order the lumber," she said as she headed for the coop.

"Need a hand?" asked her mom, but Tamara pretended she hadn't heard.

There was just enough light in the coop to read the old tape measure she found in the work bench. She extended it the length of the coop and pushed the end of the tape into the far corner, then she tried to read the number, but her mind wouldn't register it. Exhaustion was overwhelming her, and she just didn't have the energy to push through this. Betsy kept warning her not to overexert herself. Even Earl had to ask her to slow down, but when she did her anxieties about Barb and where her home should be caught up with her. And now, kneeling on the hen-house floor, those apprehensions overtook her. Her heart thundered with sorrow. She fell back against the coop wall and buried her head between her knees. It was the only defensive posture she knew against the granthyrs, but since they emerged from within, hiding her vulnerability only inflamed them.

By the time Aimee went looking for Tamara, it was dark. The hens had returned to their boxes and the coop was quiet. She could barely make out her daughter laying curled tightly in the corner. She was conscious but unaware of the filth that now coated her.

Aimee helped her to her feet. Knowing she would soon be quite soiled herself, she held Tamara as close as she could to walk her back to the house and up to the shower.

Barb was waiting with fresh towels for Aimee when she came back down the steps and ushered her into her bathroom.

When Aimee reappeared, Barb had the kettle on and offered Aimee some tea.

"She is so afraid," whispered Aimee, as Barb took her hand and led her to the kitchen table.

"As we were walking up, I asked her if anything had happened that brought this on. All she said was, 'I can't leave.' She said that three or four times. The thought of leaving terrifies her. I asked her what she was so afraid of, and do you know what she said? She said, 'Those frightening things I have to stand up to and defeat.'"

Barb went pale as she recognized the words and feared she was responsible, but Aimee waved off Barb's attempt at self-reproach and took it all upon herself.

"I know those may have been your words, but I forced her down that path. I kept pushing her back into those terrifying places expecting her to defeat this, and every once in a while – every once in a while, I think she's going to."

Aimee got up and paced around the room.

"I don't know what to do for her anymore," whispered Aimee.

"Don't you?" asked Barb.

That halted Aimee, and when their eyes met, Barb encouraged her to think about what she has seen since she arrived.

"But what about tonight?" countered Aimee. "How often is she like this?"

"More when she first arrived, but once she settled into a manageable routine she was much better. I'm sure a lot of this has to do with the uncertainties that have just come up," said Barb, her voice diminishing as she considered how her own health questions were clouding the picture. "Tomorrow should tell us more of what we need to know," she reassured Aimee.

"God, I hope so."

"That is my prayer, as well," whispered Barb.

27

ANOTHER STEP FORWARD

TAMARA CAME IN WITH A basket of eggs and washed them as Barb commenced preparing breakfast. Aimee, who normally didn't rise until after Barb and Tamara had finished their devotions was already up, so Barb began setting the table.

"I thought we might all have prayer together at the table," Barb whispered to Tamara, "or would you rather invite your mom to join us over by the stove first, before breakfast?"

Tamara agreed it would be more comfortable for her mother if they did it together. Furthermore, she didn't have the energy to direct her own thoughts in solitude or to navigate a spiritually awkward experience with her mother present.

"How did you sleep?" asked Aimee as she entered the kitchen, but Tamara didn't answer.

Neither did Tamara eat much breakfast, but she excused herself and said she had to get down to the barn.

"By the way," she said to her mom. "Betsy's coming around eight-thirty. Something I think you might want to see."

Aimee was leaning against a fence post watching her daughter take the lambs through their morning regimen of fresh hay, water, and a lap or two around the pasture when Betsy drove down the little lane in her old pick-up truck.

As Betsy parked, a commotion commenced in the cab as two black and white faces danced around on the front seat. But as Betsy whistled one sharp note, they snapped to attention and sat as still as could be.

Betsy opened the pasture gate, then her truck door, and gave two whistles to launch the dogs from their perch. They raced into the pasture, but Betsy quickly halted them, and they returned to settle down by her left leg.

"These lambs haven't been around the dogs for a while," she explained, "so we'll have to take this slow." Betsy spoke a soft command to the dogs and they walked slowly toward the sheep then lay flat down on their bellies. The lambs, already startled and on alert, backed away, then quieted. Betsy repeated the command. The dogs advanced again then prostrated themselves once more.

"Follow me," Betsy said to Tamara, and together they walked slowly to the dogs.

"Pat your right leg," Betsy instructed Tamara. They led the two border collies around the sheep in a wide arc, allowing the lambs to watch, then they walked the dogs back to the gate. From there, Betsy gave a series of whistles and the dogs repeated the slow promenade without her. But this time, when they reached the far side and were behind the lambs, they gently nudged the little flock in Betsy's direction.

Aimee was rapt with wonder as she watched the collies work the lambs. They seemed to read Betsy's mind as she moved the lambs at will wherever she wanted them to go. But the miracle took place over by the gate where Tamara had stationed herself. As the dogs swept the flock toward the old apple tree, Aimee's eye caught Tamara watching her lambs, and Tamara was laughing. There was joy on her face, brightness in her eyes, then a look of pride to see her lambs being herded by those two wondrous creatures. Soon, Tamara bore the dignified look of a serious farm woman again, but Aimee now knew there was more behind those eyes than darkness.

"You okay?" asked Betsy.

"Never better," said Aimee, wiping her eyes. She pointed in Tamara's direction. "She looks like she belongs here, doesn't she?"

Betsy rested her hand on Aimee's shoulder, then looked her in the eyes. "She does," Betsy replied. "She does belong here."

Then, seeing Tamara walking in their direction, Betsy said, "Well, want to give that a try?"

"They did pretty well," said Tamara.

"The dogs know their job. They just need to get to know you, and you'll need to learn to whistle," Betsy laughed. "Right now, I've got to get them on home."

"What time this afternoon?" asked Tamara.

"Come on over once everyone leaves for the doctor's. Then, you and Earl can go pick up your lumber and deliver that back here. If you want, he can show you how to lay the floor and the two of you can tinker with that until everyone gets back home."

"I still need to call Earl with the measurements," added Tamara, looking down, remembering she had not followed through.

"Don't worry," Betsy reassured her. "Can you do that now? It just may mean you'll have to wait while Skate trims the boards, that's all. No big deal."

Tamara nodded, then she turned back toward the chicken coop.

"You call as soon as you get back, okay," Betsy said to Aimee with concern in her voice.

"Chances are we won't know much today," Aimee told her. "This is more of an initial screening which we hope will point us in a clearer direction for more comprehensive tests later on."

"All the same," said Betsy.

As Betsy was driving out the lane toward Main Street, Aimee was going to walk down to the hen-house when she saw Dr. Samuelson walking up the path from the river.

"It's a beautiful day for a hike," he beamed, as he approached. "I hope you folks get the chance to hike up the mountain sometime over the weekend."

Aimee couldn't tell if he was being serious, but she shuddered at the mental imagery that crashed through her mind of their last experience at the overlook.

"How is she doing?" he asked.

"Which one?" asked Aimee, raising her eyebrows.

"Right," he said. "I was referring to Tamara. But, both, if you don't mind."

"Barb had a quiet night. She's inside getting ready to go. Tamara, on the other hand, is a different story. She had a rather rough evening."

"Oh?" The therapeutic tone in Samuelson's voice was unmistakable. He waited while Aimee searched out the words she evidently needed to say.

"I think she was doing just fine until I arrived, I'm afraid," Aimee confessed.

Samuelson nodded with understanding but didn't comment.

"Where is she?" he asked.

"She just went in to call Earl with measurements for a new floor for the chicken coop."

Samuelson grinned and shook his head. "Aimee," he began, but was cut off.

"You don't need to say it, too. Everyone else has," she said, looking to the heavens.

"I'm not sure that what I was about to say is what anyone else would have on their minds at this particular moment," Samuelson countered.

"Sorry," Aimee whispered. "But, before you do continue, I need to apologize for treating you the way I have lately. You have never shown anything but compassion for our daughter. And after all these years, I wonder how I never really saw that. I had such thick blinders on going in and wielded such a big stick warding off people like you who I thought couldn't understand. But the push you gave us back in the spring…"

Aimee's composure had been deteriorating from word one, but now she had imploded completely, and she couldn't continue.

As Samuelson watched Aimee and gave her room to sort out her thoughts, Tamara came out of the house, leapt off the porch, forced open the gate into the large field behind the house and started walking along the fence-row.

"Do you want to go sit on the porch?" Samuelson asked Aimee, who was taking deep breaths again.

"Anyway," she continued, "I just need you to know that our coming here last spring has changed everything. Everything," she added with emphasis. "And, I'm not sure what that 'everything' even means yet. But on some level, I know it means Tamara needs to be here, at least for the near term. I don't know how that will work, especially with Barb's circumstances, but now that the blinders are off some things are all too clear." Aimee's last statement became the leverage she needed, and a great weight began to give way within her.

"What is so clear?" asked Samuelson.

"Tamara can't go back home," said Aimee in a rush, hoping to get the words all out before she gave way again.

Samuelson absorbed what he knew to be the truth and laid a hand on Aimee's shoulder.

"But how?" Where Aimee held clarity in her mind only a moment before, now she was awash in darkness and panic was rolling through her.

"She can't stay here with Barb if Barb is ill," Aimee pleaded. "I can't stay here and leave Terrance in the city. And he won't come. He's almost incarcerated by his family and held captive by their business. And, he loves the city. Every gene in his body buzzes with New York City. Tamara will die if we take her back there. And he would die here."

"And where are you prepared to die?" he asked Aimee.

She was jolted by the question, then she whispered, "I seem to be dying in both places."

"But, of course, the real question then becomes, where will you be reborn?" Samuelson looked at her only a moment longer, then he relieved Aimee of his stare and looked back to the larger pasture.

Tamara was now walking the long edge of the field which traveled beside the river and ascended along a steady grade that would soon become a mountain beyond it.

"Have you asked Tamara how she has managed to sort all this out?" asked Samuelson. "Because you know she's been working on it. I doubt that all that anxiety has been fruitless. If I know her, she's been beating herself senseless to figure this out. I'm guessing that what frightens her is that we won't support what she knows to be the truth. Should we just ask her?"

"Before we do, there was one other thing," said Aimee. "Her medication. Now that I am seeing all of this so differently, I need to revisit that again. So, if you have any thoughts, I'd be interested in what you might prescribe."

Samuelson considered her question for some time before venturing an answer, and then said, "My prescription? Mountain air and a flock of sheep, a coop-full of chickens, an old woman to care for, and a church community to adopt her as their sister in Christ. That, deep in my soul, is what I know she needs. That is what I wanted for her from the first day I met her, or something of the sort. Medication may still play some role – I have been keeping a close eye on that prospect. But we keep muddying the waters and feeding her anxieties, I'm afraid. We could still treat those pharmaceutically and she could get on with whatever life we think is best. But then what have we really done for her?"

Aimee nodded as she took a deep breath and watched her daughter walk the fence.

"And, if I may speak personally," continued Samuelson, "this is what I would hope for my own son, if he could find half the life-wisdom in his illness as your daughter has in hers."

"Dr. Samuelson," whispered Aimee, as she processed what she had just been told. "I never knew. Why didn't you ever tell us?"

"It wasn't your place to be my therapist, or even my friend, and it wasn't mine to break our professional covenant. Now, I'm not so sure it matters. Here, those kind of formalities don't seem to be all that important. Now, putting my doctoring shoes back on, there are a few medications that might help take the edge off her depression or anxiety, and if we do feel those would help then we have to discuss it with her."

"Well, I think it's time we faced up to all of it. If for no other reason than to clear the air so we can get on with life, wherever that life takes us," acknowledged Aimee.

Samuelson put two fingers in his mouth and pierced the valley with a long, shrieking whistle that make Aimee duck.

"Sorry," laughed Samuelson. "Pamela Nazareth taught me that. Comes in handy." He pointed out into the field as Tamara turned and began walking back to them.

"Where were you off to?" asked Aimee when Tamara finally let herself back through the gate.

"I was checking the fences," she answered, then explained: "If we're going to breed the sheep, then the little pasture won't be big enough for them." Tamara looked out over the meadow. "I think Barb said there were twelve acres that stretch through there then up into the mountain. It's all fenced, but we don't want any more coyotes."

"So, that's what the dogs are for?" asked Aimee, putting the pieces together.

Tamara nodded. "Don't need them for such a small pasture as that," she said looking over the fence they were all leaning upon.

"Tamara, when your dad arrives in a little while, it seems we have some important decisions to begin making. And please, correct me if I'm wrong, but I sense you've already made up your mind about what you hope will happen."

Tamara face became white. She looked at her little flock, then she nodded that she had.

"Can you tell us, or shall I connect the dots to see if I've been paying attention?" asked her mom.

Tamara turned to look at her mom, who had a faint smile on her face, so Tamara nodded her encouragement.

"You plan to stay with Barb, keep an eye on her, and her on you, grow that flock, and harvest that garden. Am I right so far?"

Tamara's eyes glistened to hear her hope verbalized.

"So, the question is, how long?" Aimee continued. "Unless it's open ended, we'll never really let you settle in and know for sure. There will always be the specter of the city, and there will always be that date on the calendar that haunts you."

Tamara was riveted to her mom, eager for her to press on.

"School in the city is toxic. Who knows what it will be like here, though. But this is where you plan to get your real education, is it not?" asked Aimee, indicating the farm around here.

Tears were rolling over Tamara's cheeks.

"And you know, beyond all doubt, that if this should prove to be less than ideal down the road, there are other ways to start again? And nothing is lost in the trying."

"Yes," whispered Tamara.

"Now. We need to get serious. Barb may be in for difficult times, and my biggest worry is that both of you are going to be facing challenges that may require more than you can give each other. That's the piece I don't have sorted out yet, I'm afraid."

"We all help each other," Tamara responded after a moment of reflection. "Betsy, Nora, Tobias."

"And," interjected Dr. Samuelson, "I'm getting to the point where I'm up here almost as much as I am in New York these days. I haven't taken on any more clients for a year now and am gradually giving up the practice. I'm really only tracking three patients on a regular basis, one of whom is standing right here. I would relish yet another reason to tip the scales and let go a little more of the city. Frankly, I'm getting tired of it too, Tamara."

"Tamara, we still have to discuss your request for medication. That's why we called you. What are you thinking about that?"

Tamara thought for a few moments and then slowly shook her head.

"I don't know anymore," she whispered.

"We were going to see if this experience alleviated any particular symptoms and then target medication to what was left over," Samuelson reminded her. "It's still a little early – you haven't been here long enough to know for sure, but I'm still seeing signs of depression, anxiety, and a lack of sleep. Any delusions or hallucinations?"

Tamara nodded. "Just after I arrived, but mostly the other three."

"And how much of those do you think will soften if we can settle these questions about your future?" he asked.

Tamara shrugged her shoulders without looking at anyone.

"What if we started with something that might help you sleep?" he asked.

Tamara shook her head. "I have to be able to listen for Barb," she insisted.

"Anxiety?" Samuelson suggested.

Tamara nodded, and confirmed that of all her maladies it was her bouts of anxiety and the deep seasons of apprehension that took their greatest toll.

But as she fell silent again she reflected that she was seeing those diminish as she took on responsibilities that kept her focused in a meaningful direction. She was learning a lot about how to address some of her most vexing quandaries concerning faith, family, and her future. As she had taken those uncertainties in hand, stared them in the face, and found such wise people to discuss them with, her apprehensions had transfigured within her and become sources of strength. So, she said, "I'd rather try to work it out without medication, for now."

"What about your bad moods, your depression?" pressed Aimee, though she struggled to articulate the condition and used it only because it was next on Samuelson's list.

Tamara considered the question but didn't answer. She looked at her mom, and as their eyes met years of interlacing psychic battles had found their truce. They were on the same side of this. She may never get a day off from her depressive moods. But her days were now saturated with meaning, and she was sensing that the darkness now held more than emptiness or terror. She had seen evidence that it could be the very gateway to the joy she had been searching for all her life. If, that is, her darkness could be redemptive for others, and if her suffering could be placed into the service of her Shepherd.

She had learned something of what it means to lay aside one's life, and she had felt the excruciating elation of seeing another be comforted, or strengthened, even as her soul lay waste for them. She wanted more of that despite its cost. The great difference for her now was that she need not fear losing herself all alone. She was being carried even as she sought to carry others. If the pain became too acute, these people knew what a yoke was for, and they knew how to distribute their pain amongst them and shoulder it together. She had no fear of that, no trepidation for the pain it would cause her, only the satisfaction of knowing that for now it meant something. It was real. And, it was good.

So, again, Tamara indicated she would rather keep trying without pharmaceutical assistance, though she consented that they would discuss this again with Barb and Betsy, and that they be given license to contact someone if they felt it was warranted.

Aimee grabbed the back of Tamara's head and pulled her close. Tamara reciprocated and hugged her mother.

"We've got to go eat some lunch so Barb and I can leave. Want a sandwich?" she asked Dr. Samuelson.

"Thank you, no. Shelly's waiting lunch for me up the hill. Please, do call when you find out something?"

"Of course, I will," said Aimee.

Along with a truck load of lumber, Earl and Tamara brought a length of wire fence so they could build the hens a temporary enclosure just inside the barn. Earl and Tamara searched through the tool locker and found an old pry-bar, a crosscut saw, and a couple of hammers. Earl showed Tamara how to pull out the old boards and nail down their replacements.

"When you get to the studs, you'll need to trim those planks two to four inches, depending on where they lay. When you get all the way across, if there's not quite enough space, let me know. We may have to rip those over at Betsy's."

The job was slow going at first. Tamara's inexperience with tools and manual labor kept her feeling awkward. She bent quite a few nails and was glad Earl opted for the large bucket. Steadily, she found her rhythm with the hammer and saw and began making decent headway down the coop.

That's where Terrance found her a few hours later.

"I heard you were the head hen running the farm now," he said.

"Sorry, sir, we're all out of eggs," she answered him. "You'll have to come back in the morning."

Terrance hugged his daughter, and she had to endure the same looking over that her mom had given her several days ago.

"Any word on Barb?" Tamara asked her dad.

"Not much yet. It'll be a day or two before some of the tests come back. Mid-week I expect we'll hear something."

Tamara took her dad on a brief tour of the hen-house project and the sheep pens in the barn, then she let him into the pasture to introduce him to the flock.

"And I wish you could have met Lanolander," she said, as they walked past the apple tree. "I named him after that day in the zoo when you taught me why their wool makes your hands so soft."

"I heard the story," he said, now more serious in his demeanor. He stopped and looked at his daughter once more. He saw his Aunt Tamara in her, that subtle lifting of the cheeks and grace-filled eyes now lingering on a face simply remembering a lamb.

As the lambs grazed not six feet from them, and the sound of the river could just be heard, Tamara patted her thigh and whistled (though not as sharply as Betsy). Woolimittens and Lupinore lumbered in their direction. She grabbed Woolimittens by the nap of the neck, squatted down beside her, and buried her hands into her wool.

"Go ahead," she said to her dad. "You know you want to."

The dinner conversation was serious but allowed everyone to take a few steps forward into a future still very unsure for them all. Barb was given every opportunity to change her mind considering the uncertainties that lay before her, but she insisted that her offer stood, and Tamara was welcome to stay for as long as she wanted. And, yes, if enrolling in the local school was best for Tamara, then they should investigate that.

Tamara went to her room later that evening with a heart lighter than she could ever remember. Her birthday might have rivaled it, but tonight there seemed a sense of resolve among those she loved that everyone was in sync. The sluices that shed sewage back and forth between her and her parents were becalmed. She closed her door and let her eyes take in the petitions that spoke to the future she felt lay before her:

> O Divine Master,
> grant that I may not so much seek to be consoled as to console;
> to be understood as to understand;
> to be loved as to love.
> For it is in giving that we receive;
> it is in pardoning that we are pardoned;
> and it is in dying that we are born to eternal life.

So much had died, she thought, and so much had been born. And with that new birth came new purpose for her life. She would go to bed that night knowing that her rising the next day would bear the resonance of eternity. It also dawned on her that tomorrow was the Sabbath, the day of rest and reflection, a day of worship, prayer, and promise.

As she reached for the light on her desk to turn it off, her eye caught the picture of her dad's great Aunt Tamara.

"I know where that smile came from," she declared out loud.

28

A Short, But Eternal Walk

THE FAMILY AROSE IN TURNS with Tamara greeting the dawn. She hadn't slept much, but what kept her awake was the sense of possibility that coursed through her now. She spent part of the night exploring Barb's library growing ever more curious about the language of her new faith, its history, traditions, and the many expressions of prayer. She had never thought of herself as a student though she enjoyed learning when her mind would allow her sufficient focus. Long periods of reflection, however, had always jumped the rails and collided with hostile forces that grew jealous and thrust themselves into her consciousness.

Lately, however, with the discipline of work came also the discipline of thought, and she was able to take into the pasture those insights she gained during her morning devotions and allow them to mature. The lambs gave her ample latitude for meditation and further prayer. She was developing, on her own, a contemplative soul which gave her a solemn joy along with a deepening peace.

Tamara slipped downstairs to stoke the fire and begin the coffee, but she couldn't wait to check on the hens to see how they made out in their makeshift coop. The morning air was crisp, and a light fog lay about the valley.

She slid open one of the big double doors and, to her irritation, the chickens were all over the barn. She closed the sliding door behind her, tugged the pull-chain to get a little light, then she scurried around the barn chasing the hens back into their temporary enclosure. How they got out she didn't know, but she couldn't find many eggs. In the end, she located only two. Not much of a breakfast for her family. She had perfected her omelet and wanted to show it off for her dad.

As she felt a lone granthyr gnawing at the legbone of her self-esteem, she shook it off. "Ham biscuits, then," she said, though she knew Barb probably had a few eggs from yesterday. Still, they weren't today's.

After breakfast, Terrance opted for a stroll to see the lupines instead of joining the rest of the clan at church.

The worship experience still felt foreign to Tamara, but the place she had been given within the fellowship by the members of the community carried her through the service. Familiarity, even comfort, would come with time and experience. She didn't have to be in a hurry now. What she felt, intensely, was the body of faith surrounding her and the sincerity of the prayer she experienced with them. That communal mystery still confounded her even as she stood upon fresh thresholds of wonder. This was now a world she identified as her own.

As the congregation engaged in the prayers of the people, Tamara recognized a few of the voices as their requests were offered. One voice, in particular, pierced deeply her heart: "Healing for our son, Patrick," said Dr. Samuelson from behind her.

Then, from the end of the pew to her right, Pamela Nazareth stood and spoke, clear as the morning, "Lord, strengthen thy servant Barb against all manner of darkness. Heal her, body, mind, and spirit. Take the worry from her mind, the stress from her heart, and the shadows from her soul, that she may serve thee, love thee, and bless thee, all her days."

The congregation erupted with amens, but Pamela was not finished.

"And, dear Lord, we so thank you for your servant Tamara, whom you sent to walk with Barb and Barb with her. We welcome her into our family of faith, and we bless her efforts on the farm. May she know the joy of serving you all the days of her life."

A strong farm-woman arm wrapped around Tamara's neck as Betsy, seated to her left, pulled her close in a bear-like embrace and kissed her atop the head.

Tobias introduced the scripture lessons and read them from the large Bible on the pulpit. Following each lesson, he said, "The Word of the Lord," to which everyone in attendance shouted, "Thanks be to God!" Tamara joined in by the third lesson but still felt left behind by the language of Scripture and the strange concepts which were clearly so familiar to those around her.

There was so much to learn, and the more she learned, the more expansive became the mysterious regions that lay before her. Soon, she would begin reading through Barb's books, one by one, as she had time. The illustrated New Testament her mother gave her had painted a range of images upon her mind that kept informing her reading of the Bible. Often, as she read, her imagination would sketch the scenes, like the old masters of the renaissance, only her demon-possessed souls looked like people from the streets of New York. Many of the women had Tonya's face, and the neighbors she met at the General took on the characteristics of the villagers in the Gospels.

She imagined Jesus as he walked into the General to talk about lost pearls, or she saw him standing by the barn crib telling stories about sheep, or weeding the garden as he paused to ruminate about sowing seeds or tending grape-vines. There, she imagined lengthy conversations she would have with her Shepherd about where he was leading her, and how she might be of help. And, she wasn't interested in capturing her mental images in a two-dimensional medium, but in translating the insights she gained from those imaginings into caring for her lambs, watching after Barb, and helping Betsy when she could.

Pastor Toby preached a sermon on how to love others as Christ so loves us: with a vision for the wellbeing of the other, with the hand of mercy, and with a sacrificial heart. Then, once again, he invited the congregation to accept the call of grace and invitation to new faith. He invited them to prayerfully consider entering into the covenant of baptism and church membership and to join Christ in loving others as we have been so loved by him.

Tamara had stopped trying to figure this out. It was the time for new steps to be taken and fresh commitments to be made. Her family had blessed her. She had made her commitment to Barb, now she needed to make her commitment to her Shepherd. And, as she scanned the room, she became over-awed by the prospect of sharing that commitment so publicly with those who had so generously taken her in. Was she truly committed to these people? With all her heart she intended to be. She would need a lot of help if she were to keep that commitment, but that was the point, wasn't it? She was surrounded by those she trusted to help. And, she wanted to help them with what little faith and energy she could muster.

Tamara closed her eyes and fingered Aunt Tamara's cross. There were unseen forces standing behind her, just as there were mysterious movements of grace urging her onward. She slipped past Betsy and walked the few feet to the front where Tobias was singing. He put down his hymnal and warmly embraced Tamara, then he laid his hands upon her head and prayed a prayer of gratitude.

As the song drew to a close, he stood with his arm around Tamara and said, "I want to introduce to you a good friend. This is Tamara Baxter. She comes to us this morning confessing her faith in Jesus Christ and seeking baptism and membership in this congregation. She's going to be with us for a while, and I know you are going to make her feel welcome among us."

As the people began dispersing, and Tamara was hugged more than she cared to be hugged, Barb gave her the final embrace and shielded her from the rest.

"I need to spend a few moments with Tobias once he's done here," said Barb, "so why don't you and your mom walk on home. Take out the rest of the roast we had Wednesday evening and either start warming it up or slice it for sandwiches. I'll be along as soon as I can."

Terrance was waiting on the porch when Aimee and Tamara arrived.

"How were the lupines?" asked Aimee.

"Exquisite," confirmed Terrance, then he put both hands in his pocket and became introspective.

"I have to say," he ventured, "this feels like a different place this time."

Aimee was hoping for a few moments so they could talk quietly together, but as Barb walked slowly down the drive, Aimee felt it best not to engage him too deeply yet.

"How was church?" Terrance asked his daughter.

Warily, Tamara nodded that it was okay.

"Tell him," encouraged her mother.

Tamara blushed, but then she mumbled, "I'm going to baptized."

Terrance took a deep breath then nodded his affirmation.

"I promised you that you would have my total support, and I'm here to keep my word. When will it take place?" he asked.

"Probably in August. I have to get ready first," she said.

"If you can make it anytime but the 12th," he said, looking at his calendar, "then I'll be there on the bank cheering you on."

As the after-lunch conversation ebbed, Barb turned to Tamara and said quietly, "I think it's time for that walk you and I spoke about. What do you say?"

Tamara closed her eyes for a moment to mine her soul for strength, then she nodded, though she wasn't eager to follow through.

"Tamara and I are going to walk up to the overlook. We would be glad for you join us, or you can enjoy the day as you please," she suggested to the two parents.

Aimee looked a little stunned, and Terrance's face went pale.

"You don't have to," Barb assured them. "We'll go slow and take our time, but I sort of laid a promise in Tamara's lap, that she help me walk up there, perhaps for the last time. I think this old mule of a body has one more climb in it, and I would dearly love to see the view on such a gorgeous day as this."

Terrance and Aimee looked warily at one another, but both agreed that it would be best for all hands to be available, so Aimee went to change her clothes for a hike back into memories none of them cared to relive.

"I'll pack us a snack, then, and we'll be off," commanded Barb.

The gradual incline along the river was gentle, and the rise up the slope was rather easy on everyone's frame of mind until they saw the sign for the Rusty Axe Lodge. No one had any desire to take in that view again, so in unspoken consensus they pressed on. Tamara sensed the jolts of lightning igniting harsh images in each of her parents, and she saw them vividly in her own mind.

Barb took it slow, but her years on the farm bore evidence that she was bred for hard work. They rested often, but it gave everyone the opportunity to let the events of the past several days find their rightful place. Harsh memories and lingering anxieties were struggling to evolve into something new. Whatever that something new was, however, it had to push against the grim haunts that were overtaking them the higher they climbed.

At one point, it was Barb who had her hand at Aimee's back, pressing lightly as if to lend the younger woman strength to prod her forward. Barb's demeanor conveyed understanding and assurance that this, in the end, would be good for them all. Her soft, unspoken wisdom encouraged them to do the hard work of relinquishing the past for the sake of what was coming.

When they emerged onto the overlook, everyone allowed Barb a few moments alone at the small wall with the plaque dedicated to Sally Anne, Mark, and little Tobias. Then, she turned, and urged them to all come and have a look.

"You can see clear on to tomorrow, can't you?" observed Barb.

The others noted the tone of triumph and hope in her voice and took solace from it. Aimee was looking longingly at Barb and aching for whatever prospects her potential diagnosis might reveal, and Tamara had closed her eyes to the wind, which lifted her long black hair slightly off her shoulders. This time, her demeanor was placid, and the corners of her lips lifted slightly as she let the afternoon sun warm her face.

Terrance stood somewhat apart and watched the other women.

"I confess, I'm having a hard time seeing much past today," he admitted. His voice betrayed his weariness and the uncertainties constricting his heart where his family was concerned. To be standing on this old precipice, facing an uncertain future, proved to be more of a challenge to him than he wanted to acknowledge. But, he had come to trust that the three women standing between him and some unknown eternity were the only reliable navigational tools at his disposal.

"Oh, is it really so hard?" said Barb, laying a hand on his arm. "I've always thought this is a great place to find clarity about those imponderables that become so muddled up down there in the valley. But climb up here, clear your head, let your heart stretch itself for miles in all directions, and life begins to show you something new."

They all tried to milk something from that, but Terrance shifted in his quandary and still looked visibly perplexed.

"Let me help," continued Barb. "Tobias and I have been talking for a long time about what to do with the farm. I made him swear to me never to sell it, and he is committed, one way or another, to seeing that it stays in the family. And for a long time, we've been at loggerheads with one another about what to do. His wife doesn't want children or the farm."

She looked somewhat embarrassed to be saying that, and the glistening light in her eyes wasn't helping Terrance's composure.

"What do you think we ought to do?" she asked Terrance, her eyes now wet with considerable pain.

"Like I said," was as far as he got, but he couldn't keep the connection between them alive, so he glanced at Aimee, whose searching expression drained him of his last reserves of certainty.

"For many years, we have both brought this question up the mountain here for prayer," continued Barb. "But about a month ago, I came down with an answer. I never said anything to Tobias about it, though. I just trusted. And I watched to see what God would do about it. Then, the other day, Tobias came back down with the same answer. He knocked on the kitchen door and said he wanted to discuss an idea he'd been praying about, but I had beaten him to it. You see, Terrance, God sorts these things out when we think there just aren't any answers left."

Terrance just shook his head.

Barb laid a hand on Terrance's arm and said, "Tobias and I both now believe, with all our hearts, that Tamara is our sister in Christ, a daughter of the faith. She has become as much a part of our family as any child will ever be."

Barb let go of Terrance and turned to Tamara. She held both of Tamara's shoulders in her hands and looked directly into the young woman's eyes.

"Tamara, this is a big step," she said, "and it's one you will have to pray hard about and discuss with your parents, but Tobias and I would like for you to have the farm. We have no one else to give it to, and we know of no one else who could love it as much, or care for it any better, than you have. Tobias told me the other day how much he had grieved the decision he and his wife made not to have children. She refused, or couldn't, I don't really know. He told me he saw you in the field the other day and just wept for the daughter he never had. But then, he rejoiced to think that perhaps you might accept what he could never give his own child."

As she let that sink in, Barb turned to Aimee and Terrance. "I met with Tobias once more following worship, just to make sure we were both still serious about this. We decided that if everyone is in agreement, then he will call our lawyer on Monday and we'll have my will adjusted while I am still of sound mind. In the meantime, for as long as Tamara is willing, and finds this to be the life she desires, then upon my death, it will be hers. If she should change her mind and realize this is not for her, then we can make other arrangements. Tobias will have complete power of attorney over my estate and affairs, so further decisions can be made with him."

Terrance looked long into the old woman's eyes and nodded his appreciation for the business-like demeanor Barb could achieve in the face of what was clearly such an emotional moment for them all.

"Now, let's go sit down and have a snack," said Barb.

Everyone walked in silence to the large stones on the other side of the overlook where Barb began to prepare the refreshments she had brought.

"I'm sad to say, however," said Barb, "that it's not a very good time to be a farmer. A little farm like this needs something more to keep it going than a few sheep and fresh eggs every morning."

"I didn't want to say it, but that's just what I was thinking," Terrance acknowledged.

"It will take the sort of creative gifts I'm sure this family has to make it work. So, just for fun, let's dream a little," Barb encouraged them.

They were still stunned from the revelation, so Barb egged them on.

"How many sheep could you manage?" she asked Tamara with a great deal of animation.

"Dozens," Tamara said, trying to mimic Barb's mannerisms. "Three horses, and a cow for coffee milk in the morning!"

"What about that pig you were dreaming about not too long ago?" joked Terrance.

"I was just thinking," said Aimee, now introducing a more serious tone into the game, "with the lodges here, we might be able to coordinate with the Outing Club and have an artist's residency for a week or so."

Terrance nodded, then he said to Tamara, "With 'dozens' of sheep, I was just wondering about setting up a means for processing the wool. And your mom's idea might be expanded to weavers or other crafters."

"We could grow herbs and market them in the city," Aimee offered.

Then, everyone noticed how quiet Tamara had become, so all eyes were now upon her.

Tamara shook her head and stood. She turned to look out over the valley. "I think all that's too small," she whispered.

She walked to the overlook. After scanning the endless landscape that spread before her, she looked back down at the small plaque affixed to the wall, bearing the names of Mark, Sally Anne, and Tobias. This should be theirs, she thought. They should have realized the blessing of all that Barb was giving to her: the life it promises, the purpose it instills, the dreams it might have fulfilled for them.

She remembered the words that Sally Anne had underlined in her Bible:

For I am persuaded, that neither death, nor life, nor angels, nor principalities, nor powers, nor things present, nor things to come, nor height, nor depth, nor any other creature, shall be able to separate us from the love of God, which is in Christ Jesus our Lord.

Sally Anne may not have been separated from God's love, but did she know that? Something so dark had eclipsed that love for her that she lost her bearings, and there was no one to take her hand. Barb had been prevented by her father from offering Sally Anne the love she needed. But Barb had freely stepped into that darkness where Tamara had dwelled for so long. Tamara had been lost to that love she never knew existed until an old woman looked deeply into her eyes, invited her home to the farm, and gave her work to do, meaningful work, work which has already given profound shape to her life.

"Tamara," said Aimee.

Tamara walked slowly back to the others.

"What is it, honey?" asked her mom.

Tamara, already withdrawn into herself, was seeing something beautiful taking shape within her. And she knew it was meant to flourish in the lives of others.

"Other people like me should have this kind of experience," she said. "This should always be a place of new beginnings."

As they walked back down the mountain, they came to the turn-off for Lupine Lodge. Tamara stopped and said she was going to go talk with Dr. Samuelson for a few moments. She would catch up with them later.

29

THAT DYING THAT
BECOMES LIVING AGAIN

"TAMARA BAXTER, DO YOU RENOUNCE Satan and all his ways?" asked Pastor Toby.

Tamara stared into Thorafura's hate-filled face and dared the serpent to speak or even to move. Her heart beat powerfully within her. Her defense against the darkness was no longer maintained by strength of will but by an everlasting grace now at work on her behalf. 'You are defeated by these waters,' thought Tamara, 'drowned by these rivers of mercy. You may pester, and you may bite, but you cannot kill, and you will not defeat the purposes of God now at work among us here.' So, leaning against the river pushing her downstream, she said defiantly, "Yes, I certainly do."

"Do you confess Jesus Christ to be your only Lord and Savior?"

Tobias' voice was proud. He had rested his right hand between Tamara's shoulder blades and lifted the other to the sky. Tamara looked him in the eyes so long she almost forgot he had asked her the most important question of her life.

"I do," she said to pastor Toby, as he held her steady in the rapidly flowing stream. His hand, firmly pressing against her back, was the only stability she felt in the moment. All else was imitating the river flowing around her. Her life was now fluid with motion, moving forward into a vibrant, but uncertain, tomorrow.

She pictured the Shepherd who had led her to these waters now awaiting her emergence from the stream. He had led her there so he could lead her on to the next new beginning in her life. What would that look like? She leaned into Tobias and was reassured of the help she had been promised.

The water was biting cold, but Tamara had stopped noticing anything but the sound of Tobias' voice and the sensations of grace rushing through her consciousness. She was waiting intently for the next question, envisioning her Shepherd, also the Lamb of God pierced by nails of hate. Now, he stood with her and continued his work to conquer her darkness. He had trounced the serpent that slithers through her soul, and he had cleansed her putrid psyche of the crippling brokenness that causes her suffering. Was she through with Thorafura? No. But the serpent was defeated, and the granthyrs were but pitiful children of her shame.

"Do you believe that Jesus died on the cross to save you from your sins?" she was asked.

Lanolander's bloody body resting in its grave, and the Lamb of God fiercely slaughtered on the cross, both became one and the same in her mind. Both had taught her that her own value and goodness were not her own to assign. Her new worth lay bound up in her status as God's child, a status Jesus secured for her through his sacrifice, and one she would offer to others as she suffered alongside them. She had been cleansed by God, and these forceful waters flowing around her assured her that her cleansing was God's work, not hers.

She almost got lost in that rumination, but the grip of Tobias' voice clung to Tamara's awareness and pulled her back into the moment.

"I do," said Tamara, feeling the force and focus of her convictions mounting up within her.

"Do you believe that Jesus rose again from the dead and that you, too, shall join him in new and everlasting life?" asked Tobias.

"Yes," she said, now standing beside the hellish well in which she had been drowning for so long, its heavy lid cast aside, its demons routed. Now, she was ready to stand with her Shepherd at the dawn of a new day. The light that had erupted from Jesus' tomb felt resplendent in her, and the life he promised resonated deeply within.

Whatever the darkness might look like, and she had no illusions that there would be no more shadows, the darkness would not overcome the light she now knew, a light that had guided her there, a light that would sustain her no matter how sinister the night might become. She looked at Barb and knew her mind to be one of those corners of the world where shadows were gathering. But the light that stepped out of the tomb can sweep those shades aside, contain their torrents within their borders, and sustain those who must travel that way, which Tamara was still bound to do.

"And, Tamara, by the power and guidance of God's Holy Word and Spirit, are you ready to become a communing member of the Body of Christ, the church?"

She looked upon the faces gathered on the river bank, many of whom she didn't even know yet but were filled with pride on her behalf. They were blessing the new start she was making. Barb and Pamela were holding onto one another like sisters. Nora, Betsy, and Tinder stood with strong, dignified expressions on their faces that lent Tamara the assurance she needed to be able to answer honestly. Dr. Samuelson and Sherry, their son Patrick, and the four young women Tamara had seen baptized earlier in the year bore witness that their relationships were changing into something bold and new. These were her communion of saints, her family in a way her own family had never been for her. As that stark reality grabbed hold of her in that moment, she felt her legs weaken for the first time and sensed the river almost pull them from beneath her.

She could only nod in answer to the question. Her response was too encumbered by the weight she now felt as she knew herself to be one of them, their sister. No longer the only troubled child of her parents but, as Tobias reminded her during one of their conversations, she was now the daughter of a King. She was surrounded by her royal family.

She nodded again even more firmly, looking into her mother's eyes now overflowing from years of frightening uncertainty and decades of self-reproach. And her dad, whose arm was wrapped across her mother's shoulders, simply looked proud. She heard once again the blessing he had given her, and she saw the look on his Aunt Tamara's face. That smile.

Inexplicably, Tamara knew her parents to be even more a part of her now than ever before. So much was being washed downstream.

"Tamara, my sister in Christ, upon your profession of faith, I baptize you in the name of the Father, and of the Son, and of the Holy Spirit."

As Tobias placed his hand over her face, Tamara closed her eyes. Then, taking her father's blessing with her as she was thrust beneath the rushing stream, Tamara Baxter died to death, and rose again in the promise of new and everlasting life.

AFTERWORD

On the Monday morning following her baptism, Tamara, along with Aimee and Terrance, Stephen Samuelson, Betsy Nazareth, and Barb met in Tobias' office with a lawyer to finalize the formation of a non-profit board of directors. Samuelson had closed up his New York practice in answer to another calling. He had come home to begin a residential treatment program for youth with mental illness. The Outing club agreed they needed a higher purpose and began raising the money to build three new lodges closer to the farm and to provide for their upkeep, reserving the three furthest up the mountain for the club's use.

The congregation of the Blossom's Rest Seventh Day Baptist Church agreed to co-sponsor the farm project as their new mission to the valley community and the region beyond. Nora took her horses off the market and offered their services for the temporary residents who would come to the valley in search of healing. As a baptism gift, Betsy gave Tamara a puppy, a border collie.

New residents at the farm would be offered the opportunity to work the garden, gather the eggs, cook for one another, hike, ride horses, and tend the sheep. They would take their place in the community and realize just how large and loving a family can become.

Skate Matthew's brother, Ned, was the local contractor hired by Terrance to begin work on the farm-hand cottage so Terrance and Aimee would have a place to stay when they came to visit. He was adding a room which Aimee would use as a studio.

After the signing at the church, Aimee and Terrance turned right onto Main Street and navigated their way back to Concord, from which they would fly out the next morning. They would spend their afternoon with realtors looking for a new home and celebrating their wedding anniversary.

Baxter Enterprises was negotiating with a bank in the New Hampshire capital which Terrance would merge into the family's holdings and manage from there. He wasn't sure he would like the smaller city. It was too New Englandish for him, but he was too enthralled by the journey his daughter was taking them on to be any further away.

As they were walking back to their B&B after dinner, Aimee held Terrance's arm and pulled him close.

"Thank you," she said, "for all the leaps of faith you have taken these past few months. It takes my breath away to think of what we've begun here."

"I was just thinking about something my Aunt Tamara said," Terrance replied. "Following a colossal decision by the board, which half of them thought to be the very definition of lunacy, she said: 'There are too many silly things we do in this life that don't count for anything. But in the end, it's often the silliest that makes all the difference.'"

"There's nothing silly about this, though," she assured him. Her voice had modulated, as had her mood.

"You okay?" he asked.

She nodded her head and tried to add a dose of humor, but it didn't work. "I sure am looking forward to the day when you don't have to ask me that so often," she said.

"Until then, what is it now?"

But she pursed her lips, brushed it away, and refused to utter what just slipped through her mind, something about winter coming.

Tamara Baxter's story continues in *A Place of New Beginnings* in which she convinces Barb that the Fletcher farm should be repurposed to become a place of healing for others who suffer. But she is learning that living in community is arduous work fraught with challenges that continue to threaten her recovery, one of which, surprisingly, is falling in love. Yet with the help of that same community, she discovers hidden sources of grace that yield new life in wondrous ways.

ACKNOWLEDGMENTS

To Captain Dominic Zachorne, rigger of tall ships, builder of wooden boats, master modeler, and the founding member of the Wickford Shipyard Literary Society, I need to express my deepest appreciation. Dominic was a ready sounding board for ideas and shared a sympathetic heart for the concerns addressed in the story.

One day, he shared an insight that helped shape this book more than his humble heart would allow him to acknowledge. He had been working on a classic wooden ketch of historic design, now owned by a collector. He became introspective and said something to this effect: "You know, a boat needs a person, not just an owner, not a caretaker, but a person. You can always tell a boat that doesn't have a person. It looks beautiful, it's in pristine condition, but it's hollow and cold. But a boat with a person has life; it may be worn, it may not look that great, but you climb aboard, and you can feel its warmth. A house is the same way. And, a person needs a person, or they're not really all there."

As I was struggling to bring *Through a Shattered Looking-glass* into print I had the amazing good fortune of being introduced to I Michael Grossman and his E-Book Bakery. His coaching and gifts for design, his friendship and encouragement turned that experience into a joy I couldn't wait to experience all over again. So, here we are, and I want to thank him profusely for assisting me in this project.

I loved writing this story, but I'm not so good at finding my mistakes! So, for helping me resolve so many of those, I also want to thank Walter Cole for lending an eye and many helpful suggestions.

And, to my family, I am most grateful of all: Beth, Christopher, Sammi, Benjamin, and Zach, all of whom have been most encouraging and helped me walk through the emotional terrain represented by this book.

All Scriptural quotations are from the King James Version of the Bible which is in the public domain. And several prayers are from the Online Book of Common Prayer (bpconline.org).

ABOUT THE AUTHOR

Clay has served as pastor of the Wakefield Baptist Church for over twenty years.

He earned the Doctor of Worship Studies degree from the Robert E. Webber Institute for Worship Studies. His thesis examined connections between worship, spirituality, and healing. Those F*rightening Things You Should Let Win* is the second in a series of novels that will explore issues of mental suffering and the restoration of hope.

Clay Berry lives with his wife, Beth, in Wakefield, Rhode Island.

Made in the USA
Middletown, DE
22 April 2019